Table of Conten

MW01251981

Canlonen

Lightcourt Island

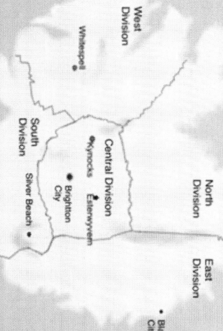

West
Division

Whitespell
*

North
Division

• Dracocoast

South
Division

Central Division

•Kynocks

•Esterwyvern

Brighton
City

Silver Beach •

East
Division

• Blackton
City

Red
Island

Prologue

It was a dark rain night, a night that seemed like any other. In a particularly rundown part of a city the sound of wet footsteps rang out in the deserted street where there were no streetlights to light the way. The sound of ragged breathing soon began echo along the empty street. A man that appeared to be in his late 30s stumbled out into the street.

Blood dripped down from his injured arm. He was in clear pain from the wound and yelled out for someone to help him. But no one heard his screams or even if they did just ignored them. But he quickly realized his mistake as his face turned pale and he started to run once again.

From an unidentified location a tall dark figure stood atop a building in their hand was a large sniper rifle. They got down to the ground propping the barrel on the ledge of the building. They pulled back the camber and dispelled the already discharged cartridge before a new one slide into place with a clear ring.

The figure looked down the sight and started to track the man as he continued to race down the empty street. Their breathing was steady as they adjusted the sights zooming closer into their target. After a few moments of the figure observing the man, they lowered their finger down onto the trigger.

For a moment their finger twitched from either nerves or in anticipation. Then with one last breath the trigger was pulled. A resounding shot of a sniper rang out in the quiet sky.

The man fell to the ground with a thud. Blood begun to pool around his head, the only eye that could be seen facing up from the pavement begun too quickly dull. His muscles twitched for a moment before eventually going still. The blood and matter that had sprayed the ground from the sniper shot started to get washed away with rain that fell.

The figure positioned on the building removed their finger from the trigger and pushed themselves up. Their clothing and the gravel from the roof clung to their body as they got soaked to the bone from the rain.

The sound of sirens soon began to ring in the quiet night towards the location of the man. It was clear that someone had called in when they heard the gun shot or maybe even before then. But it was already too late. The figure slung the sniper over their back before they jumped from the roof.

The police eventually located the man's body it was clear to them that he was shot through the head. The police began to look around cautious as it was clear to them that the man was sniped. Then suddenly as the weather slowed a figure raced by overhead and papers began to fall from the sky in front of them.

"After that figure!"

But it was no use as they were already gone. The officers that remained at the scene to case it, eventually collected the papers that fell. What was on those pages scattered around chilled those officers to the bone.

In the early morning the TV played the news in the currently loud home. A lone teen watched and tuned out all others noise that occurred around them. The news story that was currently played was on the murder that had occurred last night.

It was revealed the victim was a high ranked businessman there are a little talk about the man, but it soon focused on the suspected killer. According to the news anchors it was that the man was killed by an individual that the media had come to call the Assassin.

The reason that this has been tied to the individual called the Assassin was for a simple reason, unknown information about the victim was revealed publicly after their death. A common occurrence done by this Assassin, though that was really the only thing.

But the information about the man was damning and chilling. Unbeknownst to all was that quite good man was the opposite to who he appeared. The 'Assassin' revealed the unknown and hidden connection to the man and six missing person cases.

A common occurrence for this 'Assassin' person of the media. Like usual they shook the world with sudden unknown revelations. Little was known about this individual but most concluded that they had been dormmate for quite some time before that night. The reason for their sudden return was something many tried to speculate.

But those that believe that the media dubbed 'Assassin' was a single individual. The return brought about mixed emotions towards the infamous 'Assassin' to all. The moniker of the 'Assassin' was mainly known and connected to killed individuals that had hidden information suddenly come to light. Though that wasn't the only thing connected to the name it was the main one and most focused side the media present to people. From it the 'Assassin' was known as a vigilantly of sort that have killed those of serious crimes and or with a significant body count to their name.

From that it brought up a conflict to those above, off whether they would ever be caught or not or if they even should be caught. However, the motives and reasons of the media's 'Assassin' was unknown. Something that made some question if it truly was an individual or multiple people.

News media often flocked to this 'Assassin' like a feeding frenzy. People above always had a morbid curiosity towards such things. It brought reactions out of them, so the news covered it. But they never thought as to why they were privy to such information.

Eventually the news moved to a different topic other than the death that occurred last night. The teen that had once watched the news segment so intently had already long had their attention taken away from it. The teen that had ignored all else around them had their chair sharply moved and caused them to slam their chest into the table which caused them to let out a small quick and quiet yelp.

The table from the sudden mess became a mess as the teen placed a hand on their chest. The TV played on… even though no one even listened to it anymore.

Part 1

Chapter 1

A young woman was sat down at a table with breakfast as they watched the TV. Unlike everyone else in the house they were all ready for the day to come as they ate breakfast as they waited for the others. They were out of the way of the rushed whirlwind that the others in the home were apart of and sat quietly as they ate and watched TV. Despite this their chair was sharp and harshly shoved forward and into the table.

The young women whose breakfast have become spread out across the table looked up and caught a glance of an older women that was the only one near her. That women wore a pleased smirk for a moment one that they barely caught. She looked up and for a moment a dark expression passed the young women's face, but no one saw it. They lightly rubbed their sore abdomen from its collision with the table as they had a generally blank expression.

The young woman's name was Arianna Artusro, though those close to her often just called her Ari for short. At the time they were said to be 17 years old and had been just enrolled in the nearby high school.

The chair across from her was pulled out and a young boy sat down. This was Dave Luo a 15-year-old with who had become Ari's younger sibling not long before this point. The same went for the still asleep young man Sean Luo that was legally 'older' than her by two months.

Ari had been adopted into the Luo family of four, two weeks before this point. Though there were many questions as to why a mother and father would wish to adopt a child of her age. Ari was adopted and brought here and enrolled into the nearby school that her 'brothers' were enrolled in as well.

The family lived in Brightton City for the country called Canlonen's. The city itself existed in one of five division and was a part of Central Division the second largest city after the division's capital.

The home itself was away from the city's main centre at one of the outer suburbs. But there was a high school that was only a 30-minute drive away.

Ari watched the chaos before her with slight annoyance and enjoyment at the same time. Yavari Luo the mother of family at the time banged on the door of Sean Luo the eldest son. It was a vein attempt to get him out of bed and ready for school.

The last member of the family was Caden Luo a man that treated Ari with a kindness others of the family didn't show her and did so from the very start. He was also in a rush to leave so he could make it on time as he like the other were up late and where behind when they normally ready.

Ari glanced over at Yavari who was at Sean's door oddly angry for some unclear reason. "Sean! Get out of bed! You have school today! At this rate you'll make everyone late with you!" Yavari yowled as she pounded on the locked bedroom door.

The door eventually opened in the door stood a half-asleep Sean, he trudged himself out of his room and over to the table. He sat down at the table not even dressed. Ari glanced over Sean before she turned her attention to Caden.

Ari watched as Caden kissed his wife Yavari before he grabbed some toast and raced out the door. This was an extremely late time for him to leave so his rush was understandable. Yavari handed Sean a plate with a light meal.

Yavari for reasons unknown walked over to Ari and stood behind her. Yavari placed her hand on Ari's should and looked at her with a smile. It was a smile that to Ari that was hollow and just for show. She looked down at Ari and the two held a gaze with one another, a look between the two that was not like that between a mother and daughter.

Yavari's eyes at a quick glance looked to hold affection and love towards Ari. Whereas Ari eyes held no real show of emotion no matter how you looked at it.

Ari didn't enjoy the clear and sudden attention Yavari placed on her. "Are you getting used to things here Arianna? I know things here must be very different from the orphanage, but I hope you feel welcome here." Yavari exclaimed brightly with a cheery voice.

Ari just nodded her head before she looked away no longer wanting to hold eye contact. *Overly clingy.*

"Are you ready for your first day at school? You've probably not had a chance to go to one before now, right?"

"Yeah, I'm more than a little nervous about everything." Arianna signed in reply glancing way again. *Please stop paying attention to me. I don't want to deal with this right now.*

"It's alright everything will be fine. Your brother will look after you and help you get used to things. RIGHT BOYS?" She said with a sharpness in her voice that was directed towards her sons.

"Yes mom!" The two answered though they sounded half asleep and more than likely didn't even register their mother's words. This became more than clear a little later.

Yavari wore a closed mouth smile at her son's answer, however her grip on Ari's shoulder tightens significantly. Ari glanced over at Yavari's hand as she felt nails dig in. Ari let out a slight sigh as she looked away, eventually Yavari moved away from Ari, and she just rolled her shoulder as she glanced at Yavari Luo for a moment.

Yavari left not to long after she finished her breakfast and the three kids soon after departed for the high school. Sean was the one that drove them to school since he owned a car. It was a quiet ride with Sean choice of music.

Arianna bored and in no mood to hold a conversation looked out the window and watched as building flew by them. It wasn't a long ride but the silence in the car made it feel even long. Occasionally Ari would glance over at Sean and Dave before she would quickly move her gaze once more, she would do this multiple times over the course of the drive. *Is this a typical relationship between siblings? Is it just for brothers, because of the age gap or just something else?*

Though she tried not to Ari could help but let her gaze wander over to the two siblings in curiosity. Though as she looked at the two curiosities wasn't the only emotion that passed her eyes. But eventually she turned her attention out the wind and at the scenery that passed by.

As the car stopped in the parking lot Dave jumped out and raced off to see his friends. Ari opened her lips for a moment before closing them and glanced over at Sean. *I wonder... would he? No better, way better.*

"What are you looking at my like that for." Sean growled he was not all to welcome to the sudden addition to his family, especially since Ari was the same age as him. She had long gotten used to such so his harsh comments and snide remarks in the last few weeks didn't faze her.

Better for sure, probably nicer too.

Ari grabbed the pad of paper from her bag and quickly wrote. [Your mother told me that you would help me.]

Sean scoffed and tore the page out of the book. "Help you? Why would I help you? I'll act as if you never said... oops I mean wrote anything. Find your way around yourself I have better things to do than to help a leach." As he crumbled the paper into a ball and tossed it at her which caused it to hit her in the head.

Sean left Ari alone which caused her to let out a low sigh as she picked up the paper ball from the ground. She glared at Sean as he got out of sight before walking over to a recycle bin and tossed the paper inside. *Idiotic assholes! I show more decency to scum than what they've shown me! Those jerks couldn't even point me in the right direction.* She growled internally as on the outside she appeared calm and collected. She closed her note pad and slipped it back into her bag before she made her way into the school.

Ari walked through the main doors, and it was hard to notice the large amount of people that crowed the halls talking to one another. She held her bag close to her chest as she slowly made her way through the hallways trying to avoid being run into. Ari didn't enjoy crowded areas full of people her only saving grace was that to the students she was just another face in the crowd.

There was a slight problem however, since she didn't wish to be notice nor did she know where she was going, she was just getting swept away in the crowd. Ari would just follow the flow and with no real direction and would end up just lost. This continued till the bell rang as she was at her wits ends and was at the end of her rope of handling the large crowd in the school. When the bell rang which left Ari standing in the hall alone.

Arianna fell to the floor her breathing a little rough as she looked down at the ground. She could feel slight tears form in her eyes due to the stress but before she could wipe them a voice called out to her. "Hey what are you doing in the hall it's time for class! If you have a free period don't just sit in the middle of the hall.

Arianna looked up to them eyes filled with tears which caused them to freeze as they didn't expect to make someone cry. "Ah! I'm sorry I shouldn't have been so harsh, but you shouldn't be in the middle of the hall."

Arianna was embarrassed now with her ears a little red but decided to work with it. She sniffed and brought out her note pad. [I'm lost. I just arrived today and got completely turned around in the crowds.]

"So, you're looking for the office then that's not too hard." They said helping Ari up from the ground. "I guess you got overwhelmed by the large number of people. Yeah, this high school is something you might be surprised to learn this isn't even ¼ of the total in the area. City schools are something else."

Arianna just listened to them talk occasionally she gave them a slight nod in reply but continued to follow them to the office. "This is the main office they should be able to short things out for you."

"*Thank you!*" Ari signed with a quick bow before entering the office. The office was quiet and there wasn't to many people inside. Ari walked over to the desk she was about to use sign language but recalled that not many people use it anymore. She then pulled up her notepad again and began to write.

"Miss what are you here for?" The secretary asked glancing ups at her for a moment once realizing that she was present. Ari squinted her eyes a little before turning the note pad for them to see.

[I'm here to get my schedule, I've just been registered. My name's Arianna Artusro.] He looked over the words on the note pad before turning around. He begun to skim through a filing cabinet. He paused for a moment before he pulled out a piece of paper before handing it over to her. He then got right back to work and left Ari to do whatever.

Ari exhaled through her nose before she looked down at the paper in her hand as she left the office. She could see that classes were in blocks of time and there was a room number for each class. She walked out into the hall and looked at the number of the other doors to understand the number system.

Once Ari understood how they numbered the room it made it easier for her to locate her current class of which she was currently late for. With the schedule in hand, she made her way towards her class till she stopped in front of the door. She looked between the door and the sheet in her hand to confirm that it was the classroom she was looking for.

When she was certain was walked over to the door and knocked on it. The door eventually opened, and a teacher looked at her. "What do you want?" they asked, in reply she just turned her schedule for him to see. He looked down at for a moment. "So, you are a part of my class then?" She just nodded in reply. The teacher than moved aside to let her inside. "Take whatever seat is open.

As she walked inside the class and when she did, she noticed that everyone looked up at the door and at her which caused her to pause for a moment. Her body froze in slight fear as she looked back her eyes flashed slightly. She looked around the class a little and noticed that Sean was also in the class which caused her to turn away in a huff.

After a few moments she walked inside and sat down. But felt many piercing looks in her direction from others in the class. She looked up at the ceiling as she silently cursed displeased with the looks, they held in her direction.

Arianna was aware of her odd appearance, dark indigo coloured hair with rust-coloured eyes and lightly tan skin it was an odd combo for sure. But she didn't think that her looks were the reason her classmates were looking at her.

Desperate to get her mind off the fact she had become the center of attention which she dreaded in this state. She looked around the room and noticed that the school appeared to have a uniform.

The girls had a long black skirt, long black sleeve short coat, that underneath was a white V-neck dress shirt that could only be seen when the jacket was open. While the guys had black pants, a long sleeve shirt coat like the girls but were a bit longer underneath they wore a long sleeve white button-up shirt. Both wore grey loafers and white ankle socks. Something that Yavari had yet to get for Ari which caused her to stand out even more.

At the realization Ari slightly clicked her tongue. *How annoying. Of course, I had to go to a uniform school.*

The very moment that it was time for lunch after two classes Ari raced out of the class and up to the roof. She wanted… no needed to get away from people. Reaching the roof, she found it had greenery. Ari without a moment hesitation went into the trees and continue to walk till deep in the small roof top garden/forest.

Beautiful and calm and not too many people went up there, so it was a good place for Arianna to chill out and eat her lunch in private. The location she found was out of immediate sight as well.

Arianna sat down before she allowed a sigh to escape from her lips as she closed her eyes as she listened to the sound around her. After a few moments she seemed to notice something and couldn't stop the smirk that formed on her lips. After a few moments of thought she opened her month.

"This I don't enjoy it. If I never had to come back it would be too soon. But I have no choice! Really, I'd rather get shot again than deal with this hell. Wouldn't you agree Roy?"

Chapter 2

Arianna smirked as a figure landed behind her from out of know where. She spun around with her hands behind her back. "Still can't sneak up you." The figure sighed. Ari stuck out her tongue closing one eye looking at them. Behind her stood a man with red-orange hair and silver eyes he was a little taller than Arianna.

Ari shuffled a little as she looked up at them. "It's been a long time Roy I wasn't sure if I'd see you again to be honest." She muttered with a pensive expression. Royce Giffin is a 19-year-old that had been friends with Ari for years, the two are close enough that Ari feel comfortable to speak to him, as the two had essentially grew up together. "You disappeared two years ago; it was hard not to think the worse. You didn't even say a word before either."

Roy held his hand out and paused for a moment before placing it on her shoulder. "Sorry, I probably should have said something before. How have you been Arianna?" He asked with a sweet expression. Ari looked away as she bit her lip slightly.

"Better… I've only recently been allowed to take part of things again. I'm still not 100% but it's enough for now." Ari replied. "Though I mainly accepted something do to outside factors. I needed to accept it. So, whether I'm feeling well enough didn't matter."

"It extremely matters you don't need to." Roy looked at Ari with a glare. "I'm more concurred for your well-being than some strangers."

"I'll be alright. But I hope that you help me if I ever need it." Ari asked as she looked away before she walked over to a large tree.

"You'll probably need that help sooner than you expect." Roy added as he turned to face Ari once again. "After all things have gotten very… active lately in Brightton City. After all, the 'Assassin' been quite active."

"Shut up. The surface media pins everything on the 'Assassin' even with crimes that have little to do with them. You're doing this on purpose just to tick me off." Arianna growled as she glared at Roy. She crossed her arms as she sat down underneath the tree in a slight huff.

"All of them? What about last night?" he asked with a smirk, he clearly knew the answer just wanted to hear her say it. She looked away slight flushed face he moved over and looked at her face with a clear smirk.

"The one last night… that… that maybe done by the 'Assassin'." Arianna replied as she glanced down clearly make sure not to look him in the eyes.

"Ari, no reason for you to play dumb. It's not as if am a surface cop. We would both know it was them." Roy smirked before he sat down next to her. "You must be really tired."

Ari glanced up at the tree and let out a slight sigh. "I'm not really…" she covered her mouth to hide a yawn that begun to escape from her lips. "Well anyways… I'm currently sent here due to an 'adoption'. It's… annoying to say the least. Especially having to go to a school run surface side. It's not helping my sleep when I have those late nights either."

"So, if you're not pleased with such an arrangement why are you going through with it?"

"Eh, definitely not 'cause I enjoy it. There's just… something I must take care off. If I had it my way… I'd be… doing something else entirely." Arianna muttered. "Either way I have to deal with it is as I may."

Roy looked over as Ari took out some lunch. "Want something to eat? I don't really eat much as you, so there's more than enough to share with you. Plus, I know you'd take some anyways with or without my permission." She sighed as she placed it between them pulling out the drink.

"So how about you tell me about those you are currently living with then. You'll probably be able to sleep then."

"Sigh... why are you so concerned about me sleeping? I'm not a child, your only one year older than me." Ari huffed glancing over at him. "I understand you are worried after what happened was two years ago but I'm okay now."

"I won't stop worrying about you... after all we've known each other for a long time."

Arianna just hummed before looking away and began taking a drink. "It's a family of four not including myself, a married couple who have two boys. Currently I see no family reason for the adoption."

"They didn't tell you the reason behind it?"

"... No. They were surprisingly hush on things on all sides. So, it's not that incorrect to say that I'm pretty 'in the dark' on the whole situation though I do have an inkling on a few different things." Ari muttered trying to stifle another yawn.

"I'm not really all to welcomed either... only the father treats me kindly." Ari sighed as took a bite. "The youngest currently just ignores me. Don't even get me started on the other two." She yawned as she covered her mouth.

Ari glanced over at Roy; she knew she wouldn't yawn at the moment if he wasn't around. But since he showed up her body had relaxed, and her lack of sleep for several days had begun to catch up with her.

"Alright that's it. Lean against me and try to take a nap."

"I have class Roy."

"That's not my concern just say you got lost or something. You should get some sleep."

"Jeez."

Roy, he cared about me a lot, though on the one hand she found it more than a little bothersome at the times. But the main reason for it was due to an event two years ago. There was a major incident that occurred back then that Arianna had got wrapped up in which Roy was also a part of.

Due to that, it was something which made Roy feel reasonable for what happened to her. Even though that was far from how she felt. She found his worry a burden more so when he was around and acted in such an overly caring manner towards her.

Arianna had grown up with Roy and had known him for years as they had both grown up in the 'orphanage' together. Towards him she felt more like a brother figure due to how long they've known each other. Even despite this familial emotion towards him she was hesitant and didn't wish for anyone to worry about her.

Despite her resistance to what he said and after a few minutes of a glare contest with one another Arianna decided to cave. Ari couldn't deny she wanted to get more rest; under normal circumstances she wouldn't even humor such a suggestion. But for the moment it was safe as such she leaned against Roy's shoulder underneath the tree. She glanced over at him, "don't you dare eat all my food. I didn't even get much for breakfast today."

"Why not?"

"Half of it wound up on the table that's why."

The wind had passed them and shifted Ari's hair slightly. Roy placed his arm around her and brought her close to him. Though paused for a moment in thought she decided to let it go since it was the first time, she had seen him in a few years. "I'm glad you're alright and came back." Ari mumbled under her breath as she looked up at Roy's red-orange hair.

"What was that?"

"Nothing!" She replied sharply before for closing her eyes and quickly drifted off to sleep. Roy couldn't help but to let out slight chuckled as he looked down at her with his silver-coloured eyes as he wore a warm expression.

"And you said you weren't tired... you foolish idiot."

Chapter 3

A few weeks passed and many incidents had occurred that the news claim to had been perpetrated by the individual the 'Assassin' a claim that had now become backed by local authorities. Such a statement was something of great concern for Arianna. She claims that is out of concern for the people in the city as people will get false hope and courage when they venture out as the one called the 'Assassin' has a particular set target. Though in truth there was another reason that Arianna was greatly concerned by such statements made.

So concerned that one day during lunch at school that she had come to the habit of enjoying the company of Roy. But this day could no longer sit by and pulled out her phone. With her phone out and begun to dial a number. "Who are you calling? You don't have that many people you talk to." Roy asked as he looked over her shoulder. Ari glared at Roy as the phone started to ring in her ear.

"Hey! Been awhile."

"Arianna... been what a year since we last talk. What do you want?"

"Eh?! Why you assume that I'm calling because I want something!"

"..."

"Sigh... alright. We gotta talk, the media is getting out of hand. We need to deal with it. You know I really don't care that much about things but if we let this go on, we'll have bigger problems. Especially since one of the police departments have publicly agreed to the media's claims."

"… Haaaa your right, especially if you're calling me, it's not good. Its best we deal with it right away. When will you arrive?"

"Actually, I'll need you to come get me. I'm over at the school in the outer west area of the city. I'm… kind of… dealing with something… a little particular. So, I don't have a vehicle right now for me to use like usual. But also, suddenly disappearing would be a bigger problem."

"Sigh… seriously, alright. If you are in that school… alright, I understand. I'll come get you in a few hours."

"Come get me in the next half hour. Just go into the school and sign me out. You'll have no problem doing such a thing. I'll deal with the backlash later; this is more important to deal with."

"… Okay alright. I'll be there soon then."

With that Arianna hung up the phone and glanced behind her and over at Roy who had a displeased expression. "What?" she asked with a slight knowing look. She lowered her phone and put it away before she crossed her arms.

"I could hear his voice over the phone. Why'd you have to call him?! You could have asked me to do something. I could have dealt with the media or anything for you."

Arianna looked at him for a moment before she flicked him in the forehead. "Curb your jealousy we've been friends for years. Let's also not get into the fact they the two of you have totally different connections, with the current issue his connections are more useful than yours." She paused as she looked at him. "You probably thought to break into the source room or hijack the broadcasts. Which might I add with cause more issues that solve the current one." She sighed as she shook her head.

"N-no." Roy replied as he looked away from her. She had clearly hit the nail on the head, as that was exactly what he planned to do.

"Such away is not effective it would be more of the opposite effect than any sort of help. You know how the surface dwellers act. Unlike us or the undergrounders they do nearly the exact opposite just cause it was not done the 'proper' way." Ari muttered waving her hand in an annoyed gesture. "So don't do anything. I'll deal with it. Just rest okay Roy, I promise that if there is something you can help with, I'll ask for it."

"Yeah, as you're someone that asks for help."

"Shut it. I know my limits unlike you who just stole my phone. Now give it back." Ari huffed as she crossed her arms yet held out her hand from him to give her back her phone. He let out a slight curse and placed her phone into her hand. "Nice try. Well, he'll be here soon so, I'll be busy for the next the while."

"You did it to yourself." He snapped back with a slight glare clearly still a little mad about the overall occurrence. Ari just shrugged her shoulders in reply.

It didn't take long before the end of lunch the person she was waiting for had arrived. Dressed well in a nice suit and tie with a badge clipped to his belt he stood next to a black car as he leaned against the door. It was a young man with maroon hair and grey eyes and brought a fair number of eyes to him from the female students at the school.

He wore a bored and slightly annoyed expression as he waited, he was not all too pleased to have to come to the school. Arianna eventually walked out of the school doors and locked eyes with the man he made a slight motion with his hand, and she nodded in reply. She noticed Sean as she walked towards the man but turned away and continued forward.

"Got everything?"

"Yeah, I'm all good to go." Ari replied in a low voice. But moved her hands as if she was signing. "Did you bring what I needed?"

"Yes. If you're ready to go lets, go. I'd rather not be here any longer than necessary." He stated as he glanced around before he opened the car door.

"Not enjoying all the attention Stanly." She chuckled with a smirk as she went around to the other side of the car.

"I enjoy it considerably more than you Arianna."

"Low blow but true. It's just a school you can relax from this moment. I didn't call you here to deal with that kind of a problem." Ari replied. The doors of the car closed, and they left the school grounds and made way to the police station that Stanly was stationed at.

As the car drove down the road Arianna looked down as the small bag at her feet. Inside was a change of more formal and large clothes. She let out a slight hum of approval. "Are you sure about this? You didn't seem to wish to use such a means after last time." Stanly asked as he glance over at her.

"It's not so much a desire to do this. After what happened last time and what I must deal with, I'd rather not have to do this. However, I'm too good for my own task for such beliefs. Also, would rather not have unnecessary Light Tarrein blood on my hands." Ari muttered as she pushed the hair behind her left ear revealing a small ornate ear cuff piercing. With swirling branches in the band and in the middle was a clear gem that took up the cuff and at the bottom hung a small clear tear drop gemstone.

"My brother told me it was bad for a while."

"Bad is a bit of an understatement for what happened. I was completely out of commission for two years and slowly working back up, meaning that training I've avoided can no longer be avoided for much longer." She replied as she begun to get changed into the spear clothes in the bag being sure not to get in the way of Stanly's ability to drive. *In truth I almost died... no, I should have died that day. Not that I'd tell them that... if I did...*

Arianna buttoned up the white shirt and placed the black jacket on her lap. She fixed the pants a little before dealing with the high heels. "So, Stan did you let them know I'm on my way?"

"Of course, some of the oldies were so pleased to hear that, the PI Rouge is on her way in today."

"Pfft! You mean the old fogies that were all up in arms when I initially showed up two years ago to help with that case? Those oldies?"

"Yes. I had to stop myself from laughing. But now they all prise you as a genius and courageous. Especially for the stunt at the end of the case to save the hostages." Stan replied with a smirk. Arianna looked away they didn't know the full scope of that stunt and what it cost her.

"Are those two brothers still there?"

"Brothers? Oh, those two. No, they were transferred a few months ago."

"Darn."

As they got closer and closer to the police station Stan turned down a street that had no camera's and drove slower. She glanced at him, and the windows tinted darker with a click of a button. The gemstone on the ear cuff then started to glow and Arianna's appearance changed.

She had an older more mature appearance her dark indigo hair turns white and longer, her rust eyes also turned a dark shade of wine red. She became taller and a little more 'top heavy' with a changed figure. The large clothes she had put on now fit to her changed appearance and not nearly as baggy which made her appear professional.

"It surprises me every time."

"What the disguise cuff tech? I guess I'm more than familiar with it since I've been using it for seven years. Though then again, I'm one of the very few people that has one. So, it's also understandable." Arianna muttered as she looked at her longer nails before she grabbed the make-up from the bag and lightly put some on. Her voice sounded different from how it once did as well it was clear that the device didn't just work to change her physical appearance.

"Oh, look its Rouge."

Ari and Stan walked through the police station as they made way towards the chief's office for the police station. She could hear the whispers of the other officers but ignored them and continued to walk forward. The door closed behind them once they entered the office and someone was already inside waiting from them.

"Icarus it's been a while. Though I don't think either of us expected to meet here once again." Arianna said in a calm tone she looked forward into the dark room. She held her hands behind her back and watched as the chair spun around for the person in it to face her.

"No one else is here expect Stan you don't need to act in such a manner."

"Mmm... I understand... Uncle." Arianna paused as she spoke as though he often told her to, she felt odd to call him such at this point. She knew however it was best to just deal with it and do what she need to. "How about we get right to business rather than beating around the bush. We are both busy people after all."

"Fine by me. So, Stan told me you wish to talk about the 'Assassin'."

Ari shifted in place and looked over at Stan, who walked over to a seat. She let out a sigh and sat down next to him. She crossed her legs as she sat down. "The media has stated the recent things have been done by the 'Assassin'. You're as aware as I that it's not only the 'Assassin' committing the recent occurrences. If we allow this to occur, we'll have a bigger issue on our hands. Its already bad enough other departments officially stated in agreement with the media."

"We both know that departments corrupt and in the mayor's pocket. He just wants tourism to pop back up. Since that festival isn't that far off and that's one point that the city gets a lot of money." Icarus crossed his arms with a sigh. "It wouldn't be easy to change thing over. So, tell me everything and what to do."

"Well, the current one are by a 'copycat' someone acting like the 'Assassin' either to get more of a chance at their target or just to collect more victims... it's probably both."

"It sounds as if you have an idea of who it is that's posing as the 'Assassin'."

"I have a hunch. Many of us are well aware of the 'Assassin's' uniqueness. As such they are using it to their advantage. They like many cares little about above, just their own task. But I've looked into things… and I've come up with a… trap I'll need your help with." Ari replied calmly. "I'll make them regret using such a moniker to target students." She added with a wicked smile.

Chapter 4

Late at night where were no cameras and limited lights. A teenage girl with green shoulder length hair and golden eyes walked down along the street. They went against the police sectioned curfew set in place for the area, buy the police department of the area. From it the roads were very light with people in most places.

But there was a looming presence here that was hard for most to place. Even despite this presence as if their own world as if they didn't notice anything wrong. The teen continued to walk down the street as if they were invincible. It wasn't long till the suspenseful feeling of the street turned to a deadly quiet.

Then from the dark like a living shadow a figure clad in black that wore a particular mask appeared behind the teen. Without much delay the figure pulls out a gun and fired but the teen moved to the side before the gun even goes off. The teen who spun around pulled out a blade with a glowing edge and slashed the barrel of the gun in quick succession.

"That's quite a dangerous weapon you know. Shouldn't go pointing it in peoples back. Tsk, tsk." The Teen smirked with a familiar expression. "I'm glad it's worked out as well as I planned. The others were worried I couldn't pull it off." She laughed as she covered her mouth slightly. Her golden eyes showed a slight red tint to the colour.

The figure stood up straight an looked over at her. "Who are you?" they asked as they sent a sharp glaze at the teen. "No surface dweller would be able to do such a thing, and no undergrounder would ever come up to the surface either, normally that is. So, then you must also be a Twilight."

"First time I've been called that in a long time its normally by another name." the teen hummed as they looked at the blade in their hand. "But who am I? What a question I'm one with many names yet also no name. Unlike you. I've looked you up… Imitator, a merc known to mimic other well-known mercs on the surface to throw off the surface law enforcement. You've really gotten on my nerves."

"Oh! HAHAHAH! I got it. I know who you are! It's you. The Codeless the infamous one. So that's why you are here. But a woman? My, my, my! I didn't expect that, after all everyone has said and thought the opposite." The Imitator laughed. Their voice was smug but clearly mocking her.

She had sharp eyes as she glared at the masked face. *How annoying. Alright Arianna, keep a cool head. This guy is strong I can't let myself get lost in emotion or I'm sure I won't be getting away from this.* Ari told herself as she looked forward. "What are you feeling insecure that a codeless woman is even more famous than you. Have I damaged your apparent small petty pride?" she replied with venom

Gotta last only 20 minutes. Let's pander it out from fighting as I'm not sure if I start a fight now… She paused before she hummed. "You kept sending out warnings. I'm here, so what do you want."

"Hahah! How unexpected, I was targeting the path to the hand that feeds and the stray appears to defend." Imitator laughed as they pointed a blade in her general direction. "Those warnings, I'd say they are quite clear what my boss wishes to convey." Their voice was smug, they clearly looked down on her likely thinking the one before them was still wet behind the ears and have taken over the post, something of which was not entirely an impossibility given past occurrences.

"Alright since you won't say it, I will. Stop me if I get anything wrong 'kay." She sighed with a graceful movement of her arm as she pointed her knife at them. She didn't have to worry about any 'stray's' that might appear as she had secured the location beforehand just for her plan.

"All the victims so far have occurred for a few different reasons. Though a warning was just one of those reasons. The warning itself was to multiple individuals, the one you are mimicking in a form of mocking, the one they've been employed by, and the target themselves. Another is you just enjoy the rush, everyone below is aware of your lust towards it, after all its an open secret. You like blood and to kill, I wouldn't be surprised if you stepped up for this little job just because of it.

"Now why you chose the one the surface dwellers call the Assassin; I think you did it just because of their resurgence before the possible deadline. You wished to distill fear and mistrust towards them... because they have been the occasional thorn in your groups side for the last few years. Even though they've yet to do anything major you've come to get annoyed about them. You wanted to deal with them in a way but not directly. To sow mistrust to make it harder and cause them to lose multiple contracts. An action taken upon yourself not ordered by your leader.

"Now putting aside, the more personal reasons for it. Your actions are calculated. The Surface law enforcement are in all honesty quiet an annoyance to those that follow the rules of the underground. You've attacked a wide array of victims some of which just to throw them off and hide the real true intent and target. With the annoying surface dwellers out of the way you can act as you please and hit the true target with none the wiser.

"But this is the most important reason. To instill fear, you wanted to drag out your target with fear, even sending them away from that which they are being protected by. After all what not best to drag one out if not to threat that which is closest right? After all no matter how smart or calculating one is, it matters not when emotion gets involved." Ari recounted as she tilted her head a little.

"Normally such a tactic would work quite well. The only downfall was that I got involved. I've been around and at work for some time with many at this point. Your group on the very rare occasion have been included in my clientele, so I know that despite all that madness and brutality there is planning and intent capable in the people of your organization." She sighed. "Such perks of my profession, I can deal with anything for what I wish. Such an important thing to learn too. After all I'm unlike the others."

The Imitator started to laugh out in a maniacal way. "I really chose the right thing. What a rush with your explanation alone. Such in depth planning and thought, the very rush I felt as you stripped away every one of my actions for the past month. What a miscalculation to think you are a greenhorn by your appearance alone. After all you had disappeared for a few years but for this to happen." They laughed and bent forward as they held their stomach.

"You have that do you not? There are rumours of which, what is both artifact and tech which is to be capable of a unique ability was created and in 'their' hands. But to give it to a stray, a codeless, how crazy." They smirked as they shifted on their feet. "But I wonder how capable is this infamous codeless in a real fight!" they howled as they charged forward towards Ari.

Arianna clicked her tongue and jumped back away from their slash. She slid back when she landed before she quickly pushed off from the ground and raced towards Imitator. Narrowly she avoided the Imitator's next attack as she moved in closer.

Then when within arm's reach she attacked, she aimed from their relatively unprotected neck. They noticed Ari motives and moved slightly which caused her blade to hit their mask. There was a slight scraping sound as the unenergized blade slid across the glaze like mask and created a deep gash. They kneed Ari in the chest which cause her to slide back.

The blow caused her to take in a gasp of air from the impact, but she had little chance to recover as they attacked once again. Ari brought up her knife and had their blade slide away, they then tried to grab her with their other hand, yet she blocked it as she hit their wrist away. She flipped backwards and did an arial kick right into their jaw before she landed on her hands and flipped back to land on her feet.

Ari shifted her feet to be in a more fight like stance with the weapon currently in her hand. The blade of the knife faced out and Infront of her other hand in a fist and feet position for fleet movement as she shifted in place. They clicked their tongue in realization that they were not about to be an easy catch. They shifted to grab something from their pocket and begun to pull out an ornate kind of object with a glowing red gemstone.

Ari was quick to see the light of the gem and realized what it was. She placed her knife into her mouth before she reached to the side of her legs and pulled out throwing knives. The knives flew from her hand towards the Imitator some flew past them, and a few grazed them, but one hit right on the mark. One of the knives hit the gemstone dead in the middle, it ripped the charm from their hands and too the ground.

The knife had hit the gemstone right in the middle and it had quickly lost the clear glow it once had. She then pulled her hands back and the knives flew back towards her hand and pried the charm from the one knife and crushed it in her hand. From the charm red-light specks floated around Ari before they eventually disappeared.

This occurrence ticked Imitator off and they charged forward to attack. No longer what is powerful precise strikes rather it was a rapid flurry of consistent attacks. Not fully prepared for the first attack and unable to dodge Arianna brought up her arm to block the first slash. The blade cut through the skin quick and clean while it slightly nicked the bones of her forearm.

It was followed up with a deeper slash on her side before she was able to jump back. She begun to then defend with her knife which she had managed to grab in the middle of their attack. The flurry of attacks was too much for a single small knife to defend against, but she was able to deflect or weaken some of the strikes to lessen the attack against her.

After some time, she had managed to survive but had sustained several injuries for their attacks or just from her attempt to dodge and avoid. But that didn't mean that Imitator was completely unscathed either just not as bad as Ari was. Imitator lunged forward in for another attack likely to finish Ari off.

Prepared for this Arianna used her knife to deflect her blade in another direction before she struck with that same knife as she stabbed them in the chest. The deflection made the knife miss any vital points. Imitator reacted as well to the deflection of their blade and slashed Arianna deep in their right leg before they took out that leg with a powerful kick near the ankle with a snap. This action caused Arianna to fall to the ground.

Prone and unable to defend Arianna was certain this was the end for her. But as Imitator went in for the final blow they were stopped. A clear metallic ring resounded in the air which caused Arianna to look up and see a tall dark figure before her. Imitator's blade rang as it hit the ground from the other figure that disarmed them.

"Night… it seems the dog has come to pick up the stray they watch over. Right as I was about to finish them off." Imitator hummed as they looked at Night who was stood between the two. "What a loyal dog to protect their master's stray codeless."

"Shut up you mad bastard." Night growled as they pointed their sword at Imitator. "I'll cut you down and put you in your place!" they added anger clear in their voice. Imitator just smirked as Night slashed them across the chest.

"You'd rather let the stray bleed out as you get revenge." They laughed in a mocking tone. Night turned and looked to see the pool of blood that had begun to form beneath Arianna from the leg injury. They jumped back over towards Arianna and picked her up with one arm.

"This isn't over." Night growled as they pointed at Imitator with their sword right before the light disappeared and the two were gone.

From roof top to roof top Night jumped across as they held Arianna close to them with one arm. Arianna had her arms wrap around their neck and legs around their torso. She rested her head on her arms with her face towards the crease of Night's neck. "You better not close your eyes on me." Night muttered as they continued forward.

"I'll be okay, you have no need to freak out." Arianna replied in a clam tone. Her steady breath brushed against the fabric of the hood Night wore which caused it to move slightly. She looked at her arm that was slashed earlier to see a small wound that had begun to close. "I told you already, things are returning to normal for me."

"Don't care. You're getting treated." They replied curtly which caused Arianna to let out a sigh. Slowly her appearance begun to change ever so slightly to one more familiar.

"Your such an idiot sometimes. There's no need to do something so pointless."

"You're the idiot here. For doing something so stupid in your condition."

"I already told you I'm getting better."

"That doesn't matter."

There was silence between the two for a long period of time till eventually Arianna buried her face into the crook of Night's neck. "... Thank you for saving me, Roy." She muttered in a low quiet voice.

Chapter 5

Arianna stared at the white ceiling of a hospital room as she got lectured by Stan and Roy. *The only time the two of them aren't fight is when they are lecturing me. Nice to see that hasn't changed after about two years.* She groaned internally as she kept her mouth shut since if she said anything it just make it worse. It was a lesson she had learned after years of such kinds of lectures.

Arianna looked over at them more in curiosity if they were done and had calmed down a little. Even though she was being lectured she couldn't stop the soft look in her eyes for the brief moment she looked at them. Though that moment didn't go unnoticed by Roy. "Your being lectured here! What are you even thinking about to have such a look?!" Roy snapped at which Arianna turned her head away quickly and wiped away any emotion.

"It's nothing… Important." She replied before she added the last part in realization. But it was clear he wasn't about to drop it. He was pissed at her, so he was kind of looking for a bit of a fight with her. *He's not gonna drop it at this rate.* She concluded with a slight shake of her head. "I just thought the two of you are so much alike, kind of like siblings."

"Siblings the two of us? No way, we are nothing a like." Roy exclaimed a little annoyed on the comparison. Stan reacted differently, he stopped talking and looked away.

"Not really, you do have some real similarities. So, it's not an impossibility of you two actually being siblings." Arianna paused. "Not to mention you don't have much of a leg to stand on when it comes to your family situation as you have no idea." She added swiftly as she forced herself to sit up.

"That's low…" Roy muttered as he looked away.

"Don't care. The two of you have been lecturing me for hours. Then you got on me for how I looked at the two of you. The two of you might be older than me but I'm not a child anymore, not that I've ever really been all that childish in the first place." Arianna growled with sharp eyes. "I understand you were worried about me that's why I sat here listening to the two of you as long as I did.

"I am aware of my condition and of my ability. I understood the dangers. We do not have the liability to take things all safe and content. We needed confirmation, and information. Now they won't appear like they have been for a while I'm certain." Ari stated with a cold tone. "I can handle more than a few injuries at such a price. Besides even if you didn't show up Roy, I had a backup." She added with a slight shake of her head.

"A back up plan? What exactly was that when they broke your leg?" Roy replied sharply. Ari then pulled out a pendent in full view for the two of them to see. "That's?! How did you get that! That can't be real, can it?!"

"It's very real. Currently it's the only one in service as I'm testing it." Arianna replied as she hid the pendent again. "It's still new tech and a little problematic but I was the best one to actually test it. Before you get mad about it, I had additional plans for if it failed." Arianna let out a slight sigh, "where is she you said you told her and that she'd be here."

"Mmm. Not sure but that's what she told me." Stan replied with a slight shake of his head. "But is it really all that important for all of us to hear? If it's so important, wouldn't you tell him?"

"I already informed them while you were lecturing me. I just would like to tell you in advance that's all. Not to mention we haven't seen each other all at once for a few years." Ari replied as she looked over at the window. She didn't say anything else but had an expression that indicated she had something serious on her mind.

After some time, a young women slipped through the door and into the room Ari looked over to see them enter. "Alex you're here, I was getting a little anxious."

"Apologises, getting into a hospital without leaving a trace is a little more difficult than one might imagine." Alex replied before crossing her arms. "So why did you call us?"

The women who had just arrived was Alexandria Yuen a long curly pale pink hair and purple eyed women that is a year older than Arianna. The two at the time were close as they had pretty much grown up together, as such was one of Arianna's few friends.

"Guess you're not in the mood to catch up." Ari muttered with a slight shake of her head. "Right well I guess these no real reason to beat around the bush." She sighed as she rolled her shoulders. "I've verified that after about eight years of silence they have become an active player once again in this little song and dance."

"What? Then what are we sitting around for."

"Let her finish speaking, Roy." Alex sighed as she lightly hit him in the back of the head. "Seems you up and disappearing hasn't changed your impulsiveness." She muttered with a shake of her head. "I heard about what you're currently doing. Does it have something to do with this? Because considering your personality you wouldn't have just let this happen for no reason."

"Hold on what are you talking about Alex?" Stan asked not sure what Alex was tried to point out. Alex looked over at Ari who just shrugged her shoulders.

Arianna then looked away, "I won't deny Alex, part of the reason is due to them, but not all of it. Though I still feel the same way mind you. There are times I just wish to leave all together, especially of when I'm reminded of back then." Ari ran a hand through her hair as she wore a slightly sad expression. "But I need to do this as repayment of sorts."

"Anyways, they are back and its best we are careful. It's not about to be like it was before. But they are not the only one we need to look out for. Recently I've been hearing whispers… nothing concrete yet just rumours and speculations. But there is a chance of a new player making an appearance soon.

"They are what's concerning me. For so many centuries there has only been two. If it's true we have no idea what they are planning." Ari explained as she bit her lip slightly. "Something isn't right… and I don't think it's good. So, its best if we are all careful."

"So, what you want us to give up everything we've done."

"That's not what I said Roy. I haven't forgotten what they did to me and I'm sure you haven't either. All I'm saying is its best we air more on the side of caution for now. They've gone quiet for years. But it doesn't mean they haven't planned or prepared just like us. The rumours are another cause for concern too." Ari stated as she looked at him with sharp eyes which caused him to look away. "I'll leave it at that for now… but there is something else I need to talk to you about. I might need your help with something… relatively soon."

Chapter 6

In an unknown location there was a very dark and dreary lab. Despite is appearance it was by no means abandoned. The room was filled with all kinds of odd lab equipment there was the sounds of beeps and bubbles from this equipment. The dim lights that barely lit the room let out a low hum from their fruitless attempt to light up the lab.

The rustle of papers, the shift of movement, and the sound of low growls could easily be heard. The further in the lab you went the more some of these sounds made sense. Along the back wall was lined with a ranging size of cages, with a door to some even larger enclosers. From beyond that door the sound of distant human screams could be heard as a pair of figures look in to the encloser from a window.

Suddenly a door opened and bright light from the connected hall was let into the room. It cast light into a grizzly scene, as tools hung around the room and counter tops were coated with blood, some dry and some not, with clumps of meat and flesh all around. "Tell me about the progress on the experiment." A man growled as they walked into the room as the door closed behind him.

The figures that stood at the window was a women and man that looked worse for ware and covered in blood. They spun around was the man's voice the man covered in blood raced over to him. "Exhaled Leader! We did not expect your arrival today." The man replied in a pleasant tone as if to pacify the leader that appeared before them.

"A report is what I asked for Undead. Not some petty excuses. Or must I teach you a lesson?" He growled back which caused the undead male to flinch back. The women than stepped forward.

"If you do that much, your well aware he will no longer be of any use. Not to even mention I'll no longer cooperate." The women stated in a cold voice. She looked directly at the leader with no hint of fear of what might happen.

"Then it's you that will be punished in his stead." The 'leader' growled at her. He reached out and grabbed her by the neck, whether it was an attempt to scare the women or kill her that was uncertain.

"Even if you kill me. What you want won't work. I may not be able to die as I wish, but I'll never be your slave." The women replied. "I am not afraid of a mortal that is just using the power of a Fallen Tifan. I may have little choice in giving my aid, but I will not fall to one such as you. You will fall, the cycle will end just as it is written."

"Tsk, I will not be the one that fall but those you ride your hope with. The cycle might end but it will be us that stands on top. After all you've created that, have you not." The 'leader' purred with an evil smile. He reached up and traced his hand around her face before he pulled her towards him.

"You half-spirit. That mortal body you've invaded with aid of my power. Did you forget that I took that body's friend as my women before disposing her? After all you've already lost the blood, I'll find the other and the cycle will end with my master on top." He added as he tossed her face aside.

The 'leader' then turned to the man and begun to ignore the presence of the women. "Yes! It has been perfected a creature as you wish has be made." The undead man replied with a bow. The women looked at the man sadness held in her eyes before she turned away sharply.

"A creature of a mixture of Mythic and science. The Chimera so desired, now even if they have the elixir on their side that you are so incapable and utter refusal to make me. Even if they've managed to reintroduce such a thing to this half of the two worlds, the Chimera cruel and powerful that would be hard to deal with." He paused as he covered his smile. "They could not possibly survive and stand up against such a thing. A thorn in my side will forever be removed."

"This monstrous creature has already killed four handlers." The women muttered. "But that does not mean it's impossible to kill. Nor control." She added before she turned away and left the lab.

The women walked down the empty halls angered at which had just occurred. She held her hand to her chest with a pensive look on her face. As she turned down a corridor and ran into someone.

"Ah! Your still here. I didn't expect to run into you today." She sighed as she looked up at the tall young man with dark blue near black coloured hair and deep blue eyes. "We might experience some trouble soon. He likes the new 'toy'."

Chapter 7

Despite the extent of her injuries from the attack a week ago, which caused broken limbs and deep lacerations she returned to school with only some light bandages and tight wraps around the locations that were once broken. She sat at a desk and looked outside the window it was a cloudy overcast kind of day she found it fit well with what she had plan to do that day.

After she got injured, she got chewed out by Yavari Luo, well so did Sean and Dave since they left her alone. She told them to actually pay attention to Arianna now, as such Sean was currently glaring at her. The two since they met haven't gotten along Ari hated his guts, he was rude and abrasive towards her for no good reason, so she didn't try to improve the relationship between them and rather just ignore him for the most part.

Arianna looked down at her left arm that was wrapped with bandages. She let out a sigh as she clenched her hand a few times, it was only a few days ago that she could barely move that hand due to the injury she sustained from the fight with Imitator. Just like the injury on her arm, all her other injuries she had sustained that night were nearly healed.

This kind of thing was long familiar sight to Arianna, however not to this extent. The extent at which her injuries had healed already at this point had caused her some surprise as well. *It's faster than before. … the more I try, the harder I'm pushed back. I don't-.* Her train of thought was cut off as someone sat down next to her, something which caused her to jump as she was lost in thought.

Arianna turned her head sharply with a slight glare to indicate her displeasure for her sudden new desk mate. But the moment she laid her eyes on them her eyes widened in surprise, as next to her was a young man with a familiar tough of red-orange hair and silver eyes. *Roy?!*

Before she got a chance to question him class had begun. Arianna was more concerned with who was beside her than the teachers lecture so she used her notebook in front of her and began to write in code. When she was finished her note, she pushed it over into his line of sight and lightly tapped it. [Roy, what are you doing here? You have no need to go to school.]

He looked down at the paper Ari had indicated to him. "Shouldn't you be paying attention to class?" Roy asked in a low whisper. Ari glared as him as slide the paper closer to her and quickly wrote something down that was fairly slopy due to the fast and hasty response.

[You know, I don't need to pay attention to this, as its nothing new for me. Now cut the crap and answer me. If you were trying to come here in secret, you would have done a much better job at hiding than this even without tech. So, tell me.] Arianna replied, the look on her face was not one of worry but more of slight annoyance if anything.

[It was orders from higher up to protect you. It came about after they received your report, and due to your injuries from the last attack.] Roy wrote back. Arianna looked down at his response and her hand tightened around the pen she held onto. She brought the notepad closer to her once more and looked down at it.

After years of leaving me out to dry, now they decide to try and protect me. All they did was teach me after my fam- parents died. But now they decide to protect me once all the facts are presented to them. Maybe it's due to my use to them now or what I can do… cause it's probably not that. They never wanted to announce it, made me afraid to do so. Why I've chosen my path and why I hesitate even now. Something probably happened for him to even do this. Arianna thought as she looked away from the page with a slightly dejected look.

Arianna heard some slight gasps which caused her to turn. She noticed several heads turn away from her gaze but there were hints of a blush on their face. This instance caused her to bite her lip slightly occurrence like this has become a little more common place in the recent month which was worrisome to her. Ari at the time was on a thin tight rope of uncertainty, she was nearly an adult now in the legal sense and had to make a real choice. It was something one might consider a luxury given the chance to choose, but others in similar situations got such an option.

Arianna after a few moments her eyes shook slightly before she turned to her desk again and wrote something once more. [I'm not sure why they choose to do such a thing. Especially since I normally work alone. I ~~want~~ need to go somewhere after school, so I expect you to do well.] Arianna jotted down. She pushed it in Roy's direction and looked at the board.

[Where do you plan to go?] She wasn't surprised that was the next thing he asked. Arianna was sure he was likely to suggest for the two of them to go together next. She lightly shook her head as she rested her head on her right hand as she wrote her reply.

[I plan to go to the local Eternial temple that's all I'm sure I'll be back before dusk. So, for my well-being its more imperative you do as I ask.] That was her reply, she needed to check on something and preferred if Roy wasn't around when she did it. Arianna's reason for it wasn't that she didn't trust Roy, however there are always somethings you wish to keep from one's closest friends for peace of mind or their own well-being and this was such an occasion.

[An Eternial temple. You mean one of the temples for the Eternal religion right, a temple of the Eternal. I didn't realize you were religious or is this recent?] When Ari saw his reply, she wore a slight smile before she shook her head lightly.

[No, I'm not. I don't follow the Eternial religion, at least not anymore. I once did a very long time ago when I was young but not anymore. But there is another reason I plan to go to the temple, there no need for you to worry okay.] After her persistent resistance Roy eventually stopped and no longer asked for her reason. At the end of school Ari managed to slip away from her adoptive brothers to make her way to the temple of the Eternal that resided in Brightton City.

The Eternial religion of the world resided around the idea of two gods called Faradityx and Vysdite, their seven apostles, and the idea of an eternal cycle. All temples of the religion always resided on what is called sacred or holy ground that was above settlement level to allow the gods a place to watch over the settlement. There was a lot more to this religion than just this, much of which are difficult to recall, but for now these are the main points.

The two gods watch over those they favour and grant them true names. The apostles were the ones that directly watched over the land that the gods made. However, it's believed in the inner sanctums of the religion they've long since left with only the gods making the odd appearance and no longer granting mortals their divine favour. The cause being a war that occurred at some point in history that is not written.

At the top of the stairs to the temple was a large assortment of buildings those of which held many different aspects to the religion that the mortals had created around such concepts. Though some aspects focused on in the temples varied, the temple in Brightton City represented more on the idea of the afterlife and acceptance. Due to that the Temple was always held a vail of quiet and silence. It always felt so mournful when being there as if something was lost here.

Arianna walked over the pavilion that held the statue representation of the two gods. The gods' faces were hidden with a hood for Faradityx and a vail for Vysdite. Arianna walked over to the statue of Faradityx there was a plaque at the base of the statue where she placed some flowers. [Here in this temple lies reconvince for the loss of the last of thy Gods blood and founders of Eternial; Rotusole.] Arianna ran her finger along the engraved text which was relatively new unlike some of the other things around. *And which no body lies here. Though the plaque might make you think otherwise.*

Arianna was alone near the statues, most people avoided them since it's believed it brought forth ill omen and death due to the god that mourned the loss of the Rotusole family. So normally only tourist that came to see the statues would be near them. Ari closed her eyes and bowed her head slightly as she clasped her hands together.

As Arianna stood silent in front of the statue as if in prayer or in some form of plea a figure came up from behind her. When she heard their footsteps stop, she lowered her hands and opened her eyes. "What do you want. I came like you wanted… after all you never really ask to see me in person, well under normal circumstances anyways." Arianna replied a little sharply as she glanced over to the older man with black-purple hair that stood beside her.

"No reason for you to be so sharp." He replied as he crossed his arms and glanced at her. She turned her nose away with a huff.

"I'm annoyed with what you did that's what. Considered our relations and past I'm not pleased; it's been made quite clear your stance." She answered back as she looked up at the statue of Faradityx.

"Fine. There are two reasons I'm here." He paused as he pulled out a small chip and placed it into Arianna's hand. "It's best if you look into what I just handed you."

Arianna looked at what the man just handed her as she skimmed over the information in the chip. "A Lab? Are you certain about this?" She asked as she turned her head slightly.

"Not entirely, we were unable to verify if it was correct."

"I see, alright I'll check it out then. Now what is the other reason, if I have to guess it's not a nice friendly heartfelt talk." Arianna muttered as she crossed her arms and tilted her head slightly as she gave him a slide long glance.

"I've done what I thought was necessary." He paused of a moment. "I'm aware what has been occurring. How those around have been acting recently. It will only get worse." Arianna looked away again. "We have no other choice here, and you are aware of that. So be sure to get things ready, as you have no choice in this." With that the man left Arianna alone her fist clenched and her head down.

Chapter 8

That night Arianna made dinner for the Luo family to be a kind of repayment for the chance to join their family. That was what the reason for it was claimed to be that is. Yavari however wouldn't eat what Arianna made and claimed to not feel well. Though that was a blatant lie as she ate later after the food was gone.

The first time Yavari outwardly acted towards Ari in such away. Caden felt bad and tried to cheer her up since he thought Yavari hurt Ari's feelings. She didn't care much about such a fact more annoyed as she made things more complicated. But in the end, it all worked out and the Luo family that night they were like logs and were not likely to wake up anytime soon.

Arianna on the other hand was wide awake and well. She stretched her arm above her head after she removed the bandage from around her left arm. Her leg was still a little sore, but it wasn't something that she didn't find she had to worry about too much. Her phone that was placed on a nightstand table next to her bed vibrated she quickly flipped the screen up to see the message before she left her bedroom.

Arianna's room at the Luo family home was on the second floor without even the slightest noise she made her way down to the main floor and over to the front door. With a twist of the locks, she opened the door and on the other side stood Alex. "Hey, so what's this exactly about Ari?" she asked the moment the door opened.

"Thanks for coming so suddenly. I was made aware of something not too long ago. If the information is credible, I might need your handy work. You're an expert on picking locks after all."

"You can pick locks too, quiet well might I add. So, what makes it that you need my help?" Alex asked as she shifted slightly as she walked inside. Arianna closed the door and leaned against it.

"I'm on a bit of a time crunch and I don't know how many locks nor the type. If there are too many locks, I won't be able to do what's needed. You know how I prefer to do things alone, but sometimes I shouldn't be stubborn."

"Meaning its actually something serious and important right. Okay got it. Any idea where to start?"

"Yeah, that's the easy part. We need to be a little cautious though I made sure they'd be deep asleep, but we don't have much of a guarantee they won't wake up earlier than intended. Also don't take anything I don't want to deal with a pointless troublesome thing."

Alex them followed Arianna as she led her down the main hallway. They two's footsteps made no real sound as if they were shadows. They faced the door that was on the wall underneath the stairs to the second floor. The door opened with no issue but inside the door just looked to be storage filled with an assortment of items and boxes that were not in use.

Alex looked at Arianna in slight confusion since this was not what she quite expected. Ari when to the floor and placed her ear on the ground and lightly tapped to hear an echo back. Which meant there was defiantly something below them and not a solid foundation as the home's official building plans suggest.

Arianna then pulled out a few items from the apparent storage room to realize that the space under the stairs had a lot more space than it looked. With that they pushed thing back to reveal a hatch with a lock.

In that moment Alex was alert and realized what Arianna told her might have real merit. Alex got to work on the lock quickly as she brought out a small kit and pulled out some small tools which she fit into the lock. It didn't even take her long to release the lock and open the door.

With the hatch open it revealed a set of descending stairs. They looked at one another for a moment and gave a slight nod before they started their descent with Alex in front and Ari behind as she closed the door behind them. Ari set a timer for around four hours as they made their way down. There was a surprising number of steps to make it to the hidden floor below of an open space with some doors and chairs.

For someone that just randomly made their way down here they would think it was just a basement, secret man cave, or something of the like. With how the space at the bottom of the steps was set up to make it appear as such as it had several things that would cause one to think such, but it was more so one didn't need to make their way back up all too often. However, these two went down here for a sole purpose, as such a smoke screen like that would work as they began to look around in detail and found more than one door that was lock.

The two split off and started to work on the doors that had more than several locks. This time it took longer to open the locks. Alex managed to open her door first on the other side was selves filled with array of chemicals many of which were things that someone would be unable to obtain through regular means.

By the time Alex had opened the door she had worked on Ari had managed to unlock two of several locks. With Ari just finished the second one Alex took over the work on the door from her. Something of which Ari begrudgingly obliged eventually once she realised the locks was in fact had become more and more difficult.

Ari stood back in silence as she watched Alex tackle one lock after another. After some time, Ari started to look around the room and wonder if others in the house where aware of the space that was below them. Then Ari begun to hear a quite but distinct noise from the other side of the door which Alex was working on.

"Alex get away from the door. Now!" Ari ordered in an urgent kind of tone once she realised what it was. But Alex didn't move and remained in place.

"I can't we'll lose the pins and be unable to open it till tomorrow if I do." Alex replied. It was unsure if Alex was aware of the reason for Ari's sudden urgency. But it was clear she didn't plan to move till she finished the lock.

Ari clicked her tongue she slid next to Alex and grabbed the pick tools in her hand before she pushed Alex back and away from her and the door. As Alex got pushed away from the door an electrical current was charged and begun to run through the tools. Ari let out a low curse as she felt the jolt of electricity.

She clenched her teeth as the electricity coursed through her body. Her muscles tightened but not to the point she was unable to move. Ari fought through the pain of the electricity to finish the locked. With the lock completed it in turn cut the current that coursed through the lock. She leaned back and let out a sigh. "That really hurt."

"A timed unlock system. Whatever's on the other side they really don't want people getting in." Alex muttered her arms crossed. "Just what is on the other side?"

"Based on the information I was given it should be a lab or something. But what is being done on the other side your guess is probably as good as mine." Ari paused as she looked down as her hands that twitched. It was from a probable mix of adrenaline and electricity that had coursed through her. "I heard the ding of a timer of some kind then hum of a gathering charge. Which probably means if we don't open the lock in the right amount of time, we get 'punished'." Ari muttered as she ran her hand lightly through her hair. "Do you think you can do it?"

"If not, can you handle the punishment?" Alex asked Ari thought for a moment before she gave a firm nod. "If that's the case. Yeah, I can do it. I can just think of it as some kind of challenge." With that Alex worked on the remaining locks once more and opened those faster than before, and with it the ability to open the door.

The door swung open and on the other side the clear and familiar sound of a lab could be heard. Ari turned on the light to see counters and a number of vials, apparatuses, and notebooks inside. The two walked inside together and begun to look around. "Do you have any idea what's going on here? You're the one with the science knowledge." Alex asked, Ari walked over to a wall counter where some photos were sat. "Ari?"

Ari picked up some photos and looked at them intently, *I knew it*. Alex walked over and looked over Ari's shoulder at the picture, Alex tensed a little at the sight of one of the pictures. "Elixir... it's called Elixir. It's not a medicine rather something to make the once impossible in this world, possible."

"I've never even heard about such a thing. How do you even know about it? What exactly does it mean, or why?" Alex asked Ari looked away and was about to walk away when she grabbed Ari's shoulder. Alex spun me around and held both her shoulders and looked directly at Ari. "Arianna if you even consider me a friend. I have a right to know! I have a right to know why a picture of my dead mother is in that group picture!" Alex exclaimed her grip on Ari's shoulders was tight.

Arianna didn't say anything at first, she just looked away from Alex to not look her in the eye. "Your mother probably worked on it or worked with them at some point as a scientist. I don't know much, just it makes one able to surpass or do what should be impossible on Ashise. And that 12 years ago the most important ingredient to be able to make it called 'draggod's' blood' was lost." She lied as she looked at the equipment in the lab.

"Draggod... as in dragon god. Elixir? Could that be why..."

"Yeah... it likely was. A lot of conflicts have occurred because of it." Ari replied as she slipped out of Alex's grasp. "I'm not sure why... but Dr. Luo might currently be working on something related to Elixir."

Arianna walked over to the notebooks. "It would make sense, the hidden lab and the boobytrapped locks this is quiet dangerous stuff. Not just anyone would have been able to get past those trap locks. Without injury if it wasn't you... no, rather if it wasn't the combined effort of the two of us. They weren't locks just anyone could unlock and the 'punishments' were quite harsh." She then paused and looked over at Alex. *Though if I knew that this was what was done here... not just a secret lab. Even with her skills with locks I wouldn't have brought her with me.*

"No matter what don't tell anyone what was down here. I'll deal with it alright. When I say no one, I mean no one." Arianna stated before she grabbed a notebook. To find that the books were encoded like how alchemy and old science texts in the day had been.

"Not even Roy or Stan?"

"No not even them." Ari replied quickly. *Especially them.* Ari glanced over at Alex and added. "If Stan asks you... just tell him you helped me with something that is problematic."

"Is it that problematic."

"Extremely so. Which is why you can't tell anyone." Ari sighed as she sat down on the counter. "It's something dangerous. Something that just having even a hint of association to it means death. Something of which almost everyone wants you head just because of it. Do you understand."

Alex for the first time looked at Arianna was wide eyes with sudden realization. "T-that happened to you didn't it. It's the reason you were at the orphanage… everything." Alex muttered but that's when some dark deep seeded fear begun to form and reveal itself in Alex's eyes, something she normally kept hidden. She tried to hide it from Ari, but Ari saw it. "If that's the case just, who are you?"

"… That's the billion-dollar question, isn't it?" Arianna replied a little sharper. She had seen eyes like Alex before, she was familiar with it. But even though she was familiar with-it Arianna couldn't help but feel hurt that someone she was close to looked at her in such away. "Does it scare you. You have no idea who I am, what I look like." She spoke with an odd calm voice. Yet there was a hint of sadness in her voice.

"W-what. No, it doesn't scare me-." Alex paused she didn't finish her sentence she couldn't bring herself the say the end of that sentence. Arianna eyes darkened slightly in realization, she turned away sharply.

"Go… you know the way out… we'll talk later." Arianna said slowly but her tone sounded slightly hurt. She didn't speak or move till she no longer sensed another person near her. Arianna placed her hand down on a notebook and let out a sigh.

"How many times now have I gotten such looks now. I never thought I'd get such a look from a friend I trust in such a manner." She muttered as she looked down at the notebook. At this point Arianna had no idea how things were to turn out in the future, but she desperately wished not to lose the only friends/family she had.

Chapter 9

Arianna woke up covered in sweat and labored breaths. She hissed as her lower back hurt with a siring pain. She placed her hand on her lower back with little thought, she could feel the tense muscles in her back. She tossed the sheets aside as she stood up, she stretched her arms over her head. Today was the weekend but she didn't feel all that relaxed for the last week she had received a number of reports of some incidents of concern. Yet was told to stay out of it entirely not like she was going to argue about their decision on it.

Though that wasn't the only thing on her mind over the last while. Ever since that night her relationship with Alex had become extremely strained, which caused her a fair amount of stress. The idea for her that their relationship between each other a relationship that spanned about 10 years had become this strained from a single incident. It upset her but also made her question.

The other odd development was the slight change of heart of her youngest 'brother' Dave. He went from ignoring her to trying to become more like a sibling. Ari had no clue as to what brought about this change. She helped him with a major homework 'issue', or it could have been when she stood up against a bully for him, if not those something else she was unaware of. But after that he changed his attitude towards her.

After she got changed Arianna made her way downstairs and made herself a light breakfast as she leaned against the countertop. She enjoyed the silence while it lasted as it wasn't long till she hears a fight between the brothers. She shook her head slightly, *the two of them are just always fighting with one another they should try to get along for once. You never know when it will be the last time.* It wasn't long before Yavari begun to reprimand the two.

Ari secretly glared at Yavari as she had become sharp towards Ari recently. In all she didn't really care but had come to be on guard around Yavari as she felt like the women would try something when her guard was down.

Ari couldn't bring herself to begin to understand them in the slightest. They have been living together for a few months now at this point, and Yavari and Sean were still hostile. Rather they were even more hostile than from before. She couldn't think of anything she had done to make them dislike her or even anything she did to make them like her either. It didn't make any sense as she generally avoided interreacting with the family unless needed.

After some time Caden eventually joined Arianna in the kitchen as he also grabbed something to eat. He was kind to her from the very start though it was a nice change. Though she was wary since there was not really reason for Caden to be like this to Arianna.

To her the idea of motiveless kindness was an impossibility. But even though his kindness made her feel awkward she chooses not to avoid him because of it. Caden who had also grabbed some toast looked over at her and smiled. "Arianna, do you know about the festival that's going on this weekend?" Caden asked her.

Arianna knew about the festivals, they had an old relation to the Eternial religion, though now it was something widely celebrated in the country. *I guess it's that time of the year isn't it. It be that one… yeah, I have no desire to go to it.* She thought. However, she needed to be mindful of her answer as she was and orphan from the outskirts, not really close to any major city. As such she decided to just shake her head.

"I'm not surprised you haven't heard about it. How would an orphan hick like her ever go to such a thing?" Sean snorted as he sat down at the table.

"SEAN! Don't say that to your sister!"

"That girl is not my sister. Besides she not even saying anything to defend herself. Oh, wait it's because she's mute!" Sean growled, he was in an oddly hostile and combative mood towards Arianna for no real reason on her part. Arianna wanted to snap back at him in some way to prove him wrong but the moment she thought to open her mouth and speak she felt nauseous to the point she almost threw up.

Damn it. Arianna glared at Sean in frustration and anger. Despite the harsh words that Sean said to her aside from the single word of reprimand nothing was else was said nor was he punished. Arianna felt a little wronged for a brief moment, before her decision to resign that it was her own fate or the wrath of karma. Arianna just leaned back against the countertop with her fist clenched and turned her head away. It was clear what her place here was, and for now she needed to play it.

"A-anyways. Since you've never been to it before Arianna how about we go together… as a family." Caden coughed. The very mention caused her body to seize up. She found no real enjoyment in places crowed with people or noise, but that wasn't the only reason for her reaction.

"No thank you." She signed quickly. Ari wished to get away before they tried to stop her and force her to come, but it wasn't effective. Ari knew the idea behind the festival, and the reason the two continued to pester her to have her come with them. Sean just muttered his grievances at the very thought of going to the event with her, where Dave seemed excited to go with her.

Dave in the few weeks had actually manage to grow on her. At the sight of his excited joy at such a prospect Ari couldn't help but relent since she didn't want to upset him.

Even though Canlonen was a country that held a number of difference ceremonies and events, not all of which every town participates. But in the world, it was sometimes called the land that never rests due to such a factor. Arianna didn't really understand how the place even held such events, but it wasn't as if each event was entirely free or that people got the day off really, so it wasn't entirely impossible.

But even though there were many different events that occurred in Canlonen for Dave it was important to him to spend the first ever festival to pass since they became a 'family'. Though Ari didn't hold the same sentiments, she fell to his whims, even though she held no desire to go for multiple reasons. It was just the look he gave her she was weak to it.

Family... no I'd rather not. If I had no other choice I'd rather go alone. Arianna glanced at the two adults in front of her. She didn't get their insistence on their desired to attend such an event with her, nor did she want to go with them as a family. *What is with these people. Are all Surface dwellers like this? Or just those from Canlonen? Why do they even try to act is if we are a family... I don't understand them.*

In the end Arianna had little choice as she was quiet literally dragged to the car before she could even relent. They in truth didn't give her the option either way they were going to force her to go with them even if she continued to refuse. All for their own image, as in the country it looked bad to not go to a festival with your whole family at least once.

The event they took her to was on the other side of the city from their home, so it did take some time to get there. They didn't take her to one closer to avoid those that know them, was her thought of their reasons which more than likely correct. By the time they had arrived, the location was already packed with citizens and tourists. Forced to walk along with them through the festival Arianna didn't particularly enjoy it and held her arms and hands close to her. *Why do surface dwellers enjoy such crowded things. Too much could happen in such a place.*

As they walked around Arianna generally stood back and watched as the family explored stalls and entertainment that the festival provided. Arianna looked at the number of families that were here and most frequently took note of sibling pairs, she felt slightly forlorn at such a sight.

Would it have been like that for us too?

Despite the crowd of people Arianna felt rather lonely. She closed her eyes in thought before she shook her head lightly. Then without much so much as an indication or word of warning something grabbed a hold of her hand. This caused her to jump and nearly attack whatever it was that did it.

"Big sister you alright. You look a little pale?" A familiar voice asked her. She opened her eyes and looked over to see Dave who had clutched onto her hand. In sudden realization of the situation, she was currently in she nodded her head slightly in reply. "Is that so. Well, you should make sure you keep up or mother, father, and Sean will leave you behind." Dave told her as he begun to pull her hand forward.

Arianna looked at Dave with soft eyes. Unlike most of the others in her adoptive home Dave had become the kindest and begun to warmly welcome her. Even though it only recently it was better than before. With Caden though he was neither abrasive nor overly critical he was rarely around, so before 'home' was a place of little comfort for her.

Arianna had realized his change towards her. She was not entirely sure the reason to when he had come to try and treat her like she was his sister. *Though I don't think I could ever consider the kid my brother... but maybe a friend.* At the time the very thought of Dave being her friend; it wasn't something she thought to be possible for several reasons. But she couldn't help it with how nice he was to her despite how they even came to meet or get close.

Arianna looks at Dave as she followed behind him. *Though I know the circumstances and the difficulty. For the kindness he's shown me, whatever his reasons might be. I'll be sure not to let anything happen to him. After all, not even my closest friends...* Arianna shook her head lightly. She smirked slightly and pulled Dave back and up into her arms.

"Whaa?! B-big sister? Could you put my down?" Dave asked as he stuttered slightly most likely from surprise or embarrassment. Ari shook her head and put her finger to her lips to indicate to him not to say anything. "I'm not a kid you know I don't need to be carried around like this. Beside am I not heavy, for you to keep carrying like this?" he mentioned but once again she just shook her head.

After he resigned in defeat Arianna continued to walk to find the others of Dave's family. The two eventually found them in the audience of a performance, as they walked over Ari put Dave down and stood next to him at the very end away from the others. Yavari begun to mutter something to Dave which he protested to and defended her. Yavari though she acts like a kind mother to Arianna she was relatively two-faced though she acted kind at times, she was extremely harsh to Ari, and she often blamed Ari for things, nor really trusted her in the slightest.

A mother like that... It doesn't surprise me she has a son like Sean... Dave must take more after his father then. Arianna couldn't help but think as she turned her head towards the performance that the other in the family decided to come see over the insurance that Dave or myself was with them. The light of day had begun to fade so she was curious as to what act could even be performed.

The moment she turned her head to the stage however that question was answered as a jet of flames shot out from the man. This caused Arianna flinch back and stumble slightly. The performance was of fire minsters, performances that build a performance over/around fire and flames something that wasn't an unusual sight here.

It was something brought from the Eternial religion, though there is considered multiple different elemental affinities there are four core elements that are the bases for every other aspect excluding light and dark. It was believed that the 'apostles' of those core four were closer to the gods even though the others were 'apostles' with the aspect of other elements, that some extremist of the religion call only mutations. Either way due to the Eternial religion that originates from Canlonen as 'element' minsters that preform like this exist as it comes from that aspect of the religion's old ceremonies and dances.

Arianna didn't expect to see fire minsters considering the time of year it was, as she didn't even realize what this festival was. Her body had begun to break out in a cold sweat, and she had begun to unintentionally grip harder onto Dave's hand of which she still held on to. Dave let out a slight noise of discomfort and pain. He asked Arianna to let go or loosen her grip, but she didn't hear him. At which point Yavari act and pulled Dave hand out of Ari's grip and caused slight injury to Ari of nail marks and bruises.

As she no longer held on to Dave's hand, she brought her hand to her chest and begun to shake slightly, and her breathes became more rugged. She made slight noise as the flames went in her direction and stepped back. Dave held onto Ari's arm, "Sis are you okay?" She shook her head with her eyes closed.

Sean who had also noticed this suddenly realized what was wrong and smirked before he started to laugh lowly. "I got it. Arianna is terrified of fire. How could you even fear something like that that, the vary basis of life." He laughed as he held his stomach and begun to tease her. "Oh, I know, how about I help you get over your fear. Maybe then you'll look at me." Sean stated with an evil grin.

Arianna flinched and covered her eyes as he stood behind her. Sean then grabbed Arianna's wrists and pulled them away from her face and looked her in the eyes. Arianna could see an odd shine in his eyes which sent a shiver down her spine. Sean then started to push her closer towards the performance, Arianna was so fearful that she had no strength at that moment to fight back against him.

Arianna was pushed closer and close to the front of the performance her body begun to tremble as a leaf. She closed her eyes, but it didn't help, tears begun to form in her eyes and a whimper like noise escaped her lips. As she opened her eyes all she could see was flames that were in front of her and shot towards her. In her eyes something shined in them and turned dark; tears fell from her eyes before she let out a loud scream of fear.

Arianna spun around and knocked Sean to the ground, and she raced off. Caden went over and grabbed Sean by the arm and dragged him away from the crowd. "You took it to far this time Sean. Way to far." Caden growled.

"It was just a joke! It's not my fault she reacted like that." Sean replied sharply with a look as if he was the victim in this situation. Caden slapped Sean in the back of the head with a sharp look.

"You should have stopped the moment you realized she was terrified. She shouldn't have had to do that" Caden snapped. His eyes were dark clear with disappointment, he was furious.

"You saw how she was too. You could have done something to. But you did nothing. It's not my fault." Sean snapped back. Caden probably wanted to deck Sean at the moment, he glared at his wife Yavari indicating his displeasure in what he was currently faced with.

Caden knew Arianna had a few major burn scars on her back and Yavari knew this as well. Caden was very displeased with his wife at that moment for how she acted at the time. "Your right I should have done something, but I didn't as I thought you'd be reasonable adult and stop. Clearly I was wrong about my eldest son and don't know him as well as I thought same for my wife. However, the fault still entirely falls on you." Caden replied as he dropped Sean's arm.

"You're not really choosing that kid over your own son, are you?!" Yavari exclaimed as she pointed at Sean. Caden spun around and glared at Yavari his fist clenched, he was angry at how his wife acted in this moment. Even if she didn't know his speculations, Arianna was a child they agreed to take in.

"Arianna is also our child we decided to taken. It's clear where your priorities lie is not family but blood. I didn't even know someone like you even still existed in this world." Caden growled as he turned away. "I'll find Arianna by myself."

"Wait up Dad I'm coming with you!" Dave exclaimed as he chased after Caden to help look for Arianna. The two both left Yavari and Sean behind without a second thought alone in the festival grounds as night drew near.

Chapter 10

Arianna eventually stopped after a few minutes past. She tried to wipe away her tears that had streaked her face as she hung her head down low. *They'll probably leave without me. Damn it, why couldn't I just hold back, I ended up causing a scene. Granted Sean forced me into that situation. But… I just couldn't curb my fear when the flames came at me. Now he knows I'm terrified of fire and is going to us it against me. Fuck! Fuck, fuck, fuck! I'm such an idiot for letting someone learn of this weakness of mine.*

Arianna ran her hand through her hair in frustration. Her tears had stopped at this point, but the image hadn't really left from her mind. She walked with her hands in her zipper hoodie pockets with the hood over her head, in a real melancholy mood. Night had started to fall by now as she continued to walk down the festival streets filled with a generally cheery mood which was in complete conflict with her current mood. It's not like it was an occurrence that was completely new to her at this point in her life.

At this point in her life Arianna disliked several different things; a fair number of them about herself. One of which was her 'excelled' memory, as there are several things in the past that haunted her that she was unable to forget, and she was unable to forget things unless blocked out. As such this was likely to be another thing that would haunt her till the end of her days at this rate. She kicked a stone along the ground with a sigh to release some of her frustration and watched as the stone tumbled away out of sight from the force and number of people that were also on the street that night.

That joyful atmosphere of the festival didn't last much longer however as suddenly there was a noise followed by one scream than another. People were thrown into a panic as they begun to run away in the opposite direction from which the sound and screams had come from.

Arianna on the other hand made her way towards that spot. When she got close enough, she realised it wasn't something to be taken lightly.

Arianna ducked away out of sight and changed her appearance to that she used in for the Police station Rouge. Arianna was forced to change some of her physicality due to the lack, of a change clothes that would fit if she made it was the full normal physicality she chose to have when she was Rouge. With her appearance changed and she made her way back to the location.

There were a few people that hung around the area, but the most obvious sight was the bloody body that was on the ground. *I can't go right to poking the body that would cause some suspicion to be cast on me and cause problems. Guess I gotta take charge for now.* Arianna sighed as she removed her hood.

"I'm Rouge, Private Investigator and occasional consultant for the western Brightton City police. Has anyone called the emergency services yet?"

"Y-yes I have. Though I'm certain a number of others have as well."

"Is anyone still on the line with emergency services here?" She paused for a moment. *It would be a good idea to talk to the operator if they are still on the line. That way I'll be able to explain the situation more and give the EMS better information to go off of.*

"N-no."

"Sigh… alright. Can anyone tell me what exactly happened? I only heard a scream which brought me over." Arianna asked in a calm collected voice. Her arms were crossed her shoulders back and head up as she looked around. Some might say that she was oddly calm to be on a scene such as this one.

"I was here, a-and saw it all."

"Alright would you be so kind to fill me in on what happened."

"It's not much to be honest. It was just like it normally was for the festival nothing seemed wrong. Then suddenly that body fell from the sky."

"It fell from the sky? Did you hear any planes, helicopters, or even screaming?"

"No there was nothing like that."

Arianna crossed her arms and held her chin as she closed her eyes for a moment. *There was no scream, so they likely didn't jump from anything. Nothing was in the sky that they noticed… hmmm, let's take a look at the body.* She thought. She thanked the person for their time and told them they should stay nearby as police would likely also want to hear their statement.

She then went over towards the body and pulled out a pair of gloves she had left in her hoodie. With the gloves on she took a few pictures of the scene. However, she was quick noticed the camera quality of a camera phone was lower than what was desired for a crime scene photo.

She looked around and notice someone with a professional grade camera. Arianna thought for a moment to use that person's camera but decided against it since it wouldn't be good to leave crime scene photos on a civilian camera. So, she chooses not to do anything major that would greatly hamper an investigation.

Arianna begun to look at what was in front of her specifically the body. *There doesn't seem to be much impact damage to the ground, nor do I see any bruising present or forming at this time that would be likely from a fall of significate height. So, they probably didn't fall from that far to here.* She thought as she shifted. Right as she was about to stand and look around, she paused.

"Wait…" Arianna muttered as she looked at the body again. *A fair amount of the blood's dry… that explains the lack of major blood splatter or even pooling blood.* She realized but continued to work more. At this point she actually touched the body; it was already cold to the touch and stiff. Arianna looked more at some of the wounds and noticed a distinct pattern. *These wounds… are they claw marks? I'm not too sure but the spacing fairly is uniform and the gashes are ragged not clean like the work for a blade or bullet.*

Arianna then moves closer to the face that was hidden with cloth of their clothes. It causes Arianna to pause. The individual wore something like a helmet not just that; one that was familiar and not something you could find on the surface. *What… no way.*

Arianna knew media sources would likely arrive first before the police. At this point she had looked enough at the body to satisfy her curiosity for now. Since she was fairly sure she wouldn't be allowed to work on this she had no choice but to change her approach.

As she finished, as if timed, security guards showed up with blankets. "Great timing. You with the blankets come over here and help me lay them. Then five of you gather up witnesses and watch for symptoms of shock. The rest of you set up a 600m parameter for now… yeah that should be enough. Let not one through expect EMS and the police."

"Who are you to give us orders."

"Rouge PI. I've worked as a consultant for the Brightton police before. As the only one here that has worked with them, I think I have a good idea what they might want done. Aside from that the most important thing is preservation of evidence." Arianna replied with a firm tone with sharp eyes. *It's something those skilled on both sides know well.*

"So, don't you think it be best to follow the directions of someone that's worked on such things before."

With that there was no argument, Arianna with the help of one guard covered the body with a blanket. She noticed their completion, "first time seeing something like this?" she asked with a calm tone.

"Y-yes."

"Well considering what you do, it wouldn't be the most common sight. Word of advice for now don't breathe in through your nose. It's not a pleasant scent. Also keep your gaze here to a minimum. Don't think about it alright."

"How can you be so calm?"

"Well, I've seen my fair share at this point. Besides some people handle it better than others that's all, not unaffected just suppressing such emotion really. Go help gather witnesses and when EMS shows have them look you over as well since your pretty green."

With that all dealt with Arianna waited for officers to show as she kept a close eye on things. As she thought media arrived first since they were closer than the nearest police station. Given the time she decided to look up and confirm something she had speculated.

Above was a tree it was not incredibly tall that a fall from it would normally kill a person rather just break something. She looked over the tree and though it was dark she was able to notice something in it. But the police and EMS arrived before she could do anything else. "Rouge what are you doing here. You have no reason to be here."

Arianna turned around to look at the officer who looked as if he was trying to protect his turf. "Believe me it was a stroke of luck. I was in the area when it happened that's all. You act as if I can't come to enjoy a festival when I'm in the country.

"But when I got here, I knew it was going to take you guys' a while, so I secured the scene that's all so far. I've even gathered some witnesses, so I'd say I was quite helpful rather than a problem as you always make me out to be."

"Because you are a problem."

"I'm hurt." Arianna said with a pained expression that turned into a smirk. "Can this problem go home then?" She asked with a sigh.

"Hold on, I need you to give a statement." The officer stated as he grabbed her arm. She gave him a displeased look which caused him to flinch slightly.

"But I didn't see anything." She replied in a bored tone. They wanted her to leave anyways, now they just wanted to know what she figured out and take the credit. No matter where you went, there were always parasites like this.

"That's not it, tell me what you know."

"Fine, let me go after this then." She sighed with cold eyes. She was more than annoyed with people from above though that by no means meant below was that much better. Just a lot less occurrences like this and what she's had to deal with for months now.

"Fine. The blood was already dry and their muscles stiff when I arrived. I didn't arrive long after the initial scream since I was at the festival. So, my guess is that they were already dead, but I have no idea how long though exactly. The thing is the injuries I could see were weird. That's all I got for you." Arianna replied to the officer. After a few moments he waved his hand after she signed a paper and left the perimeter.

Yet even when she left the perimeter Arianna wasn't done, after all she left out a certain piece of information/hunch, the tree. Arianna managed to get over to the tree from another she climbed up and got the location that she noticed something hanging from.

It was a small bag she opened it and begun to look through. After a few moments she pulled out a small card. "I thought so, since I recognized the helmet, this had to be the case. But what the hell happened?" She muttered as she shook her head.

She removed a few other small items from the bag before she got down from the tree and left the festival grounds. As she made it to the base of the stairs to see a familiar figure stood there in wait. "Stan? What are you doing here?"

"Waiting for you."

"Okay but why… no, how?"

"The family called in."

"What? Hold on called me in as missing. Who did exactly?"

"Caden Luo."

"Ah… you already knew where I was probably because of that call right. Sigh… but I'm guessing that's not your only reason for being here."

"Your right. I was asked to give this to you." Stan replied as he handed her a sealed letter. Arianna looked at it for a second before she opened it. While she read the contents of the letter, she had an odd, then soon dark expression as she let out a long sigh.

"Great. Of course. I'll be calling in a bit of a favour soon it seems." Arianna paused as she looks off in the distance. "This really is a great time for this, but I don't really have any choice in this matter anymore. Especially with what's been going on. Damn it, I just can't catch a break." She groaned as she squatted down and roughed up her hair.

"You know about the body, right? The occurrence I had I just come from. There's more like that isn't there? That's why you and everyone else has cut me out of the loop.

"Whatever did that isn't human… I don't know exactly what it is… but somethings not right about that either." Ari groaned out loud before she stood up. She then handed the items that she took from the bag over to Stan including the 'ID card'. "I was able to grab this before the police. You can deal with it properly unlike me."

"What? Annoyed about being a codeless now?" Stan asked as he took the items from her. He only briefly glanced over but he would know that wasn't the reason for her frustration.

"No, I don't care that I've been left out on certain things going on in your organization. After all there are certain things, I can do that you can't as a codeless. No, I just… I don't like this. I'm not exactly sure how to explain it." Arianna paused before she shook her head.

"This might be just the beginning for what's to come. Whatever the thing that's done this, and whoever is using it… they going to be dangerous, and it is unnatural." Arianna then walked with Stan to his car and got in. "Whatever I guess I won't be going 'home' tonight then or for a while for that matter either. I need to clear my head anyways." Arianna muttered as she looked out the window as they drove off.

At the time Arianna didn't understand it or the feeling she had, nor on what she had seen. But a tension had formed in the world and the stage was set. A game long in the making was nye ready to being all it was waiting for was a main actor's choice. As things had barely just begun.

Chapter 11

A week had passed since the festival and Arianna had not been seen since that day. Even though Arianna had disappeared in the Luo house; there was no real indication of any fear or worry about her were abouts. There was the occasional mention of it from Caden and Dave over the past week but there was nothing aside from that. The house appeared to be content even.

On this night most of the family was on the main floor, all except Caden Luo who had gone into the hidden basement. It was a dark night with no light in the sky, and the area was oddly quiet. However, this clear oddity went unnoticed in the Luo home.

Dave had been pacing that night he didn't like how his brother and mother acted towards Arianna's disappearance. Yavari wanted to act is if nothing was even wrong in the first place, while Sean was more or less in complete denial of the events. Dave wanted to go and search for Arianna himself, but he wasn't allowed.

Tonight, he planned to sneak out and start a search by himself, he partially felt he need to make it up to Arianna especially after how he completely ignored her in the beginning. Even since that day he realized he was wrong about her, more so he was proved wrong. He had been swayed by his mother and even brother and thought she had ill intent towards them even though the family had adopted her. But that was wrong, they were wrong about her, so he wanted to do something right for her and find her. Though he didn't even get a chance to even do that.

There was a loud rumble that got louder and louder with each moment that passed, till the point that things inside the house begun to shake like that of an earthquake. The tremors got worse with each moment as the three hid as instructed in the event of an earthquake. Though such actions that they had taken were an ultimately pointless endeavour.

A wall burst open into the room and sent rubble inside, and the power inside the house went out. The large gust of wind that was attributed to the destruction of the wall caused the three to fly back away from the hole that had formed in the wall. Downstairs the noise it caused, and the cut of power was noticed as well.

Caden at this point raced upstairs to where the crash and his family were. A major hole was created in the side of the house which despite the major damage to the wall still stood. From the hole a large, towering figure forced its way inside the home despite the tight fit. The figure looked nothing like anything they had ever seen before in person.

The figure was extremely large, on all fours it roughly was about as tall as the ceiling of the house which make over 200m tall. Not only was its massive size that caused the family panic, but the sight of the figure did as well even in the darkness it was possible for them to see a slight outline.

Along with its massive and bulky form it appeared to have a tail like that of a scorpion, with giant wings like a bat. It had massive paws over half the size of the average person, and clear sharp and large claws and fangs. It had the main body of that akin to that of a lion in some form but much larger. It was a clear appearance of the first created form of a Chimaera.

The Chimera let out a loud roar that made one's ears ring if not prepared. Its golden eyes glowed in the light as it begun to scan the three people that were in front of it. It's very gaze caused shivers to travel down their spines. *Where the hell, are they?*

It may not have found who it searched for as it didn't move for a few minutes. Then with a growl and a slight shift of its body it reached it's claw out towards Sean. It was slow and clear it was in no real rush.

Caden clenched his fist before he stepped out from the hallway. "HEY! I'm the one you want! Leave my family alone!" he yelled as he waved his arms. It let out a slight growl before it swung its paw at Caden and slash across his chest with its claws. The force of the attack sent him into a wall, but the wound was not that deep.

A groan escaped from Caden's lips as he placed his arm on the wound on his chest. He could feel his blood seep through his fingers. But he also noticed a numb sensation that begun to spread from the wound. *Poison!?*

Yavari held back Sean and Dave away from Caden who had drawn the attention of the Chimera. Dave fought to try and protect his father as Sean was frozen in shock. "Stay here. He's doing this to save us." Yavari replied sharp and coldly there was little to no worry in her voice.

"Let me go. Dad's going to die at this rate." Dave exclaimed as he struggled against his mother. Dave hit his mother in the side and her arms, but she didn't budge in the slightest.

"That doesn't matter. All that matters is that we survive. He'd rather that then all of us die." Yavari said. Her voice was cold and so was her expression it scared Dave who was used to his kind and sweet mother. She had never acted in such away before in front of him or the rest of the family.

Dave shivered before he pushed away her arm with all of his strength and slipped out of her grasp. Yavari reached out to grab him by the collar, but her hand missed. Dave raced out from where they hid and stood in front of his father.

Dave stood in front of his father with his arms extended out to block the Chimera's sight from Caden. Dave's legs where shook like a leaf but he stood firm. Dave paused for a moment as he opened and closed his month, before he yelled, "leave my family alone!"

The Chimera primed to attack Dave and swat him away like a nat, paused. It didn't move or really didn't want to move. Then there was a high pitch sound like something begun to charge and the sound of and electrical shock could be heard. The Chimera yowled out before it's paw raised higher to strike.

"Dave move!" Caden yelled but Dave was frozen in fear. Caden couldn't move he was to injured to pull Dave away. Dave closed his eyes as Caden looked away as the giant paw swung towards Dave.

Another dark figure raced past the Chimera from the hole. The figure raced forward and went in front of the Chimera as it tackled Dave to the ground. The figure turned as they fell and fired a pistol at the Chimera and shot one of its ears.

The figure rolled away from Dave before they got up to their feet and stood in front of them. "Stay here. Don't even think about moving. I'll handle this." A voice that was different from what they expected spoke. They positioned their feet and the sound of rubble crunched beneath them as they shifted. "I'll take care of this just don't die in the meantime." They added as they shifted their body weight and center of balance down towards the ground.

With all the strength they could muster the figure then pushed off the ground and lunged forward. They flew between the Chimera's legs before they kicked up against the ground a little before the mid-section with a similar force of strength. With this tackle like motion, they threw the Chimera backwards and caused it to tumble out of the house and caused more damage to the wall.

The figure stood in front of the hole in the wall as they pulled out a blade from their back. Even outside there wasn't much light as the power to the entire block had been cut but that wasn't much of a problem for the two opposing parties. "So, you're the new thing that's been causing amok among the city lately. Never would have guess it was such a thing as this." The figure muttered.

The Chimera roared and swung a paw at the figure. They brought up the blade to brace rather than to dodge the attack. For a moment they held up against the attack but then their feet that were planted into the ground begun to slide and kick up dirt.

The moment their feet completely lost their place they were hit and begun to roll along the ground before they came to a stop. They had been only lightly grazed by the Chimera's claws but noticed the numb sensation at the wound and realized it had the capability to use poison. A realization of which caused them to click their tongue in annoyance.

They forced themselves to their feet, but they didn't a moment for reprieve as the Chimera attacked right away. The figure hadn't noticed the attack of the scorpion tail that had shot towards them, before their eyes flashed for a brief moment. The figure jumped backwards, and the tail dug itself into the ground.

The figure not about to miss a beat brought up the pistol and fired. The bullet hit the Chimera in the chest but didn't seem to really phase it. Once more the figure's eyes flashed, they went to roll to the side but were a second late as the tail shot up from the ground and pierced into their left arm.

A low curse escaped their lips, they dropped the pistol in their hand and pulled out a dagger. They cut the barb of the tail off from the chimera to stop it from pinning them down or them to give them a chance to be dragged. They clenched their teeth as they felt a sensation as if their blood was on fire.

They left the barb in their arm since they knew they had no chance yet to deal with it. They got to their feet. their hand gripped tighter around the blade as they put away the dagger and grabbed the pistol once more. They took a short breath before they lunged forward towards the Chimera. In kind, one of its paws shot towards them, and it's claws gouged into their side.

Rather than fall to the pain that was felt from the deep slashes in their side they spun around and swung their blade with all their strength. With a slash of the blade towards the Chimera's paw though with a short momentary resistance the blade severed two toes. The figure then slid across the ground on their knees. The Chimera spun around as it tried to attack again only to have it miss and fly over them.

The figure rolled as they fired their pistol to hit it in the foreleg before they continued to move towards the Chimera. It snapped its jaws at them suddenly, and they pushed to the side to have its jaws snap down onto their right arm. The Chimera lifted them up in the air as it hadn't severed their arm in two. Blood flowed down their arm an into their face as they dangled from the Chimera's mouth.

Not one to give up in a fight till they were out of options or dead, they swung their left arm up. With the blade in hand, they stab the Chimera's eye which caused it to roar out in pain. They dropped from the Chimera's mouth to the ground below. What land beside them was the pistol. They had trouble to move their right arm from the bite injury. So, they just put the pistol away since their right arm was now essentially useless for the time being. After they delt with their second weapon, they forced themselves up and off the ground.

Blood had begun to drip down the Chimera's face from the eye wound and it had staggered back away from the figure out of pain. The figure grabbed their blade once again before they jumped, for a moment they disappeared before they landed on the Chimera's back. The grabbed onto the structure of one of the creature's wings and pulled back hard.

The Chimera bucked backwards with a yowl as its wings opened as it to go into the sky. The figure turned the blade in their left hand and stabbed into the thin membrane of the wind and made holes and gashes in its one wing. The Chimera begun to move roughly at which it had become difficult to remain on its back. So, as the figure was thrown off, they stabbed into the side of the Chimera and dragged the blade down as she fell.

They landed a little hard but rolled away quickly as the Chimera went rampart and slammed into another building. They stabbed their blade into the ground as they pulled out a second pistol and fired at the Chimera again this time at the points of injury and its wings. The Chimera roared at the figure its eyes were red with anger. But rather then lash out its anger it turned tail and disappeared into the cloud of dust it had created from the collapsed house.

The figure stood for a moment in wait but then they put away its weapons. As if a string was cut, they collapsed to their knee the moment they sensed that the Chimera had fled. They wiped their month clearing a slight trickle of blood, while their breathes were a little rough. Then in a few moments, it returned to a relatively normal rate. They leaned back against the broken wall with their eyes close. Though they didn't act like it they were in a fair amount of pain.

"Dad? Dad!? Wake up!" Dave exclaimed it was loud that it roused the figure. Dave tried to what Caden up but it his method wouldn't work. If something was done in a few moments Caden would die from the Chimera's poison or the wound it had inflected.

Right poison…he had a wound didn't he… must have been from then. No rest for the wicked it seems.

The figure got up from where they sat and walked into the house through the hole in the wall. They looked down at their right arm and raised it. They clenched their right hand into a fist as they could slightly move it once more as if it wasn't limp just minutes before.

They looked up into the house and saw the figures of Yavari and Sean both wrapped in fear from what had occurred. Then they turned their attention to Dave and Caden. *Kids pretty brave, brave but stupid really. Though its defiantly those two but… no, I'm not mistaken. So, this must be the reason for the lab then for such energy to come from them. If only it was the kid, much more promising among other things. If he has such promise… I could use him… no.*

The figure stopped before Dave and Caden. "HEY! G-get away from them!" Yavari yelled but the figure paid her no mind. Well, expect that they wish to send her a death glare at them for such a reaction when in consideration of what they had just done.

"P-please. You have to save my dad… I don't want to be left alone with my mother." Dave muttered with a sad expression. The figure had no problem to see what was in front of them and could tell that Caden's face was extremely pale.

"You don't wish to be left with your mother?" they asked as the figure reached down by their leg. "She hasn't done anything to you though. So why?" they questioned. They pondered for a moment as they thought about their current wounds but decided it was more troublesome.

"… She scares me. Cold blooded-." The figure stopped Dave from the additional whether out of sympathy or another reason entirely it wasn't entirely clear.

Sociopath? No probably not maybe some tendencies… well it matters very little to me, but something clearly has happened recently.

The figure held a dagger in their hand as they looked down at Dave. "Though how desperate you wish to save him is moving. Whether you asked me or not, I would have done so either way." The figure replied. Then in a quick swift motion the figure slashed their right palm. Blood began to form from the cut in their palm.

The figure pressed their fingers into the cut to apply pressure and cause more blood to form and pool. Then they held their hand out over Caden's body. After a few moments they turned their hand and allowed the blood from their hand to spill and land on Caden's injury.

In normal sense of logic adding blood wouldn't work, not to mention be potentially more harmful than it would do any good. However, that kind of logic had rarely come to show its face to the figure for quite some time.

The figure allowed and made it so that their blood to cover Caden's wound completely before they stopped and brought their hand away. They held their wrist for a moment as if to message it, then they wiped the blood away from their palm to revealed unmarred skin as if the cut never existed in the first place.

"The wound won't fully heal but it won't be life threatening anymore… and the poison will be neutralized as well. None the less I should get going there are things I have to deal with." The sighed as they held their right arm that was still is fairly rough shape.

Caden semi-conscious reached out and grabbed the figure by the ankle. "Wait… don't leave… you are… I-." he spoked before he lost consciousness once more. However, that brief moment to cause them pause.

It delayed just enough to change things from how they planned. As right when the figure was about to leave and quickly get out of sight, the generator started as if the interference stopping it from starting was gone. Power returned to the home and with that the lights turned on. Something of which caused them to click their tongue.

Chapter 12

Nothing wants to go my way does it. I knew I should have used my tech again, darn it. No there wasn't enough time after that delay as I didn't expect this. No point in regret now just means things got more complicated.

"Arianna?!" Dave exclaimed as he looked at her in shock and surprise. This caused Yavari and Sean to sightly come to their senses and look over at her. Arianna couldn't act as if it was someone else either she was still covered in significant injuries that there was no way for her to explain them.

Yavari got up from the spot she hid in and raced over to Arianna. She grabbed a hold of Arianna's right arm and held it tightly to cause her a significant amount of pain that caused her to let out a groan. "It's because of you that thing came. I knew we shouldn't have adopted you. All you've caused is problems since you arrived." Yavari growled the look in her eyes as truly mad. Arianna couldn't help but let out a laugh.

"Finally showing your true colours to me no filter. I knew something was off but oh my. I can see his reasonings now. HAHAHAHA! If I didn't come when I did it would have been over. It wouldn't have left you alive. If you're lucky that Chimera would take you too." Arianna laughed as she wore a crocked smile. With her left-hand Arianna grabbed Yavari's fingers and pulled them back near the point that would have broken them as she pulled Yavari's hand off her injured arm.

Arianna then stepped forward with a straight posture she couldn't stop herself, the cat was out of the bag after all so there was no point of holding that 'mask' anymore. After everything that has happened to her at this point, she couldn't control her emotions. Emotions that she had kept in check for years, but at this moment of revelation the cracks begun to show. Her anger and pain burst out from over the many years not just that which the Luo family had been attributed to though it was directed towards them.

"I'm not here cause of some sham adoption proceedings that if you knew anything you'd be aware it wasn't in anyway legal or true. No, I'm here cause it's my job. It's my job to deal with things like today, not like it's my only thing I must deal with. Seriously for fuck sakes!

"My first contract assignment in a few years and it's this. Even those surface richies I worked for before had more common decency towards me than you have." Arianna growled as she held her right arm. Her gaze was sharp though her face had become quite pale in a few moments.

"Arianna are you okay your looking kind pale. Are you poisoned too?!" Dave gasped as he walked over to her and grabbed her left arm. Arianna patted Dave's head lightly with a kind expression.

"N-no. I'm okay it's not the poison. My bloods already dealt with most of it... aside from that of the barb." Arianna paused as she just remembered that the barb was still in her arm. She pulled it out and tossed it to the side. "Just let me get all this out." She muttered as she clenched her fist.

Arianna then pointed out as she held Dave closer to her, she was pointed in the general direction of Yavari and Sean. "Never in my years as a mercenary, have I been treated in such a manner. Some 'real' darn high and mighty surface dwellers we got here can't even have kindness towards another being.

"If it wasn't important, I would have left long ago. I honestly have half the gull to kill you right here after everything." Arianna raged as if she could breathe fire, she was too angry to care about her fear. This was the most emotions the family had actually seen from Arianna.

Someone who was normally composed and didn't say anything. After a few moments she let out a deep breath and calmed down a little more, she placed her hand on her face over her left eye.

"A mercenary so you're a mercenary. Those aren't jobs, not to mention I've never heard of one so young." Yavari responded. Whether she just wanted to be combative, or it was an actual question of concern was uncertain. But it was clear that Yavari didn't like Arianna at all, so it was likely the former.

"No shit sherlock. Of course, they're jobs; they just aren't a surface run thing. But young… I guess. However times are in a bit of a change right now, if you can't tell with such a blatant attack as it was tonight." Arianna replied with a calm expression.

"Honestly it was luck this was all that happened. They really planned things out. A sleeping agent released in the area, cutting the phonelines to prevent incoming or outgoing communications. A jammer to signals, also taking out the power for a significant amount of time. Just be glad they didn't burn the house down of all things. Even after all of this. No one above will know what happened tonight… well expect you so… don't say something that make you look crazy 'kay." She muttered as she tilted her head slightly.

When Arianna heard cars, she let out a slight sigh. *Took a little longer than expected. No matter it gave me a chance to express my grievances. It's not my place to care about them for the next while anyways.* She thought as she went over and opened the front door.

On the other side of the door was a familiar individual with black-purple hair. "You had me worried when you went off like that." They stated as they walked inside. "Wow they certainly did a number on this place. Surprised the ceiling hasn't collapsed with such a giant hole in the wall."

"Well, it's not like I had time to explain when I got the information. But yeah, the thing was huge. Pretty heavy too." Arianna paused. "I'm pretty sure it's the same things that's been giving you trouble recently."

"Are you sure? It could be something else. Could be anything."

"You're not wrong it could be… but I'm pretty sure. It did a number on me, and it fits what little else I know." Arianna replied before she glanced over at him. "There was no way you could expect to hide such a thing from me forever Dark."

Dark looked down and noticed something. "You didn't put your shoes on… now your feet are all cut up." He muttered as he shook his head slightly.

"It's fine, I couldn't if I wanted too anyways."

"Are you ready to head out then?"

"Yeah."

"Wait! Head out, so you'll leave us here. Didn't you say you were hired to protect us. So where do you think, you are going? Are you really going to leave us here? What if that thing comes back?" Yavari exclaimed as she pointed at the two of them. There wasn't really any way to win this situation Yavari was going to displeased either way, Arianna knew this, so she didn't stumble.

"I have something more important to deal with. Don't get me wrong that thing isn't gone. It will be back for sure. That was just the start and there is only two way it will probably end. I've prepared something take my place as I'm otherwise disposed. They are quite good so worry not. Let's go Dark." Arianna spoke calm and clear. She turned and begun to make her way out the door.

"Arianna wait! Please don't go."

"Sorry Kiddo, I don't really have much choice in the matter. Everything will be alright till I get back. My strong friends will be around to keep you safe till I get back. Be good okay." Arianna told him as she pat Dave's head. "Also, I know Sean can be a jerk sometimes but try not to fight all the time. In times like these you never know what could happen."

"Arianna let's get a move on!" Dark called out. Arianna pat Dave's head once more as she turned around and made her way out the door.

"Yea, yea! I'm coming, you impatient old man!" Arianna replied as she rolled her eyes. She gave a slight wave before she walked out the door and walked over to the car that sat there with Dark. Arianna climbed into the back seat and as soon as the door closed the car drove off.

The car drove throughout the night as Arianna slept in the back, only to wake once the light of morning hit her eyes. She sat up and groaned slightly as her right arm was still hurt, but she rolled her shoulders anyways as she stretched a little. Her body snapped and popped from the odd position she slept in as her wounds healed. Though some found such a sound unsettling to say the lease, she neither cared nor minded.

Arianna then fiddled with the ear cuff a little as she looked out the front window. The light of the morning dimly lit up the cabin of the car. The cuts on Arianna feet had held and in clear view on her left foot and around her ankle was a fresh tattoo of a black dragon with red eyes, but there was also an addition ear pricing as well. *Is this the future they hoped for me… probably not.*

"Why did you take on that mission? I didn't force you, especially after what happened I wouldn't task you with such a task right away. You had no obligation. So, tell me." Dark asked as he glanced at Arianna in the review window.

"Your right, but I'm not doing this for you or the organization. Its repayment."

"Repayment?! What are you talking about?"

"It doesn't matter."

Arianna turned to look out the window again, so she didn't have to look Dark in the eyes. Something that had become a habit to her in the last week. "I surprised you managed to talk in front of them."

"Don't remind me. I don't feel great just thinking about it. But I didn't have much choice. Then that woman ticked me off. Gods I think I said more than I ever have in that moment than I normally average in three months." Arianna replied with a groan as she covered her face.

Arianna was aware Dark tried to make a conversation happened between them for some reason. She never really tried to talk much to him and his brother much especially when she 'learned' something she 'shouldn't' have a few years ago. Though such a thing would become something she would eventually regret later in her life.

The pair continued to drive down the road to an unknown destination. Dark would occasionally look back at Arianna, but she never looked up at him rather she just tied a blind fold that she had in her pocket over her eyes. Even so the car continued to drive down the

Chapter 13

Not long after Arianna left the house, those which she had mentioned arrived at the home. By this point Caden had begun to regain consciousness. He sat up with a start before he frantically looked around. "Where's Arianna?" That was the first thing that he asked something which displeased Yavari.

"What does it matter to what happens to that bitch. She lied about everything to us and had the audacity to get mad at us after everything we've done for her." Yavari replied sharply as she crossed her arms and looked away. Dave walked over to his father after he glanced at his brother Sean for a moment. He questioned due to what Arianna had told him, it was strange and made him wonder why she wanted them to have a better less combative relationship. But that's as far as he went in his thoughts about it at the time as he turned his attention towards his father.

"Arianna, after she healed you... well someone arrived, and she left not too long ago. The one she left with was someone named Dark or that what she called him." Dave replied as he helped his father slowly get up from the ground. "Dad, Arianna mentioned that she was here due to a job. Do you have any idea what she was talking about?"

"A job... so that's it." Caden muttered to himself before he looked at his youngest son. Caden noticed that Dave was calm after everything that just happened, and it was clear he did care about the well-being of Arianna, so he decided to answer what Dave asked. Dave helped Caden sit down in a chair, he looked at his chest to where his wound was to find it was only some light cuts. Even despite the seriousness of the injury not even an hour prior it was like this now. That was likely a confirmation to him of some kind towards the events that had transpired.

"Yes, Arianna was hired for a job, though till now I didn't know it was her. I hired Arianna; I did so months prior to when she entered our home. It was not long after I received a threat towards myself and those around me. The threat was all due to my part in something I took part in quite some time ago." Caden replied as he looked off in the distance.

"There is much you don't know about our world and what's truly going on around us all. Sigh… the threat was not something to take lightly. It was sent by an extremely powerful group. Even though it was a threat on my life and others there was no way I could take it to the police either. With no other option, I hired a mercenary from a group I trusted. That's the reason she came here. But to think-." He added as he closed his eyes as he cut himself off.

"So are we just lucky then that she was here to save us, that we even met her!" Sean exclaimed suddenly as he got up from the ground. "How could I believe something so far-fetched. Even if it is true what are we supposed to do since she's left. We don't even know if she will even come back." He growled his eyes and words where sharp, an attempt to deny all that had occurred.

"Sean, Arianna already said she didn't leave us alone." Dave replied quickly. "After everything that just happened how could you even act like that, she saved our lives with her own on the line. Just like a character in a video game or a hero in a story. I'm sure she has a good reason for everything she's done, especially for lying to us. Arianna isn't as bad a person as you and mother make her out to be."

"How are you so sure. You're always like this as if you know everything. Father said it himself, Arianna is a mercenary and I'm sure just like in stories she has killed people. Not to mention we know nothing about her as probably everything we did know was a lie. Also, you saw what happened, do you think a normal person could do what she did or heal so quickly not to mention how she saved father." Sean snapped back at Dave. "Besides what's the reason that someone is trying to kill us!"

"That's quite simple really. It's something coveted by both those below and in between. Something that had nearly been completed around 16 years ago. Project Elixir, a project which my younger half-brother brought you abord to despite your surface origins." A man spoke the front door was opened without a knock and a small group stepped inside. "Been a while Caden. You seem to be doing pretty well for yourself. Though still surprised you married that woman in the end, after everything he told me that happened before."

"Well, is pretty relative at the moment. If you consider the circumstances of what's lead us to meet once again. On that other thing however… I think I'm starting to wish I listened to him." Caden reply as he leaned back and looked over at the sudden visitors. "But why am I not surprised that you are one of the people to arrive. We're getting up in the years it seems if someone that could be my own kid's my saviour. Shouldn't you and your brother consider retiring the two of you are much old than myself." He muttered as he ran his hand through his hair with a slight smirk.

"Always the cocky one, but then again, my half-brother always enjoyed your wit. No matter, we have more important matters than catching up. Since the operation is revealed to your family a proper introduction is in order especially since you'll be unable to tell anyone anyways." The man stated as he crossed his arms.

"My name is Icarus Altshuler. I am the head of the Yano's Surface operation branches. The young man next to me is Stanly Klipp one such agent that works directly under me. Then that is Night and Thief they are Yano agents." Icarus introduced the small group. "These three will oversee your protection detail temporarily and tell you more if they deem you worthy of such information. Though you don't really need to tell you anything. I'll fill you in on… recent developments."

"So, tell me, Icarus. How the hell did they learn who was involved in the project first it was his family, and now they are after me after so many years. It's quite different from what was said." Caden asked his voice a little low clearly displeased by the currently flow of events.

"To be honest with you Caden, we have no clue. No one has leaked the information not even our prime traitorous suspect hasn't spilled. Not as if many people knew about such a thing in the first place. All we know for sure is that they have targeted four people now."

"This is a right mess. I don't even think your brother remembers me. We only met a handful of times all which nothing to do with it too."

"Probably not. He always has his hands full. He's barely treated that kid right after all that's happened. Things have been even more of a mess since the youngest passed." Icarus replied his arms crossed as he shifter on his feet slightly.

"You brother hasn't treated them right. You're not serious. Didn't-" Caden paused as he looked up as Icarus who nodded his head to Caden's unspoken question. Caden looked at him with wide eyes and stood as if frozen for a moment. "Thank the gods. I suspected but... I'm so happy, thank you for letting me know and confirming my suspicions." Caden sobbed for a moment as he covered his eyes. Icarus then looked over at Yavari and Caden's kids.

"Icarus Altshuler and Stanly Klipp! I recognize those names. They two of you work for the Brightton City police department. I don't know what this Yano thing or what you are talking about but I'm sure it's illegal the moment I release this to the press you are done. So, tell me where that bitch is and lock her in jail right now if you don't want the same fate." Yavari exclaimed. Night (AKA Roy) the moment he heard that nearly jumped at Yavari and slashed her throat, he would have if Stanly didn't hold him back.

Icarus smirked amused at what she said to him. He slowly walked over towards her as he applied silent pressure to her with his own strength. "Oh my, this is why it's such fun dealing with you surface dwellers sometimes. Your arrogance is laughable, you're not even someone of high standing on the surface. It's just because you think we are beneath you. She wasn't wrong when she speculated you were a rose bush." Icarus laughed.

Caden looked away as Dave hid beside his father. What was in front of them wasn't hard to miss that anyone could sense it. The very blood lust full and dangerous aura that emanated off Icarus and those behind him.

Even with this situation Caden didn't help his wife out of it and let her face the brunt of it. "If you wanna live, I suggest actually learning the truth of what's going on. Cause you, Yavari, no matter what you say to people, it won't matter. We have a better reputation and backing stronger than anyone on the surface. Rather it be so easy to just kill you with no repercussions.

"The laws that you surface dwellers hold so proudly are that of a long bygone age that haven't adapted to the current situation on our world. Not just that you very act is quite a disgust. Even the average surface dweller doesn't act like such scum as you. We face different rules and ideas than you. So, if you don't want to die just shut up before I take away the voice... permanently."

After a few moments Dave swallowed his fear and stepped out from behind his father. "Mister Icarus sir. There is something I don't really understand would you be able to explain it to me please." Dave spoke and made sure his voice didn't waver and show his fear. Dave was restless and was unable to stop himself as he shifted in place.

Icarus turned and wore a slight smile as he looked at Dave. He likely reminded him of his nephew who would act similar when face with such a situation. "I can't promise to answer them, but I'll answer what I'm able to tell you." Icarus replied as he moved away from Yavari, the pressure disappeared in its entirety. The moment the pressure was gone Yavari fell to the ground unable to stand up.

"There's a lot I don't get, and I don't think I should ask about the Elixir thing. But there are things both you and Arianna said like calling us surface dwellers, being a mercenary, and this Yano thing. There's a lot more I wanna ask but I feel these are the most important." Dave spoke as he looked up at Icarus in the eyes. This caused Icarus to let out a slight chuckle in amusement as he found Dave quite fearless but could tell there was something else to the kid as well.

"Alright kid but how about you answer my questions first. They're really quick."

Dave nodded as he continued to look at Icarus. "Kid how are you able to read people so well. It's not as simple as knowing the person, no there's something else to it. Your brother mentioned it too, it's not like you can see the truth either. Care to explain." Icarus questioned but the moment he said this Caden flinched Stanly looked over at him which stopped Caden in his tracks as his eyes held a slight threat and reassurance.

"Um... it's kind of hard to explain. It just really this feeling I get, and sometimes I see slight colours around them too. Arianna never felt that she wanted to hurt me or the family, something told me I could trust her. Though I didn't believe it at the start till she protected me not to long ago." Dave replied as he thought about it. Icarus glanced in Stan's general direction.

"I see. It's kind of like you can see a person intention in a way. It's quite a useful skill, could you always do this or was it sudden?"

"Always."

"Interesting. What about your older brother can he also do something others can't?"

"Yeah, I've seen it. Plants and nature respond to him in a way. He also told me that he senses things too." Dave replied Sean glared at his brother. It was something Sean had tried to keep hidden but Dave had told that man without little hesitation about such things that would likely have been shunned by others above.

"Stronger then... hair colour too. Hmm, maybe she was on to something. But we still have nothing yet." Icarus muttered as he crossed his arms. "Alright kid, as for what you asked." He paused as he shifted in place a little.

"The Surface thing's kind of self-explanatory. You live of the plants surface, from the surface, dwell on the surface. People like us though often to describe you as we aren't the same. Those of the surface are blind but not in the literal sense. We also say they often have unretained or wiled pride and they claim to have 'peace'.

"But even though we are on the surface it doesn't me we are of the surface. It's a mixture of things really. Though it's not uncommon for those from other dwellings to use it like an insult." Icarus replied though it was a very rough and incomplete explanation about it.

"Next mercenary yes... I'm sure you've heard of it those that would do nearly anything for money. That's what it is, though mercenaries no longer exist on the surface as a job it still is one. People on the surface use us too, to get things done in... other ways from dissatisfaction you can say.

"Mercenaries are the only ones that still travel between really. Mercenaries work for money and under a contract normally. Well, I should probably explain the other thing to as it is tied to it.

"The Yano in all rights is a mercenary organization, and just one of many groups like it though one of the more famous ones. Different from their rival the Marione. Groups like us are a part of what you of the surface call the underworld or even black market. Most crimes that have gone on for years and never been caught are normally the work of a mercenary from an organization." Icarus explained.

"So that probably would include the Assassin, right?" Dave asked as he remember the name of someone that fight what Icarus described.

"The Assassin's a special case… they aren't even called the Assassin to us like how the media and you of the surface call them. Main person that they call the 'Assassin' well they are currently not affiliated with any organization. Honestly if you want to learn more you should do some research or prove yourself." Icarus said as he scratched his head.

He wasn't too sure what he should tell Dave as it was like a mine field in ways but, he also knew Dave was likely wanted to learn more about Arianna. He also noticed that Sean was also listened to what he said as well. Though Icarus knew the relationship between Arianna and Sean was like a cat with water. Though he had no reason not to let Sean listen to what he said either.

Dave then went over to the other three. "You're probably the friends Arianna told me would show up. Even if it just because of her thank you for keeping us safe. However, I do want to ask you something that seem a little random. What comes to mind when you think of Arianna?"

"Pff. What kind of… you like her or something kid." Stan chuckled slight as Dave's face turned red slightly as he quickly shook his head. "Alright I'll play along. Quiet would be the first thing I'd think of. Though she probably has her reasons she doesn't talk all too often though she's quite capable of it." Stan replied as he looked at the kid before he turned away.

"Secretive, doesn't tell people much, and avoids true conversation about her personally. In truth we know little about her too." Thief replied bluntly their arms were crossed as they looked away.

"C… cute. She's cute." Night replied as he quickly looked away Stan chuckled lowly. "Shut it. Don't you dare tell her I said that either."

"That's the best you'll get. I'd go with smart; she learns things quick." Icarus added on. "Anyways we got thing to do so let's wrap this up. People will come to deal with this, in a few hours. We have set up a place for you to stay till things are fixed." He added before he led the group out with the Luo family behind them.

Sad, lonely, afraid, kind, strong, hurt… that's…

Chapter 14

A few months had passed since the incident with the Chimera. Like Arianna had told them, no one knew what really happened that night. It was claimed that what happened that night that destroyed a number of buildings and killed a few people, and the cause was claimed to be due to a localized earthquake that occurred in that area.

This caused several changes around them due to the destruction of multiple buildings. One such was some new students that arrived at the school and one in particular that had come to latch on to and annoys Sean to no end. Dave felt that his brother deserved it for what he did to and his sudden change of tune towards Arianna now that she was gone.

On the other side of things, the new guard detail of Stan, Roy, and Alex asked Caden a few more questions. Though he was stubborn for the most part he did answer a few of their questions. One such question was about the secret lab below the house. Caden revealed that as Arianna had speculated that it was to help create the Elixir or really something similar.

Caden revealed the truth that the Elixir had several hidden side effects. Side effects that apparently no one on the project knew about. Even though it was not done the very exposer of it was quite drastic as if it was something like radiation that doesn't seem to be as deadly. Though rather than the researchers, it affected their children. Caden at the time tried to create a counter of sorts to give to his kids.

The reason that the Imitator had attacked teens as their main focus, was to be a threat to Caden. In this way stated that if he didn't comply his family was next. Something which Arianna had realized but didn't reveal it to any of them. It was hard to say if they felt betrayed or not by such a thing as it wasn't a new occurrence, Arianna had done similar things before.

Not only that but the ever since that day that Arianna disappeared the relation between Caden and Yavari had turned out for the worse. Yavari was vindictive but since Arianna wasn't around, she took it out on Caden. She was harsh and started to blame everything on him. It truly was everything that went wrong not just the attack that occurred, even the smallest things he would be blamed for.

Whether it was a twisted sense of self subvariant justice or was how Yavari always was, that is a bit unclear. Yavari was like a rose bush or another name for similar was a white lotus, someone the on the outside acted all nice but was the opposite and hid their hostility behind a kind or innocent facade. Arianna did notice there was something off as she had said and at one point made a comment that Yavari seemed like a rose bush, pretty appearance but hid sharp thrones.

Now Yavari had turned those 'thorns' on Caden which had caused their relationship to detreated even faster than it already was. It made it that anyone returned to the 'house' promptly to avoid the situation and Yavari. This made things difficult for the three to give them better protection, their only grace was that nothing had happened since the Chimera appeared months ago though that created its own set of problems.

Since nothing had happened Sean no longer wanted to fallow the orders of house arrest. Eventually one day Sean decided to sneak out to meet up with friends, something that was a bad decision on his part.

No one that was sent to protect him would have known he had left as that point in time that he left there was a slight gap in the rotation that made it possible for him to leave. But there was an unexpected factor in Sean escape and that was Dave. By chance he learned of his brother's little plan and watched as he left.

Out a mixture of being petty and slight pay back Dave called Roy. Like Sean, Dave didn't think anything would happen, so he called just to get back at Sean more than anything and convinced Roy to take him along with them to get Sean. Dave was on Roy's back as the two made way in the direction he heard about till the eventually met up with Thief. But of course, the moment one lets their guard down is normally when the enemy would strike.

A loud yet familiar roar to Dave echoed through the empty streets. "That's the Chimera's roar." Dave exclaimed as his grip on Roy's shoulder became stronger. He never could forget the sound of that roar.

"Are you sure?"

"Yes."

"That's in the direction you said your brother went. They were waiting for this. If we're lucky it will just be the Chimera."

"They were just biding their time. Tsk, they may act like savages sometimes, but they're not stupid like you'd think such would be. They knew sooner or later things would lighten up which would give them the prefect chance to strike." Roy stated as they made their way closer to the location. "Thief you ready?"

"Yea, if it's only the Chimera the moment I get the chance I'll take them away with the tech Arianna let me borrow. I know the plan Night." Thief replied as they landed in an alley nearby.

"Stay here out of sight we'll take care of it."

With that Night and Thief disappeared but of course Dave didn't really listen. He moved closer to where his brother was. When Dave could see Sean, it wasn't hard for him to tell that his brother feared the Chimera in front of him and his friends. Not that Dave blamed Sean for it either he was also scared of it.

Dave watched his brother not sure what he should do. That was till he noticed the ground below his brother. Small stalks of plants begun to grow up between the cracks in the ground. Dave knew he had to stop his brother from as they weren't the only ones that could see this. "Stop." Dave exclaimed as he tackled his brother to the ground.

"Dave?! How did you get here?"

"I followed you idiot." Dave replied as he looked at his brother before he learned next to Sean ear. "There are other people here, that don't have good intentions so don't show off not matter how scared you are." He whispered before he got to his feet. It wasn't a large group with Sean only about five of them in total.

"Now what? We got your brother now, our chances of getting away are defiantly zero now."

"I'm not dead weight jerk, I can run by myself. Besides when did I ever say I was alone."

With that the loud bang of a sniper went off. The other's panicked at first as they thought it was aimed at them. The Chimera staggered as the sniper round priced through its skin and sprayed some blood. With the Chimera staggered a figure jumped down from above and landed on the Chimera's back as they stabbed their sword into its back.

"Wait? Is that Night?!" Sean exclaimed as he noticed the person on the Chimera.

Then another figure appeared before them. They were slender and wore clothes that were slightly lose, a long scarf, a hood over their head and a lower face 'mask' like helmet as well as something over their eyes that made it look cat like. "We'll talk about going against what we said later." Thief said as they glanced at both Dave and Sean.

"Wait you're a mercenary! If that's Night, you must be Thief." The one from earlier said. Thief glanced at them for a moment. "If the two of you are here…" they trailed off.

"Shut up, just stop talking." Thief replied sharply as it grabbed the five friends of Sean's. "I'm getting you out of here." They added as they pulled out a pendent. The pendent glowed in response before the group of five disappeared in thin air.

Night was thrown off the Chimera's back and slid and stopped right in front of Sean and Dave. "Seems it was able to take them all." Night muttered as he turned his attention back to the Chimera.

Night raised his sword up to block the Chimera's large paw that swung at him. The force of the attack caused him to slide a little, but he held his ground and weapon. Then he shifted his blade that allowed him to deflect its paw.

Night jumped over the paw and swung his blade and slashed the Chimera on the wrist though not deep enough to sever it. Night attacked powerful and fast this made it, so he was able to push the Chimera back albite slightly. Night charged forward and avoided the Chimera's attack before he jumped and kicked it square in the chest which pushed it back.

The Chimera roar and swung its paw down at Night to squish him like a bug. Night quickly moved the blade in his hand and held it above him. Its paw slammed downwards onto Night's sword which caused the blade to pierce though and out the other side. Blood rained down on him as he held himself up against the strength of the paw that tried to squish him. Night fell to one knee as his body started to buckle under the weight.

Night then used all his strength to stand up once again. Then Night moved out of the way of the paw and pulled his blade out in the same motion before it slammed to the ground. The Chimera closer to Night than before tried to bite him. He dodged to the side before he sent and upper cut into its jaw which snapped its month closed.

In the next moment Thief appeared in front of Sean and Dave. "Just in time." Night huffed as he grabbed a hold of Thief who grabbed the brothers before they disappeared right before the Chimera, with no trace of them left behind.

Chapter 15

On a faraway abandon rooftop Sean, Dave, Roy, and Thief appeared. Roy let out a sigh as he let himself fall to the ground. Roy took off his hood before he removed his helmet. "That thing was no push over." Roy sighed as he took a deep breath. He ran his hand through his hair to hide the slight tremble in his hand. "How did she manage to drive it off?"

"What are you doing? There are other people here Night!" Thief hissed when they noticed that he had removed their helmet. That little comment caused Sean and Dave to look over at Roy's direction which made it possible for the two to see his face. Sean didn't initially recognize Roy, but he did eventually.

"Calm down. A side from those two there is no one else around. Not to mention the two of them are in no real position to give anything away nor could they even if they wanted too." Roy sighed with a wave of his hand. "Your hesitation and worry are understandable but Alex there is no reason or way they can do as you think. So, relax and take off your gear."

"Yeah, not gonna happen. Even she probably wouldn't do this." Alex (AKA Thief) muttered with her head in her hand. "I don't understand your reason in confidence to do such things. Do you do this with all your clients?"

"No. But it's not like they are normal clients now, they have connections with such a high-level thing, along with some knowledge of classified info." Roy replied. He then got to his feet and stretched his arms over his head. "Enough with that we have another matter to take care of. These two went against us."

Alex then turned towards the two brothers and shifted her attention to them. "That's true. Sean went against the rule to stay at home. All so he met up with some people at night without telling us and nearly got all of them killed. While Dave left the area, we designated to his brother almost getting himself killed in addition." Alex agreed with her arms crossed. The two were aware that it was probable that the Chimera wouldn't have killed the two brothers due to their usefulness as hostages over corpses.

"Exactly my point. So, I think they deserve punishment due to their abundance of energy that they have which brought about disobedience." Roy replied with a smirk as he crossed his arms. The two brothers' probably felt a chill down their spine from that small gesture and sentence. "You take the eldest, I'll take the kid."

"What! Why do I have to take him? I'd rather the kid he's cuter." Alex replied with a slight huff. Roy reason was calculated not just something based on a mere whim or preference.

"That's why. Your always soft and partial to the younger ones especially when it comes to punishment." Roy replied as he walked over to her and placed his hand on her shoulder before he leaned in towards her ear. "Also, if I'm in charge with Sean's punishment I might just kill him for what he did towards Ari." He whispered in Alex's ear.

"And how are you so sure I wouldn't do something similar. She's my friend too." Alex replied to him, her eyes a little sharp. Roy looked at her but didn't say a thing for a moment.

"I've seen how you've acted lately. Don't think for a moment it gone unnoticed Alex." Roy replied in a low tone. His eyes were sharp like a knife and act as if just pure ice, his voice held no kindness or warm that she could use to ease herself.

"R-right I understand. I put him through some rigorous training. That way no one has to remain with them all the time then once we're done." Alex replied, Roy removed his hand from her shoulder. Without a moment of hesitation Alex moved away from Roy at a fast pace with her face slightly pale. Alex grabbed a hold of Sean arm and disappeared with him.

Dave then looked over at Roy with a nervous expression. "Um... am I also going to be trained?" he asked, he shifted in place. Dave was I mixture of nervous and excited, he had seen what Arianna and Roy were capable of. He saw them like they were a character from a video game that fought against unknown forces. Dave wanted to be similar to them in some way as he thought the two of them were cool. It was an innocent admiration a breath of fresh air to the normal reactions people had.

"That's part of my plan since you seem so egger. But there are other things that you'll be doing for the next few days. We'll use that to tire you out for the night." Roy paused as her crossed his arms. "Just be sure not to tell your mother. She'd probably have a conniption." He sighed with a slight shake of his head. "You act more like your father towards such things. It's a nice change of pace for once."

"So, you are going to train me then! I promise not to tell her!" Dave exclaimed his eyes had a sparkly look to them. Roy wasn't too sure how to really deal with Dave, but he decided to just bite the bullet and just do as he wanted to.

Roy ruffled his hair slightly. "Nice to see someone so egger. But how to fight and defend yourself isn't going to be the only thing we are going to talk about." He stated clearly with little expression.

"Don't care, as long as your tech me cool things like you and Arianna can do it doesn't matter." Dave replied earnestly. Roy probably felt a little burdened by Dave's response, it was different from the normal response and so innocent in comparison. However, it was something that Arianna suggested in case there was something problematic.

The reason was that no matter who it was to present such information to those of the surface as she had suggested would captivate them. Roy decided to do such a thing for Dave since he was the calmest about the whole ordeal and more likely to accept and listen to what Roy planned to say.

"Alright then. Before we start training, though not everything we'll talk about is relevant to a fight or skills people like me use. We'll start with this; I want you to tell me what you know about the country we are currently in Canlonen." Roy stated as he looked at Dave. This was something like a test. It was well known knowledge to those like Roy that what those of the surface knew was fairly limited, and when one has to deal with something like this its sometimes best to start at the very start.

Dave didn't get the reason that such a question was the block to the start of the training he was offered, he had lived in Canlonen his whole life. "Canlonen is the smallest of the eight contents, and only one of the contents that is also a country and not split. It is divided into five divisions The central division we currently reside which also houses the capital city since the divisions surrounded by mountains. The other divisions are the North, South, East, and West division each that have something to bring people to the country.

"Canlonen uses two languages Cadish the main language and English which was adopted in as a second once the rest of the world learned of Canlonen's existence something that took some time of unknown reasons." Dave explained a very light and summarized version of what he learned about his home country.

"What else?" Roy asked which caused Dave to flinch slightly. He explained it like one would have on a geography test that asked a similar question, though Roy wanted something in particular. He didn't want a general summary though some of what he said were important.

"Um... Canlonen is the home and birthplace of the Eternial religion that worships two gods. There are many myths and legends steamed from it and mention of a creature called an Elder Dragon. It brought about seasonal festivals around elements which also has dances attributed to them from said religion. That's all I can really think of."

Roy sighed as he shifted on his feet slightly. "You aren't wrong. Such information is important to consider if one works on Canlonen soil. Knowing the main culture and language makes it simpler to blend in and work." Roy replied with a slight nod. "But there are some other things as well. Eternial while the main religion and can be used to hide, not everyone practices it in the way that those at the temples do, often taking a more passive approach if at all.

"Canlonen is said to be the starting point for the currently system used below. Then there are the most important people in the country. The Rotusole family, they were the most influential and important people on Canlonen. Many major things in the country the family had a hand in. It's also said that the family was the one that brought about the religion of Eternal. But not only that they have been said to be involved in many important things in the world." Roy told Dave. "Though considering how the surface is run I guess the last to parts of information wouldn't be well know."

"I've never heard about the Rotusole's if as they are as important as you said. How is it possible I've never heard of them? Such people couldn't be that powerful to completely erase such a family's entire history and influence." Dave asked it was a reasonable question.

"Well, it's believed they had outside help. It's not only the surface that the family's nearly been lost to history. All that's left that's known about them know is that they were extremely influential on all fronts, they were very wealthy, and they lived on Canlonen which they've influenced the most. Probably only because of their ties to the Eternal religion is the only reason there are even traces left of the family name. There are probably a number of families that have been lost in such a way too." Roy explained with a slightly sad expression.

"So then not just here but the entire world such a thing could happen. Are you trying to tell me such a thing could happen to my family?"

"It's possible that might happen. Your family could be wiped just like the Rotusole's with no blood remaining or done for protection."

"I understand. Do you happen to know how exactly the Rotusole family was destroyed?"

Roy looked at Dave, he could see the slight fear and nervousness on his face. The kid was pretty brave, normally at the very thought your family would be wiped from the records of history they'd be fearful or despair as it meant they were likely to die. "No one really knows but it's thought to have happened within the last 100 years since their name still exists in whispers. But from what I've heard the most common reason was that they were murdered." Roy answered, he was calm when talking about such an occurrence. "Knowing this do you still wish to train?"

"... Yes. It's all the more reason to do so. To try and not let such a thing happen to my family." Dave replied which caused Roy to smirk slightly. "... was that some kind of test?"

"In a way. It was to give me an idea for what the surface has taught you. But also, if you have the nerve to face a fate so dangerous head on. Such a story is often told to the newest recruit to test their nerve. People fear death, and even more so for their entire existence to be destroyed and forgotten, it's a pretty effective test." Roy replied with a slight shrug of his shoulders.

"Then is the Rotusole family even real?"

"Very real. I just used them as an example for you." Roy sighed as he glanced at Dave. "That's enough learning and test for today. Let's do some actual training now. I've deemed you good enough to learn, you have a good attitude as well. So, I'll personally train you rather then pawn you off. I can see why you've caught Arianna's interest as well. Don't worry I'll train you well and good. Not just physically and with skills but also that unique ability of yours too." Roy told Dave with a smile as he walked over to Dave. Roy patted Dave on the head for a moment before he picked him up and leapt from the building.

Chapter 16

For multiple weeks on end, at night Alex and Roy trained the brothers Sean and Dave. Though Alex was pretty lack luster as she trained Sean, she couldn't deny that he had a unique ability. This was reinforced when it was confirmed to them all that the Marione was the organization they were up against and that it had begun to focus on Sean more than before determined with help of how Alex had 'trained' Sean up to that point.

On the other hand, however with the 'attempt to get rid of energy' the efforts had been fruitful even with this short time frame. Not only had it become clear though they had threatened the entire Luo family Dave wasn't on their radar rather more an afterthought or just baggage. Even without the new information on the enemies goal the weeks had been useful.

Dave despite his slightly weaker physique in comparison had made progress in what Roy had put him through. Dave being in his teens at the time did help with him retaining what Roy had taught him. But it wasn't just how to fight that Roy had taught him.

Roy who had seen Dave as a sort of surface student had taught him a few other things like he did the first day. One such thing that was more about mercenaries and their organizations. Like the Yano and Marione the two most powerful organizations out of them all.

The Yano and the Marione similar to one another yet also different. Two organizations that were bitter deadly enemies with one another. No one knew how long they had been enemies with one another, but it was for a very long time. As such the fact that it was the Marione they were facing once again after many years was not much of a surprise.

Roy looked at Dave pleased as he practiced the sword technique that Roy had taught him. It was one that focused on light swords, so it worked well for him. "You've done well today, Dave. You've shown great improvement from when we first started. Let's stop for the night, there some more I want to tell you."

"What is it? You've already told me more about mercenaries, the organizations, the Yano and the Marione."

"What I've told you is barely even surface level information really just general knowledge."

"Then is it more as to the reason you've often emphasized how I'm incapable of certain things."

"I don't think I've said such a thing that often."

"Often enough."

Roy looked at Dave for a moment. "Sigh… well no that's not it but it's nothing major. It's just due to our ancestry and such, you know bloodline. So, there's different things we can do, that's all. Like height, in a few years you'll be fairly taller than me."

"Wait what? Really."

"Yeah, that's a bonus for those of the light."

Dave paused for a moment. "How you said that. It's not like someone individually."

"You're not wrong. But this isn't a biology class." Roy sighed as he shook his head. He felt like it was like 20 questions or something. "Can I say what I want to talk about?"

"Let me try once more. Hmm, is it those things I've seen you and Alex use before?"

"… oh artifacts… or are you talking about tech? Well, it doesn't matter, but no. It's not something I can tell you about anyways. They are things that are beyond what's known and understood, on the surface anyways. There's a little more understanding below. Though that doesn't mean that below we completely understand artifacts."

Roy ran his hand through his hair as he let out a sigh. "Now let's start. What I'm going to talk about isn't something that interesting, but since it's something that has been used a few times, I thought it be best to talk about." Roy explained as he sat down in a chair. "Actually, Icarus recommended that I talk about it since it's possible that such a thing could happen to your family."

"This is something that has happened multiple times throughout history. Fire something dangerous yet it is calming and beautiful if not destructive. It's been used before to kill or hide things. In the last 50 years such an occurrence had become more common on the surface Many of them have been tied to an individual that's called themselves Fiarago." Roy explained, he leaned back in the chair, to Dave his gaze looked a little distant as he said this small amount. "Fiarago is believed to be involved in many more incidents than they've claimed."

"How is this important. Their just an arsonist are they not?"

"No… its more than just that. From what I heard. They've done a lot more than just start a fire. They attack, kill, torture, and at some point, set the place on fire." Roy told Dave. Dave took an oddly deep breath as he heard this.

Cast in the light of the flames of the building that had been set ablaze, before him stood a tall figure cast in odd shadow. He couldn't move but something told him this wasn't the first time that the figure before him has done something like this.

Despite the inability to see the figures face or anything that would define them. They showed him a crooked grin that sent chills down his spine. Whoever it was enjoyed the scene that was before them, they relished it. Then with little warning there was a loud noise, and he could feel the pain that raked his body.

He could tell his body was in poor state, unsure the number of injuries that were present, but could feel his body was shaking. Another figure then stood in front of him, all he could tell was that the person was older than him, but he felt a familiarity to them. He could hear what was said but knew they were talking.

Then the conversation was cut as the large figure before them lunged forward and grabbed the person before him by the neck as the figure knocked him back. Without a second though he got back to his feet and attacked. He bit down on their leg hard and could taste the blood that entered his mouth.

They tossed the other person aside before they grabbed him. They hit him hard in the side of the head which cause him to let go. He felt fear as the figure held them to their face. Their grip around his neck tightened, then the figure threw him. He felt as his head hit something hard followed by his body before he fell to the ground.

It was painful and he could feel himself about to lose consciousness, he glanced over at the other person who appeared to be screaming out to him. Then right as his eyes begun to blur and couldn't keep his eyes open any longer another figure appeared from the flames clad in black.

Dave gasped as he leaned forward. His head was ringing, and something felt weird and off. He placed his hand on his face as his thumb and index finger rubbed against his temple.

"Is everything alright. You suddenly went very quiet." Roy asked as he placed his hand on Dave shoulder which cause him to flinch. An action which surprised Roy as it was something he never done before. "Are you alright?"

"I don't know." Dave muttered in reply. His eyes were a little out of focus as he sat back up. "Not sure how to even explain what just happened. No what I saw." Dave added as he shook his head slightly. He remained quiet for a moment before he was hit by a sudden realization.

"It could be that... there's only one why to check." Dave muttered with a serious expression. It was different than his normal cheerful laid back yet expressive expression he often had.

It was fairly similar to the expression his father often wore. "Roy, could you talk about the incidents related to Fiarago again. But don't talk about the same thing as last time."

Though confused Roy had no reason to refuse his request. Roy said it was similar to how I would get sometimes so he thought it was best just to follow along with. "Okay, just don't do something that will get you in over your head." Roy answered with a nod of his head.

"Some people have said that there have been times that Fiarago has purposely left people alive that way they would be killed by the fire or smoke." Roy explained, Dave then felt a sudden shiver up his spine. He felt this one was to be different from the other one as if it was to be some kind of test for him.

This time he wasn't 'in the front seat' for the action rather outside and watched like an observer. He stood outside in an unknown hallway. In the room he stood next too he could hear some kind of noise but was unable to see inside, as if trying to block from sight what had occurred.

There was then the sound of a very slight creak of a door. He turned to the direction to see the door at the end of the hall open. In the opened door all he could see was what looked like bright red eyes that appeared to glow. Then without a sound a small figure with the red eyes quickly moved through the hall over to the door.

In front of him the small figure peaked into the door. Though still unable to see inside he could see the despair, horror, and fear the figure had at what they had seen inside. Unsure how long it was the figure at some point as if they broke out of their trance and pushed the door completely open.

On the other side of the door was the master bedroom that had been destroyed. Furniture, broken destroyed or with massive gashes in it. Not only was that all around blood was everywhere as well. The room was covered in the splatter and spray of blood, the bed itself was mess the sheet were soaked in blood, and on the ground were two more figures that blood begun to pool around them.

In the broken window stood was a slightly familiar figure with the same creepy crooked smile. They had one foot on the windowsill as they looked towards him or rather at the smaller figure. It was possible to see blood drip off the figure and from the blade that was in their hand. The figure eyes shined from some twisted delight as the smaller figure let out a broken hurt scream as they fell to the ground. They laughed before they jumped out of the window and disappeared from sigh.

The figure fell into one of the many pools of blood which caused the blood to fly, coat their limbs and face slightly. Their pained sorrow filled screaming sobs echoed, they looked at the blood that covered their hand and they began to shake and tremble. Eventually flames caught to the home and quickly begun to engulf the home.

The broken window filled with flames and the light of the flames lit the room more and made it even worse. The full sight of the smaller figure's parents was in view with their broken twisted and mangled forms. The flames also revealed a vibrant purple violet colour the small figure had.

The small figure turned their head then crawled and scrambled over to one of the figures. He had no idea what they said but it eventually allowed the small figure to move from place. However, the house was already greatly engulfed in the fire.

Despite the physical and mental pain, the figure felt they left the master bedroom. The smoke had yet to reach where they were, but the fire was strong, and the roof had already begun to collapse and the main entrance that was behind and below him became blocked by wreckage covered in flames.

The small figure covered their mouth with a clear cough as they descended the stairs. They tried to escape the house every exit they tried was blocked. Till the ceiling collapsed above the small figure. He could hear the small figure's muffled pain screams that the flames tried to consume as it surrounded them.

Dave begun to cough and covered his mouth, he felt as if he had been choking on smoke. Dave rubbed his irritated throat for a moment before he explained.

"I forgot about this. It's another ability of mine… it's only happened once before this. But for some reason and somehow, I get to see events the fit what you described." Dave explained as he looked at Roy. "I have no way to know if it's real or not."

Roy thought for a moment before he said anything. "It's likely an event from the past, you probably can see such a thing due to in part your other ability. I think your ability in general is more of what we call a physic ability rather than a magic one. But based on your reaction you don't really have all that much control over it." He muttered.

"This ability of yours could be very useful let get to working on it right away."

"How would it be useful?"

"Just trust me on this. There are many things you could use it for if its refined. We'll start tomorrow so be ready." Roy replied as he clenched his fist. He smiled as he looked over at Dave not about to take no for an answer. Dave lowered his head in defeat was he raised his fist to mimic Roy.

Chapter 17

Sometime passed the weather started to become colder and tree leave begun to fall. Sean walked down the school halls quickly before he ducked behind a corner and into the stairwell.

Roy happened to be in the stairwell to send out a report when he heard someone enter to find it was Sean. He looked out of the double doors that closed off the stairwell to see a woman that looked a little familiar race by she looked around before she took off in the other direction.

Sean phone then started to buzz which he quickly answered. It was difficult for Roy to hear the other half of the conversation since the stairwell caused a slight echo, but it wasn't hard to figure out. "Barely, that girls like a bloodhound." Sean muttered as he sat down on the stairs.

"Dude you think I want this. The girl's crazy I swear. You think she'd go back to her old school now that the damage was repaired. But no, now she's stalking me at my house. She lives four blocks away and I've seen here on my street.

"Why do you think I have an idea, it all started when she ran into me that day. I wasn't even nice or anything and she's clung to me since." Sean groaned it was clear he was frustrated with the situation.

Roy recalled the girl that Sean was talking about at the time. Her name was Alyssa, she was one of the people that caught in the aftermath of what happened with the Chimera the first time. The girl was the near perfect definition of an obsessive stalker from what they've said. Despite the ability to return to her old school she remained and chased Sean around like a lovesick puppy even after he had made it very clear to her that he didn't feel the same for her and asked her in all different ways to leave him alone nothing worked.

"Don't say that you ass. I don't want her to break into my house. Wha-?! How could you even suggest such a thing? There's no way in the world I could use Arianna as a fake girlfriend to keep her away.

"Why? Cause she would kill me; I'd prefer to just date someone in our friend group. What when I wasn't around, she said none of them are worthy of me. The fuck is wrong with her." Sean growled as he hit the wall with the side of his fist.

Roy leaned against the wall as he closed his eyes. The problem many people when they tried to deal with Alyssa was that her parents' significant figures in Brightton City. Though Roy didn't like it the person on the other side of the line was right. To resolve it in a more peaceful way at this point Arianna was his best bet.

If Sean wished to resolve it fairly peacefully, he need someone that no one in Brightton City couldn't really touch. Which really means someone out of the city or a merc.

Alex didn't care enough to do something like that, so the only way she would have been is if she got paid a significant fee. She had to not only act as if they were dating but also deal with whatever Alyssa wanted to throw at her.

At some point Sean eventually hung up the phone. His head was in his hands as he let out a sigh. "If there is still a god in this world, could you deal with Alyssa. I don't care how just make it, so I never have to deal with her again." Sean muttered. After a few moments Sean slipped out from the stairwell which left Roy alone.

"Pfft. So fed up he's gone to praying to a god he doesn't even believe in. You got to really mess up something really bad to cause something like that." Roy chuckled as he crossed his arms as he muttered to himself. He shook his head slightly as he looked out the window in front of him. Roy had become bored with school especially so since Arianna was gone.

"Well either way the chance something even happens to the girl as he wishes are slim. I'd say he's getting his just deserts." Roy muttered he glanced at the time before he moved away from the wall.

At the time his only real enjoyment was when he trained Dave and couldn't help but be conscious of the time while at the school. "I get why Arianna was so annoyed now with having to be here. Something like this has little value to people like us. And for her that's done it a few times… yeah she has good reason for her displeasure." Roy mumbled with a slight shake of his head.

For Roy for the last while he found that the sessions that he had done with Dave to be the most enjoyable. Dave was enthusiastic towards the sessions that he has done with Roy, he listened and tried out anything that might just help him improve.

It was something that even when Roy once worked with the typical trainee of the Yano that had rarely occurred. Each person of the assigned protection detail agreed that both Caden and Dave were different from the typical surface dweller they delt with, something of which they found to be a breath of fresh air.

Roy thought back to a few weeks prior, Dave was in a particularly curious mood where he asked a lot of questions. Dave asked anything and everything it didn't matter whether he got an answer or not. It was a good thing it wasn't Stan who acted like that really.

"Come on is there really nothing you can tell me about Arianna?" Dave asked with a slight huff roughed up after another lose from a fight with Roy. Roy looked at Dave he had asked a fair number of questions this session. Except these weren't the typical questions rather a little more personal.

"Even if you are currently like my own personal apprentice. To answer personal question like that isn't possible." Roy replied as he stuck his sword into the ground. "For what reason are you asking such things? You already know that such information is not just handed out." He asked as he leaned against the hilt of his sword. Roy looked down at Dave in question it was odd, and he couldn't determine such a reason.

"… is." Dave mumbled as he looked at the ground. By how he acted it was as if it was something he was embarrassed to say out loud.

"What was that? Speak up so I can properly hear you."

"Latris! It's because it will be Latris soon." Dave yelled back before he quickly covered his hands with his mouth with a red face from embarrassment. Dave looked to the side, but the red blush wasn't something he was good at hiding.

"Latris… that sound familiar." Roy muttered as he placed his hand on his chin in thought. "Ah, I remember. It's one of the Eternal holiday's is it not. It goes on for a week during the winter month normally around the second month of snowfall, or to be correct three weeks after the official first day for the winter axis. The most devoted of the religion head to a temple on the first and last day with their house."

"Ah, yeah. Though not everyone celebrates in such a way. During the middle of the week there is the custom to exchange gifts with people, especially those special or have done something significant for you in the past year. It's a holiday heavily celebrated in Canlonen so most things close and people spend time with their family." Dave muttered in agreement while he also added to what Roy had said.

Dave looked down at the ground. "Because of what you, the others, and Arianna had done for me I wished to get you all something meaningful that you all could use or keep."

Roy didn't say anything for a moment as he had his eyes closed in thought. "You don't really need to get us such things. We aren't doing this out of the goodness of our hearts or anything we are getting paid for it. Besides, most of us don't celebrate such a holiday nor practice the Eternal religion. Even Arianna, I can't recall he actually celebrating it for as long as I've known her."

"… fine but I'll still get something for you and Arianna. You two have done a lot for me in the past year it wouldn't be right not to. So please humour me so I can get a good gift. After all you had to done something before you worked with the Yano." Dave pleaded with shiny eyes. Roy looked away as he felt the sudden pressure and wave of emotion, it was something Dave learned how to do over the past few months. Roy looked away to try and not cave but, in the end, it was a fruitless attempt.

"Damn it, using the ability I've been teaching you to control against me like that." Roy grumbled as he ruffled his own hair and annoyance. "Fine, I'll tell you. It's not as if it's something big or anything. To be honest there isn't much about Arianna's past that I know about. Even to me she's extremely guarded, and she's yet truly open to anyone even though we are close. So, anything about her past or what would look good on her anything like that I have little idea as she's that secretive, however I know she likes cute things and soft textures." Roy muttered in reply. "When it comes to me… it's just as mysterious."

"What do you mean?"

"You asked about my past before the Yano. I don't know it. There was some kind of accident before I joined the Yano, so I don't remember." Roy replied in a calm tone with no real emotion in his voice.

"Oh, I'm sorry to bring it up."

"It's fine, it happened a long time ago. Like for Arianna, though since I can't remember it's probably not as painful. Arianna was the one that told me my name and saved me. As such it doesn't bother me, nor do I really care all that much anymore." Roy replied with slight wave of his hand. He looked down at his sword and noticed a tassel and recalled something.

"Then your name."

"Well, it might not be my actual name. Though I think it probably is... it's what Arianna called me before she knew I lost my memory."

"Then does that mean Arianna knows about your past?"

"Maybe, no she defiantly does maybe not everything, but she knows." Roy replied as he shook his head. He knew he had said a fair amount, but it was way too easy to do as such with Dave. Maybe it was due to his ability, but it was easy to talk and tell him things naturally.

"But you haven't asked... you also are close to her too."

"When we were younger, I did but she never said anything. They only reason I knew she did was that she'd bring up odd things to correct me but never expanded on it." Roy sighed he touched the tassel that was attacked to his sword. "For the first few years... I was very mean... and hated her for not saying anything since she clearly knew something. She gave this to me back then and I just yelled, attacked, and hurt her."

"Then how did your relationship change?"

"Arianna though she did distance herself after that... she can be very kind which was odd considering the environment we lived in. It took some time and after seeing her one multiple occasions, eventually I realised she didn't tell me anything probably out of some kind of pity or kindness but also probably due to the request of another.

"That was when I realised, I had the entirely wrong impression of her. She's more like a hurt animal fearful to all with something holding her back. She puts up a strong front but that's all. You've realized it too, I'm sure." Roy said as he gave Dave a slight smirk at the end.

"So, I guess now you don't really care about the memories you've lost." Dave replied as he looked at Roy.

"Yes, whether they return or not, is something no longer I concern myself about. I've learned and gained just as much as what I lost really so it doesn't matter that much anymore. Not to even mentioned its more than likely my family had died a long time ago now. Even if it was annoying at the time that such a choice was made for me... though it might just be blind faith. I trust whatever decision that Arianna makes."

Roy then shook his head, a little out of disbelief he even told Dave about such a thing. After a moment he glanced at Dave maybe he saw the younger version of Arianna or something else, but he spoke up once more. "If your so determined to get me something... a weapon or something for it will be fine." Roy told Dave with a smirk as he ruffled his hair.

Roy opened his eyes as he let out a sigh. He looked out into the hall to see Alyssa. He realized she must be trying to get something from him for Latris, like Dave did. He shook his head a little as he let out another sigh.

No one could deny that at the time Alyssa had become a thorn in everyone's side that were involved with Sean (expect Yavari), as it made everything that much more difficult due to her obsession. It was both an annoyance, a distraction, and just an overall problem now.

But no one would have expected what would come nor happen a few weeks after this occurrence. When Alyssa up and disappeared, most at first assumed she just went back to her school as she left one day and no one in the school realised anything happened to her. Not until a few months later did people hear anything.

Chapter 18

Months had gone by now since Arianna had disappeared that night. The season had changed twice since. Snow had begun to cover the ground and the presence of slick ice had started to appear. Winter had long since appeared in Brightton City and the festive time was soon to approach.

Snow crunched beneath Sean's feet as he walked through a deserted part of the city where the path was not managed by the city. Sean's usual nightly training session what abruptly cut short as Alex was forced to deal with something. Though she told him not to leave as it wouldn't take her longer, and even if it did Stan would arrive to take him home.

However, as the impatient jerk that he was he didn't listen to or follow Alex's instruction in the slightest. As such rather than wait for a few moments he decided to walk back home instead. Whether just pure arrogance, a complete disregard for what occurred before, or over confidence it's hard to say his exact reason for his action but it caused unnecessary problems in the end.

Since Sean was brought to the location they trained at by Alex, he didn't have a car to use to drive himself back. Though even if he had the option, the roads to get to the location they used were rough so he probably wouldn't have wanted to drive there in the first place. Which brought us to the situation in which Sean walked down such a street despite every reason for him not to.

It was a cold and dark night that day, a chill that one didn't easily forget. Sean walked down the road that had no streetlights, only that of full 'moon' that peaked between the mixture of buildings along the way. That night the cold one felt itself on that road that night was as if

133

it was sign of what was to come, as it was more than just the regular winter night chill.

Sean let out a deep breath which formed a small mist cloud. It was quiet aside from the crunch of Sean's footsteps, but the air was tense. Sean could feel the tension in the air that one could cut through with a knife he thankfully wasn't that dense. So, he knew something was wrong around him, though not sure what it was that caused it at that moment.

He picked up the pace and begun to walk faster down the road. Though such action wouldn't have been much help as it was still a very long walk both ways with a significant amount of time till he would either be able to run into a crowed street or his home. As if some god had been watching out for him a notice about his plight was sent out to all involved with his protection about this moment in a relative time.

The sound of footsteps begun to come from behind Sean and pick up pace. He felt something was wrong either from instinct or something else he reached into his pocket. Sean hand grabbed what was inside and spun around and blocked a blade with a small knife. His arm trembled under the strength of the strike as he slid back slightly with one of his knees collapsing and forced him to kneel.

The figure that attacked him became lit up from the light of the 'moon'. Their face was covered by a mask, but he could feel his attacker's excitement. Eventually Sean legs fully collapsed, and he fell into the snow. Their blades disconnected and the attacker went over Sean's head before he spun around.

Sean was in completely shocked from the other individual's immense strength. It was similar to what Roy had shown to him before. "Oh my. I'm surprised you managed to block that. You surface dwellers are normally quite useless in such a front. Though your attempt was quiet poor either way… you must have been given some training. Must be them as they are always a thorn in our side, they'd do anything to screw us over even train those of the surface." They hummed as they shifted in place. "For such a fruitless accomplishment, you'll learn how hopeless your fate is. Codename Imitator front and center to come deal with you." The Imitator introduced themselves.

Sean remembered the name Imitator it was a name that's been mentioned a few times in the last year. But that name had also come up in conversation with him not to long before this, Alex had warned him about such an individual. The Imitator was one who had caused some significant injury to Arianna. It wouldn't have been a surprise if Sean was scared, most people probably would be if in his shoes at that time, not that he would have ever admitted to it if he was.

Imitator begun to walk towards Sean at that point, but Sean had yet to get back on to his feet. In a quick second escape attempt Sean scooped up some snow into his hand and threw it at Imitator's masked face before he tried to scramble to his feet. "Ha! Nice try!" Imitator laughed out in a tone that mocked him. Imitator then threw and knife that priced into Sean's leg which caused him to fall back to the ground and scream out.

"Hoho! What a lovely scream, much better than that codeless bitch who didn't even make a squeak of pain from our fight." Imitator laughed joyfully. A thought of which would have sent chills done most people's spine. "It's so sad I'm not allowed to play with you like the other's since you are the one, they want. They say I can't lose such a weak and prime specimen ripe for the picking." They said in a dissatisfied tone with such a notion. "If we're lucky they will let me be charge of integration and punishment. What a lovely thought." They muttered as they traced their finger down Sean's jaw and chin.

Then the sound of a sniper shot broke through the silence of the night and Imitator staggers back holding their arm. "Who was that! You promised me a chance to enjoy the hunt! I'll kill you for interrupting me!" Imitator growled. This time around they were much more unhinged than before. The Imitator held their arm as it was dripped blood from where they were shot.

A building a fair distance away Alex looked up from the scoop of her sniper and touched the side of her helmet. "Missed a direct killed shot but I bought you a few minutes to get over there Night. Be careful they really stepped up their game this time after the multiple failed attempts since they brought that mad man in. But something tells me that not all." Alex muttered as she picked up her sniper.

"Understood. If another high rank agent shows up, I might require back up Thief."

From the shadows Night jumped out and grabbed Sean. As he was about to make his escape Night barely avoided a gunshot that shot right in front of him. "Ah, ah, ah! I won't be allowing you to make your escape with the target so easily like that experiment or mad mimic." A new voice teased as they walked out from the shadows.

The new individual had a complete upper mask that didn't cover the bottom of their face rather it cut off below the nose but made it look as if they had fangs. The white mask they wore had splotches and stains of red all over it. Though the mask was distinct their clothing wasn't anything special with dark red colours that fit them a little lose and were baggy.

Night stepped back slightly with a click of his tongue. "Bloody... you're not someone I expected to run into."

"Well, someone has to pick up the slack for the old timer and lab experiment that only slightly better than a brick wall." Bloody replied as they crossed their arms. "My addition to this little task was more like an additional after thought."

Bloody then glance over at Imitator the look though one couldn't see it was bone chilling. "Seriously old timer, get your head on straight.

Haven't you realized there is two high classers that you're facing, not just the guy in front of you." They clicked their tongue. "Seriously, it's a good thing that Codeless isn't around this time."

"Codeless?"

Bloody looked over at Sean who muttered that. They saw him flinch the moment they faced him which caused Bloody to smirk. "Yeah, the Codeless. The one the surface media has taken to calling the 'Assassin' for an absurd reason. Why give a codeless such a name when they have no right to have one with their choice? Besides if that was the name, I had to go by I'd die of embarrassment. Oh, yeah, you'd have no idea what they are. Codeless are the mercenary of mercenaries, but that one is always such an annoyance."

Night didn't want to deal with this even with Thief as back up. He had to fight two attackers that were decent in a close fight while he also had to protect Sean. Thief was in no ways a good close-range fighter when it means to exchange heavy, and numerus blows. Once more he tried to get away as the other two were distracted, but a gun shot hit the ground right in front of him.

"You would be able to get away from here. They aren't the only thing we have either." Bloody replied as they waved their hand slightly. The motion was followed with a rumble and roar as a now familiar beast appeared before them. "We have this thing as well. The boss doesn't wish to pass this chance by any longer, so he has allowed us to pull out a fair number of stops to make sure things go our way."

The odds were overwhelmingly against them in this moment. But even in the face such odds didn't matter all that much. To Night and Thief one thought crossed their mind. If they were going to fail, they were going to take out/do as much as they possibly could to weaken those they curse.

Thief appeared above Bloody as she attacked with an Axe. Bloody barely avoided Thief's attack as they spun, and Thief's axe clashed with Bloody's cleaver like blade. Night then lunged forward and attacked Imitator. "Move now." Night growled at Sean.

"No, you don't get them!" Bloody ordered the Chimera. It moved forward towards Sean, he stepped back for a moment couldn't make himself run. The Night and Thief pushed the two high ranked agents back and away from Sean, but they had no way to deal with the Chimera as they were a person short. Though against the Chimera not just anyone could stand up against it.

The Chimera was about to attack Sean he closed his eyes out of fear ready to be jumped, but as he did that, vines broke through the pavement and bound the Chimera's legs. "It's bound move!" Thief growled out an order.

Sean opened his eyes but was afraid to move from fear of the sniper that shot at Night earlier. "Don't think, run!" Night grunted as he fought against Imitator.

"You should pay attention to me! Let out a scream for me!" Imitator laughed as he attacked Night with a hard swing of their weapon. Night held his ground against the attack and stood firm. Thief did have more difficulty against Bloody than Night had with his opponent, but she made sure that she didn't let Bloody get away from her.

Sean jolted by Night's roar turned to run and escape from the location. "I have no idea what exactly did this to the Chimera but it's not important!" Bloody muttered as they hit away Thief's attack. "Don't let the target escape! Sniper team aim for the legs make it so he can't run anymore."

Even with Bloody's command nothing happened. Thief then pushed them back with a strong attack which they let out a curse. Sean begun to make his way away from the fight and range which worried Bloody, but they were unable to do anything as with each moment they made an opening Thief rounded back without much time to spare.

Neither Bloody nor Imitator at the time were in a position to chase after Sean. The Chimera begun to struggle more against the vines, and they began to snap away. The Chimera was strong but also large, so the moment Sean got away into an alley, it had little chance to go after him.

It fought hard and broke the vines in succession then right as the last vine snapped a large dark figure swooped down from the sky and slammed into the Chimera and took it away out of sight. The figure moved fast so none of those on the ground could see exactly what it was but a streak of red against the large black figure that appeared. Sean was frozen in surprise that something was able to do that to the creature that had haunted and hunted him for months now. He feared the notion of such a creature or being capable of tossing the Chimera like a toy existed.

"Run you idiot! Now's your chance!" Night yelled before he was tackled to the ground by the Imitator. The two begun to wrestle on the ground with one another. The Imitator was whole focused on Night and cared little about Sean that much was clear. Though for what reason that was unclear.

"Sniper's if you want to live to see tomorrow shoot the damn kid! You can't let him get away! Now's our chance with them gone!" Bloody howled as they fought Thief. "Kill them for all I care!"

There was a sudden crackle over the two opposing forces radio frequencies. There was a sudden breath over the radio and a pause as if in thought of what to say or maybe even hesitation. Then after a few moments as Sean was nearly out of range an odd new voice broke in over the channels and spoke.

"Sorry Bloody. But there's no one left to follow your orders."

Chapter 19

The full 'moon' hung in the sky a figure cloaked in black stood a top of a tall building. Just behind them lied a corpse with a broken sniper in hand and its blood that had begun to pool upon the roof it lied on. The figure looked around slow and meticulous, as if they were in search for another victim for them to slay.

They then stopped as they saw what they were in search of. Their hand reached behind them as their gloved hand wrapped around the hilt of a blade that rested there. Without second thought the figure jumped from the building wind rushed past them and caused their long coat to flutter in the wind. They positioned themselves in the air to align with a planned landing location in mind, till they eventually pulled out the blade they grabbed hold of before they jumped.

An individual on another building that had kept their eye to the sight of their sniper in wait for the right moment. Then they began to hear rush of wind the flutter of a cloth, these noises caught their attention away from their sight. They began to look around to find the location of the sound. Before they realized to late and looked up.

From above the figure landed their blade managed to slash through and price into their leg as the figure landed on top of the sniper. This action not only greatly injured their leg but also cracked a number of ribs and injured multiple organs. The sniper gasped and coughed out in pain.

The figure pulled out the blade from the sniper's leg before they stepped off them. The sniper only had a brief moment that allowed them to painfully gasp for air. As the figure spun on their foot and kicked the sniper square in the chest which caused them to roll across the ground and hit the side roof ledge.

The figure then looked at the sniper. They brought their sword up towards them which cause the momentary 'moon' light to shine against them and the sight of their black helmet. Then they run their hand along the blade and a slight humming could be heard along with the sizzle of the blood that had coated the blade.

They turned the sword in their hand before they stabbed it into the sniper rifles main body and cut the barrel itself off. They destroyed the sniper to make it impossible to use again.

As they focused on that the sniper, they had kicked wasn't dead yet. They pulled out a gun and fired but the figure as if already aware of the threat spun around right before and dodged the bullet to which they threw a dagger which embedded itself into the sniper's chest.

But another noise took the figures attention away from the sniper and they jumped onto the ledge of the roof. They could hear the sound of a roar. They looked towards the direction and watched as the Chimera struggled against the vines that had bound to its legs. They took in the situation before them and watched the figure that raced away from the main fight.

They knew the Chimera would break free and chase the other figure that tried to flee from the location, they would get caught. The cloaked figure raised a hand and down from above a large figure appeared behind them and completely blocked out the 'moon' light.

It looked down at the other smaller figure with its red eyes. Its eyes held pride, anger, contempt, and dissatisfaction towards them, but the other figure cared very little about it. Then with a quick motion of their hand they waved and pointed at the Chimera, the other figure huffed out in a prideful like arrogance before it took to the skies and dove towards the Chimera.

The cloaked figure watched on to see what the other figure would due. Before they could witness what was to occur a dagger was stabbed into their lower leg and grabbed a hold of the other with their hand. The sniper dragged themselves over to do this something the other large figure saw but ignored.

They looked down at the sniper in annoyance and kicked off their hand before they stabbed it to the roof with their sword. They jumped down from the ledge and kicked them in the stomach and avoided the dagger that was still embedded in their chest. The snipers other hand reached out to try and pull the blade out of their hand. They pulled the dagger out from their leg then threw it down and into the sniper's other hand which pined that one to the roof as well.

The figure then pulled out another blade, twin to the first from behind their back hidden by their long coat. They walked over to the sniper and stabbed the sword into their spine at which point they screamed out. They twisted the blade a little before they dug their heel into their back.

The figure then leaned forward and grabbed the sniper's head and turned it up to look at them. They tore away the low-grade mask and looked at the snipers tear streaked face. "Not much fun when your own low acts are used against you is it."

"P-please. H-have mercy." The sniper sobbed their body trembled from the immense pain. They looked at them in silence for a moment.

"… mercy. Funny." They muttered before they pulled out another dagger. This one however rather than use it as another sort of pin it had another intended use. The figure dragged the blade across the sniper's neck and let go of their head. The sniper looked up at them in shock before their eyes begun to blur and dull before they collapsed to the ground.

The figure then retrieved their blades before they collected the mask they tore from the sniper. They did look at the mask for a moment before they decided to take it with them since they had collected a number of similar masks already today. They wiped the blood from their twin swords off against their legs before they put them away.

The Sniper's radio then crackled to life. "Sniper's if you want to live to see tomorrow shoot the damn kid! You can't let him get away! Now's our chance with them gone!" The figure heard a familiar voice from the radio. So, they turned to the sniper and swiped their radio before they attuned and connected it with their unique helmet, with unknown origins. They stood on the ledge of the building once again and looked out over to the battle ground. "Kill them for all I care!"

The figure was certain and felt a slight moment of enjoyment at the certainty of who they faced. They waited till eventually they connected with the new frequency, and everything was in tune. The crackle of the radio as they waited could be heard over both frequencies as they worked to connect properly. Then a notice appeared before their eyes. "Sorry Bloody. But there's no one left to follow your orders."

"Who are you?! How did you access a secure frequency!"

"Tsk, tsk. Can't figure it out… there's no need for me to inform the ignorant of how." They replied. "But oh my. Fighting over such things, I wish to have under me. Won't let you do that now. As I'll be the one to take it all." They hummed as they begun to jump across roof tops towards the fight.

The figure whistled out with a clear sound into the air. "Get the kid." They ordered as they motioned in the direction which Sean went. "No need to fight anymore now. Time is up the match is done." The figure then said over the radio as they jumped from the building towards the fight. "The fight is over and won. It's my game now."

The figure from above kicked Imitator off Night and slide across the ground before they pivoted and lunged towards Bloody. The figure swung a blade which Bloody jumped out of the way of danger. But the second blade came out which forced them to block with their weapon and a sharp clang as they weren't ready it likely stung their hand.

The figure then moved quickly over to Thief and swiped the necklace they then whistled once more. "Katia now!" They yelled out before they grabbed both Thief and Night by the collar and pulled them closer. From above a jet of odd flames cut between them and the two enemy agents.

"Don't let them escape." Bloody howled but hesitant to face the flames themselves. The Chimera on the other hand made its way over, it would try to go through the flames to reach the other side. From above Sean was dropped before them and the figure grabbed them as well.

The figure held the necklace in hand, and it begun to glow slightly. The large black figure then wrapped itself around the four of them which hid them from view as energy gathered. Though still unclear to the others surrounded by it for a moment as the light got the most intense it was possible to see the glisten of black scales.

[Its blood was disgusting. Very pitiful like you. ... what has the universe come to that a great one such a me must follow a low being such as you.]

I'm concentrating. This thing's completely drained and must do it myself through it. I'm not in the mood to fight with you now. So, shut up I don't care how you act, you lost I proved my worth. We both have to put up with one another Katia.

[Hmmm. It wasn't propre nor has thing been fully done. ... You'll die at this rate.]

I almost have it.

[Your out of time.]

That's fine I got it now, let's go!

The tech begun to activate, and light begun to surround the group. *[Thought you'd never ask.]* A prideful feminine voice replied. The large reptilian like figure that surround the group begun to move then lunged towards Bloody and the Imitator with it's large sharp jaws opened to snapped on them. But as the reptilian creature neared to snap down on them it disappeared. At the same time the group disappeared in a flash of light right before their enemies' eyes.

Chapter 20

In a flash the small group of four appeared in front of a house. The home was located on a street with several streetlights which made it possible to look at the unknown figure a little better. The figure was dressed head to toe in black gear that was aimed for the idea of combat and reconnaissance primarily done at night. But even with the light it was hard to tell anything about the figure as it revealed nothing only that they are someone that fights and the gear they wore was relatively new as it was fairly clean and undamaged.

Before anyone of them could speak a word the door to the house burst open and a person rushed out and hugged Sean. "Oh, thank goodness you're alright. You are okay right my sweet baby?" Yavari exclaimed and begun to look Sean over franticly. "This is all the bitch's fault! Leaving us in the hands of such people. We never should have adopted that child all they've brought is misfortune and problems. Never should have brought in such unknown blood here, nor even accepted her in." she ranted as she gripped Sean shoulders tightly.

"Mother stop it." Sean muttered embarrassed and possibly ashamed of her actions. However, he never said a word of argument nor defense. His expression didn't really change much as she said such things. Either out of agreement or due to the simple fact that Yavari had acted in such a way numerous times at this point.

Night and Thief looked away likely due to a desire to kill Yavari. The figure however begun to laugh with their shoulder that trembled from their vain attempt at stifling their laughter. "My god you truly are a two-faced bitch. You act as if this an ancient era, with the very thought that raising a child without blood relations is bad or something of the short. The fact you dislike one not with your blood or of different origin. I've never met a Surface dweller as bad and utterly disgusting and horrible as you. You act as if the world revolves around you, and you can never do anything wrong… its hilarious." They laughed as they held their stomach.

The figure suddenly straightened up with their head turned up as if they looked down at them. "You hated the girl the moment you took her in but hid it at the start with overly sweet actions. That's how you work you act overly sweet and attentive when angered, hatred, or annoyed. A sweet act you put up for others to hide your true nature. A rose bush or white lotus such person could be called." They exclaimed before they turned their head down a little and pushed Yavari back from Sean. "It was probably a real blessing that girl was the one brought in and not another. Such a person like you would devastate and hurt them. As you threaten, treat them poorly, constantly blame them for what goes wrong, and even threaten to send them back to where they came, but often pull them back in with sweet kind acts."

The figure clenched their fist. "Such a person as that girl could care less about you. Someone that couldn't even thank people for risking their life to save idiots like you. Idiots who wouldn't think twice and expect them to do such without nothing in return. I have no idea where even such a notion of entitlement came from, maybe it's due to our races long history, but it's so pathetically stupid, so stupid that it's both laughable and pitiful something thinks they have such entitlement or worth. You are nothing to me, and I could kill you anytime I wished."

"Y-you can't treat me in such a way!" Yavari stammered as she stumbled back. She pointed at the figure, but they couldn't care less about the women. "We're paying you! I also have great backing!"

"Payment… you are not the one that is paying us rather your current husband is. Also, a women kicked out of their home and disavowed for a long family of Eternial figures has little ground to stand. Besides I have more backing than even one of your pinky fingers." The figure replied as they stepped forward. "You are a person that makes anyone but yourself into a sinner to save yourself, even children who've done nothing wrong. You mask has cracked Yavari

you are so blind you are unaware of what is going on around you."
They said in a tone that chilled those that heard before they leaned
forward.

"The day that you are to die. I hope to be the one responsible or
even get to watch as the light leaves your eyes and face Faradityx. As
even below people like you are hated as we have standards even though
we commit such acts unlike you." The figure whispered even with their
manipulated voice Yavari probably was able to picture who it was then.
"You act clean, but you have a secret. I know what you and she did. -."

Yavari froze their blood ran cold as they stumbled back. They looked at
the figure with wide eyes and filled with fear. The figure though you
couldn't see it was pleased with the look they wore. But it wasn't long
before they felt immense pain which caused them to flinch slightly.

From the door two more figures appeared. "Night! Thief! I
know you could do it! Your so dumb Sean! They told us already it's no
longer safe for us! What made you think walking home was a good
idea. They won't give up after multiple failed attempts." Dave lectured
his older brother a sight that caused the figure to smirk despite the pain
they felt. "But who is this?"

Night and Thief looked at one another, neither of them was familiar
with the figure who came to their aid. Even with a helmet it could very
well have been swiped so they couldn't say who it was other than they
were currently friendly. With no answer from those two the figure
spoke up. "Unlike them I'm in a different situation. I have no name like
they do for I am what is called a Codeless. I was in the area is all and
have an amicable relationship with the Yano over the Marione, so I
decided to help."

"Could you be the 'Assassin' then? I heard the 'Assassin' is a
codeless and works with the Yano." Dave exclaimed he was oddly
excited in the figures point of view. They wanted to end to conversation

quickly but knew for now it was better to hold out to hide their urgency to leave.

"Assassin, eh? I might be, might not. Who can say? I am just a Codeless most of us are considered the same. Though some agents find some of us more annoying than others. The more important fact is of one's capability." Codeless replied with a shrug. They were careful and didn't reveal anything other than they have no true affiliation with a single group.

Dave looked at them for a moment intently. "Stay here for a moment, I want to give you something before you leave." He stated to Codeless before he raced inside at which point Caden walked over.

Caden ignored Yavari as she took Sean inside the house. "I apologize for the action of my sons. I'm grateful you are putting up with them and teaching them." Caden said with a slight bow. Codeless glanced over at Night and Thief unaware of the fact that the two boys had begun to train with them. "I should thank you as well. A codeless like yourself had no need to aid in such an occurrence but you did and saved my son and helped those that are protecting us."

"You don't really need to thank us. Though it is nice to hear. We are being paid after all. Besides I quite enjoy training with your youngest he's become akin to my apprentice at this point. He is quite enthusiastic in learning what I have to teach him and receptive, so it's become quite enjoyable." Night replied as he waved his hand slightly. He looked away as if he was slightly embarrassed to receive a direct thank you.

"Sean is tolerable. He learned part what I've taught. But he doesn't keep his pride in check. This is not the first problem that's happened. But today we were lucky." Thief muttered with her arms crossed. "He acts sometimes like it is just a joke."

"I hope he hasn't been too much. It seems he takes after me with his passion to learn what interreges him." Caden chuckled slightly as he rubbed the back of his head. "Also sorry about him Thief, all of you are working hard. It's something I know well. But from what I grasp what happened today was extremely dangerous." He added which the other two nodded in response.

The Codeless let out a slight cough to remind them they were still present. "Ah! We'll continue to talk about this later." Caden realized as he glanced at Codeless.

Around then Dave ran back out was a small case that looked like a first aid kit. He then pushed it forward into Codeless' chest. "You need it. Be sure not to ignore it or it will probably end up much worse." Dave told them.

"Ah...! Thank you very much for your kindness. I'll be sure to use it well." Codeless replied as they took what Dave handed them. "... word to the wise. Be wary of the women you call mother. She is not someone trustworthy, a snake in the grass that would sooner turn tail than help." They muttered. With that Codeless turned around and walked down into the street before they jumped up and kicked against the streetlight and went off into the night.

A figure jumped from across the sky above like a shadow in the night as they left no trace of their path behind them. After some time, they came to a stop a top a tall building, as they felt a jolt of pain through them. Their hand went across their chest as they knelt to the ground.

It was hard from them to breath and the helmet they wore was no help on that front either. They dropped the box to the ground as they reached up with a hand that shook slightly and touched something on the side of the helmet.

The helmet that was securely attached with not clear way to remove it begun to change. The metal like face part that covered all but their eyes begun to slide back and open which allowed for its easy removal. They pulled off the helmet and tossed it to the side as they gasped for air. With the helmet gone their long hair fell onto their back.

They began to cough and spit out blood after a few moments. In this moment it was a clear sight of how injured the individual was. But these injuries were not from the fight they joined to but from something else entirely. They could feel that inside of them something wanted to break out something powerful. It twisted inside of them impatiently as it waited, something that was easy to feel in their current state.

Their body begun to shiver, and it felt as if their blood run cold. They had no energy left, nothing and it tried to grasp for something. They couldn't move and it got harder for them to hold themselves up as blood trickled from their month.

"What do expect was to happen when you overdo it like that? If it was anyone else, they'd already be dead. Not only have you've gone over your limit, for a while now, but you also didn't finish what you needed to." A voice familiar to the individual spoke from behind them. "Just like Ryna, you burn yourself out to the point of ashes. I should call you Ryna, it fits well."

"... Shut up... that's not... I will not be a warrior of flames. I didn't have much of a choice. I certainly don't enjoy this in the slightest. But if I didn't things would have gone worse. I can handle it... even if it's only partial. For now, it will have to do... I can't let... that happened... too... so I have to..." they muttered before they passed out and fell to the ground unconscious.

"Sigh... pushing yourself to this point. You remind me of Freya in many ways. Rest now while you can. I await your decision dear; *Aria* of flames."

Part 3

Chapter 21

In a bedroom of a secret location there lied Arianna. The first thing that she registered was pain and the odd yet slightly familiar heaviness of her body. She opened her eyes slowly before she forced herself to sit up and look around the room.

This is one of my safehouses… she thought before she winced in pain. She looked down to find that she had already been covered in bandages, though she could still taste iron in the back of her throat. *Well, I'm not dead.*

Ari lifted the covers off herself, she was in a pair of light sleep wear a tank top and shorts likely so they could get at the bandages. As she pushed her legs over to the side, she could tell how bad it was, the pain and the heaviness was very clear at such movement. Though the pain was something she was able to deal with, she didn't enjoy this familiar heaviness to her body overall.

I over did it. My body that is naturally in tune and entwined with mana… completely empty. I shouldn't let them know… I can't worry them. Damn it… I didn't get to do everything either. She groaned with a light shake of her head.

Ari reached over to check the date as she turned on and looked at the screen. *Latris is it really that time again… no it had been a while. But it seems I was out for a few days either way.* She thought before she forced herself to her feet. She balanced herself against the walls and table as she made her way out of the room.

In the small apartment like safehouse there was no one else inside which was a slight relief for Ari since there wasn't a break in. She made it to the main room which had a window that allowed her to look outside and see the snow-covered city and ground. *At least I wasn't left outside.*

On the counter she noticed a note and a box. She limped over to the counter and sat down in one of the 'bar' chairs and looked at the note first.

[Took you, too you're closest safehouse. Dressed your wounds. The state you were in couldn't wait let it heal the normal way. Didn't want my little flame to wink out on me. It might be around Latris when you read this. Don't stay inside and mope, go out and do something… at the very least go out and eat. Till next time. – Fang] The note read; she tore it into pieces before she disposed of it.

Arianna was a little annoyed about the end of the note. *Who said I was moping? I just don't do anything… not like I have anyone to celebrate it with anyways.* She thought with a huff before she glanced over to the box. It didn't look like much, but she brought it over next to her and tipped off the lid.

Part of the box contain medical supplies that looked to have been used recently. The other half of the box contained a smaller bag that had wrapping paper that stuck out. The tag on the bag read Dave.

Arianna looked around like a kid about to do something that would cause them to be scolded by their parents. She grabbed the small bag and placed it in front of her. She reached into the bag and felt a soft texture brush against here fingers, she quickly grabbed hold of it and pulled it from the bag before she placed it down onto the table.

What sat down on the table in front of Ari was a small to mid-size plush wolf doll. It was very soft and cute she looked at it for a moment before she reached out and touched it. *Cute and soft. But how did Dave know I like such a thing? I've never had nor looked at one when he was around.* Ari muttered as she held the plush in her arm. Though she couldn't the plush completely against her bare arm due to the bandages she was content either way for the small amount.

*No one alive knows about it since I avoided it after that day…
wait. Actually… one time when I was younger, I couldn't stop myself…
someone might have been around at that time. How embarrassing.* She
thought as she covered her flushed face with one hand. Ari then glanced
down at the plush and brought it to her face to feel the soft fabric, with
it so close she was able to catch the scent that clung to the fabric. She
let out a slight chuckle and wore a bright but light smile on her face.
When was the last time I received a gift like this?

Ari placed the plush back down on the counter and closed her eyes for a
moment. *I'm not allowed… nor wish to return to that house with Yavari
there or I might just kill her. Which though I care little about such a
thing… it's the opposite of what I was contracted to do, and its Dave's
mother…* She paused, a low laugh escaped from her lips as she opened
her eyes and leaned against the table. *When did I become so
sentimental…? I shouldn't allow myself such a luxury. I'm just going to
get hurt if I keep allowing myself like this.* She muttered as she felt a
numbness in her chest.

Despite the pain she quickly stood up from her chair and went to the
fridge. When she opened the door, she found there was nothing inside.
She pondered for a moment she did think for a moment, not to eat and
face people that were out and about to enjoy Latris since it wasn't
something she couldn't do.

But Arianna's stomach was not in agreement. She hadn't eaten
for days at this point and for the last few months had sustained herself
with very little food and water. As she went too far it seemed she had
used up the last of all the reserves she made for herself and was only
able to function on the small fumes that remained.

Ari looked down at her hand but more at the bandages that had
wrapped her. She was in pain that was for sure, but she was certain she
could manage it and keep her limp to a minimum.

My powers are completely exhausted, like what happened a few years ago. My body is in such a state that it's incapable of healing such wounds at the usual rate… which means my body is weak again not long after it start to improve. Though worry some it should return to an acceptable level in a few weeks that I can return to my job and deal with what forced me to return early. She hummed as she flexed her hand a little and her pain tolerance.

He'll be mad I left with little word but once he learns what going on I'll be fine. But I really did go too far, I've never exhausted myself like this before. It's too much like what happened to me a few years ago expect it feels more stable and just exhaustion rather than… She trailed off as she looked out at the window again.

I should just go eat… a few bars should be open despite it being Latris. Hmmm in this state I should be able to get drunk could help take the edge off and numb the pain. Not that it's a real solution but I might not get another chance like this anytime soon.

Arianna after she decided what she was about to do begun to suppress her pain and straightened up. After she tidied a little, she took the small plush to her room with only a slight limp before she went into the bathroom. When she entered the bathroom, it was hard not to look into the large mirror on the wall. She was able to see that she had been covered in a fair number of bandages wrapped around her body.

As she removed some of the bandages she found that some of her wounds where still open. It was likely that some of them had opened when she moved around. Ari shook her head a little as she missed her healing ability at that moment. It wasn't good for her to let her blood spill to much with its ability, but she also didn't enjoy pain even though she had begun to learn to numb herself to it, more for combat and stealth reasons, but she still disliked it all the same.

Ari then looked up in the mirror at herself. She hadn't seen her real appearance in years, and she frequently used the one before her. Such an appearance that she had long grown accustomed to which had become so familiar now. She wanted to run but at the same time she couldn't bring herself too completely do so especially at the beginning when she burned with anger and hatred.

At times she did wish to just disappear completely and try to forget it all. She feared her past that she was desperate to forget it and leave it behind but couldn't. Whenever she tried to resolve herself, something would bring her back to the cruel reality she wished to forget. She couldn't forget and feared ever day the truth would be revealed. A fear instilled in her for just as long as her fear of fire. She didn't truly want to die at the time.

She leaned towards the mirror and covered one of her rust-coloured eyes. Though she was disguised, and her true appearance and eye colour were hidden as she looked into her own eye. She couldn't help but to picture the real colour and true appearance one she rarely allowed herself to express. Her eyes held sadness as it was something that she could never forget about her past nor simply leave alone.

The Tamer's cursed eyes. A charm like thrall, or even somewhat like hypnosis as it that made others more susceptible to those with side eyes. Essentially it made the person more likeable to others in general, but the eyes in particular are the most dangerous. Though the general charm was something one could ignore their eyes were another matter. One look into the eyes and the person is in thralled, at the time there was very few know that could resist it. The stronger they were the stronger the 'curse' was.

It was something that couldn't be denied was useful in some sense but disheartening for the distrust of another's emotion towards them. The question would always be 'is this true or an illusion? Do they really feel this way towards me?'. For some the curse was not as bad or they could control it to a slight degree, however for those that were not as fortunate there was another way to mediate and dimmish the curse's effect on others.

It was direct eye contact, if direct line of sight was cut the effect was demised or completely gone. Once the curse was awakened one learned to avoid eye contact or wore things like glasses to act like a barrier with the 'barrier' method being the most effective as long as their eyes were blocked it was fine.

The curse was related to her past. It was something she could not ignore once it begun to be expressed more clearly and affect those around her. Her true eye colour was indictive of her blood and the curse even in the worlds current state.

Arianna sighed as she lowered her hand and turned around. *I can't forget the Virtual Holo-display specs (VHDS), not after all the work to get the proto-type done for me to use. Hah, though I could just use it to get some free drinks.* She snorted before she begun to clean up and ready herself to leave.

Chapter 22

Arianna walked around the snow-covered city for some time in search of an opened bar/restaurant. She was dressed lightly in comparison to what most people around here would wear, in a sweater, a hat, and some light boots. She was naturally unaffected by the cold, so this was the best she had in her safehouse. Despite her condition she was pleased she was still unaffected by the cold in her current condition, though it made her wonder if her goal would pan out.

After about an hour as she walked around the city in search, she located a place that was open not long after it begun to lightly snow some more. With little thought and care she went inside the establishment. Inside she took a quick glance around as she dusted herself off and took a seat as it was a 'seat yourself' establishment. The place was light on customers which was on no real surprise to Ari due to the time of year and the country it was.

The place didn't really have a warm and welcome kind of atmosphere. With some of the glances she had gotten from other patrons as she had arrived had rubbed her the wrong way and made her hairs stand on end. Ari just ignored them however and just removed her main outer winter gear. Her hand brushed her left ear as it grazed what was one of two pieces of tech that was wrapped around her ear out of sight, hidden, light and small.

Though she didn't enjoy the eyes of some of the other patrons whose eyes remained on her, she chose to just ignore it as she wasn't in a state to deal with it cleanly. Eventually a waitress came over to her and handed her a menu.

"What could I get you to drink?" the Waitress asked before Ari had much of a chance to really look over the menu let alone the drink part of it. Ari thought for a moment hesitant to speak, she couldn't change her appearance, so she just sprayed some temporary black colour spray in to darken her hair more. But she hesitated since was in this appearance she's gotten comfortable with. She was limited in what she could do with her body's current state.

Come on, I can't rely on others for something so trivial. Nor anything else if faced with worse situations later. Just like talking to the others or when I got mad at the Luo's, it's just a waitress I can do this... even if it's with your real voice. Ari told herself as she placed her hand on her chest to calm her heart that raced from this simple notion. She let out a shaky breath to calm her nerves and put herself in a different mindset and as if it was a different situation than what she was. "Vodka tonic and water... please." She said in a quiet tone.

"Alright sweety, look over the menu to decided what you want as I get that for you." The waitress said with a kind voice. She looked like she wished to pat Arianna on the head like a small animal. Arianna found it a personal victory she was able to say such thing to the waiter.

Arianna begun to look at the menu. *I should get more than normal then I have leftovers. That way I don't have to go to the store till a later date. Besides I'm very hungry.* She decided in a quick conclusion as she begun to look what exactly to get. When her drink arrived, she wasn't all to slow to drink them as she was fixed over the menu.

As turned her attention to the items on the menu, the door to the restaurant opened with a slight ring, a noise which caused her to glance up in the direction. A man that was only few years older than herself walked in. She got a pretty good look at him from where she sat, she thought he looked handsome with fine strong features, it was like an illustration done by a professional artist in the flesh was in front of her.

But that was all she did and turned back to the menu. Arianna at this point had already seen her fair share of good-looking people both guys and girls at this point, not to mention that most would say she was such a person herself, though she wouldn't agree to such. Even so she cared very little, as though she found them ascetically pleasing to the eye that was all. So, she was unlikely to spare a second glance at a person unless needed to really.

After some time, the waitress arrived with her drinks. "You ready to order sweety?" she asked, and Ari just nodded her head. "Tell me what you'd like." Arianna then listed what she wished to eat which consisted of an appetizer, a salad, and a sandwich. "Are you sure you can eat all that? It's quite a lot for someone your size."

"Mm. I need leftovers." Arianna replied in a soft voice. She held out the menu to the waitress which she eventually took.

"So, you're thinking in advance then? I see, its defiantly better than going out multiple times. What would you like to drink next?"

"Another vodka tonic and a rum with any kind of dark pop."

"Alright then I'll bring you everything once its ready."

Arianna nodded her head in reply. With nothing to occupy her and little interest in what played on the TV she pulled out a novel and begun to read it as she drank the water before her. Even with the book she was still mindful of her what was around her. That included the occasional stares of different kinds that would come her way.

"What you think? Get her drunk and take her. I'm sure the boss would like her, or we can do as we wish to her." A low voice spoke the caught Ari's attention. He was huddled forward as he whispered to the guy across him, they person that spoke was a few booths away from her. But it was clear who it was he spoke of, as aside for the waitress, she was the only female patron in the vicinity, and they had glanced over at her a number of times already.

"Well, she's quite a pleasure on the eyes. Liked her when she walked in." Arianna was a little annoyed at this point and glanced up at them with death glare. She could see them shiver in response and one looked directly at her and paled a little. "She seems a little fisty…" they spoke a little quieter at that point and the volume of the TV was raised so was unable to hear what else they said. Arianna looked over the table and picked up a toothpick that she then sent towards them and into the cushion of the seat right next to them as a sort of warning before she turned her head away.

Arianna found the two's talk more of an annoyance rather than as something of amusement. To her the idea of someone like her being sold or used in such away on the black market was a bit of an insult. Though the thought to take care of a 'ring' like them was a task she wouldn't mind doing, but she was in no shape to do so at the time.

Arianna chose to act unaware of their little conversation for now and focus on her novel. After some time however she did hear a chair move but passed it off. That was until in the peripheral of her vision a figure sat down in the seat in front of her. Ari looked up and to her surprise that man who entered earlier was now in front of her. She gave a slight look as she closed her book.

"I apologize for being late I didn't realize you had already arrived." The man said clear and easy to hear. Arianna looked at him with no real expression but her one eye was raised to indicate her question towards his action. "Don't give me that look darling, I was distracted I hope you didn't have to deal with anything troublesome before I arrived."

If she was any other women, it would be a bit of a surprise to them before they decide to quickly play along, even just fall in love, or the like, just due to his act. She looked at him in contemplation then her eyes narrowed. She looked at the man a little more up close with a keen gaze with no judgement after a moment smirked as she suddenly realized something. *Such a game to try and play. Fine I might be able to make use of such a thing no matter who you are.* She decided calmly before she shifted in her seat. *Let's see how good he in word games and run arounds.*

"Oh, it's quite alright, I was very content with the thought that my lover jolted me without so much as a word. After you've been gone for so long too." Arianna replied with an annoyed tone but changed in the end so sound as if she was hurt. She noticed he was a little stunted, maybe from her different tone from the meek one she had prior, maybe even questioned if she had actual plans with someone.

"That wasn't my intention. Something just came up suddenly that I didn't have time to let you know."

"This is always your excuse ever since you left school." Arianna muttered before she begun to tear up. "Your never around anymore. I'm already alone as it is. But it feels like you're avoiding me, and it hurts." She started to sob as tears slowly fell from her eyes as she looked at him before she turned away with her hands on her chest. "You're probably seeing other women or something. After all they have always told me that I'm not good enough for you… you probably feel the same way."

"What?! Other women! What asshole told you such a thing! I'll kill them." He growled with a sharp gaze. Arianna was surprised at how well he was played along with her, which confirmed her suspicions even more. "You're the most beautiful person in the world. I could never think of leaving you for another." He said sweetly as he pulled her face to face him. He begun to wipe away here tears with his thumbs, but they just kept falling.

"You're the only person I'll ever love." He said was he leaned over the table and brought his face towards hers. He leaned in close to her face she could feel his breath brush against her check. Then something she never expected happened. He leaned in close to her than licked the tears that trailed down on the one side of her face. "Is that good enough for you." He whispered in her ear, his voice was very deep and low, a voice that was quiet a pleasure to hear.

Arianna's eyes widen and her face started to turn red out of embarrassment. She wanted to slap him, but it would be counterproductive to what they just did, same would be if she rushed to the bathroom to wash her face. "Crazy conniving asshole." Arianna growled under her breath so only he could hear and heard him lightly chuckle as he leaned back into the seat. *He 100% did that on purpose. Probably to get back at me for that like act.* She growled before she glanced in the direction of the two men to see that they've moved further away.

She grabbed some napkins as she wiped away the rest of her tears and her face. Her face then returned to normal as if she didn't even cry in the first place. The man across from Arianna was taller than her by a couple centimeters, along with his good looks and deep voice he had dark blue hair that looked more black than blue, which one wouldn't realize it was blue in the first place unless it was in different light. With his deep-sea blue eyes that held a very slight silverish tint around the iris' he had quiet the memorable appearance to her.

The waitress came over and placed down my food with a smile. "Mind telling me, your secret on how to attract hot guys." She smirked with a playful expression; Arianna just shrugged. "Oh, what I would do to date a guy with looks like your boyfriend." She sighed with her hand on her face with a slight blush. He smiled at her, and Arianna could hear her gasp. "Um, do you need anything else?" She asked Ari just pointed to her drink. "Got it what about you ho- sir?"

"A beer and a sandwich like what she has." He replied with a polite tone. The waitress nodded her head quickly and raced off with a flushed face. Arianna glanced at him for a moment with the thought that if he had a lover, they might be jealous as he seemed to be a kind of playboy. She moved her book to the side and brought the appetizer closer to her before she took a bite of one and realized how hungry she was as she wanted to eat the entire thing.

Arianna tipped back her drink to clear her mouth and look at the man across from her. "Thanks for the help in dealing with something annoying. Now what do you want?"

"Why do I have to want something." He replied quickly. Arianna glanced at him and grabbed another appetizer. She thought there was a chance he would leave if she didn't play it right. But in a few moments, she realized what way he wants this potential 'relationship' between them to be. But she wanted it to be a little more benefitable for her, and too bad for him she has a lot of experience in dealing with contracts and contractors that try to screw her over.

"No one truly helps a person with no goal in mind. To look good, relieve guilt, get closer, stuff like that. That statement runs even more true for people in our field of work. Normally its money but something tells me that's not you're aim." Arianna sighed as she tossed what she grabbed into her mouth. "I am more than likely to agree, but I just need to know what I'm getting into… for my own well-being since it's likely 'dark' work considering."

"How did you know?"

"That's easy. Your build and certain physical characteristics like height, told me your race. They don't match a light Tarrein, and the dark never come above ground. Not to mention the dark are quite short, so all that leaves twilight. Then your hands are calloused, movements trained, and are very quick to adapt act right for the situation meaning you are a merc." Arianna replied simply as if it was nothing.

"You approached me for a similar belief, though from probably a different rational." She added with a shrug. He covered his mouth to stifle a slight chuckle and a slight smirk that appeared on his face.

Chapter 23

The man in front of Arianna shifted as he regained his composer. "This is a first. I've never met one with such skill." He stated as he flashed her with a smile and touched her hand, as he let out a slight cough. She glanced over at it but didn't do anything rather she noticed something else from the sudden contact but kept a straight face despite the concern it caused her. "I want to make a deal, one that would be beneficial for the both of us."

"A deal what kind deal? What does it entail? Why ask a stranger you know nothing about?" Arianna asked as she tilted her head to show her interest. She continued to eat as her salad arrived and begun to work away at that as she continued to listen to him.

"I need your help with it, as no one close to me can do such a thing. But whoever said we'd remain strangers I would like to improve our relationship. Since we'll be working together and all." He told Ari. He was clear in his flirtatious acts and Arianna knew what he wanted to happen. Emotions were easy to use when looked at objectively and the one that was best for him to use was love and attraction.

"So, you want us to talk about ourselves then or something, I guess. Oh, and I guess you wish to exchange names as well." Arianna said shyly. Though it wasn't how she felt. Rather she acts how she thought would fit better with how he probably thought of her at the time. A fox against a dragon; a battle of wits between the two.

"But of course, Lennox; though I'm also known as Aether." Lennox replied without much thought or hesitation. "What are the names of a beautiful women as yourself."

"Ah… Lennox you didn't let me finish I would have told you." Ari muttered as she pretended to be flustered. "I don't actually have a real name like you." She mumbled and made herself look like a lost puppy.

"Y-you don't have one. Not even one people just call you." Lennox stammered as he realized his mistake. Below one's name was important, and one's codename was normally only shared between close allies in the same organization. He made a blunder that its only savour was that it was only his first name he gave.

"Yes, I'm sorry. I in truth in all legality currently have no name. I lost my parents young so… I'm one of many names and no names." Ari paused. "If not the normal term, people will call me Ari at times." She muttered as she covered her mouth as if a child telling one a secret. *I've pulled this one over him, but to put some ease, I should be more forth coming with the other part he talked about.*

"Ari… so that's which you wish to be called. It's hard to say a name fits one as beautiful as you. Rather I thought it be angel." Lennox complimented as he really tried to charm Arianna. She shifted in place and looked at him as she let out a slight laugh that was very fake. "However, with your other comment. I'm to take it that you are a codeless." He said in a low voice which she gave a slight nod.

"Does it not work out better for you. We Codeless can-do things you Affiliates can't after all. Which would make me all the more able to complete what you wish." Ari stated as she tilted her head slight was a small polite smile. Lennox looked at her for a while before he let out a sigh likely out of defeat since she was right. Codeless were freer mercenaries in a sense when in comparison to those that are a part of an organization, though did come with a set of numerous downfalls.

As the next part of Arianna's food came it became quiet between the two of them. Though it was more like a silent war of attrition in a sense. If nothing was said by either side especially from Arianna it meant Lennox's deal attempt fell through before it even got off the ground. Arianna knew this she just wanted to make him nervous.

Though Arianna couldn't care less about Lennox's flirtatious acts towards her, in hope to ensure her cooperation there was something else on her mind, really two things. First was she didn't like how kind Lennox had treated her so far. He was nice to her but found it was more than what she probably had a right to. Even if it was an attempt at flattery, only her close friends at the time had treated her in such away. So, it was more she felt uncomfortable though she hid such thoughts.

The second reason was harder to explain. The moment that Lennox entered and came nearby Arianna felt this odd kind of connection. It felt as if her own energy and life force was anxious and wanted to reach out. But it was clearer once he touched her hand. It was a feeling of an odd bond between them and a sense of odd familiarity. An odd spark you could say she felt the moment at his touch that she almost wanted to take her hand away.

However, she didn't to hold the faced. She didn't know if Lennox felt this odd sensation either, but she found it oddly confining. She knew they were opposites from one another in some way and that in itself should have caused her leave without a second glance, but she didn't. Despite every oddness she felt from when she met him for the first time in such a way, her instincts told her something that caused her surprise.

Her instincts which have never really failed her and helped her survive many long years. They told her to stay, listen, and maybe help with equal return. She didn't feel anything towards Lennox at the time other than the odd familiarity with his energy/life force. The only reason this relationship between them began after his aid was Arianna's instincts. Her very being that told her that he would make what she desired most be possible, become a great help to her, and well if they joined hands make something thought impossible possible.

Arianna closed her eyes and placed her fork down after she rationalized and sorted out all she had felt in that moment in time to return with a clam head and good sense of reason. She didn't want to faulter in arrangement of a deal that was supposed to be a disadvantage to her in every way.

But she also had to ready herself for the next part to make sure she held his trust. Even with his name in her hand he could back away from the deal as he had nothing from her yet but a false name. She heard Lennox across from her shift which indicated to her he planned to leave the table as he thought he had failed to secure the deal.

Arianna's eyes opened and she looked at him with a clam expression. "You said you'd like to get to know me more. Do you really plan to leave before I said a single word?" Arianna said with a clear smirk as she learned back relaxed. "I already mentioned, I am quite famished. I didn't wish to speak with a full mouth. It must have made you nervous as you sat and watched, I apologize."

Arianna shifted as she tapped on the table. "In truth for the last while I've been a very poor state, so this is the first meal I've had for some time. My condition was so bad that I did not leave bed for several days as if dead. With my chance though a danger I wished to eat out and hopefully drink as I find Latris a painfully dreadful time of the year."

"So, you've been ill for some time. But did you leave only since it is Latris?"

"You could say that. Though I had no plans on going somewhere during Latris. I often say in my home... in... melancholy as someone close to me said. Even so after all this time due to my unique skill the pain of that day is still very fresh. You'd think after more than 10 years the pain would lessen... but it might just be my own fault as I let the 'wound' fester and scar with guilt... even if it's not entirely clear currently." Arianna sighed as she looked down at the table. Even if it was to build up trust it was something hard for her back then, and something she had kept locked up inside her.

Arianna could feel her hand tremble at the thought of even a conversation of such that was light. She closed her eyes, but she couldn't handle the thought of when another learned of such an occurrence, but more so talk of such in a public area. It made her chest tight and felt extremely weak. Though she had put up the strong front she used when acting as any of her other personas this story was too close to her and made her want to throw up.

Lennox maybe aware of her condition as her complexation that begun too greatly pale, had placed his hand on top of hers and rubbed his thumb against the back of her hand in comfort. The reason he did such a thing back then was hard to say, but he did so with little thought apparently, no sympathy or empathy, nothing but real instinct for his action.

Arianna who looked up at him with slightly clouded and teary eyes could see it in his eyes. The face and eyes that had approached her with such emotion and expression. His eyes in that moment as she looked directly into them were hollow and void of such emotion or sentiment.

Arianna with her cursed eyes once they awakened could always read a person's true inner self, for her the expression the eyes where the window to the soul was very true and literal. Though she couldn't see everything unless desired, she could always read the persons emotions. Lennox the moment the illusion he held dropped and Arianna looked at him for the first time she saw it.

Even though he looked at her with no emotion or sentiment it wasn't due to affiliation or anything like that but something else entirely something buried deep below. For a second, she pictured someone else she saw with such eyes a very long time ago that was in a worse state than the man before. But he was clearly no puppet and acted in accordance with his own will.

If it's him… it will be fine. She could feel that which made her steel her nerves. Though maybe partially her own instincts she felt such on her own. She didn't want sympathy or empathy, she wanted someone to just listen to what she said and didn't care in anyway about it. It was a scar, but it was something she no longer wanted. After so long as there was no real way to heal the wound anymore even with everything said and known. *Maybe Fang knew this might happen.* She thought with a slight smile.

Arianna placed her other hand on top of Lennox's. Her hand he would recall was warm yet understanding in some way though exactly how there was now real clue, as he would never go into great detail about it and just look away as if embarrassed. "Thank you… I'll be alright now. No please close your eyes and tune out what I'm about to say till I touch your hand again." She said with a calm voice. Though she was alright with Lennox she didn't want anyone else to listen to what she said even if it was very little.

The last of her food and another drink was placed down on the table before Lennox closed his eyes as she asked. Arianna reached behind her ear and turned off invisible holographic glasses (the VHDS). *"You will hear nothing the two of us say till I snap my fingers. You will also leave us be till then as well."* Arianna's words at that moment, an order of sorts were odd. An ability that allowed her to simply command the unassuming. It was as if she made a barrier of silence around the two of them at that moment.

Arianna then closed her eyes and tapped Lennox's hand lightly. "What did you just do?" he asked quickly as it wasn't hard to notice the change in the place. It was as if they were no longer there or really their spot didn't exist to others.

"It's nothing big. You don't have to worry. Just don't look at or into my eyes okay. We agreed to talk about ourselves a little so I just made it so there is no need to worry about the rest of our conversation. That's all, if you are worried about their wellbeing, they will be fine." She muttered. "Now let's finish this up alright. There is no need to dawdle anymore, whether we say everything or not. After we talk about ourselves lets close things."

Chapter 24

"You are being quick to the point."

"Well in my current state I can only manage this for so long." Arianna muttered a reply without much thought. "What you want is not really to get to know me it's something you can use. I typically don't deal with such clints, but I owe you for the aid and like, so I'll budge."

Arianna looked up at the ceiling and let a sigh escape her lips. "I've never really talked about this… I never thought I ever would in truth. But I will tell you somethings that not even those closest to me knows about. Something I've never told anyone. Then tell me something light about yourself in compromise. Then we'll talk about the deal how's that?"

"That works to me."

Arianna let out another sigh. "Good… I will tell you something dangerous… something that makes it, so you essentially hold my life in your hand. Even without this small amount it has such weight." She paused as she turned and took a bite of her main meal. "It's such a thing that I'm heisting to say it despite being one to choose to do so."

"Some time ago I once had a fairly normal happy family life, though hidden from the world it the happiest and brightest moments of my life albeit very short in comparison. Mother, Father, dog, and my twin brother. The moments back then were truly happy and full of love and warmth, even though we were different and force to hide it didn't matter. The times together from back then for those short years are always one that I can't help but look on. Even now I probably wanted to have a family like back then or to have my family back even though it is impossible.

"As I said my time with my family was very short… sadly short, something I wish could have gone on longer. But I guess why the time back then is so impactful and important to me if what follow to bring me life to this point. A night that was to bring forth a joyful day… shattered it all. I lost my mother, father, twin brother, and home that night with a scar to serve as a bad reminder.

"I could never tell anyone what happen… never reveal who I am, never admit who my family was. All in to survive. I was meant to die… and my existence was denied.

"That day I lost everything and was abandon once again… all I wanted was revenge on that who did this to me. To kill them before they kill me… get vengeance for my dead family. It might have been funny for such a young child to burn with such hatred. But I couldn't stand the thought of doing nothing back then. I was sent to an orphanage and trained to the point I am today on the path as a codeless.

"Most of my emotions from then have cooled now. I have come to sit on the fence you could say. Should I leave everything behind and live the life my parents might have wanted for me, or should I continue a path similar to the one I've been running down for many years. I guess you can say I'm just tired now." Arianna sighed as she leaned against the table.

"I'm a terrible person. I haven't gone to their grave sites once. I've let people think the entire family has died, no one knows about the exitance of me and my brother. Greedy, selfish, vindictive. I am the one that should be dead. That good enough for you?" She added as she looked up. She placed her head on the palm of her hand. "With little amount my vary life is in the palm of your hand the most dangerous thing to me. The fact that I am the one that should have died so many years ago."

Arianna wore a small smile though her eyes held a deep sadness. For the parents she lost, the brother she loved but choose to hide, and the very life she could have had but left behind. She almost looked over at Lennox but stopped herself. She shook her head lightly. "They are the reason you've come to hate Latris."

"Well… it's not as if they died on Latris, no they died on a different day, time entirely. Just this day… I can't help but think back to such time with them. I have been left with lonely days… and no one has ever tried to help or ease the pain. As such it a time that I can't help but find myself reminiscing. Maybe it's just pathetic… its be so long but." Arianna paused as she looked at the plate before here.

"That's who I am the one that should be dead. A scared orphan that certain people wish gone, a codeless that came to be just because of what happened so long ago." She added with a slightly sad chuckle she hated herself at this time and for the first time to anyone that self-hatred was clear. She claimed herself a little and made herself expressionless once more before she motioned to Lennox.

Lennox didn't say anything for a few moments. "I see. Well for me there isn't much to myself like for you. As you already know am a twilight and an affiliated mercenary. One of my father's many children, though only half siblings as my father killed my mother when I was a child. I'm… 21 years old, and currently favoured by my father as he gave me this." Lennox listed off before he placed an amulet on the table.

Arianna looked over at the amulet and gasped in surprise. "That gem in the amulets completely made of Elem! It's such pure quality too! This is one of the hardest things to get." Arianna paused and glanced at her hand and the amulet. "Could I possibly take a look at it?"

"Go ahead." Lennox replied. Arianna took hold of the amulet and felt a refreshing feeling wash over her like a wave. She looked it over her eyes shined as she did so.

"This is defiantly pure water type elem gem. All of them are rare but those of the major four element type are especially so. Do you know how to use it?"

"Kind of… it's hard to explain. What about you?"

"I can't use elem gems. I can sense it and everything but for some reason I can't use it in the slightest. Well, it's not a big deal in the grand scheme, but it is a little sad."

Lennox looked at Arianna. "You seem to like things like this… Ari."

"Oh its… just a passing hobby."

"… do you know anything about gems that change colours?"

"Gems that change colour. If you are sure they are like gems or gemstones… there are two that come to mind. Soul gems they are gemstones that are the representation of the soul of the one that wares it. Though uncommon it does change colour and can when a person wares it, they have clear distinct colours.

"But they are rarer than elem and proclaimed as a legend. It's said no one knows how they come about. The other is the gemstone of fate, they are essentially things of myth. It's said they are first clear as glass and once joined to a person they will change colour. But they are to never change after that, the gems colour represents one's fate overall in life, so only death would probably cause change."

"Quite the knowledge for a passing hobby."

Arianna laughed a little as she scratched the side of her face. She looked at the amulet some more for a few moments before she placed it back down on the table. "Now what is it that you want from me?"

"I want your help to overthrow the current Marione leaders, elders, and many of the high-ranking officials" Lennox said which caused Arianna to flinch. This was something she never expected, not to mention the implication of it.

"Not completely destroy them but overthrow. You're planning a coup that's what you are telling me. Which also means that you're affiliated with the Marione." Arianna asked to make sure. *Though his codename was a clue to his affiliation before he even said such a thing. But its surprising.* She had never heard of a coup in a mercenary organization let alone for the Marione which is up there.

"Yes. That's why I need outside help. Someone that can cause chaos that will throw them into a mess." Lennox replied as he crossed his arms. "I'll give you any information I can get my hands on that will make it possible to cause problems. Anything and everything, all I ask is that you don't kill those that are working with me to overthrow them."

"... fine I'll agree to that. When facing a group like them additional information can be quite helpful. Though I can't make any promises on the later part, I'll try but my life is paramount."

"That's fine." Lennox replied as he handed Arianna something. She looked at it and nodded. "Contact through that point. The agents here are going to be more active, apparently they have some plans underway, but I don't have all the details."

"Alright, pleased to work with you mister Lennox." Arianna smirked, he looked at her for her words. "What your tw- three years older than me." She shrugged with a snicker. As she was joking around, the waitress tripped, and her tray fell and hit the edge of their table and sprayed the two with drinks.

Arianna looked up a little surprised before she begun to laugh. She grabbed the drink brought earlier and tipped it back. "Yeah, this is a fine way to end a day like this." She laughed with a slight tone of sarcasm. She then realized she locked eyes with Lennox and her face paled in realization. *Shit I just managed to close the deal too!* She screamed internally as she ruffled her hair in annoyance.

As she tried to think of how not to make an utter mess of this deal that could be useful to her later. She felt odd before she could think of how to fix this. Ari felt as her body and face begun to heat up, her vision begun to blur slightly, and her mind got a little fuzzy. She knew it wasn't the alcohol that she had, she only felt a slight buzz at that point, no it was something else.

Ari could feel her pulse race and felt even more acutely aware of what was around here even more than normal which begun to make her overwhelmed. Her leg then brushed against Lennox's, an action that she normally didn't care about caused her to flinch. She felt odd and couldn't think straight for a moment. She covered her face to try and cool herself off, she managed to tune out all that was around her to let herself think. It wasn't hard for her to connect things and realize what happened.

"Fuck! Seriously I can get a break. Those fucking bastards managed to put something in that drink." She muttered as she covered her face that begun to flush even more. It wasn't something simple either, but it was made even worse because of her current condition. Arianna turned and grabbed a container behind her and put the food in it. She placed down money on the table that should more than cover the cost of her meal and drinks.

Damn I need to get home before I do something. If I… no that's just rude… I shouldn't do that to someone charmed or that I plan to work with. She groaned. She glanced over at Lennox again. *Damn he might not want to work with me cause of this. Allowing chance like this slip away really sucks. But I have no choice, I need to get away before I lose my reasoning and rationality… or even worse.* She shook her head as she got up with her eyes lowered. "I'm sorry." She muttered before she raced off covering her face and could feel shivers in her body.

If I wasn't in this state, what they did wouldn't have worked. Even ignoring that... I can't believe I let something like this happen. I'm going to kill them for this. She growled as she raced the door and snapped her fingers. Arianna then raced off down the street as soon as she left bar.

Chapter 25

As Arianna tried to run off away back to her safe house a hand grabbed her wrist. The action caused her to spin around and fall into the persons chest. "Why are you in such a rush?" Arianna was about to attack the person till she realised it was Lennox. She pulled her hand away as she felt herself started to flush more as she was able to feel his muscles.

"W-why are you following me." Arianna managed to stutter out. While internally she was cursed up a storm from anger at her current state and how she wasn't in complete control of her body. She clenched her fist and dug her nails into her palm. She winched slightly but was able to act how she liked though her face was extremely flushed.

"Is everything alright? You're really red." Lennox asked as he went to try and check her temperature, but she moved back. Which caused him to glare at her for a moment. She turned her head away to find her breaths were a little more rugged.

"…" she tried to say something in argument, but it was caught in her throat. Then despite herself she told him the truth though she had no plans to tell him such. "Before I said. That I was not well. I'm still not in top shape and a little weak so I planned to get drunk since it was a good chance to. As my resistance is weak right now." She mumbled as she grabbed her arm. "That drink they managed to put something in it. Really strong… don't think its surface. I'm barely holding on to reason and consciousness right now."

"There was a new drug made recently. Hard to say for such but it could be it." Lennox replied. "But if what I heard is true it's a surprise your able to hold a conversation."

"Exactly, I realised my state rather quickly. But that's not the only reason something else happened. You don't feel weird or anything with me."

"No, I'm fine, but I think you should worry about yourself."

"I'm not worried." Arianna replied as she glanced at him for a moment. She ignored the reaction she felt and looked at him. He really wasn't affected despite the direct eye contact. She really felt odd at this point as, for as far as she knew, there was no real immunity. She shook her head violently. "Can you let me go before those men come to chase after me. I need to get somewhere safe as I deal with it."

"I wasn't trying to pull a Cinderella act or anything. I needed to get away before something happened, and I embarrassed myself. Sigh… I just came out for a good time to relax before I have to get back to work even harder than before and this happened." Arianna groaned as she covered her face. "Aaah! I want to kill them! Gods this is annoying! I can't even look at you without feeling weird."

"A group, Delta was one that made the new drug. But apparently it wasn't originally a drug just made into it… for some reason."

"You mean this is just a trail kind of thing. If it has this kind of effect on me currently." Arianna muttered and felt a shiver down her spine. "But again, Delta, this isn't the first time this groups name has come up recently… just what are they planning."

"Have you calm down a little. You seem able to talk despite only a few moments have passed."

"No not really. If I don't look at you, it seems I can suppress it to some degree."

"Maybe you've fallen for my looks."

"I'm not cheap… and you're just teasing me now." Arianna muttered. "I'll admit you are ascetically pleasing and have a good body thanks to mercenary work. Defiantly something most women would like in a partner." She mumbled with a low growl. "It's not something for me. Looks are nice but there are more important things. But to be honest even then, though I lean towards men in terms of preference, I've never felt such away before."

Lennox looked down at her in some sort of intrigue. Though vague in what she meant in some ways, others were more clear. But he wasn't the only one Arianna despite her current state was also intrigue by the man before her. They both had several reasons for such, but to Ari it was more of a back burner thing than the current issue at hand.

Lennox held her by the waist and close to himself. Ari was sure he might have realized some of the affects at this point, and it took so much from her not to completely fall into its affects. "Will you let me go now I'm still…"

"No, I'm making sure you're alright."

More like observing, and probing information out of me. She retoured. "Whatever that drug is it isn't natural for here. I can't explain it but… its defiantly not. It's not that, as… rather just how it feels. It's not easy to explain… what I mean it's not right and anyone would feel similar." She huffed as Lennox dropped his coat on top of Arianna's head.

She could feel the body heat and his scent that still lingered on the coat something that didn't help her current condition. Ari stepped back and out of his gasp as she held her arms crossed in front of her. It was hard for her to ignore the coat he just put around her despite how, whatever it was she was that the affect made her feel or how it made her want to act. It honestly made her feel torn in two from the affects and annoyance to how it affected her.

"… if I tell you that I've heard of a way to deal with it faster than just waiting it out as you freeze in the snow, would you agree to it?"

"Yes, but not due to the cold or anything. I have things to do that are quite important that could be done, over just sitting here for who knows how long."

"No matter what happens? You won't do anything."

"… sigh… fine yes."

Arianna ran her hand through her hair as she stood up straight and wrapped the coat around her shoulders more, so it didn't fall off. "So, tell what needs to be done?"

"Before I mentioned that this drug wasn't originally a drug. According to one of my allies it's more like a curse that was made into a drug."

"So, you've been looking into it, and not just that but have someone knowledgeable of curses."

"Wanted to see if I could make use out of it. But that wasn't the case, aside for that odd occasion that it makes people speak more truthfully."

"So, you did know… I feel used."

"I didn't pry that much."

Arianna huffed with her arms crossed. "Don't be like that. I didn't know initially. So, it wasn't fully intentional." Lennox said looked at her.

"But you could have done more, it's just annoying that this had to happen when I was in such a state. But not just that I know there are people that would try to use such a thing just for that alone." Arianna muttered as she quickly glanced at him. "And the fact it was used against me ticks me off."

Lennox covered his mouth to try and stifle a laugh. "Pfft... a-anyways from what they've told me there should be a few different ways to deal with the curse part before the drug actually wears off. Though because of that there will be back lash. So how about it?"

"Fine but first, I want you to tell me something truthful. Then I won't care what exactly it is your about to do."

Lennox smirked as he grabbed Arianna by the waist and pulled her close to him. Her face quickly became flushed. "But of course. That's quite easy. Before me and the others were in a rut but with your help, we'll be able to do more than before. After all the Codeless the surface has come to call the 'Assassin' is now on our side."

"I have no idea what you are talking about I'm just your typical Codeless." Ari replied in a calm tone. She looked up at Lennox ignoring how such an act affected her. "But we'll see whether or not this agreement is beneficial for the two of us. If it goes, we will continue this deal." She stated calmly as she held her pointer finger under his chin and forced him to look directly at her.

The two both knew that they could use the other to achieve their goals. To each of them the other was a means to an end, but they didn't wish to lose the other just yet. Arianna could see past the well-placed natural mask that Lennox used, while it was clear that Lennox knew that Arianna herself was more capable than she presented to him.

They each wanted to trap the other in a sort of cage, or lock so they couldn't escape due to their use. No matter what condition or affliction Arianna was under to her it always was the completion of a goal or desire before anything else. She planned drop Lennox the moment she realized that he was of no use. Though he held her most guarded secret she could adapt to protect herself that was something she learned over the many years how to do. But she was also aware that Lennox had similar sentiments.

Arianna knew what Lennox had shown towards her has all been an act. She never easily placed her trust in another nor her heart and was never swayed emotionally towards someone she held no trust in. But thanks to her ability she knew it was an act, the sweet words and actions all done to tie her to him and make her easy for him to use. It was a strategy that would have worked on nearly any other girl based on Lennox's looks alone.

A game of emotional manipulation. A game which both were strong players of. Intrigue didn't matter in the end.

For this game Arianna acted similar to how he wanted, to get what she wished out of the deal. She didn't plan to lose the potential golden goose that had appeared before her. She would do what she needed to hold on to this potential edge she managed to find. She looked at Lennox with resolute eyes with an expression different from any other he had seen from her before.

Lennox looked at her and smirked. "Good, you have a will and resolve as strong as I've heard. Even in such a state." He stated all the while. It was something that gave Arianna momentary pause as it was very real not just some mask, it was the first occurrence either. "So different yet so similar. I like it." He whispered. As if destined to meet one another, the very words never said.

Arianna could feel Lennox's strong arms on her back tense before he pulled her in closer leaving very little room between them. He then tilted her head up and looked into her eyes. He wore that same smiling smirk, then for a moment she saw something. In his dull and listless eyes that she could only see for a moment as they begun to shine with something that she didn't have a chance to identify.

Lennox leaned down towards her and kissed her. Arianna eyes widen in surprise as her face begun to flush even more. Despite the shock, surprise, and embarrassment she felt from such an action, she felt that something that had been wrapped around her snap and brake. Right as it broke, she felt she had control over herself once more.

Arianna was frozen in place for a moment before pushed Lennox's chest to forced him back. As they separated, her face and ears had become bright red, and it wasn't due to the cold. "I-I... my first kiss. Couldn't you have at least told me what you planned to do." Arianna muttered as she looked away.

Before Arianna could do or say anything else she felt a sharp pain in her head that then racket her body. Her vision black out for a moment as she stumbled and held her head. A groan escaped her lips as the pain hit, it was as if something had bashed her in the back of the head. Her legs collapsed and her vision started to black out as she begun to fall.

Lennox stepped forward and caught Arianna in his arms. He looked down at her as she leaned against him. She was still conscious, but her version was blurred, and breathing was rough at the time. She placed her hand on his chest as she tried to fight against herself from falling unconscious. Her arms than trembled once more as another wave of intense pain hit her, at that point her body went completely limp against Lennox as she fell unconscious.

Lennox lightly touched his lips; Arianna still had some light traces of the drink that was laced with the curse drug on her lips. He found it was as strong as she implied as he felt slightly affected for a moment. "She's stronger than I thought if she could hold on that well against something this strong in such a state. It's as she said, I seem to have found something I needed here." He muttered with a smirk as he picked Arianna up in his arms and carried her off.

Arianna awoke to an unfamiliar ceiling and location about a week had passed. She placed her hand on her head that still had a slight dull ache. *Breaking that dame curse was more painful than expected.* She thought, though she was sure if she was in an even slightly better condition she wouldn't feel as if she had been hit by a truck as she did at that moment. *It seems Lennox took me somewhere safe after I passed out. I guess I should be grateful that I can at least trust him to this extent after a first meeting and just formalizing a deal together.* Arianna sighed.

She rolled over on to her side and noticed her jacket that rested on a chair just in reach. Her body felt to be in better condition than when she first went out, so she knew more than a few days had passed. *It seems he found out I was injured too. I should properly thank him for his help since it seems he took care of me all that time.* Arianna muttered as she closed and opened her hand. That pain in her body vanished entirely and her wounds lessened at this point it was certain her body had reached a more normal state since this occurred.

Ariana could hear something buzz from the chair her shirt and jacket rested. She wanted to ignore it for just a moment longer, but it was incessant and continuous, so she knew it was something serious. She reached over and pulled out a phone and opened it. At that moment she was flooded with messages. As she went over them, she quickly sat up in surprise as she yelled out.

"The fuck... no way." She cursed. The simple mission that Ari had taken on had become black level and high priority and danger. Nemours death reports of different agents where before her none were off those, she was particularly close to but in such a short time since she was a part of it the mission had turned out like this. "Elixir... it's all because of elixir... damn it. Crazy... such chaos for something like this." Arianna arms trembled slightly not out of fear but rather frustration and guilt.

[All agents and contracted codeless this are an advisory and warning. An Active battle between the rival Marione organization is currently under way in the Canlonen central district's Brightton City and surrounding area. It has become a blacklisted danger zone for all. All with active jobs/missions in this designate area use extreme caution. Combat against the antagonist organization is highly likely, along with a dangerous experiment at their disposal. All organizations and the codeless alike are in danger to be caught up in the fight. You have been warned. Death count: 37 mercenary operatives (Allied and Outside).]

[Yano Job requests: Priority Level: High/Top; Survivability: 6%. Location: Surface, Brightton City, Canlonen. Requestor: Yano Leader, Dark.

Details: A surface individual disappeared near a month ago that had been around another high target individual that has had those connected to them attacked just due to their association with them. Evidence has been found that the disappearance is connected. No family connected to the disappeared individual has been seen since till two weeks ago. Individuals that claim relations has plead for their return. The claimed connection has been found to be false. Odd readings have begun to come from the attached location. Immediate investigation of the location needed and reported due to likely risk to the high priority target in the area. Deaths/failures: 11.]

Arianna stood up with clear eyes, bandages around her body were untied and fell to the ground revealing healed but slightly scared skin. She pulled her shirt on and grabbed her jacket. *I… no I can't let this sit any longer or else something worse might come to pass. I wish I could say it in person but…* She sighed before she shook her head then she wrote a note and left it on the table.

Arianna knew this was a pivotal point. The first battle between the Marione and Yano in many years. It was signs to what was to come. An indication of a new age to come as a war between the two always brought about.

As a Codeless she had every right to leave the two to fight it out. She had already handed her job off, even if she returned early, she had no obligation to jump into it again now that such a notice had been released. Arianna could help but think of Dave that kid that had no reason to be so nice to her, and to Caden who she needed to repay. She touched the ear cuff attached to her ear and changed her appearance.

Arianna looked back at the apartment that Lennox had graciously brought her to after she passed out. She did feel bad to leave without a word after what he did to help her. She wanted to and should thank him in person, even if he might be a part of the Marione as she had come to suspect after their conversation.

She was a codeless and made a deal with him so she thought he probably wouldn't kill her despite the battle occurring in Brightton City. Even with such a feeling of obligation to properly thank him, she had little choice. She pulled her hood over her head with her phone and novel in hand she left the small apartment and disappeared as if she was never there in the first place. All that remained was a note, the bandages, and food she had left behind.

Chapter 26

Arianna looked down from roof she sat on at house. She wore dark clothing, with a helmet that covered her face and hid who she was. Where she was, wasn't far from the tall buildings that mainly populated Brightton City it was visible distance. She didn't like how close the house she looked down at was to the Luo's residence. It was only a few blocks away at best a 25-minute walk away from one another. That fact didn't sit well with her when faced with the situation before her.

Her arms where crossed as she looked at the house. Outside nothing looked wrong or out of the ordinary. Though she knew that wasn't something she should place her trust in when you consider what she does. She didn't notice any alarm systems and the virtual display indicated there was nothing like that either.

If they didn't have an alarm system of any kind, it's likely the family was grabbed here. Since there's a history of activity in the area too, it's all the more likely. It's like they are just inviting someone to come in. Arianna thought as she shifted slightly on the roof. *I don't like it but there isn't much choice. It's too suspicious, and close to the Luo family, so I have to check it out.* She groaned as rolled her shoulders.

Arianna stood up before she jumped off the roof and over to the house. None of it sat well with her but she had to push her worries aside to do the job before her. She landed next to a first-floor window. She couldn't hear and nearby movement and didn't notice anything when she looked in. With a click of her tongue, she pulled out a small case that had several tools.

With one of the tools, she cut a small hole in the glass that was large enough for her to fit her arm through. With the hole she just made she slide her arm through and reach up to the lock and opened it. With that the window slid open with ease. *I know other mercs have different ways to get into places… but I don't see any signs of another person breaking into the place.* She stated. *I don't like this.*

Even after her grips of dislike and wariness of everything Arianna still climbed in through the window. As she stood inside, she could clearly see and smell signs she didn't like. Dents, chips, lacerations, scuff marks things knocked over and glass on the floor, a fight had occurred here. She placed her gloved hand on the wall and noticed dried blood and blood streaks from a poor clean up attempt. These indications one might think it was caused by an untrained individual, but Arianna knew they were left and done on purpose.

Then if you ignored the drag marks that lead to the living room there was a distinct smell that she was unpleasantly familiar with. The unpleased and clear smell of a rotting corpse, a smell that had begun to permeate in the house. Arianna found it hard to ignore her initial guttural reaction, which was caused from the strong scent that was havoc on her sensitive sense of smell.

After she took a few moments to collect herself, she followed the scent down through the halls of the house without a single sound till it eventually led her to a single room. She stood in front of the door that she was certain the smell came from. After a brief pause to make sure nothing was on the other side of the door, she opened it.

The sight on the other side that greeted her was grizzly. The room was covered in blood with several bodies that littered the floor some older than others. Some of the bodies were open, others torn apart, but aside from the oldest bodies before her they all appeared to have experimented on in inhumane experiments. Chest cut open limbs and organs removed all kinds of things, she felt chills run down her spine at the realization.

They used the connection and the fight that had occurred between the two major organizations as a means to the end. So that they could gather up lab 'rats' for them to use. For what purpose their experiment had, it was unclear at the time. She begun to gather/loot useful items from the dead mercenary bodies, but there was very little even though this was the room that they dumped items and bodies.

The door was then kicked in. "Hahaahh! There you are little rat. I wonder where you scurried off to. When knew you had come but you didn't follow our trail we left. A very special rat we've drawn in." they laughed. "You must be special or dumb to make it here after ignoring the clear signs we left. What a dilemma you put us in."

The individual that appeared made her skin crawl and bristle. She was in danger, extreme danger. Arianna stood up and spun around to face the foe that appeared before her. They lifted a weapon and fired. Something priced her skin before a current of electricity coursed through her body and caused her to scream out. "Get our special new rat. I have a feeling we might have a good one on our hands. One we can really use this time."

With that, two individuals walked into the room. Arianna fought against what her body wished to do and got to her feet. She kicked one into the other, but the kick didn't have nearly enough power and they just staggered. "What the hell are you mad men planning." Arianna growled as her arms twitched from the electricity.

"It's a simple idea. I'm sure you are aware as any twilight is of the abilities that have begun to appear. After all that was the idea of Elixir. To bring forth the abilities lost and latent in the blood. That's not all I want! I want to bring out the latent potential that lies within twilight bodies. Think about it the Dark have unique trait and so does the Light, but we adapt, its little in comparison. The very basis of science is shaken due to the existence of the three different races of the same species and everything else that have been found.

"I want to find it and take it, then send it to one. Then have one that is stronger for the overall goal and end time. So many people, so many failures to make one. My life work is here, and the leader choose to hand over leadership to that fink over me, after they managed to create that creature that proves the very basis of my theory just like Elixir. I've worked many years on this, he won't even hand over a specimen that has clear roots to Elixir that could add leaps to my research.

"But now you're here. My special mouse. Not just anyone could have done as you have, to get in here, to come here, to fight against the weapon that should be debilitating you at this very moment. Your bloodline is strong just like the leader. So, get them your puppet dolts we can't lose such a great specimen."

The 'puppets' lurched and stood up as blades appeared from their hands. Arianna could barely move she managed to turn as one lunged forward at her. The blade slashed Arianna across the back deeply. She howled out as she was thrown to the ground. The 'scientist' watched as the wound begun to close slightly and fight against the poison that had been laced on the blade.

"I am right. You are one. I will have many fun games planned for you." They laughed as she slashed her across the back with another poison covered blade before they dragged her away. She fought as they took her to the room, but the poison and electricity had done a number to her, so it was hard to break free from the 'puppets' grasp. They tied her to a blood coated operating/medical table.

As she was tied to the table the barbs that she was shot with were removed, but they let the back wound festered. She slightly regretted not wearing her long coat jacket when she entered now though it was smart on the chance of a sense or something like that it could have hit.

A 'puppet' then tore open her shirt and at this point was pleased that she used the disguising tech to hide the bindings around her chest. The scientist than begun to attach nodes and sensors to her body as the other 'puppet' tried to remove the helmet but was unable. They pushed the 'puppet' aside and went to try remove the helmet themself.

Before he had a chance to try and open the helmet, the door to the room opened again. "Clayton! What the hell are you doing! We are done for the day." A women's voice growled as they entered the room.

"A-attendant Lisa. What are you and the others doing here?" Clayton questioned as it was clear he thought the others had left. He spun around and rung his hands. Arianna glared at the man who acted all high and mighty just moments ago.

"It seems another Mercenary has shown up. Your little act has brought so many flies that soon we are going to be faced with one that we can't stand against. We should move locations now before that happens."

"W-w-wait! Before that we should use this specimen. I'm certain this one gives us some of the results that my research is looking for. I'm certain this one has a regenerative ability. If we just discard it as you want, we'd lose valuable data that the leader wants, and we might be able to make something similar to Elixir or make the most powerful agent as I suggested."

Lisa looked over at her with their partial mask. Arianna glanced away as she felt she might get caught. They looked at Ari for what felt like hours but was only really a few minutes. "A regenerative ability... did they express anything else?"

"Not that I saw attendant, but I didn't really give them much time to do so." Clayton replied. Lisa looked at Ari again with the same pricing gaze that felt could see past any illusion or disguised she had.

"Alright. All hands-on deck we are going to quickly work on this new... specimen that Clayton's managed to pick up. It will be the full works and final stage as well if things don't work out properly." Lisa order Clayton turned to try and remove the helmet from Arianna once again.

"Clayton ignores the helmet. We need to work quickly it's not in the way. Besides I'd rather not see the face of another specimen face against your experimental procedure again today. Be sure to coat things with poison it will slow the regeneration enough for us to work. We will surpass any of the specimen's previous limits and get the data the leader desires."

"Yes, Attendant Lisa!"

Given neither a chance of resistance nor rest as the other lab workers descended onto Arianna. There was no talk or exchange of words, nor a moment of rest. Her limbs were tired down onto the table tight as more items were attached to her body till eventually tools placed on a table that was pulled over next to her. They didn't even grant her the luxury of anastatic as they cut into her with their poison coated tools and blades, as if their main goal was to cause her the most pain.

Flesh and bones cut and broken, with poison that burned her flesh to impede her capability to heal. Electricity coursed through her body on the odd occasion as if to keep her conscious for the entire ordeal that felt to last weeks to her, though the exact time wasn't all too clear.

Though they claimed it to be for an experiment it was more like torture as blades burned and twisted. They made sure she experienced the most amount of pain possible. Limbs and chest cut and stabbed into as they prodded and worked on anything they could. Her blood that had begun to pool on the table eventually ran off the table.

They at first didn't understand why after so much blood was lost, so much pain inflected that cause her to cry out, that nothing happened and that she was still alive. Then they recalled the ability she was said to have, regeneration or advanced healing. Pain was still inflected, and electricity coursed through her, they wanted to push her over the edge. Even with her screams and body that still held to life after all they had done and the large loss of blood it still wasn't enough.

196

That was the moment they decided to see the full extent of what she was able to heal. They no longer 'held' back on her, she screamed out as she saw what they planned to do but they cared little about what she said. Their goal was to collect data and see how powerful her abilities were and far they went.

Grave wounds even worse than before begun to be inflected upon her. It was to the point that even her black clothing begun to show blood that it had collected. They cut her throat to cause her to bleed but she still lived, and body healed itself... as such they then decided to cut off a finger.

Arianna fought violently at this point shocked with electricity and tied down she was unable to escape. Some of the lab workers went over and held her down. They then cut it off she screamed out in utter pain; she had long gotten used to the taste of blood that had accumulated in her month from the continues 'experimentation'. But even with her extreme pain and continuous action preformed on her that was near mind breaking, her near exhausted body they would inject more energy into her.

As such no matter what they cut so far, fingers hands, legs, they reformed as its prior turned to ashes. The clear indication was the blood that had soaked into her clothing. She felt her insides boil and bubble and wished to destroy everything around her, a flame that tried to climb out from the recesses inside Arianna that locked away. She couldn't let the power out, as it was one, she locked away to forget.

Even though she didn't let it out subconsciously they saw the change of power. At this point they tried to take her power. The pain she felt from this was worse than anything they had done up to this point as it felt something had begun to tear into her soul and being before they shredded it after. A pull and rip that felt but could be seen the pain caused Arianna to scream out more than before as she couldn't stop herself or supress it.

The continued this she felt blood and bile in her throat and her wounds tore open and slowly no longer healed themselves. But no matter what they did they couldn't remove her power.

"It's not gonna work. It seems this one's power and abilities are tied to their very life. If we take them, they will die."

"Why does their death matter. We shouldn't care about the life of a lab rat."

"That's not what I meant Clayton. To remove the power would kill them and likely also destroy the ability you desperately wish to remove and use. We've clearly cause significant damage if you look at the data and vitals, they've decreased even blood levels that had rarely show fluctuations are going down significantly now." Lisa paused as they pointed at the screen.

"We have been at it for days. We've confirmed the existence of these abilities you hypothesised as it is. So how about we try the opposite as you proposed in your theory. They are barely alive as it is, so I say it's a good trail run."

"I'll admit you have a point. But it's nothing more than that."

As they said they moment they begun to try to remove the power's, Arianna's body got weaker. Her voice course from the screams, her breaths were shallow. She barely clung to life even despite the utter pain she had been faced with. Her eyes were clouded over and felt lethargic, but that didn't last long as she was bombarded once again, and her body shocked.

At this point there was nothing left that could keep her awake. Her body became weaker and weaker. There was nothing that could be done as darkness consumed Arianna and a droning noise rang out.

Chapter 27

A women stood alone in a dark inky blackness and stood on a reflective dark watery surface. She wore only a white dress that was ripped and torn, with the blood from her wounds that clung to the white dress and her skin. When she looked down despite the surface that looked to be reflective, she couldn't see herself, she wasn't able to picture herself either.

Her body was covered in injuries, but she felt nothing. Her body felt oddly light as if her body held no weight. She looked around calmly, but she felt lost and confused. Eventually she begun to walk forward there was little sound aside the light jingle of the tap from her bare feet as she walks along the watery like surface. The longer she walked a question begun to form in her head. *Am I dead?*

There was no one else around that she could see after she walked for who knows how long. All that was around her was darkness and the sound of a light jingle. The longer she walked the more distorted things became too her. It was a numbing like sensation, but also felt nothing but a calmness inside her.

But her sense of self also begun to disappear as her eyes begun to cloud over and just continued to walk. After some time, she turned suddenly and walked in that direction way till eventually a figure appeared in view that sat on the ground. She couldn't really make out the figure at this point as she didn't really register it, but she sat down behind them her back faced theirs's.

They leaned against one another she didn't feel any heat from them but could feel life from them. Something she realized her body lacked, which brought a sudden set of realizations. She lacked life as if frozen, and that her existence had become torn and damaged. Her form was transparent and flickering as if this form was hard to hold. She felt her energy was drained but she could take in some of the energy from the figure.

"Broken" she muttered in an unfamiliar voice. She couldn't recall what she looked like and begun to realise the longer she was here the more that became unfamiliar to her more than it already was to her torn existence of self. The figure that she rested against as their body trembled.

The figure lifted their head and turned to see the faded flickering figure of women that was hard to determine. "Who are you?" A male voice asked from the figure she leaned against.

"... I... I'm not really sure anymore." The women replied as she held her knees to her chest. She did feel anything but felt comfort doing this. "... Something happened to me. But everything's foggy... and becoming foggier. But it doesn't bother me."

"You're dead, aren't you?"

"I think so. But I'm not worried... it's like relief but also some concern. Maybe I wanted to see someone who passed, but there was something I was supposed to do." She muttered as she leaned her head against her knees. "I feel like how I came to pass was bad too. Even with that... I wonder if..." she trailed off as she looked away as she felt she should say what she felt.

She had yet to turn around as she closed her eyes as she felt the figures energy entre her and give her more strength. "Why are you here?"

"I've been trapped here while they us my body for themselves like a soulless puppet. They can't enter it but uses it. I can see and feel myself but can't move it while here."

"How long have you been here?"

"I'm not sure. First they used something on me... till more recently I've appeared here in this dark void."

"They? Where you kidnapped and forced to work for them?"

"They are the one who controls in many ways and a shadow organization they started to use more recently. They of shadow, one goal, and alteration... have begun to use... Delta."

"Delta..." She trailed off. "You call this a void... so it's not the afterlife or purgatory."

"I don't think so. It's the place they sent me to, to make me feel hopeless as I watch... to make me lose hope. A space they control, where nothing really exists... it tries to destroy and make you lose yourself. They must have pulled you here too as they felt you are a danger to them and their goals. They wish to completely destroy you."

She turned for the first time to look at the figure as her vison became a little clearer. "They wished to destroy me, and you... so they made this place to deal with that they deem troublesome, and a threat." she mumbled.

Her vison clear she could see the figure before her even though only darkness surrounded them. He had light skin with short dark purple hair and deep red eyes around his neck was a black prism necklace. For a moment she pictured another person before her, but her eyes didn't leave him and shock slightly. "Knox." She spoke without thought or reason, the name just fell out of her.

His head spun around to her, and he begun to glare. "Where did you hear that?" he growled. His voice was sharp and pointed as he looked at her.

"I-I don't know. It just... the moment I actually saw you with clear vision... that came out of my mouth involuntarily." She stammered at the sudden hostility. She looked away nervous.

He grabbed her fade shoulders; she was surprised he could do such a thing, but his grip tightened around her shoulders. "I need you to tell me! What happened to you. You need to remember!" He asked he sounded desperate. But she could only shake her head,

"Then how long ago did you die? No how old are you?"

"... 19."

"Can you remember what happened to you that brought you here?"

"... I-I went, I was grabbed..." Her shoulders trembled. "... they killed me... it wasn't fast... it was very painful."

His grip tightened even more to the point it might have broken someone's shoulder. "Who."

"... Marione, they said Marione."

"I'll kill them." He growled his eyes became dark. "I'm on your side. I'll pay them back for what they did."

She could feel an odd chilling energy flow into her body and set itself inside her before it budded. But some energy from her flowed to him that was warm and did the same thing. Like they had exchanged energy with one other or something like that.

He brought her up to her feet with him and looked at her. "Don't lose yourself. Don't let yourself break. Just hold on to what you can. Please." He asked as he placed his head on her shoulder his voice held the sound of a plea in desperation.

He let go of her shoulder. She opened her mouth to answer black tendrils shot out from the ground and wrapped around her body.

They looked at one another in surprise, before they pulled her down and into the dark water. "---!" his hand was out and yelled something out as she disappeared down below.

There was no direction just darkness all around, no sight or sound it was utter nothingness. Till a light appeared and enveloped. They were no longer trapped in a suffocating darkness. It felt warm.

"Now is the time for you to choose. You must make a choice, the choice we put off once before. Leave behind the past, those near you, the past you wish to ignore, what you fear, what you don't want to face, they fact of what they done, those you care, just leave everything behind, as what they wish to come to pass, as you chose to leave everything. Or live, and embrace it all, challenge what they wish and stop it. Regain what was lost. But it will entail many hardships challenges and choices, that are extremely hard, it will not be easy and pain with follow. No longer would you be able to deny it… and fate will be cruel. All in order to do what must be done.

"Nothing has changed always repeating, granting time, as I grow weaker, till there is nothing left that could stop them. It matters little how it's done but what will be the results. There are only two choices for you now. Denial or Acceptance of fate and destiny. But even if you don't take it there is another to turn to. Or will you take on that burden for that who is close? You must choose. Will you bring froth a new beginning or allow an ending to take place?

"Denial or Acceptance? Will you become a new piece in a stacked game and be the ace or the joker? Fate can no longer wait."

From the flames Arianna fell to the ground. She took a deep gasping breath with her hand placed on her chest. It felt as if it was here first breath of air, and her heart was pounding. She wore nothing but a torn white dress. Her limbs trembled and her eyes were clouded and unfocused.

Then from the other room Assistant Lisa kicked in the door and stepped inside. They looked down at the collapsed Arianna, her gear and clothing had been removed personally by Lisa however she was unaware of ear cuff. Lisa's eyes shook and she turned around without a word, then promptly returned with everything they took from Arianna's body including her helmet. "Get up. You need to get out of here." She said as she dropped the items in front of her.

"… N-not… yet."

"I'll deal with everything here. I can't let them use you after you finally appeared. You are the one I have been waiting for. So, get out of here and rest." Lisa stated with clear eyes. Arianna just shook her head. "Once they heard of the success, they've decided to pull off a missive heist in the southwest. They will get multiple surface dwellers involved. They plan to firebomb the school that kid is."

Arianna's muscles tensed. "You don't have much time, so you need get away before they see you. This place, the building, research everything I'll take care of. You are in no shape to do anything right now. I'm sure what you just did and been through has taken everything out of you. I'll help you don't worry. So, you need to leave… I'll see you again." Lisa stated before placed a one-use teleportation orb between Arianna and her items.

Arianna looked up with clouded eyes at Lisa her head was still muddied but she realized something right as the orb activated and she disappeared to another location that was not inside the building. "I thought I would never see them. I could protect him… and her… but this is the least I can do till we cross paths again soon. I truly am cruel… but I'll be there when I'm freed and so is she." Lisa muttered. She then tapped a few things on her bracelet.

"I need your help, to destroy the lab, its research and Clayton. We can't let anything escape." Lisa stated with a calm voice.

"Why are you suddenly going against his order's you've been working hard to get close."

"They appeared and got entangled in the experiment. We can't let them get their hands on the data and the Lab must be silenced. I'll give myself a perfect cover don't worry."

A lone figure with bright blood red eyes sat on the edge of a tall building in black garb. They sat relaxed as they look down at the small home that was consumed in a roaring blaze. The cloud moved the 'moon' was revealed. The light of the false moon shined against their back as a cold winter breeze blew by and caught their long purple violet hair, that though managed and clean was hard to say when it was last cut properly and in a little disarray.

There was a slight bubble inside of them, whether anger or something else it rose and formed. The tips of their hair change colour to an icy blue but its didn't change all their hair just the tips. This very appearance one could feel and odd power an increase around them, one that was clearly not natural to the current world they resided in.

Their very pale skin was easy to see as they rest their chin against their palm. They had fine yet delicate features that could turn a few heads, a beauty that had several charms. However, at this moment they looked dangerous as they looked down at the house that was in flames impassively with no clear expression. The only slight indication was that sudden change in her hair and the slight creak that came from the object held down by her legs that rest against the wall and ledge.

No call had been made about the house till it was clear it was too late. The roof had caved in on itself that caused them to shiver slightly. No one left the house from when they started to watch. It was near luck that no house next to it caught on fire rather just slightly burnt. Though the large space that was mandatory between houses likely played the greater role in that fact than just luck on its own.

By the time firefighters had arrived the house was a collapsed mess of flames and rubble. There was no chance they would be able to find anything inside by this point. It was clearly intentional as well; it was made to look like prior the cold case on serial arson events that ravaged the world over 12 years ago.

A sigh passed their lips as they place the item down next to them on the roof. Their hair returned to its violet colour as if the icy colour never existed. They had been there for hours to watch as the house collapsed and burned. They opened their mouth and a light voice passed. "They really did." They mumbled. "If that's the case then that..." they trailed off.

They turned around and stood up they didn't notice any stiffness from the position that I had held for hours at that point. But even if they felt stiff that wasn't about to stop them. They covered their eyes and shook their head a little. They felt extremely odd in a way that was hard to described, something wasn't right, but they didn't plan to let that get in the way.

There were only a few hours left before dawn by that point. They clenched their first before they looked back at the house once more. Fire fighters worked to quell the blaze that had begun to die down and made sure it didn't spread to other homes as well. *They will have a busy day.*

The item that rested on the ground was picked up and placed on their head. It wasn't closed nor did they work to bring their hair into the helmet either. *Busy for many people really, myself included.* They walked over to the other edge of the building before they jumped off and disappeared into the night.

Chapter 28

The light of morning had cut its way through some of the gloomy clouds that had covered the sky. Arianna found it fit well with everything around her. School had already started, and students had returned from winter break. She knew that Roy was likely with Sean at this time which was good since he was the target of the Marione, but that didn't mean she wasn't worried about Dave.

She had no plans to return to the school after she returned, since the adoption act was no longer need. But if what assistant Lisa told her was true then the Marione planted at least one firebomb at the school to cause chaos and grab Sean. But the other students were in just as much danger, so she needed to take action no matter what happened. If she froze here, it would be the end.

It didn't matter if she was in a bad condition, they weren't about to wait for her to be better to carry out their plan. A true moment of acceptance and action over just allowing such a thing to occur due to her condition.

For years Arianna had felt trapped, with no escape or way out of her situation. It was as if she was on the edge of a cliff for a very long time. After all, the idea that anyone could turn on her and kill her had long been instilled. To her. the world and its people were all enemies but at the same time the very people that would ultimately need her one day.

It was a double edge sword, she knew it. At first all she wished for was revenge and to survive as it was her mother's last wish. It was something that come to chain her down. She was afraid, but she wanted to make a change, she wanted to bring forth a change. Even if in the end when it was all over, she would be killed or that only death would await her. A change needed to happen.

Arianna looked up to the sun and closed her eyes as she tilted her head to it as she sat in the parking lot. The light didn't emit heat like it once did, but she wanted to feel the light against her skin like this once more, a moment of true bliss to her. It was the last moment Arianna could feel such away.

Despite her bloodline, race, and origin, due to her past she was able to experience something unique not just to her kind but to all. It wasn't easy and caused her pain but in the very end of it all she eventually come to never regretted the life she had come to live. Able to experience all aspects, but also had a preference to work alone over working with another. But things needed to end one day, as all things must.

Arianna stepped off her motorcycle as she turned towards the school and looked at the building. A sigh escaped her lips, and she felt her hands tremble ever slightly. The building would be gone, the moment she stepped forward it would truly begin, and there would be no chance to run away any longer.

Did you know this would happen one day mother… you always had an uncanny ability to always know like that. You always had that sad look… I'll never forget you or father… but I'm not going to let it hold me back anymore. I'll accept it all… it might take time but… one day… one day I'll hold my head high as myself when I come to see you.

I'll pay back the man… but I'll no longer pine for the past that can never be. I'm going to do what I think I should not what I think you would have wanted. I love you…and goodbye. When I come to see you both in person, I will be free from the chains of the past that have bound me for so long. No matter what pain may come or will bring me… I'll face it and not look back again. I'm sure you'd be proud. Arianna thought as she looked at the sun again with her eyes closed.

She opened her eye with a sharp look, though she was still afraid she had steeled herself. Ready to face what was a head with those she had come to trust and rely on. Actions towards fate had begun and started to move once more in earnest. Arianna turned and walked towards the school; any moment she knew she would receive a message that would inform her, and it would begin.

Arianna walked towards the school a shoulder bag strapped over her shoulders filled with what she needed. The halls were empty since classes had already long begun, and it was still hours before lunch would begin. She walked down the hall to the office, she looked at the familiar secretary, her hand trembled. *Just act like Rouge… or that I'm talking to the others.* She told herself.

"… I need… I need to speak with Dave Luo. It's an emergency." Arianna spoke in a quiet and slightly shake voice that all at the front office could hear. They looked over in shock, even though she had only been to the school for a short time, Arianna had become known due to her disappearance and the very belief that she was mute. "D-do I have to repeat myself. Call Dave Luo here immediately." This time Arianna spoke in an authoritative tone.

"R-right away!" the one secretary stammered shocked by her sudden tone. They never expected that Arianna could have such a tone, it was obvious she was nervous, so they saw her as a meek being after everything but that wasn't the case. After a few minutes Dave raced down the hall and into the office.

Dave's stood in the door in surprise, he never thought he would see Arianna again. He raced over and hugged her. Arianna who had a straight face the entire time formed a slight smile as she placed her hand on Dave's head that was placed in her chest. "You've grown quite a bit since I last saw you. At this rate you'll be taller than me in no time." She chuckled lightly as she ran her hand through his hair.

Arianna couldn't deny that despite the short amount of time she had become close to Dave, she wished he was her brother though if he heard that he might have been a bit discouraged. Dave's ears were slightly read as his face was in her chest. "Let's go out I have something important to talk about."

Ari held Dave's hand and took him outside. She smirked as she looked at him, "I don't have to bend down any more it's a little weird. Your lights grow so much at this age." She sighed with the slight shake of her head. "Now's not the time for such things."

"Yeah… why did you come here Ari? I didn't think you were going to come back."

"Ah! I see you've gotten stronger… yes, your right… originally when I left, I lied… I didn't think about returning then. But that's not the case anymore. I don't have time to explain, you just need to get out of here right away."

"What?! I need to leave! I've been training I can help you Ari."

"Not with this, and you're not that strong just yet Dave. One day but not now. But even if you were strong you can't help with this."

"Why!"

Arianna looked at Dave with a slightly sad expression. "The Marione has planned a full out attack on this end of the city. I only can do so much so I came here. They are going to attack surface; many civilian buildings will be caught up in it. But there are two main targets, one being this building, and since you two are guard well the attack here is more extreme." She started.

"They've placed firebombs around the school. You're the least protected so I wanted to get you out first. I'm gonna deal with the rest of school right after. I'll try to reduce to casualties that would otherwise occur."

"I can help you! So let me." Dave exclaimed as he looked at her with sharp eyes, she just shook her head. "If you're not gonna let me help what was the point in training me. The point of learning what I have."

"Dave, at the end of the day I was tasked to protect your family. You are still very green; you are not ready to be a part of a full-blown battle between the two organizations yet. I have seen many people die Dave some many. So please. There is no way to prevent the fall of the school and what's about to happen to this part of the city. I'm just about to do damage control. Wait to join the rest of the school that's the best thing you can do right now.

"One day I'm sure you'll be on my side but today is not that day. If you truly wish to follow down this path even after all you've learned and seen, it's your choice... Royce has likely told you where you could go to follow this path. But please think about it no matter how tempting it is right now, is it truly what you want. So please do think as there is little chance to turn back.

"I don't doubt you or anything... but this isn't a game its dangerous and you can die. It is different, we are very different and dangerous people from you." Ari paused for a moment as she looked at Dave with sad yet kind eyes. "You have been kind to me unlike those two. Not only that but in truth I owe your father a debt for something a very long time ago. That is what allowed us the chance to meet.

"I'll never forget the kindness you've shown a person like myself, which is also the reason I wish to see you safe. I can't stop what you choose it is your choice and life, just don't rush into it because of how 'cool' it seems and such, all I ask is just think about it.

"We won't get another chance to talk like this for a very long time after this. When we can meet again under different circumstance even if you had come to hate me by that point for all I've done. I'll be more than happy to welcome you with open arms even so to repay you.

"Please know this... no matter what happens or how long. If you are ever in serious danger and need my help. I'll come right away all you have to do is call that number I gave you before, just like you did before. You already know how it works."

Dave looked at Arianna his eyes glossy he understood at this point Arianna was serious. He didn't want to part like this. He wanted to get to know her more, the women with a large and unique aura to her. Someone who always showed him something unexpected.

Someone he knew no matter how strong she currently showed to him was on the verge of collapsing and breaking like glass. And he was sure she was aware of this as well but still made this choice for herself.

"Arianna, I know that there is very little that I actually know about you. I know we've only known each other for a short time. Your someone I've come to care about alright. You probably just see me as a kid, even though I'm just a few years younger than you.

"I won't stop you and will listen to what you say even though I don't want to. But please place some trust in me like I trust you. No matter what happens please know I'll always be on your side like you have been for me and my family. I'm willing to be there for you if you ever need it!" Dave exclaimed as his face flushed red before he raced off.

Arianna smiled a little as she watched Dave run off. *If only Sean was a little more like his brother than I wouldn't hate him as much. It doesn't matter anymore. The youngest with the skill to see one true personality, thoughts, and feelings with a coloured aura… and the eldest with weak plant magic. Though small something people desire, and people here would fear if outright known. I do hope when we next get to meet it would not be in such circumstances… but with how things are now it's hard to say what the future will truly hold yet.* She thought as she turned and made her way up the stairs.

It was mere moments till chaos would break out. Ari's footsteps resounded through the stairwell and hallway. It was almost like an abandoned building with how quiet it was, she felt a kind of peace and reassurance from it. The silence and loneliness or being alone have been long friends and comfort to her and always would be in the end.

As she reached the top floor, she walked down the hall she could see classes going on as she walked past and even noticed the few glances from other students in class. The surprised and shocked faces that some had as they saw her. She found it to be amusing. Some people left the classrooms it was odd for them to suddenly leave class for such a reason but when considered that they've seen a person who had been missing for about four months walking down the hallway.

Arianna turned to the fire alarm that was on the wall. She hummed for a moment in wonder whether she should wait for the message or not. Someone them grabbed her arm. "Where have you been! Don't you know your family been worried sick." A teacher exclaimed as they held her wrist tight. Arianna looked at them with a side long glance.

[They are on their way.] She glanced up at the message that appeared at the top of the glasses. She let out a hum as she tore her wrist out of the teachers grasp with ease. She then turned to face the teacher.

"I care little about such a thing, an where I've been matter's not dear 'instructor'. There are more important matters." Arianna spoke in a monotone voice as she reached behind her and pulled the fire alarm and at the same time an EMP blast went off in the area.

Chapter 29

The teacher looked at Arianna in anger and students begun to file out of the classrooms due to the sound of the fire alarm. "Everyone! Return back to class!" The teacher growled as they swiped their arm in emphasise.

"Dear 'instructor' that I do not recognize, did you forget that in this district by law, its illegal not to leave as designated unless impleaded for any reason; well unless of course that alarm is in action against the procedure of another code. Oh, but then again it is just a surface law so of course you wouldn't know 'instructor'." Arianna chimed as she tilted her head. The 'instructor' bristled as their arm went into their jacket as they spun around. Arianna's hand went into her bag.

The two swung at the same time as their daggers caught on one another. Arianna turned her blade slightly and locked them together. "Move now!" Arianna yowled as she applied more strength to her arm.

She glared at the people that stood around gawking at the two of them. But that wasn't much help. "Tsk. Idiots still don't get it." She muttered as she separated and knocked the 'instructor's' arm back. Ari sent a strong kick and sent them flying into a locker, though that much alone was difficult at the time.

Ari lunged forward and placed her arm against across his chest. "Enough games. Where are the bombs you planted?" She growled this caused people to panic and move as people started to run down the stairs. "You were planted here to set the firebombs and make sure no one left, but not just that. You were to ensure that the target was grabbed during this event. A low level sent to die. Just tell me and you won't die." They didn't say a word and just smirked. "Shit!" she cursed in realization.

Arianna jumped back right as a firebomb explored from that locker. The blast sent her flying back into the lockers of the other side and fell to the ground. Then one after another the firebombs exploded throughout the school. But somehow the blast was mediated and avoided causing anyone any serious injuries, though the flames caught to all the walls.

Ari looked over at the charred body of the 'instructor' and clicked her tongue as she pushed herself up from the ground. Even though she took a direct hit from the blast aside from a few nicks and slightly burnt clothing she was alright relatively speaking, uncharred unlike the 'instructor'. Roy raced over to Ari and helped her stand as he looked her over. "I'm alright Roy. We need to get people out of here." She murmured as she brushed him off.

Ari then begun to help other make ways down the stairs, with Roy, Sean and his friends help. Though she wanted to question why they and Sean decided to help she choose not to and just get people out of the building. As the number of people trickled down Arianna looked around the fire had become extremely intense. The very scene just made her skin crawl as she looked at it.

"Roy, there will be more. Head down protect Dave. Sean and the rest of you should head down as well I'll do a final check." Arianna told them. Roy didn't argue and started to go down right away. The two looked at one another for a moment. Though it took longer Sean's friends eventually started to go down the stairs. "What are you doing?" Arianna asked Sean.

"Two are better than one."

"You should go. I-"

Arianna could hear creaking from above and glanced up. "Look out!" She clicked her tongue and pushed Sean with all her might down the stairs towards his friends as she fell backwards. Pieces of that ceiling that were a flame had fall right where they stood and on the top of the stairs. Escape had been blocked.

Ari glanced down at her hand confused as she felt something odd, and it wasn't the first time today either. For that moment she touched Sean, she felt an odd rush of energy. She had felt something similar from Dave as well. It wasn't something that she could explain or understand, but for the most part she did feel like she had a little more energy at the very least.

Arianna stood up and walked towards the stairs and looked down between the flames she could see Sean and his friends on the second-floor landing collapsed. Sean slowly got up holding his head, which had begun to bleed a little, as he seems to hit his head from the fall. Sean then looked up at and had a look of surprise. "Arianna!"

"Pff. The first time you've called my name in earnest concern." Arianna replied as she looked down with a clam expression. "Things are starting to collapse from the flames. The stairs will collapse soon too. Follow after Roy... don't worry about me like you usually did before." She said with a smirk as she closed her one eye. Before anymore words could be exchanged more of the ceiling fell before her and completely blocked the stairs. Sean screamed out for her, but the flames consumed the sound.

Ari looked at the flames and as they licked her clothing, she flinched and closed her eyes. All she could picture was another time as she begun to tremble and fell to the ground. She held her shoulders as she trembled, and her breathing became heavy. As she felt the flames lick her arms she screamed out, "noooo! Get away from me!"

The flames then moved back away from her and formed an arch about her. The embers fell around her. Her trembles slowed and she opened her eyes and looked around her. Her eyes held sadness and a realization. "T-that's right. Flames... I have power of fire... complete master... fire magic. Its stronger now... but..." she muttered as she looked down at her hand.

"I forgot... cause. After... my magic... power awakened that night which is why I survived but it reminded me of that night... the part of that night I sealed away. I was burned and trapped almost like this. Hahah... how cruel fate is. It forced me to remember it all... everything from that night... the trauma that I tried to forget but had been haunted by since. I tried to forget that and my powers." Arianna muttered in a sad voice. Tears begun to fall from her eyes as she covered her face. "My fears all... everything from that one incident. Damn it." She cried out in despair from/for memories that had returned.

Sean held his bleeding head as he and his friends arrived where the school had gathered. Roy was next to Dave as they looked at the burning building. Roy turned his head and saw Sean; he went over right away. "What happened?"

"Arianna pushed Sean down the stairs."

"What? No... well, she probably wanted to do it for a while anyways... but either way she wouldn't have done it for no reason."

"The roof on the third floor collapsed over the stairs. She pushed him out of the way."

"But then what about Arianna doesn't that mean she's trapped on the third floor." Dave asked as he came over his tone was worried and slightly panicked.

"Where is the fire department or any emergency services for that matter? Sean hit his head pretty head when he fell."

"I'm fine. But we need to help Arianna." Sean muttered his tone was pained and his one eye was closed with blood dripping down his face. His face was pale, he was unable to hide the amount of pain he was in as by his expression alone it was clear it was immense. He held his head; it was a miracle he was even conscious. Roy could tell by his eyes that Sean was in bad shape as his eyes were extremely cloudy. Roy probably wished he paid more attention to emergency first aid training at that time.

"But let's go back for a bit. Since when could Arianna talk. I thought she was mute. Also, Roy the two of you seem to know one another well."

"Arianna could always talk… no let me clarify. There was nothing physical that made it so Arianna was incapable of speech, she can speak perfectly fine."

"If that's the case, why didn't she do so from the start it was more inconvenient for everyone."

"I'm not sure the exact cause or reason for it. But whenever she tried it makes her sick and she told me that she just couldn't. That's normally how it is but sometimes she can speak if she needs or forces herself, she's usually in a bad mood later if it was in that case. Now in concern to the two of us we've known each other for many years that's all."

Before the conversation went any further vehicles drove towards the school at a fast pace. A quick glance one might think they were police cars, but they weren't. "Look EMS. Finally, that took forever. Come on Sean you need medical treatment right away."

"Wait!" Roy exclaimed but was too late to grab the two. He grabbed Dave and pulled him away into a tree. Dave looked at Roy in shock, but it soon became realization and understanding.

The cars skid to a stop and the doors were kicked open. People with masks stepped out guns in hand. Sean saw them, as someone that has run into a few like them prior knew what that meant right away and stopped as he pulled his friend down. "Shut up don't say a word." Sean hissed as he pulled a hood over his head.

A few seconds later one of the masked people shot one of the clamoring students that were trying to get help from them. Screams erupted; the other masked person next to the first smacked them on the back of their head. The masked people begun to move their guns drawn. "Sit down and shut up! Lest you want a bullet pierced into your skull."

A few people quickly sat down. "Who do you think you are! This is an education facility! -" that was all the male teacher got out before they got shot. There was screams especially by those around the teacher that got sprayed with blood and matter. At that point everyone got down on the ground.

"We are looking for someone. You surface dwelling shmucks should be honour the chance to be able to interact with the great Marione Mercenaries. A once and a lifetime opportunity for you surface dwellers, probably… and come out alive of the interaction that is. We are looking for someone in particular… so shut up and you won't be the next to die."

Students begun to whimper, some begun to recite prayers, or sat in stunned silence. Like they said anyone that made too much noise was shot and killed so that became real clear, made everything and everyone fairly quiet.

Roy was without his gear or any good weapons, all he could do was sit in the tree with Dave and watch as events unfolded. This went on for a long time as they looked, till eventually, they arrived at Sean.

"Remove the hood. I want to see your face!" they growled as the barrel was point at him. He was barely conscious at that point.

"M-my friend got injured in the fire. The hoods begin used to control the bleeding. He's applying pressure see."

They looked at Sean only glancing at them for a moment. "I don't care." They growled as they bent down. They grabbed Sean by the throat and lifted him up before the hood fell, and they smirked. "Found you, ya little weed."

At that moment everyone turned towards Sean. Sean barely had his eyes open as he looked down at the masked person that held him by the throat. He didn't even have the strength to struggle.

As he thought that it was the end for him, a shot rang out. The person holding Sean staggered and dropped him, which caused Sean to collapse to the floor. The masked person fell to the ground bleeding as they held their neck, blood seeping between their fingers. On the other side from where the shot rang out, stood a figure cloaked in black.

Chapter 30

Arianna shook her head slightly. "Now's not the time for this. There are more important things to concern myself with right now." Ari muttered as she pushed herself up from the floor. She wiped the tears that streaked her face. She looked over at the satchel, before she removed it from her shoulder and place it on the ground.

Arianna opened the bag and begun to pull out what was inside and took out familiar black combat style clothing. Quickly she changed into her combat clothing without anything on her head or face, then glanced over at the school uniform she had just removed. After a few moments she grabbed the clothing and tossed it into the flames.

Then she pulled out her weapons and attached them to the belt then finally grabbed something to cover her head which was none other than a helmet. The gear was mainly new with the helmet being only a little older than that by a few months. It was the second time she changed gear like this in a year, with the first time was to distance herself from the old legacy that had come to be attached to it.

Though the recent occurrence was due to the prior clothes that had become drenched in blood, and more than a little torn from what happened just yesterday. Even though the clothing was able to self-repair to a degree it would take time. But since it was so drenched in blood that she needs to use the spare due to the time restraint.

The satchel then disappeared before Arianna put the helmet on and close it around her head. She begun to look around for a classroom door that hadn't been blocked by the collapsed ceiling. Eventually she spotted a door that was only blocked by fire.

Arianna walked over to the door and waved her hand and the flames moved. The flames still caused her to tremble sightly, but she had begun to suppress all her emotions, so it was done subconsciously. The handle was wrecked so she couldn't open the door the normal way, she tilted her head a little before she rolled her shoulders. Energy begun to surge and collect in her body, and she could feel her weak and tired body get stronger. She glanced down at her hands for a moment and shook the thought off.

With that she pivoted slightly so she was parallel with the door with her feet planted. She lifted the leg closest to the door up before placing a powerful side kick right below the handle. The door let out a solid creak as frame itself bent and buckled. The door swung back into the room; it was possible to see the slight bend that was in the door frame and the locking mechanism as well, destruction which the kick had caused and had ultimately allowed the door to open.

There weren't too many flames inside the classroom. It made sense as Surface schools back then made sure that multiple rooms in a school building had some fire 'proofing' capabilities to slow the spread. It was to make it easier to insure the rescue of trapped students. Thought it only worked up to a certain degree, but thanks to it the room was generally untouched by the flames caused by the firebombs.

Arianna looked around unconcerned, at this point that only thing of worry was the oxygen supply which the fire was consuming. But another thing of worry was whether the building was about to collapse on top of her, something which she had no desire to experience again. With such problems that were laid out before her and the fact that she had become completely trapped on the third floor at this time her main and near only option was to escape through a window.

It was possible to escape other ways, like descending the building from the roof, but it had a higher chance of been spotted since it was daylight. Or she could wait till the part of the third floor collapsed so she could descend to the second and maybe subsequent first floor, but she was already in her mercenary gear due to clothing being resistant to fire, so it would hard to explain why she was already inside the building, not only that it was hard to say when the floor would even collapse. As such the best option before her in a logical sense was to escape from a third-floor window, and she wouldn't get hurt as she was more than accustomed at descending at such heights

Arianna looked over at the window then at the objects that that littered the classroom. She knew that the school's glass was strong so using a chair to break it open probably wouldn't work even with her strength, it would take multiple hits at the exact same spot or hits in the location that the window was weakest. As there were no dents or any of the sort it would spend a lot of the already limited amount energy, she currently had to try such a thing.

Arianna after some thought she pulled out a pistol from one of the holsters. She rather not wastes to many bullets as she had no idea what waited for her when she escaped, but it was a necessary action to her at this point. She fired two quick shots into the glass a certain distance apart from one another. It created two large shatter like cracks in the glass, it was enough at this point she'd be able to jump from the window.

Ari put away the pistol and went towards one of the chairs. That was when a message popped up in the corner of her visor. [They've arrived and already investigating. You best get there quickly.]

[I managed to get two of my people in the group. If they see the target, they will pass over them. But I can't promise you they will be ones to find them first.]

[So, it's best you intercept them as soon as possible. It's in both of our best interest that they don't get their hands on the target]

[My allies will make opening and opportunities for you when the fight breaks out. They will likely make it look they are attacking you but will miss or graze their shots to avoid suspicion. Hopefully this will be enough.]

Arianna looked over the messages before she replied, [for now that is good enough. It's best they don't get cast under suspicion right away after we decided to co-operate with one another.]

[However, would you get me the current location Marione base here? They will more than likely get a hold of scientist as I didn't have a chance to get a protection detail on them. So, I'll probably have to infiltrate the base later.]

[Got it. I'll send it to you after the battle. Is there anything else you need?]

[Well, a mana, stamina, and health potion would be nice, but no way I'm getting that right now.] Arianna replied sarcastically. [But in all seriousness, could you tell me what your allies masks look like, so I don't kill them in the fight?]

Mercenaries are generally faceless with only their codename being the thing spread and occasionally their form of dress as well. Mercenary organization however came up with 'proper' yet good way to tell allies from enemy when in the heat of battle. Since an ID/tag check is impossible during such a thing they needed something to prevent the chance accident deaths of allies from their own team members.

The organizations made it, so they have a set of gear that is designated to them. All agents wear during missions and combat to be a distinguisher from others, especially when a war between organizations broke out. For example, the Yano uses technological helmets of all kinds, while the Marione uses masks.

Once you reach a certain level in an organization you get a unique designated piece of such gear that is only dedicated to them that another other cannot use, (essentially though there are some slight scenarios that deviate for such).

Codeless however do not get such gear, they hide themselves in other ways that varies in methods. But when working with an organization they do get a 'temporary' loan of such gear. Arianna a codeless herself is a very special case when it came to this, however. Though she often would swipe such gear when her paths crossed with agents, she either killed or had already passed. Recently she had been given her own unique helmet by the Yano organizations leader Dark. It an item of which she was currently using, and it was a fact that very few people are aware of.

[One has a full-face mask slash mark across the right and a crossing line below it, somewhat mimics an upside down cross, they are a lower rank but the only one of the cross divisions there. You don't have to worry about mistaking them.]

[The second individual will be easy to tell as they are high rank. They have a complete upper face covering mask. It doesn't much of the lower jaw area as it's cut off right below the nose, but it is made in a way to look as if they have fangs. The colour of the mask is mainly white mask, but it has splotches and stains of red all over it.]

That second one… he defiantly just described Bloody. So that means they are a part of the resistance group in the Marione… it's a little surprising. But in hindsight they've always acted different from other agents of the org that I often crossed paths with. Well, I know what they are capable of so it's a good thing that for now we are on the same side. Arianna thought as she grabbed the chair. She dragged the chair along over to the window while in thought, *I wonder how many high rankings people of the Marione are a part of his group. I never thought of the inner working of an organization before… but is it really such a mess in the Marione for such a thing to occur?*

Arianna shook her head she was let her mind wander more then quickly reigned it in and focused to the task before her. That was before a complete suppression of herself was possible for Arianna, though that wasn't really the case anymore.

Arianna lifted a chair up and slammed it into the window as the leg of the chair hit right between the two bullet holes. Then around the area where the glass had become cracked but still stood just shattered. A large hole had formed in the window as glass fell to the ground, the hole that was made was large enough for Arianna to escape from.

She tossed the chair back behind her before she walked back. She rolled her shoulder she looked at the window. The condition to land wasn't that ideal but there was no point to complain about it. After a moment Arianna sprinted towards the window and jumped. Her legs tucked in towards her chest, her one foot slight extended and arms crossed in front of her as she jumped through the window. The creaked glass that didn't fall at first was then brought out with her as she went through the hole.

The fresh breeze from outside she could feel it as it grazed against her. Escaped from the burning building but she was still falling so changed her position mid-air to prepare herself to land. She put herself in the best position to land on the ground without injury. Initially spread herself out to slow her descend even if only slightly and for a few moments before she moved into her landing position as the ground got closer.

As her feet touched the ground, she quickly tucked herself and rolled, this was to spread out the shock from of the landing at such a height. There was a slight numbing sting in her body, but she ignored it and got right on her feet in a few moments after she landed. Ari knew she didn't have time to just sit around due to such minimum pain (in comparison to what she has felt before). The school building by that point had become even more engulfed in flames. There would be no chance to save it at this point since EMS wouldn't have shown up to the school, they probably had no idea that the building was even on fire due to the EMP.

Before Arianna had much of a chance to do anything else but brush herself off glass and dirt, she heard the resounding yet familiar sound of gun fire. She lifted her head up, the sound had come from the other side of the building where the parking lot was located. *So, trigger happy. How many people have they killed already?*

Ari adjusted her clothing a little as she begun to walk towards the building. As she got closer, the flames could no longer hide the loud voices of the Marione agents and the cries of students. She hid herself out of sight, as now wasn't the time to reveal herself.

She looked at what had begun to occur in front of her. The Marione agents through the fear of guns forced all from the school down on the ground. She counted the number of agents in front of her, there were 12, and she knew two of them were her allies. Ari also was aware that Roy didn't have his gear or any significant weapons on him at the time so he was unable to help during the fight that would occur in board daylight.

That would mean that Arianna had to fight 10 Marione agents on her own in a poor state. Even with her abilities in her current condition that would be impossible. Something Ari was well aware of, so she needed to be cautious and strategic at the time she made her move. She couldn't miss a shot or miss an attack as she would become quickly overwhelmed if she did.

At the point she had arrived that she could see the students, the Marione agents had long begun to search for Sean. She couldn't see Roy and Dave amongst the people kneeling on the ground. But she also had trouble to locate Sean as well. *Alex trained him well enough in the art of stealth and blending it seems. He's probably keeping low… he knows his hair is a real giveaway too.* Ari thought as she scanned a little more cautiously at that point, she found Sean. But so did a Marione agent as they walked towards him.

Chapter 31

"Remove the hood. I want to see you face!" they growled as the barrel was point at Sean.

"M-my friend got injured in the fire the hoods begin used to control the bleeding. He's applying pressure see."

"I don't care."

Shit! Of course, that wasn't gonna work. You made them even more suspicious of Sean... and angry. Ari cursed as she realized the situation was about to turn south. She quickly pulled out her pistol and cocked it, then her free hand moved under her long coat to the hilt of one of her 'assassin' like swords.

If his friend didn't say anything to cast suspicion, Sean could have lifted the hood up just enough to show his face and some of his hair. In the shade of the hood, they wouldn't realize his hair colour at a quick glance. The Marione is looking for the colour not the face. She groaned, they had to check over a thousand students, so they would only cast glances.

Arianna had planned that if they didn't realize or see Sean, she was going to trick them and inform the agents Sean was at home and not the school. Since they planned everything for this part of the city Sean would have been safe when she misdirected them. She clicked her tongue lowly as she raised her gun. She had to wait for the right moment to get the best results, though she knew it would probably go awry due to the students.

Arianna watched as the agent reached down and grabbed Sean by the throat. They lifted him up in the air which was more than likely constricting his ability to breathe. Her hand gripped the pistol tighter as she looked around at the Marione agents.

This was not about to be an ideal situation that she was about to face. The arrogant agent lifted Sean up into the air, around then with Sean's feet just barely touching the ground. The hood was loose on Sean's head as he no longer held it, and with was a slight gust of wind the hood fell.

Arianna could see the blood that had trailed down Sean's face and realized that he was injured. At the time she wasn't sure but she guessed it was probably from when she pushed him down the stairs so they wouldn't get crushed from debris. She wanted to curse as with each moment what was before her got worse as Sean couldn't fight and was possibly about to pass out at any moment. "Found you, ya little weed."

At that moment everyone turned towards Sean, at the realization that he was the one they wanted. Ari couldn't see Sean face at this moment, as the arrogant agent basically begun to show him off like some kind of prize. Arianna walked out from where she hid, no one noticed the new figure that had appeared in the distance.

With one foot forward and had turned herself slightly to make her a smaller target and raised her gun. She begun to aim down the barrel at that arrogant agent. Marione agents though as strong and capable as had one major flaw when it came to their combat gear. A single most exploitable yet difficult weakness, they didn't protect their necks in the slightest.

Her pistol aimed right for the arrogant agent's neck and directly at the carotid artery. Ari took a deep calm breath before she pulled the trigger. There was the loud bang of the pistol as the fired. The bullet pierced into their neck and blood quickly started to trail down it.

The arrogant agent staggered, and they dropped Sean. They stepped back as they brought their hand to their neck as blood begun to gush out from their throat. Blood begun to seep though their fingers before they collapsed to the ground and started to bleed out.

Arianna stood tall and confident as she looked forward at what was before her. They all turned toward her, for she where she had fired, had remained there on purpose. They couldn't see Arianna face, but she made sure to give off the proud, confident, arrogant, and cocky appearance. "I came to crash this little party you were having. Setting off an EMP here in the city. Tsk, tsk, how naughty. You really gone and put a damper on what I was doing." Arianna spoke though the voice that came out was in no way anything like her own.

"Hey! We have hostages, do anything and they are all dead. I know how much you Yano softies like to avoid unnecessary bloodshed." One agent claimed as they aimed their gun at the students and the others followed suit. I could see a slight tremble in some of their hands. A side from Bloody, no one on the Marione side recognized her, but they believed her to be an unknown high ranked Yano agent. Though that wasn't the case in anyway.

"Hahaha! How cute! Why should I care about such things? Surface dwellers are of little value to me other than a potential source of income." She replied with a laugh as she tilted her gun up slightly as smoke still rose from the barrel.

Though it wasn't exactly a lie what she said, it wasn't exactly the truth either. The main goal was to get the hostages from the school out of the way. It was a preference not to have an entire school of people killed in front of her and become something akin to a near genocide. "You got in the way of my job... so I'm here to pay you back."

The agents at that point realized their mistake and pushed them aside. "What?! No way! A Codeless?! Fuck why did we have drag in ourselves a Codeless!"

"Leader! A Codeless garbed in pure black, with true aim that never misses a calmly aimed shot! Their outfits different from what it had been previously but… I'm certain we just pissed off the most powerful Codeless down below. I'm sure of it they are the one the surface dweller's call the 'Assassin'! They are the only one capable of getting something like a helmet off a Yano."

At the mentioned of the Assassin the surface dwellers looked up at her. One who had never been seen before. "Assassin? I have no idea who you are talking about, and the strongest how funny, is that what they are saying now a days? I am but a Codeless one with no name as of yet. Is that what the surface dweller's come to call me or is it someone else or maybe even many of us Codeless you never know really. You can't really trust the surface dweller's points of deduction now a days really." She said nonchalantly and completely dismissing such a notion that they in away were such a person.

However, it was true. Arianna a codeless after many long years, missions, jobs, and the like on the surface, she was the one the surface once called the Assassin. She was the only one expect for Dark and a few other trusted individuals aware of this. The first ever codeless ever to receive such a name, as embarrassing as it was it was proof of her strength and ability. A feat that granted her the vary right to have a name without any affiliation to an organization. Though she had yet to officially choose her own name to use below.

Arianna then aimed her gun again. "Now what do you plan to do? Will you run with your tails between your legs like the loyal organization dogs you are or actually fight?" She mocked them as she fired. She purposely missed to graze the neck of the agent, which let the cat out of the bag of who she was. A sort of payback before she killed them you could say.

"Get the target and hold off the Codeless!" an agent order, it was of some surprise it wasn't Bloody in charge. Which meant they were either higher rank than Bloody or they weren't in command since they were added on as additional. But it didn't matter in the end as she looked forward and smirked.

Chapter 32

Arianna pushed off the ground and moved towards them quicky she fired at one's hand as she felt a bullet graze her arm. She pivoted and twisted around before pushing off the ground and jumped into the air. Then unsheathed blade with a metallic ring. It was an item which she had been holding on to since earlier.

The momentum from was used as she swung her sword and slash the blade. With the powerful swing she slashed the agents open neck. As she landed on the ground, she moved her blade and a bullet hit with a ring.

Arianna fired another shot and moved to get to where Sean was. But the lead Marione was closer. Sean was limp in the leader's arms; it was clear he passed out not long after the agent was shot. The adrenaline had more than likely worn off at that point, with the sudden relief of being saved. He likely no longer tried to focus and keep himself self-conscious. Ari didn't wish for the leader to go far and shot them in the leg, but he was quick and begun to us Sean as a shield before she could get another shot.

The leader more than likely had come to realize that Arianna also wanted to grab Sean as well though they obviously had no idea as to why. But what it meant to the leader that they could use Sean as a meat shield since she wouldn't wish to hit him. At this Arianna couldn't help but click her tongue as she got blocked by more agents.

Ari tilted her gun and place it into one's chest as she fired which caused them to stagger. That guy then got 'accidently' shot by the crossed mask person. She then turned, as her senses told her of danger from behind and deflected another bullet. She shifted her blade as she caught another person's dagger with her sword.

She looked up and notice that two more agents that had started to help the leader of group and usher Sean into one of their vehicles. Ari didn't want them to capture Sean as that would mean more problems later. As if they captured Sean then she would have no choice but to infiltrate their base, which ever one was the closest to Brightton City, since that was where they'd likely go.

She pushed the dagger back and brought her gun up before quickly shooting then under their chin. With that the person limbs went limp from the sudden shock, and she kicked them to the ground. Ari could hear the sudden screams of the students that were around her, but she paid no mind, as she more focused on the enemies that were in front of her and wanted her dead.

Ari start to move forward and but once again blocked by the two enemies that remained to protect the leader and the other two that had been in the process of kidnapping Sean. She quickly holstered her pistol and pulled out her second blade from her back and blocked the two's weapons. The metal screeched in response to the clash of their weapons, and they slide down her swords.

The two before her moved back and she then was by the four attackers she had yet to properly deal with. While the two allies had backed off closer to the vehicles. Ari looked at the two before her, she could see that they were high ranked, but she didn't recognize them, so it was likely they recently obtained their position.

Her hand clenched the hilt of her sword tighter, she needed to gain a slight upper hand with what was before her. A sigh escaped her lips before flames appeared and wrapped themselves around her swords and coat them with flames. She slashed one blade towards the ground near her feet and singed the grass. Like she had hopped it cause the agents surrounding her a moment of pause.

With that she lunged forward and brought both blades down in front of her and cut down a less experience agent behind her. The agent that was cut down with the flame cover blade had flames that flickered from their wounds. Ari held her blade down as she stood straight up and tilted her head slightly as she looked towards the group leader. With the flames from the burning school building behind her, it was slightly chilling sight.

"You three! Hold that Codeless off as we extract the target. Do not let them get a chance to follow us. Either kill them or sacrifice yourselves. The boss won't accept any more failure on this simple job to grab a kid." The leader ordered. Ari wasn't too sure if in her current state she'd be able to take down two high and a single low rank, Marione agents. She had spent a fair amount of energy as it was, and she couldn't let herself slip in a fight against them.

"Sir, over Aquaria, I think I'd be a better match in a fight against a Codeless. Not just that I've fought Codeless before after all." Bloody spoke up as they glanced over at the leader. It wasn't even something they gave much thought to before they replied.

"Fine, go ahead Bloody. Maybe you can redeem yourself to the boss that last failure a few weeks ago." The leader replied, though Bloody glared at them for such a comment but it went unnoticed. Bloody then walked forward and took the agent called Aquaria's place.

Arianna stabbed one of her blades into the ground before she grabbed her pistol and fired at the vehicles trying at the very least to pop a tire. But the two remained weren't about to let Ari get too much damage on the vehicles or the departing agents. The high ranked lunged forwards and attacked which she blocked with her sword. The two clashed weapons as the low ranked got into a different position, at which point they fired.

Arianna dodged their shots as she pushed the high rank back. She brought up her pistol once more in a last-ditch attempt to do something before they escaped with Sean. With a pull of the trigger the gun fired and hit a window of one of the vehicles which cause a shatter pattern on the window, but it didn't break.

For such an action gave an opening that in normal circumstances she wouldn't have. This allowed the high rank to slash Ari's arm. But she moved in response and shot them in the foot, as another shot grazed her side. She placed her pistol back in its holster as she retrieved her imbedded blade. All she could do as watch at the corner of her eye as the vehicles left with Sean inside them.

Annoyed as the vehicles were out of sight, she kicked the high rank square in the chest hard enough that they slid back. At which point Bloody shot the low rank next to them point blank and killed them instantly. The high rank looked over in shock.

"What the hell are you doing Bloody?!" They growled their tone clear with shock and anger. "You're not turning traitor are you! After everything the organization has done. To get yourself to such a position of power, and more."

"I have no idea what you are implying with such a statement. What exactly has the current Marione done for me that is significant?" Bloody answered it was clear that their question was rhetorical but for whatever reason the high rank was surprised by Bloody's response.

"I'll tell you; it has forced me to kill fellow trainees and allies for little reason. At the slightest hint of disobedience against the head it almost certainly leads to death. The head is a true tyrant and unfit to lead. I don't wish to follow such a man who thinks such idea that he holds.

"Nor a man that thinks even less of their own flesh and blood, who encourages them to torture and kill one another for the position as the next head. Who could care even less if one of his own kids became a mind and soulless puppet, a man that would be delighted at notion?" Bloody growled. "I'm done following such a man as the head of the organization, a place which has only gotten worse over time. I desire change to the leadership."

Arianna glance over at Bloody. She was aware that the Marione was a less than stellar place to end up in if you weren't a mad killer, a complete physio, a blind follower, or someone that completely lacked certain morals. It was a dangerous place where one wouldn't be surprised to be backstabbed by your own allies for the slightest chance of premotion, heck it was almost encouraged sometimes. Ari has worked with the Marione on very few occasions, and it was never a pleasant experience.

It had been run in such a way for near eternity at this point. Though the similar could be said for the Yano on how things were run, both organizations have been around for so long at this point. But it was curious to what caused such a sudden change. The Marione has always run things with lack of humanity and common decency to themselves and to others. Even if it wasn't such a new concept to which the idea of a resistance to how things were, it had never really happen nor become active like this in the past.

Arianna allowed the flames on the blades to dissipate as she slowly walked towards the high rank. "Would you like for me to deal with them Bloody? I have no qualms about it." She asked.

"No, I'll help fight them rather. As I said such actions are commonplace for us after all." They replied with a slight shrug of their shoulders. The high rank at this point scrambled and picked up their weapon. But it had become useless for them to fight, with the wide gap in skills.

Even with Arianna and Bloody's shoddy teamwork that could hardly be called such. They still easily fought against the young high rank. In the end Arianna slash open their stomach and Bloody stabbed them through the chest as they saw the light leave agent's eyes.

Arianna sighed as she wiped the blood off her blades and put them away in the sheathes attached to her low back under her long coat. She crossed her arms and looked over at Bloody. "I would have never thought we'd be on the same side in such a situation. Especially since a fair number of people I'm close to downright hate your guts or just you in general."

"The sentiment is mutual. I never taught he would hire a codeless, let alone the one that got me in trouble a few weeks ago. But I trust his judgement though I'm not particularly found an idea." Bloody replied as they looked over at her.

"I'd think any Marione would have similar sentiments. The Yano and the Marione have never gotten along from what I'm aware, always bitter enemies. The Marione has also always disliked Codeless as well. Got two for two against me since I'm a Codeless with good relations with Yano." Ari sighed as she shrugged her shoulder. "Just remined him to send me what I need since they've got the target. They've already grabbed the other one, haven't they?"

"Yeah, but you were already expecting that." Bloody replied they then walked closer to Arianna. "The EMP effects are going to nullified in about 20 minutes. So, I don't suggest sticking around to watch the building fall." They added in a whisper as they place a slight bloody hand on her shoulder.

"Got thanks for the heads up and subsequent aid you had provide."

"Just make sure your worth all the additional aid he's given you. We have a goal in mind after all, and that your actions are just apart to make them possible." Bloody replied sharply. Arianna just waved her hand in response before Bloody left completely.

Ari then rolled her shoulders and glanced over at the school building. *I'll have to make a lot of calls now to deal with this. I am not looking forward to what's a head... I have a bad feeling too.* She thought as she glances back at the people that were around her. It was hard not to think that things had become a real mess, when this mission was originally supposed to be a cake walk.

Ari shook her head slightly; her concern right now was to get out of here. Talk and mulling over thoughts could be done later. At this she turned around and went to the parking lot, she walked by cowering people that acted as if they feared the very ground she walked. Without a single moment of hesitation, she got on her bike and drove off. Behind her she left the burning school, the scattered students and faculty that was in a complete mess, and confusion of everything that just occurred.

Part 4

Chapter 33

At the edge of the treeline of a nearby forest there was a slight ledge that rested four individuals. Arianna looked down from the ledge they rested at to the large warehouse military like base the was down below them. The base had several rotating guards, and the four of them had been posted out here for the last six hours, she had got the shift rotations from Lennox when he gave her the location of the base. It was likely Bloody had told him her plans of infiltration and retrieval, not that she was one to complain about such a thing it just meant less time spent on reconsent.

With the six hours of observation, she did confirm what Lennox had informed her about the guard shift. She had even managed to find a good entry point through a low air vent that they could climb through, however their escape would require a different route. She had long been changed into her gear and fully prepared with everything she normally ran already started. As she staired at the building she felt a hand placed on her shoulder she looked back at the other three that were with her.

Arianna initially planned to come by herself and do a lone infiltration, as less people meant less traces. However due to the situation she had very little choice in the matter of the approval for such a thing.

Arianna walked out from the shower as she dried her hair. Her clothes were being washed clean of the blood that had come to cling to them. She picked up the earpieces for the VHDS and turned them on as expected the message she had been waited for arrived. The coordinate location data for the Marione's nearby base that was confirmed to have her client and charge. Not just that but also information on some of the outer defences and the guard rotation outside the building.

How resourceful.

With this data that had just been sent, it was just enough to formulate an infiltration plan to use. But there was a slight problem, as this area had become a blacklist zone due to the increase of the fighting between the Yano and the Marione, and the job itself that had become a problem between them.

As the organisation between the two most willing to work with outside sources, it made it, so that area was technically under the Yano direction. Codeless like herself could not act without direction or digression like they normally did. It had become a life-or-death thing.

As such Arianna had no choice but to call Dark the leader of the Yano. She let out a sigh as the towel she used for her head draped her shoulders. Her still wet hair dripped slightly, though most of it was caught by the towel. She placed a disc like object down on the coffee table as she sat down on the couch and started to brush her hair as she waited.

After some time, the disc came to life and a holo-graphic screen popped up as the familiar figure of Dark appeared on screen. "What is it, Arianna? Why are you calling me after you ditched both the training and your job?"

"I have valid reasons for my actions and decisions, but you don't necessarily need to know them. After all I've just a painful thorn in your side… or a threat to you, as you once said to my face." She replied coldly, she could see Dark visibly flinch, but she didn't care. "I have different reasons for calling you work related ones. SO, I think you'd like to listen to what I have to say and not cut the call like you normally do."

Dark looked up to try and defend himself but froze as he actually saw Arianna for the first time during the call. "W-w-what!? Why are you calling me in such dress?" He stammered quite thrown in a loop.

"I have no idea what you are talking about."

"... Did you purposely call me in a bath towel to shake me. I would never stoop so low. Even though your mother was a beauty, nor would I no matter whatever form you take with that disguise tech."

"Really? Even if I took the appearance of your traitorous ex-wife you've protected." Ari purred with a visible smirk. She was purposely getting under his skin at this point as she changed her appearance to that which she used when she went out during Latris. "Now stop glaring... we both know it to be true. But I have more important things to talk about then that women."

Arianna shifted in her place as she placed her hair brush down on the table. "I have managed to find the location of the Marione's out base that is currently holding Caden and Sean Luo. I request permission of the acting Yano leader Dark to allow right to commence an infiltration and rescue mission on the base."

"Denied." Dark replied without missing a beat. Arianna shot up and slammed her hands on the table.

"Why not! I'm aware this will aggravate things here, but we cannot allow them to hold on to those two for long!" Ari exclaimed with sharp eyes. "Caden worked on project Elixir directly, they will not let him go for long. We're lucky if they haven't already killed him. While they are clearly aware at this point that Sean has been affected by the aftereffects of Elixir. As such it's only a matter of time before they kill him. You never get in my way like this before so don't even try to act all familial towards me after everything."

"I will not send you off to die for such a reason. It's the least I should do for your father. Going alone to an enemy base, no matter

how good at stealth one is, it's just suicide. You are right we cannot allow the Marione to hold on to those two for long.

"They've already created Chimera's and have manage to gather a fair number of powerful artifacts. We can't allow them the chance to also learn the secret of the Elixir of strength passed down in your family's history, knowledge which Fang gave personally." Dark stated with a serious expression. "I'll put together a group of high ranks for the infiltration. Just give me the data you have."

Arianna glared at Dark, no matter their relation, Arianna had long lost such faith and trust in Dark. But she also understood another thing as well that he was willing to send a group of people. "No. If you want this data, I must be a part of this group. I'll cooperate, give me three high rank Yano agents to work with on this infiltration. That's my condition for the information."

Of course, things worked out in the end which allowed her to be a part of this mission. Though Dark never did pay attention to Ari's wording of things. Whether it was low expectations, trust in her, or something of the short, Dark didn't think of Arianna as a real true Codeless, the wanders and true masters of negotiation and manipulation.

Ari looked at the group before her. Dark had put together a good group for her to work with for an infiltration mission. Night Ari's close friend Roy a strong fighter and not one easy to take down, though stealth missions usually aren't his cup of tea, he wasn't too bad, had great teamwork with Ari, and was here just in case the worst occurs during the mission.

The next was Thief AKA Alex another person that Arianna had known for a long time at this point and worked well together. For Thief stealth missions are her bread and butter. Her combat capabilities maybe a little lack luster in comparison to others but she could slip into a place like water or a shadow and was skilled at dealing with alarms and locks.

The last agent was someone Arianna was not as familiar with but knew about them. The agent called Angel, they were 50/50 on both stealth and combat, but they were skilled none the less. Angel's greatest skill is ability to deal with hostage type situations, they can keep their cool and calm demeanor during such occurrences and is well versed with combat medicine. So, their above average stealth skills were the reason they were placed on the team.

"It's an honour to work with you. I can brag to my friends I got to work with most famous Codeless. The Codeless with the highest success rate that the surface even had come to give you a moniker."

"It's it really such a big deal?"

"OF COURSE! You're really famous, even though no one knows what you look like. But when the Leader offered me such a chance to work with you, I couldn't pass it up. Who could pass up the chance to work with such a famous person? Your so cool, not to mention the only Codeless ever given the chance to choose a Codename without an organization affiliation. If you held my hand, I could die happy."

"I don't really get it. You are aware this is essentially a suicide mission, right? All of us are more than likely going to die if not get seriously hurt or lose something precious. Dark didn't even want me to even take part in this. So, I don't understand why the three of you volunteered for this."

"If you are a part of such a mission, I'll follow by your side through it."

"I have similar sentiments as Night, and I will try to make sure we get out alive."

"For me even if I die it doesn't matter since I've been given such a chance. But I guess the rumours are true that you have a close relationship with the Leader, Codeless, along with some of the other famous Yano high ranks."

"I wouldn't say my relationship to Dark is close, even though I have the right to call him by his name. It's... a special case... same with most of the others. A chance of faith... it was highly possible I'd never have such relations with such people." Arianna replied as she looks away towards the base. "This mission is not going to be easy... it's going to bring forth a change to many things in the future once its finished. This will be... a very hard thing... and maybe even feel extremely long.

"We are about to enter the lion's den... the chance we'll run into a friendly individual is slim to none. I will not hold it against you if you wish to leave. We are about to partake in the hardest class missions the Yano offers, infiltration and protection escort, in the Marione's own base." Arianna replied as she stood up from the cliff edge.

"We are with you Codeless."

Arianna closed her eyes as she could feel the wind blow against her and move her coat. "Alright then. We will infiltrate the Marione base through a near ground level vent in between the guard rounds outside of the base. Once inside we will have to locate and make our way to the cell blocks. That is where they should be holding our targets. After they are secured, we will make our escape.

"We will avoid unnecessary combat to avoid detection for as long as possible. Due to the vent's location its likely we will be unable to escape from there not to mention the difficulty of taking our targets back through it. Hopefully we can use a stair exit but if not, a window might be a good bet. If we have no other choice but to use a window, I have a backup plan for our escape so we can make it.

"Our plan is riding on avoiding detection for as long as possible. The sooner we are detected the harder things will be, for one we could be easily cornered. It would be best if I take the lead on this. Though Thief and Night are by right the highest ranking here, my skills as a Codeless are more valuable here since this isn't an ordinary stealth mission.

"I know Dark even put Thief in charge due to the heavy reliance on stealth this mission holds. But this mission will more than likely end up with us being discovered at some point. And Night to be honest, though you work well solo and with certain people, your leadership skills are less than stellar during combat as you often get absorbed in it.

"I am also aware Angel is here, but you have the least experience out of all of us in such kind of mission. I don't think having you as leader for it would be a good idea. Though I'm not sure how well I can manage a group since I normally work solo personally. As such I think the best choice for our leader in this operation is myself or Thief."

In the end the group choose Arianna as the group's main decision maker and leader, with Thief being the commander in stealth situations. With such things covered and decided they quickly got to work and started their infiltration on the Marione base. With ease they managed to slip between the guards during they're rotations around the building and slip into the low vent leaving behind little trace of their presence.

Chapter 34

The group crawled through a dusty vent till they reached a vacant unused room that they could drop down into. Arianna moved to the other side as Thief delt with the screws that held the vent in place, the screws hit the floor with a slight tink noise. Arianna could have melted the vent cover with her flames, but she was still hesitant to use them, not to mention she knew it was best to conserve her strength and mana energy.

With the vent free Arianna turned it then brought it into the vent shaft and allowed the others to jump down first. When it was her turn, she slid out to only end up being caught in Night's arms. She looked at him for a moment but didn't say anything before she lowered her legs to the ground out of his grasp.

Ari moved over towards the door and stuck her head out and looked around. She didn't see anyone nearby which was of slight relief. "There's no one nearby. But I have no idea where the cell blocks are. Unless we can hack into a terminal and get a map, we'll be moving around blind." Arianna muttered as she crossed her arms.

None of them were hacker's and the Marione's firewall was equal to that of the Yano's. Arianna had some skill with such a thing, but the Marione's firewall was beyond her skill level. So there only choice really was to obtain a map from inside the building even though it wasn't ideal.

Without any warning the groups communication channel crackled. "A map you say… I think I can help you all out with such a thing and do you one better." A familiar voice purred. The others pulled out their weapons ready to fight. "Now, now. No need to be so on guard. I'm friendly, the dear codeless should be aware of this after I helped her last time."

"… Assistant Lisa… how did you gain access to this channel. This is not something easily hacked." Arianna replied. She pat Night's shoulder which was to tell him to lower his weapon. Though he didn't do so right away. "I also don't think this is a coincidence to be meeting like this again either."

"So precise, so calm. Quite well adapted to things. I have my ways into things, but I learned of your enviable arrival from an ally."

"I see they have quite loose lips."

"Well only to me really and they only told me about this. Nothing else between the two of you. Not like they'd have much luck hiding things from me in the first place." Lisa replied calmly. "Now let's get down to it. I can help you rescue your targets and avoid any trouble."

"What's the catch?"

"… Later. I will tell you later. It's not something to difficult so you do not need to worry."

The others looked over at Arianna. "I don't trust them." Thief stated first.

"I concur. They could only be a Marione if they are able to off such help."

"I don't really trust them either… but it's up to you Codeless."

"… They are sincere in giving us aid… I can tell you that. They did not lie when they said to have saved me not to long ago. I can't necessarily say I trust them… however their aid will be invaluable… and if they are talking about who I think it should be alright for now since no one else knows. I'm going to take their help; time is of the essence we need to take a gamble. Worry not if anything happens, I'll be sure to properly deal with it." Arianna sighed at which point they put their weapons away. "Alright Lisa, I'll trust you here. Tell us where they are and where to go."

"My pleasure dear Codeless. Your targets are on the fifth floor where the cell blocks are located. I'm unsure of their condition but I do know they are alive. I'll be able to lead you up to them and help you avoid any agents if you follow what I tell you. Treat me like your operator for this." Lisa told them.

"I understand, we'll follow your direction then."

Lisa informed them that were they were currently located was almost the furthest away from where they are as they could have possibly been in the building. As they begun to make there move the group was quiet and didn't even make a single sound as they made way through the halls. "You'll make your way to the stairs that will bring you closest to their location. It's the only one I'm able to unlock from where I am currently. Its farther than what you'd likely prefer but we have little choice." Lisa told them Arianna gave a slight nod.

Lisa watched them from the camera's and had sent a looping feed to all other sources. Lisa was clearly well adapted to technology to be able to do as such with ease. It made Arianna very pleased that she was on their side at this moment. With Lisa's help they had managed to avoid a fair number of Marione agents that were roaming through the halls.

To avoid those in the hallways that near they either hid around the corner or in a room till they passed. They've yet to be sighted thanks in part to this and Lisa's help. Things were going well till the stairs that is. As the group made their way up the stairwell there was little talk, due to the design of the stairwell, communications in and out were difficult thanks in part to the walls. They relatively blocked near all signals. So, they were all walking blind at this point with no chance of a warning from outside.

Arianna did have a map of the building displayed to her on the inside of her visor in the form of a mini map, so they weren't going to enter the wrong floor. As they climbed up Ari heard a sudden noise, as the door handle of the nearby stairway door turned. But the door didn't open and appeared to be locked. They were near the fourth-floor landing so close to the floor there were heading for. But it was the fourth landing where the door tried to move.

"The damn doors jammed again." Someone on the other side groaned. Arianna froze and had someone run into her. She grabbed the railing to stop her fall and looked up, she nearly went to sprint up the stairs at that moment.

"Again Seriously?! That's the third time this week. Sigh, move back."

"Dude what are you about to do?"

"Mmm, break it open of course. If the base commander gets mad about it not my fault. Should have had the door fixed right away. Besides we could just blame it on Alton, like everyone else does. Only use for a useless fighter."

"Alright… Speaking of him… how the hell is he even alive still."

"No idea. Move back, I'll break it down."

Arianna turned and motioned for them to quickly move back down the stairs, but she was further up than the others since she tried to race up above the fourth-floor landing. The others already managed to get out of sight, but she was in plain view. She clicked her tongue and grabbed the railing.

Arianna heard something colliding with the door. The door that begun to groan as the lock started to bend. It would only be moments before the door gave out. She heard another slam when she jumps over the railing, as the door was thrown open. They only saw a brief flash of black in the middle of the stair well but thought nothing of it. She fell down the middle of the stairwell for a moment before she grabbed the railing of the third-floor landing.

She pulled herself up and over the railing but had no real chance to take a breath as she heard descending footsteps. She pointed at the door and raced over it and pulled it open. They slid out of the stair well and let the door close behind them. But they weren't safe yet as the pair was heading towards them. Arianna looked around quickly and found a room. *No one's in there.*

Ari moved over to the door, and they hid inside just as the pair opened the door. Ari took a slight breath in as she listened to what happened in the hallway. When the footsteps were finally gone the slight tension, they had faded a little. "Sigh… I thought we were about to get caught for a moment there." Angel muttered as she placed a hand on her chest.

"Why are you all on the third floor?"

"We nearly got caught in the stairwell. Some agents broke in and entered between floors. We'll head back over there in a few moments." Arianna replied as she clenched and unclenched her hand to deal with the slight shock they got.

"No, if they broke open the door, you shouldn't use that stairwell. There is another one not much further I can access. Use that to make it the rest of the way up. I'll lock the doors again, hopefully such a thing won't happen again."

Night walked over the Arianna and placed his hand on her shoulder. "You alright that was quiet the sudden drop. Or is there something wrong with your hands?"

"No… no. I'll be fine. I just shocked them a little bit. They'll be all good soon." She replied though she knew that here hands were going to be covered in multiple bruises as she had broken some of the blood vessels in her hands from that move not just shocked the nerves as she said. Ari shook her head a little as she pushed herself up. "Lead the way, Lisa."

"Certainly."

This time they had no problems and managed to make it too the fifth floor where the cell block was located. "Alright Lisa, we made it to the fifth floor. Where are they?"

"The kid is in block D cell five, and Caden is at block B cell seven. Block B is where you currently are D is a little further. All the doors are electronically locked."

"Would you be able to unlock the door for us?"

"No, I don't have access to the door controls here. But I can deactivate the alarm systems, so it won't go off when you go in without proper clearance."

"Block B if it's holding Caden likely will have stronger security due to what Caden has and can do for them. Thief, I know electronic door locks like these aren't so much your things, but you work on Caden's? I'll deal with the other door. Angel you're with Thief, Night you're with me, the two of you are our lookouts as we deal with the doors."

As they walked a little bit away from Thief and Angel, Lisa spoke up. "They've started on the lock. But… though you're right the door for Caden is more challenging the one on the kids more dangerous. But you already knew that didn't you."

"… since they suspect him to have unnatural abilities for our world, they would be more cautious. Though I don't think they know what ability he has. The Marione are not ones that often take such people lightly." Arianna replied. "If I mess up while trying to unlock the door… I'll be okay." Though that what she said Night didn't really like Arianna's reasonings she said to Lisa.

The two eventually came up on the cell door. Arianna looked inside to see Sean inside lied out on the bed with a bandage wrapped around his head for his head injury. "Well, they at least treated his wound." Ari muttered as she moved back from the door. From the strap on her arm, she pulled out a long thin needle. She moved over to the panel and slid the needle in between the gap that was present between the panel and wall.

As she made the gap slightly bigger, she pulled a dagger from her boot and slid it under the panel and removed the face from the wall and had it hang down. Ari picked up the needle that had fallen to the ground and slid it back in place. She then begun to look inside the panel which was a mess of wires, and circuit boards.

Following wires and looking over the circuits she begun to cut a few wires with her dagger. After she cut a few wires there were only three left to cut but the wire she was working on she was stuck between two wires. Eventually she decided to just cut one. But she chose wrong, and it shocked her bad. Night hit her aside to remove her from the current, she let out a groan as she fell to the ground.

Chapter 35

"T-that hurt." Arianna groaned as she tried to push herself up, but her arms were weak, and she just fell back down and cursed. "Fuck."

Night looked over at Arianna, "are you alright?" He asked she could tell from his tone he was worried about her.

"Ye-yeah, I'm alright. Just give me a minute. Then I'll unlock the door." Arianna replied as she took a breath. *So, this is what she meant… it really does a number though. I guess I really don't-* Arianna's thought was cut off as she saw Night walk over to the panel. "Wait!" she gasped, she didn't want him to use a gun, though that would probably work in unlocking the door it would be very loud. But that wasn't what happened.

Arianna forced herself to her feet and grabbed Night's hand and blocked what happened from the camera. Water formed in Night's hand before he tossed it into the electric panel, it sparked and crackled before it created a large jolt of electricity and smoke raised from the panel. Arianna looked over at Night in surprise. Though she had a hunch there was something, she didn't know what it was as things were still quite unclear back than with everything.

Arianna touched the side of her helmet and turned off her com and voice modifier and reached over and turned his off as well. "Water magic… you can use water magic. No… right now isn't important… we'll talk about this later. Cause this isn't it right… you can't just use water magic can you."

"… yes."

"… I won't ask if you don't want to answer. For now, I'll act like it was me. My use of magic classed abilities is already known at this point. I thank you for the help but for now avoid using it again, anything could happen. You don't want to know what they would do to you if they knew about this in the worst case."

Arianna turned around and turned her voice modifier and coms back on. "What are the two of you doing. You don't have time to spare you know." Lisa huffed as soon as Arianna's coms came back online.

"Yes, yes. We're aware, I still had a charge in me. I shorted them out for a moment."

Arianna then walked into the room and over to Sean. Ari looked down at him she reached her hand out but paused, as she thought at what happened at the school. She closed her eyes that placed her hand on his shoulder. This time she didn't feel any rush of energy or the like but felt something inside her flicker in response. There was something oddly similar about it.

Ari quickly shook his shoulder to try to wake him, but he didn't wake up. She removed her hand and felt a slight chill. Sean was still alive she checked to be sure of that. "Hey get up! We're here to get you out. Stop fooling around." She huffed as her voice got a little more desperate.

"He's been like that since he arrived." Lisa told Arianna; she felt her muscles tense. "He apparently passed out on the way here and hasn't woken up since."

Ari stepped back a little as she held her hands close to her chest. *Oh, my gods, th-this is my fault. Cause I pushed him down the stairs. Even if it was to avoid the collapsing ceiling… I could have pulled him with me but… damn it.* Arianna thought as she clenched her fist. Night stood behind her and placed his hands on her shoulders. He likely knew what she was thinking, and shock is head.

"You didn't do anything wrong. You only tried to save him. He knows that too. Don't blame yourself for it."

"But… I didn't mean for him to end up unconscious from my actions. Even if you try to justify it for that it's for what he's done to me for the last half year or so… it's too far… too much for what he ever did. There's nothing Angel could even do for him right now. We need a hospital doctor or a certified medical one at the very least."

Arianna clenched her fist tight to the point her knuckles were white. As she looked down as Sean, she saw something. More something flashed in her vision, and who was in front of her wasn't Sean anymore but someone else. Her blood ran cold at the sight, as her breathing hitched for a moment.

Night looked down surprised at Arianna's sudden condition. He grabbed a hold of her shoulders and stopped her from falling. After a few moments she lightly touched his hand. "I'm okay now." She muttered but her voice was a little weak, but it wasn't because she was tired.

"R-… Night…" Arianna spoke again off coms. "If… if something like this happened to you because of me. W-would you hate me…" she paused as she looked at the white floor. "Would you hate me if I couldn't kill you… but rather choose another method after you got captured by an enemy."

"That's a rather odd question. What brought this on?" He asked as he looked down at her. But Arianna didn't look up at him in response her hand still held his and trembled slightly. "Something like that would never happen."

"P-please… Night… just please give me an answer."

"… At first… I might be mad, after some time I might come to understand like before."

"… even if your feelings… emotions... the like, fade or disappear…"

"A- Codeless what's gotten you so shaken up to ask such questions all of a sudden?"

"I-it's nothing… probably just my imagination."

"Sigh… even then yes. I might be mad or angry. If you give me an honest answer, I could never hate you."

Arianna looked down at the ground. When she closed her eyes, she could still picture it, bodies around her as if she left a trail of death in her wake. Then before her, knelt a man with clouded over eyes that were empty. Somehow, she knew what happened to that man was her fault, and what echoed as one word: [Monster].

Arianna even at her weakest moments after she became a Mercenary had become generally numb to the hate, and death of others. But when it was people, she was close with, she was extremely weak to then as she had a tendency at the time to rely on them emotionally. But that felt so vivid, the voices and the man felt so familiar it shook her to her already unstable core, as unlike how she occasionally would act had emotions.

Ari closed her eyes again to closed off and take control of her emotions again despite her weak grasp on it and the skill. "Night could you carry Sean for me. We are going to meet with the other two." She said as she removed his hands from her shoulders and left the room.

260

"Of course, I'll follow you in a moment." Night replied and Ari gave him a slight nod as she went in the hall and leaned against the wall.

Ever since a few nights ago more and more strange things had begun to happen to Arianna. But she had no explanation for it. She didn't know if she should be afraid or excited about it but there was one thing she could agree with. She felt that she had begun to become more like a monster.

Ari shook her head a little to get rid of the images and thoughts. She was sure her friends, the ones that she's been with since they were kids would be on her side. Even without her telling them her past, even when she tried to avoid them, they eventually became friends and she responded to them in kind with her inner most feelings and trust. She had yet come to realize how desperately she relied on and held to them for her own sanity and peace of mind. To her they had long become the family she had lost, the people she could truly rely on and trust.

Night walked out of the room carrying Sean on his back. Arianna had her eyes closed lost and thoughts, Night lightly touched her shoulder and she glance over at him. *Hmmm… knows not the time to wallow.* She thought as she forced herself to stand properly. "Let's go meet with the other two they should be done at this point. Then we'll see what to do next." Ari stated as she begun to walk back to where they left Thief and Angel earlier.

Once they arrive, they find Thief and Angel inside the cell. Angel was treating Caden's extensive number of wounds they had gotten. It was unclear if he got them from when he was captured or afterwards, but they were extensive. "Do you think he will be able to walk on his own?" Ari asked as she crossed her arms and leaned against the door frame.

"Mmmm, probably not by himself. Thief will be able to help him walk though." Angel replied quickly, with also offering up Thief as the one to help him as well. Ari nodded her head in reply.

"We have what we came her for so let's go there is no reason for us to stay longer other than to get caught."

"Before you leave there is one thing, I want you to do." Lisa spoke in a calm voice. "As payment for my help of course. I would like for you all to come and meet me."

"What? Are you crazy! As Codeless said the longer we stay will these dead weights the more likely it is that we'll get caught." Thief growled as she lifted Caden up. She probably wanted to glare at Lisa but of course that wasn't possible.

"Oh, is that what you all think?" Lisa asked her tone was playful, it was clear though this was just a game to her. Night and Angel nodded in reply, but Ari didn't respond as she didn't like Lisa's tone. "Really now? Oh, my I guess I should just tell the others about the two useful specimens escape from their cells with the help of Yano agents of course. They will love it and I'd get a promotion."

"WHAT?! Total bullshit! You'd take us this far just to back stab us!" Angel growled, she slammed her hand into the wall out of anger and made an indent.

Arianna wasn't surprised she thought this might be the case, she was ready for such a possibility of being backstabbed after the rescue. The problem was the condition of those they saved, at this point they were just dead weights for them. Which would make a sudden escape that they would have to do if they went against Lisa now utterly impossible.

Lisa knew this to, it was a battle of wits, planning and knowledge; and Lisa had it all from the start. She knew that the two were in such bad states that the group would be unable to escape if they were suddenly caught and was aware of their desperation to get them out due to their value overall. Though she also knew that she was more than likely going to get hit from this once they meet but that mattered very little to her.

"… you planned this from the very start. You acted with such certainty… as if you can see the future. You knew everything would lead here. I have no idea why though. Why go through such trouble."

"Now, now. No need to ask such question now. It's a simple decision, isn't it? If you don't want to be caught now all you have to do is come and meet me. I'm not asking you for much. Besides codeless you own me."

Arianna sighed this was no point for her to get mad. They had no real feasible option before them as all other lead to certain death. "Fine… where are you?"

"fourth-floor, the one just below you I'll guide you."

"A- Codeless! What the hell are you doing!"

"Making an executive decision, so shut your trap." Arianna growled this was the first time she snapped in such away at them. She rarely snapped but that just hit it home for them how bad this situation was for them. "Do you need all of us… or do you just want me, Lisa?"

"Well, your allies are more than welcome to come along. But in truth you are the only one I want Codeless, after all you are someone, I've been waiting years for. So, as long as you come to meet me, I'll be more than please."

"Alright I'll be down soon." Arianna replied. "You three take them out of here. I'll meet with Lisa by myself."

"Are you fucking crazy! Meeting someone from the Marione alone in their own base! Its suicide!" Night growled as he glared at Ari. She could understand his reason for it, but Ari had her own reason for it as well.

"Getting them out is the most important thing. They only want me. I'm a Codeless not a Yano. Even though I'm trespassing on their grounds without authorization, I could make it out of here alive just because of that currently. But the chance of any of you doing that is very little.

"Lisa's goal is not our death, rather something else. Even once they find out about the escape, I'm certain that Lisa doesn't plan to let me just die. As a codeless I can act as if I was here prior at Lisa or someone else behest.

"You guys don't have that option. The Yano at the end of the day is they're enemy, they will not let you go if they caught you. Please understand I'm doing what's best for all of us."

"We are not allowing you to go alone."

"Don't follow me and get out of here." Arianna growled as she turned away. "That is all I ask... so leave." She muttered as she began to walk off. But despite her best wishes for them and for the best outcome for their current situation, they still decided to follow her to where Lisa waited.

Chapter 36

Arianna walked into the room that Lisa lead her too and could see three figures in the darkness of the room. She didn't sense any form of hostility towards her from them so, she remained relaxed. However, that wasn't the same for those that followed her here despite her order.

Night pulled her back behind him, and the others pulled out their weapons to fight. Arianna placed her hand on Night's arm, "it's fine. They are not hostile towards us, you guys who mind you should be fleeing, can relax."

"You gotta be crazy to think I'm going to relax. This is clearly a trap." Angel growled as they stepped forward. "How could you even be so relax meeting any Marione in the first place. After everything they done! I've heard they are the reason you're a codeless in the first place and from a young age at that. They killed your family did they not. How could you be calm!"

Arianna looked at Angel, she expected this kind of reaction. The Yano and the Marione have real bad blood between the two. Thief and Night would likely be more outwardly hostile towards the three unknown if Arianna hadn't stopped them personally. After all they've known one another for a very long time, they knew not to go against Arianna at this point.

The three figures then begun to move closer to as they had noticed their arrival, so they likely planned to talk. However, this lone movement Angel didn't like, and they got ready to attack. The three didn't even pause for a moment at the sight of Angel's hostility which made it even worse.

When the three figures didn't stop and were only a few meters away Angel jumped forward to try and attack them. Arianna however expected this and acted quickly, she grabbed Angel's arm and pulled them back which slowed their movement. Then she kicked their feet out under them to tripped them. With Angel body essentially at her mercy Arianna slammed Angel down to the ground.

Arianna motion caused Angel let out a gasp and drop their weapon, she them place her foot on their back and pulled their arm behind them in an awkward position pinning them to the ground. At first Angel tried to squirm out from under Arianna but the more they did the harder Ari pulled there arm back to the point it almost popped out of the socket. "W-wh-why?" Angel asked it was clear they were in tears or close to it. "They are Marione. Why are you stopping me?"

"I told you before to stand down, but you didn't listen." Arianna replied with a sharp tone. "I don't care about grudges between organizations. An though you are correct that it was the Marione that had a hand in death of my familial relations, I have no desire to kill every Marione that appears before me.

"I want the death of one man, to watch the light leave their eyes. I will use any means necessary and take care of anyone that gets in the way of it. Do you understand now... I don't care who they work for if I can use them for my overall goal I will. So, unless you wish to die here and know I suggest you shut up." Ari growled she was purposely being harsh to get the point across. She needed to make it clear to them that she was not one to cross no matter what state she was in.

Arianna didn't even have to look back at the other two to know how they felt from this. Night would have been annoyed, similar to Arianna he didn't really care about killing off all the Marione or fighting them at any chance he got, though he was more likely than Ari to get into a fight with them at this point in time.

Thief had a different stand than them. She would have been mad and displeased with Arianna, she wanted to jump into a fight like Angel but didn't since she wouldn't only be against Arianna but Night and the Marione agents before them. As such though not happy about it she decided to do nothing rather than to pick a fight.

The clap of a pair of hands could be heard in front of them. Arianna looked up as one of the three figures walked forward. "I'm happy that you could make it over here Codeless it's been a bit since we last saw one another in person. But I see your teammates came along with you as well." A familiar voice spoke, it was Lisa. "I didn't think you had it in you to be so harsh. Though from what I've heard your often cold and act cool headed." She added, the women the stood before them was tall with long black hair and eyes. Arianna remembered them from the incident at the lab where she first had a chance to meet Lisa.

"We last saw one another a few days ago it wasn't that long. But what did you think I would allow someone following my orders to go against me? I maybe a codeless but I know when to put others in their place." Arianna replied as she let go of Angel's wrist and shrugged her shoulders. "After all it's the reason you didn't let you friends out as you thought I could handle it."

"Hahah. Very perceptive. I'm very happy you came to meet with me as I requested."

"Not like I have much of a choice in the first place."

Lisa started to laugh out as her head tilted back. She looked younger than they acted, but Ari had already come to notice that like her, Lisa hid her real appearance with some teach. Lisa waved her hand to her two allies that stood behind her, "let me introduce my friends here."

"This one here is Alton Faciana, he is from a long line of crafters, that lived in Antarctica. The Marione killed his family a few years ago and kidnapped him in hopes of having him create knew teach for them. He hasn't passed training as others are against him so he's yet to get his own codename." Lisa explained as she pointed over to the younger man next to her with jet black hair though he wore something over his eyes to hide the colour. "This is Aether, you may have heard of them before."

"Aether… they are in the top 50 rankings." Angel muttered as they pushed themselves up from the ground. Arianna looked over at them to look at their black fox-like mask that had false long silvery-blue hair attached to it. She didn't say anything and knew that Aether looked over at her as well, maybe curious of what she was about to do, but she just looked away.

"I don't think you forcibly called me here to have a nice little chat and introduce me to your friends. So, what is it that you want from me?" Arianna asked, she was quick to the punch as she didn't want to waste any time since the others decided to follow her here.

"Now, now, there are a number of things I need to talk about with you. Wouldn't you like to have more information as well?"

"Sigh… alright I get it. Speak then."

"But of course."

"You of the Yano have a fair amount of information on the Marione due to the rivalry between the two. They've likely forgotten its rooted in an old link between the head of the clans that's escalated to this.

"You may have heard about Elixir, first one might think of the one known as the Elixir of life. This one's a little different, rather it's the elixir of hidden strength. The Yano in more recent years started to work on it. Marione went in another direction to create beings, control beings, and ensure abilities persist.

"Recently it had become much worse. Anthelm has tripled the efforts and will not allow failure, he also desires elixir and more power. They've always been bad… but it's gotten worse so much worse. It's what had led to a number of deaths even… like a kind of madness."

"Anthelm... I recognize that name... yes. That's the name of the Marione's leader... a name from what I understand is passed down." Arianna muttered but she held her tongue. *But reports and records of the Marione isn't the only place I've heard this name... it's also appeared in legends passed down. One of the few my father managed to impart onto me.*

"Yes, you are correct Anthelm is the name of Marione's leader. They are extremely dangerous in a number of ways." Lisa replied as she looked away. But the looked in her eyes was odd; it was something that Ari caught.

"Anthelm is the reason behind the creation of the Chimera's... but you're the one that created them correct. But that just one in a number of experiments he's had commissioned correct."

"Yes, and not only experiments... but most of what Anthelm has a direct connection two... is not pleasant. Even on originally normal levels for this group, beings are not treated like anything but a tool for him to use."

"And many follow with it yes? That one... taking from so many. The innate abilities that rest in most twilights, that was such. You're lucky I haven't done something for that one alone."

"You're right... there are many experiments that Anthelm promotes around that which does not originally exist in this world. But... there's more to it than that. As I said he sees people as no more than tools. He desires people under him that are nothing more than a tool with no will a puppet, and more." Lisa trailed off.

Arianna knew about the clan that lead the Marione, which included one secret, that a very limited set of people knew about. Lisa didn't lie when she said that abilities classed as supernatural didn't originally exist on the world of Ashise. But there was a secret to it as well. "There's something else isn't there... they others can hear it, it's fine. Say it."

"Are you certain… it is a secret that been hidden for a reason."

"Yes, it's fine. Something tells me such will not be the case in the future anyways."

"I'm aware that Codeless knows this but it's unlikely anyone else but Aether would be aware of it. The abilities that begun to appear more when elixir and other experiments like it begun. But they are not the only abilities that exist on this world. Some are dormmate but some are not. I won't go into it as it's a long story. But Anthelm is one with such an ability." Lisa begun she appeared hesitant to talk about this, but it made sense. This was something that has been a secret for a very long time.

"Anthelm has the capability to revive the dead to a certain extent. Not like they are undead but… something else. There is a catch to it though, the dead can only be revied in a certain time frame, and not all can be revived. Each time this is done the more the soul and mind of the revived breaks as well. Those he can revive are normally under his complete control with some exceptions." She explained Ari clenched her fist, she was not aware of Anthelm's capability to revive the dead.

"Anthelm will often kill and revive people to use… and surrounds himself with such people and people he can control. But he also wants to have useful people by his side. The ability isn't perfect but it's still extremely dangerous… one that defies natural law even. How he got such an ability is unclear.

"Not everyone in the Marione is one that has been revived by Anthelm. There is a limit in range and such so the number of those alive still out number Anthelm's undead. For note all I work with like, Aether, and Alton have not been touched by Anthelm. It is likely to be so unless something drastic happens. But I'm sure you know Codeless this isn't Anthelm's only ability." Lisa explained.

"Yes, I'm aware. I expected as much even. An ability like mind control he might have. But that isn't all. You said all you work with are not undead, those I'm sure are those people and you are the one that has given them direction so far. But there is one thing I want to know. What about you? You didn't include yourself."

"Haha… you really are just as sharp… no. Even more than… sigh. Your correct, I'm not like them… but I'm also not like the others. Lisa is a fake name as I didn't give Anthelm the name to call it. This body has died before, and Anthelm forced it to return to life… but well."

"Something happened unexplained. It's why you hid your appearance yes… please show me. It's part of why you called me yes."

"Are you sure you want to know." Lisa looked at Arianna her eyes filled with worry and compassion.

"Yes… I'm no longer going to run… besides, I already have a feeling at this point. I want confirmation. Then an explanation."

"Alright."

Lisa closed her eyes and removed the ring she wore. Her current appearance flickered for a moment before it completely disappeared. The women in front of them now looked very different though they had several scars all over some on the neck and even her face, but it was clear she was a foreign beauty. They appeared a little older as well, they had white, blonde hair, amber eyes, and slightly tanned complexation.

Arianna turned her head the moment she saw them and closed her eyes, but she wasn't the first one to speak up. Caden who at some point regained consciousness looked at the women in front of him in shock. "S-S-Slaine?! H-how is this… how! That fire… your children… my friend… everything. How?!" Caden asked his voice nearly breaking. Slaine[?] just looked over at him with sad eyes.

Chapter 37

Arianna couldn't look at Slaine[?] for a while, but she saw them and the moment she did see them she didn't want to believe it at the time. But when her eyes landed on the true appearance of Slaine[?], she felt it, her instincts told her that what was before her was not of human or mortal descent.

"I am not Slaine Farin Rotusole. That women died a very long time ago, but this is the body of that women who died." Slaine[?] stated she glanced over at Arianna who had yet to look back. "… as you believe. That women had died with the rest of the Rotusole family in that fire many years ago. But Anthelm got a hand on this body. He tried to revive this woman, but her soul had already passed so only fragments remained… but something needed to be inside on the body as fragments can't control a body. His revival power grabbed I who was close by, a spirit.

"Who I once was, fused with the fragments and memories of this body, given things never before forced to live. Anthelm was cruel he wished for the elixir that Sliane and the other had been working on, but we wouldn't give it to him. He killed the other many times, but he couldn't control me due to what I once was.

"But I also couldn't die, I'm unable to die as Anthelm will not allow me for the use this body's memories have for him. As such I'm trapped in this body. Forced to watch Anthelm deeds and what he did to others. I eventually decided to sow seeds for the future."

Arianna eventually opened her eyes and looked up over at Sliane[?]. "So, what you're saying is. Anthelm attempted to revive the women Sliane due to elixir but for some reason Sliane's soul departed from the world very quickly and left only fragments. But the body wasn't past the point, so he was able to use his ability which grabbed you an original will-less spirit that had become forcibly fused with the fragments and memories of the body." Arianna sighed as she looked up. "But even like this, the body has useful skills Anthelm wants. So, he's kept the body alive which has trapped you in this form unable to escape as you've been fused. You are not human, nor undead, you can't even be considered mortal either."

"Correct. With no real hope for escape at the time I decided to try and kill Anthelm to give me a means of escape. He has no idea of such plans or way to control me as well, so it was fine. I just followed mainly what he wanted, and I generally was given free rein. I did slow things down, but things would end eventually, there was no real way to stop it from happening."

Angel put her hand up. "Hold on I'm a little lost here. Can you explain more. How could this Anthelm person revive the dead. You even said it wasn't a skill due to this elixir thing. How is such a thing even possible. I know we have advanced tech down below, artifacts, elem and the like but reviving the dead isn't possible. So, stop speaking bullshit." Angel growled as her voice got harsher at the end.

"No… actually… it's very possible, just not for mortals normally. Have you heard of the myths and legends from the Eternial's?" Arianna replied as she shifted in place. She crossed her arms; it's something that was not easy to explain back then. Not evening going into elem and artifacts, no one really displayed supernatural or magical ability out in the open after all.

"Yes, I'm aware of them. It is the only religion that actually has temples down below."

"Well… though not exactly word for word or truly accurate partially due to time and just well religion itself spinning it to fit their narrative. Um, well some of them… they… hold water… er fact. Ah, they hold some truth in them. After a long time, it's hard to say how much of it but well." Arianna tripped over her words a little at the end not too sure how to say it. "There are very few that have abilities like this now they are unlike those that are classed as supernatural skills and like. Honestly its almost non-existent at this point even, but they exist. But they all surpass what humans and descendants of them would be capable of."

"But Codeless how could you even believe such a thing without seeing it. I know about those other things, but they've only begun to appear recently. If what you're stating such things have been around longer, how has no one learned of it. Our world is a world of science after all."

"Yes, you are right. Ashise our world is a world of science, the supernatural and magic did not exist here originally." Arianna agreed as she shifted. "But our world isn't a closed system. The reason I can believe such a thing is because… well, I also have abilities.

"The reason people are unaware this fact is partially likely because of the Yano and the Marione by the way. There is a reason they are so powerful and always clashing. After all information is power, so till the right moment this fact is wished to remain hidden." She sighed as she uncrossed her arms. "Now let's continue."

"Right… well really I want to ask you a few things. To start would it be possible for you to remove your helmet?"

"My helmet… you should be aware I probably also hide myself as well just like you do. So why? I'm not going to remove my disguise like you. Unlike you I have more to lose by doing so now."

"It's fine, your helmet is enough. I may have this form, but I still have my prior skills and that which this body had."

"You're not seriously thinking of removing your helmet, are you?!" Angel gasped but Arianna just ignored them.

Arianna stood in thought for a moment. She didn't really want to remove her helmet but for some reason her instincts told her the opposite. If she removed her helmet there was much for her to gain.

Ari then gave a slight nod as she reached up and pushed the buttons on the side which opened it. That then allowed her to remove the helmet cleanly.

Her appearance was similar to the one she had used when she went out on a day of Lartis. Arianna held the helmet in her hand as she moved her hair back, her hair was a slight mess from the helmet. She looked slightly down with half closed eyes as she reached into her helmet and placed two earpieces around her ears which formed the VHDS.

Ari looked up at Slaine[?] to see her with slightly glossy but also relieved eyes. "It's real." Slaine[?] muttered as she slightly covered her mouth. She shook her head quickly to quickly bring herself back. "Thank you… I now know you are indeed the one I have been waiting for."

"But why were you waiting for me? Like I had a feeling it was something like this as you became fixated with me ever since we first met but why."

"Because you are the head. The only one capable of preforming the thing I wish."

"… I see."

"With that I have some requests for you. First would you take Alton and Aether with you out of the Marione. Alton is in danger often here not to mention he doesn't wish to be here, and Aether's in a similar situation though stronger they are in danger as well. I've been keeping them safe but soon that will no longer possible. So, I'd like you to take them out of here and protect them."

"You want me a codeless to protect them? Not the Yano?"

"Yes, you can take them to the Yano if you wish but I want you to protect them outside. You're the only one I can trust for such a task. It's not a hasty decision nor a rash one. I know what you can do... I know you."

"If you give me the chance to leave this place, I'll follow you. I defiantly can help you out to so please." Alton stated. He looked at Arianna with shining eyes. She looked away slightly as she felt a little guilty.

She looked to the side to see that Caden had been preventing Angel from being able to speak, she couldn't guess how long but it made sense why they hadn't said anything for a while. After Night and Thief knew better than to speak unless it was important, or they really wanted clarification. "Ah fine... but I'll only take them with us if they want to. We don't need dead weight with and unwilling charge." Arianna replied she said this, and she felt Aether didn't want to go.

"I'll be staying back." Aether confirmed what Ari had thought.

"What? Not Aether you can't I won't be able to protect you afterwards and you barely broke away last time. If you go with her, she'll be able to help you." Slaine[?] told him, she was somewhat like a worried parent. Arianna had no idea what it was that the two meant, but she knew it was something of significance. However, she had no plans to force someone to come with them, it was something she didn't care to do.

"They'll need someone to guide them out. The group also needs a leader with you gone. It will be fine." Aether replied to Slaine⁽ʔ⁾. She looked up at her and glance down.

"I see, I can't do anything if your so adamant." She paused before she grabbed his hand, "… help you. After everything… abilities…! Not just that… I'm sure you noticed it. You'll understand one day." Ari couldn't hear everything that Slaine⁽ʔ⁾ had told Aether only bits and pieces. She then turned around and walked over to Ari.

Slaine⁽ʔ⁾ then pulled some items out and placed them into Arianna's hand. An old book, a unique pair of earrings one that had a crystal that hung on the end of one of the strands, an account of money, and the last item was a card.

Ari looked at the card in surprise, in her eyes one might have thought it was something from some kind of card game but that wasn't it. "What is it you're holding? I can see an outline of something but… it's just clear." Alton blurted out. Arianna felt shivers in realization.

How? How is this…? She thought as she felt a slight squeeze on her arm from Slaine⁽ʔ⁾ it was a silent gesture as in this is the best I can do. This brought Arianna away from her thoughts and she quickly put the items away as Slaine⁽ʔ⁾ walked back near Aether. "I understand… thank you for the payment… now what is the last thing you want from me… after all that's the reason for these as payment."

Slaine(?) looked up at Arianna in the eyes with clear eyes. "This is my last request for you Codeless. A request of which you are the only one capable of doing for me now." She sighed as she placed her hand on her chest. Alton looked away, and Aether though didn't change it was clear they also knew what she was about to ask from Arianna.

"You will know where. You will be able to go through. You are the only one… because of who you are. You can free me." Slaine(?) stated. "I want you to kill me."

Chapter 38

The request was a surprise. Arianna clenched her fist looked down at the ground, her hands trembled slightly, it wasn't out of fear or anger it was hard to describe but the closest might have been sadness. Caden looked at Arianna eyes filled with both sadness and sympathy.

Her eyes shook a little, but she tried to hide the emotions she felt at the moment. "… I know it's a cruel request for me to ask from you. But I have no choice. As side from you aside from this moment I will not get another chance to be free for many years. I can't handle it anymore… sooner or later I might give Anthelm what he wants. You're our only hope… so please."

Arianna closed her eyes to calm herself and cool her emotions to no longer let them show. After a few moments with a sigh Ari lifted her head and opened her eyes, which were clear. "Alright… I'll grant your last request with the payment that I've received from you." She stated as she looked at Slaine(?). Ari's eyes begun to emit a slight red glow and she was able to see the core that rested inside the body which Anthelm had created.

The core that Ari could see was right next to where the heart should have been in the body, but only the core was inside them. Ari then pulled a sword out from her beck as she begun to walk towards them. "At the very least I must say this before the end moments. Thank you for everything. I'll be sure to do as you asked from me." Ari stated and Slaine(?) nodded in reply.

"I know were once a spirit, but you don't happen to have a name, do you?"

"Spirits have no wills. We are more collections of one of the two true energies. Collections of the true energy of Order. We will follow and fulfil the request of the ones that can wield order's energy. Without will or real thought we also do not have names normally. It is rare when beings of energy like I once was get a name, a will or form. We are like orbs of light would be the best explanation. But this experience is something special… I'll be by your side and watch over you I promise."

"… If that's the case its only right to have a name since you have your own will. It will be something to help keep you grounded similar to that of a true name. For all you have done for me and those trapped in the darkness that consumes the Marione giving them a point of light and hope to follow.

"You have been the light for such people to give them new hope and a chance to bring forth change for them and their group. You did what was not just best for yourself but also them. I don't know how you have helped Alton or Aether, but I know it's significant as I've never seen such people trapped in the Marione like this have such looks or even reasoning.

"You have become a bacon of light for many and will continue to be such for them as they strive for what you put forth. No matter what is to come I do not wish for that light to dim. As such I'll give you the name Lumina to be a reminder of that light you have brought to the people here even during your relatively short time here." Arianna spoke her voice was strong and held a certain weight to them.

"Lumina… my names Lumina." Lumina muttered with a slight smile. Though unseen by most there Arianna saw it as a light attached itself to them. Arianna stood in front of Lumina with her blade drawn she took a slight breath and raised the blade above her head, but her arm begun to tremble slightly. Lumina touched Ari's shoulder. "It's okay. This body has gone long past its time. I'm more than ready to return as well. You are giving us our rightful peace."

Arianna looked at Lumina the fused spirit who had taken root in the body of Slaine Rotusole and had become known as Lisa. She thought it was odd how fate twisted itself to bring such occurrences. She couldn't help but be curious yet also fearful of what was to come.

With her blade raised above her, will steeled and nerves calmed icy blue flames had begun to wrap itself around it. The flames flickered and moved with life the blue colour to it almost felt like it could chill one to the bone yet also burn. With her free hand Arianna grabbed Lumina's shoulder and turned the blade in her hand. Then in a swift movement the blade of flames moved downwards and pierced into Lumina's chest.

As the blade pierced her chest some kind of resistance appeared that tried to stop Ari's blade. The force of the resistance caused large gust like pressure waves that knocked those weaker or unprepared back. The ground beneath the two begun to show odd patterns and symbols as if to scare them off to show that it was something powerful and not easily broken. The only other person that remained in place was Aether as she stood near the two and watched though neither noticed.

Despite the blade that slowly went deeper into Lumina's chest there was no blood that fell to the ground. The further the blade went in however the more sparks, gusts, and force that appeared and tried to act/attack Ari to protect itself from her. The space was not proportionate to Lumina's body as Arianna's blade had almost completed entered her chest.

But eventually the tip of Ari's sword managed to touch the sphere inside Lumina. The sphere that granted both life and energy to the already dead body, but also trapped and held the soul/Lumina's spirit to the body. The moment the sword touched was when the strongest attack occurred against them. It was strong and painful as it was Arianna didn't move back.

Lumina as if aware that this was the end as it couldn't stop Arianna. Lumina leaned forward towards Ari's ear and whispered something. Tears begun to form in Arianna's eyes but even then, she forced her sword forward and into the sphere pricing it right through. There was the sound that rang similar to that of when glass shattered, and Arianna's sword then pierced out the other side of Lumina's chest.

Arianna could see the energy the sphere orb provided disappear and disperse from the body. At that point Ari turned her head away and closed her eyes as a single set of tears ran down her face as the body of Slaine turned to ash in her hand. Then in the pile of ash that formed before her the shattered fragments of the orb fell on top of them.

Arianna could feel a pair of eyes on her. She turned her head in the direction and opened her eyes to look at them to see it was Aether who hadn't really moved. Ari felt flustered from Aether's gaze and quickly wiped away her tears and put her helmet on that she attached to her belt. At the time she didn't realize Aether's slight outstretched hand as she was more flustered that he saw her tears something she didn't want people to see especially those she knew.

The flames of her blade had long gone out since the moment it priced the orb, so she put it away and turned around. "You'll be able to guide us out of here right." Arianna asked as she closed her helmet.

"Yeah... it's not my strong suit as I don't normally handle this but as long as you get out before it's too late, I should be able to manage." Aether replied dryly. Though even for him it was odd, as if a little disappointed. Arianna nodded her head as she crossed her arms.

"We probably don't have much time then. This took up a fair amount of time after all." Ari replied as she walked over to the others. "Get to your feet you guys we need to move now." They slowly got to their feet; Night passed Sean to Thief as Caden leaned against Night in tandem. Arianna glanced over at Aether for a moment before she quickly turned back. "Let's go." She sighed as she turned on her coms and left the room.

The group ran down the halls and it wasn't long till an alarm began to sound and Marione agents begun to scramble into action. Arianna couldn't help but inwardly click her tongue, she feared this might happen which was why she told the others to leave without her but now they were faced with this.

Aether didn't lie when they told her that they weren't great at the operator type job which involve directing them away from trouble. He did manage to help them avoid a few groups but eventually they got spotted. At that point it became a flurried race to try and get away as long possible, but it was only a matter of time till it caught up to them.

They raced down corridor after corridor, Aether had pretty much lost them at this point and gave them no really directions, so they had no idea where the nearest unlocked room or stairwell was. Till eventually they got cornered at a windowed T-intersection with groups of Marione agents on all sides. Arianna looked around franticly at the hopeless situation. "Combat positions shoot to kill. Try to create an opening for us." Arianna ordered; they were cornered she knew this but there was nothing they could really do.

Arianna didn't get the chance to inform, nor did she really think to in the moment to inform them that she wouldn't last much longer if she needed to do something crazy. With one ruthless crazy moment after the next with little chance to rest she was really pushing herself. She could already taste blood in the back of her throat. She was given no chance to heal her body properly or restore her energy. At this point her movements had become a little sluggish and slow.

Arianna realised there was no way they could break through as more and more agents made their way to their location. She glanced behind them at the window and make a split-second decision. "Thief and the two you start breaking the window." Arianna suddenly ordered as she reloaded her pistol.

"What?"

"Break the damn window open!" Arianna snapped as she fired and two Marione agents dropped. Since Thief was the least combat oriented out of the three it made sense to have her placed on the job to break it open similar for her thoughts on sending Alton and Caden to do that job as well.

Arianna would slash and gun down agent after agent and it was getting harder for her with each moment that passed. "Look out!" Angel exclaimed as she yelled to Arianna. She spun and blocked the blade and shot them down. But she heard a gunshot and turned to see Angel fall to the ground as they took a bullet to the chest.

Arianna swept her hand and created a wall of fire blocking the hall Angel guarded. Alton dragged her back as she and Night continued to fight. The window was thick glass and after a very long time it finally begun to crack and brake but Arianna was barely holding back her line. She begun to get grazed and cut a lot more at this point. She was breathing heavy as she sensed something bad was about to happen to herself, she couldn't move to block or dodge.

Arianna got pushed aside to the ground as Caden was deeply slashed across the chest severing a major artery. She cursed as she created flames walls to block the remaining walls, she pulled Caden back and was aware he wasn't going to survive, and Angel was gravely injured. Caden squeezed her hand to tell her it was okay before his body went limp. Arianna stood up as she let go of his hand. She looked at the others, they weren't in good shape at this rate they were going to die.

Chapter 39

Arianna couldn't let this go on any longer. But the window wasn't open, and hallways which were blocked by numerous Marione agents so currently they had no escape. Ari decided, in order to get the other's out she will use every last bit of power she had, just to give them that chance of escape.

Determined she stabbed her sword into the ground. "Night step back now." She ordered as flames formed and gathered at her fingertips. "Even if this hole situation is because you idiots don't listen or trust me enough. I will not let this end here." Arianna said as she stepped away from Caden's body.

"These idiots that care to much for a worthless life such as mine. So, this will be repayment for their dumb act. I will give them a chance of escape." She added as she swept her hand in front of her. She created three blazing walls of white, blue flames that blocked the hallways and the Marione agents off. The heat near the walls was stifling to others. *Even at the cost of my own life.*

Ari turned and looked at the window with sharp eyes. The small number of cracks that was in it proved how strong the glass was. She let out a sigh as she walked over and stood before it before she raised her gun. She started to gather some of her magic energy into her gun as she begun to power it with her ability.

When the energy gathered and wrapped itself around the gun and bullets. She fired at the window seven times which caused it to shatter and create and opening but there were still large pieces of glass still around the small hole she just created.

Her fist begun to be coated with flames and she slammed her fist against it. The blue and white flames spread out and whatever part of the glass didn't break by her fist melted. At this point there was a giant hole in the window large enough to walk out of which was what they needed since they had to drag/carry out immobile people.

Arianna closed her eyes. *I can't leave them here or Anthelm will do to them what they did to Lumina. We can't jump either with too many injured... I have no choice. But to do this now.* Ari thought. She was going to perform a summoning part of the ability granted by her father's blood line.

There were a few different ways summoning's were done at the time, with a unique card called a mythic card that acts as a medium or a ritual, a direct link or partner summon which was common now, and a few others. However, but there was one way it could be done, one that was more dangerous but faster than the others and could break many of the restrictions that others held on the summoner and/or summoned.

"Make sure nothing breaks through or interrupts me." Ari stated as she stood at the edge of the window. She looked before her at the pitch-black night she closed her eyes and took a breath. This very well could kill her but that wasn't about to stop her. Arianna raised her hand as magic began to form and create a magic circle.

"The Divide between worlds that bends to my will. I seek to part the vail and create a passageway for thy who is bound to my soul. With flames and ice in my hand, and elements that flow to my will, and time that I command, the space between worlds that I desire to have bend to my will for my blood wills and avails.

Granted the name –, by my fore father, and the one that hold the ancient blood title of Tamer from the days of old in this world. Few can stand against me as all follow my command, I the one that can call forth any manner of being as I see fit. No world can bind me as I break these chains that did. I the parter of the vail, and summoner and tamer of beings. Allow it so I can open forth the vail before me at my will!" Arianna spoke in the long forgotten ancient language, as she slashed open her palm.

The winds begun to shift, and you could feel the charge in the air. The look of the sky even changed. The very sight of Arianna standing before then as the sky begun to crackle with purple lighting was chilling, as the extend of the ability of those with ancient blood and ancient magic abilities became frightening clear to those that could see. Though they had little idea the cost that such a skill and ability truly held.

"Thy of ancient blood beloved and more. Great and powerful, with much a head to come. Thy of new beginning. You are granted the right to part the vail. From now on at will thy may open and close the vail as seen fit. I take thy offer of blood, and the price for such act." A deep voice replied in the same language. The blood from her cut hand as collected in an orb and disappeared. Then a flash of purple 'lightning' shot from the sky and hit the back of her left hand then warped around it which caused her to let out a slight hiss of pain.

After a moment as the sky cleared and the lighting around her left-hand calmed Arianna looked up again and turned her left hand. *"I part the vails and call out. Come forth at my summons; open a path to thee; my soul bound partner; Elder Dragon Kailivrania!"* Arianna called out in ancient tongue. As slight dark flash occurred in the sky and a figure appeared from it and begun to grow larger as it approached. It then covered the entire window with its black scaled body then it turned its head and a large red eye looked into the window at Arianna.

[Why have you called me puny being. You seem to wish to die, once again, and in an even worse state than last.]

I'll live, I can promise you that. But we have no time for a 'pleasant' chat of bickering. I need you to take these people out of here.

[What of you tiny?]

I'll remain, they cannot learn of your existence, nor the fact were able to cross the vail. Now isn't the time for such information to be revealed. I also must remain to keep the flames strong till you are out of sight. I'll be okay... so please.

> *[... For a small thing you are very brave I'll give you that. Fine if you survive this endeavour of your own making... I will be more willing to listen as you've truly proven yourself and your worth.]*

Arianna looked at Kailivrania and nodded her head as she lowered herself enough to allow the others to climb on her back. "Take the immobile and dead onto the dragon's back. Escape will be with her help. Be sure to hold on to her and those that can't." Arianna ordered as she stayed in the hall holding the wall of flames and blocking anything that pierced through with a magic barrier.

"Codeless what are you doing get on." Night asked as he looked over at her. She shook her head.

"I can't, I barely have enough energy to maintain this. If I leave now the flames will die, they'll see the escape and the dragon which can't happen." Arianna replied as she shook her head, Night then jumped from Kailivrania's back, and back into the hallway next to Ari. "No, get back on there."

"I'll stay behind with you. Don't you dare think I haven't noticed. You're in no shape to do this as you suggest. I'm the only person strong enough right now to do this. You, giant lizard you should go know if you don't want Codeless to die."

[When I get far enough away, I can maintain form for about two hours. I'll drop them off away from here.] Kailivrania told Arianna as she moved away from the window.

Wait?! You traitor! Why do you listen to him so well! Arianna exclaimed out of injustice of what was occurring before her. Kailivrania opened her three sets of large bat like wings, the very motion caused a large gust. Kailivrania two tails twitched then her wings flapped down in a powerful move and shot up into the night sky and started to disappear.

Arianna leaned against the wall by the window as she focused most of her energy to maintain things. They two of them both knew that the wall of flames wasn't going to last long enough. The colours of the wall had already begun to change to yellow as it cooled. "They're going to get through. We might both end up being captured." Night let out a low chuckled as he shook his head.

"That's way I told you to leave." Ari muttered as she rested her head on her knees.

"You knew this and still planned to stay."

"I'm too weak to jump from this height. To be honest with you the moment I let myself relax and lose focus I'll pass out… that's how bad it is. I haven't let myself get a good rest since I returned. I've gone way past my limits. But even because of that, it doesn't mean I can stop. A moment of weakness right now is all they need for them to succeed and take something from my hand."

"You talk as if you're playing a game… or a leader commanding troops. But I don't get why you're so willing to sacrifice yourself."

"Because my worth is deemed very little. Sigh… it not important I'm going to run out of the last of my power soon." Ari sighed as she pushed herself to her feet. Night who was looking out the window looked over at Ari.

Night without a single word walked over to Ari. She questioned him but he didn't stop. He stood in front of her and opens the mouthpiece of her helmet. Night then reached up and removed his helmet to reveal that he had changed his appearance.

"I won't take off your helmet since you've turned off your disguise to save energy. I made a backup plan in secret. Before we left, I knew that you were in a very bad condition. Even then, you didn't stand down and rest." Roy paused. "How could I sit back and watch as you nearly kill yourself."

"… you're an idiot. A real idiot Night! I'm not someone worth all this trouble you go through to help me. Why don't you give up on me like the others? I'm a monster. I don't deserve to be saved and just leave me in the dust." Arianna muttered her fist clenched as she looked down.

"You're just a girl who's lost everything as if it was a price you had to pay. You are someone that guard themselves with thorns to keep other's away and keep people at a distance. If you're a monster than you're the most beautiful monster I even known."

"You already seen what I can do… I've never told you much about me or what I know. I'm not a good person."

"Who is?"

"… You're acting like we are going to part and never meet again." Ari muttered but Roy doesn't reply. She turned her head suddenly and looked at him. "You're not serious are you. Tell me it's a joke. I'm not about to let you do that."

Roy pulled her towards him near the window and held her hand lightly. He then removed the glove of her right hand. "You are the most important person to me. The thought of letting this happen to you. The two of us have very different feeling for one another. That much is certain, and it doesn't matter whether you accept my heart or not. You are and always will be someone for me to protect.

"You were the person that gave my empty life meaning after I lost my memories. You have saved me from death multiple times even when we were just strangers. You held out your hand to me, and even though you've always kept most of your secrets close I do know we both have come to rely on one another for support.

"So, for everything you have done for me and will do for me in the future, I'll protect you with this life of mine, even if my feelings change. I'll always feel the need to protect you as well always be friends and family to one another." Roy told her as he looked up at her. He held her right hand tightly as he knelt to the ground. "I may not know your real name appearance or even true name but that doesn't matter. I know who you are as a person and know your more that deserving of my loyalty. As such, I pledge my warrior's oath to you, and take you to be the master of my body and soul that I'll always protect." Roy swore as he kissed the back of Ari's hand magic then from Roy traveled and laced around her right wrist and connected back to Roy before it disappeared.

"Back when it was my time to choose my codename, even back then there was much you had done for me. I wanted to be your knight and protect you. I choose it as a play on the English word's similarity sounding and since we worked in the dark of the world." Roy muttered before he looked up at you. "I can never betray or hurt you now after giving you, my oath. I'll always trust and protect you and can never kill you. So, no matter what happens I'll wait for you. But for this moment... I'll be greedy and do this one thing for myself."

Roy then turned his head and kissed her on the lips. Ari looked at him in shock as he kissed her. At first, she noticed an odd rush of energy, but her mind raced more about other things than the sudden opposing energy that flowed into her. Rather all she could do was think of the shock and surprise of the sudden kiss from Roy.

Ari didn't realize he had feelings for her to such an extent. She had some idea but thought it was more like as a friend or family, it was because she could never think of herself at the time with another person as she thought bad of herself and highly of others. It was hard for her to believe someone could love her in such a sense at the time as she thought everyone had a motive. But she knew Roy wasn't like that, so she felt like a bad person, for two different reasons.

One was towards Roy the other to a person who was in love with Roy as she knew them. Roy moved back and looked at her with calm eyes, but he didn't look hurt either. "This was just my selfish wish… nothing else. When this is all over, we can talk." He sighed as he put his helmet on and as she closed the mouthpiece of her helmet.

"But right now, we have something more important to do. Both of us." Roy added before he pushed her out of the window. Arianna had no strength, so she had no way stop or support herself to prevent from falling out the window. The flames died down and allowed the Marione passage, Roy/Night turned to face them.

Arianna fell into the back of a truck, and when she managed to climb up, she saw as the Marione agents captured Night. She didn't have the strength to climb out or make a noise before the truck drove off with her in tow.

Chapter 40

The truck eventually stopped at the edge of the forest near the base for an inspection. Arianna hearing this scrambled out of the truck and into the forest without being seen. In the forest she stumbled around for some time. It was hard to stopped herself from falling unconscious, but she needed to do so till she knew it was safe even if only slightly.

Arianna was in a very bad state and position even with her summon no longer using her energy. Long had her mana run dry and she over drawn herself, then there was the sudden foreign opposing mana that forced itself into her body. Everything had piled up on her, now it begun to slow clear physical signs of this, one being in a state of exhaustion. Eventually her body was so sluggish that she tripped over her own feet and fell to the ground.

A groan escaped from her lips as she fell and now could barely push herself up. As she turned her head to find a hollowed out opening in the roots of a large tree. She knew that it wasn't ideal, but she also knew that couldn't move for much longer. If she passed out right, there in the open was much worse than to rest inside a tree hollow. Ari dragged herself over to the opening and tumbled down inside of it.

Ari shifted around to get into a more comfortable position or as comfortable as one could get in such a place. That followed with the removal of her helmet that was place on the ground and her long coat that she used as a sort of blanket. It was still winter and there were multiple dangers for her to worry about than just the Marione now, but in the end, all of this was far from her mind. It didn't take long as she crossed her arms across her chest and allowed her mind to eventually drift off.

The sun had begun to set as Arianna's eye fluttered open. A slight groan escaped her lips as she moved and popped to remove the stiff feeling she had. Her body still didn't feel the best, but it was better than it was a few hours ago. Ari in all honestly would rather not take part in another mission for a while or fight but she understood wasn't possible.

They still have Roy… with whatever chance I have… no that I need to take it. I can't let them take him away for multiple reasons one being that he's my childhood friend, that I consider as family. Ari thought as she placed her head against the root of the tree. She glances over and out the hole for the ground. The snow was light which just a small blessing.

A slight melancholy look as she gazed out before she closed her eyes in thought. Her thoughts couldn't help but go to the events that took place in the hallway. The kiss and the last moments before and after they parted.

It was clear to Ari how Roy felt towards her at this point, and she felt guilty, though less because she knew someone else held the same kind of love for him. No, she felt guilty for a different reason, not that she didn't realize his feeling sooner.

Ari felt bad she could reciprocate his feelings for her. Roy to her was a very good man as well as a person. As both a friend, someone who cares about him, and as a person that considers him family. All she wished for him was his well-being and happiness. But Ari herself thought for many reasons she couldn't, and her viewing Roy in the way of family wasn't one.

Though Arianna considered Roy as family, she was aware they had no blood relation with one another. She had no qualms over the notion of such a relationship between orphan children 'families' they made with one another. She knew several that had done such. Even with that relationship between acting as a family neither of them went far and respected one another as a man and women once they were older.

No that wasn't what troubled Ari. Ari knew she was a woman with many faults, she couldn't trust another person for one. She had never even told him about her past... as even if it was that long ago it was something that important and dangerous. To others, Arianna knew she was essentially poison or a ticking time bomb that was prime to kill just about anyone. One wrong misstep could kill anyone close to her. She didn't get how a person could even fall for her at the time.

But the biggest was she didn't understand love especially back then. She understood familial love she remembered it from before she was forced to the orphanage. No, it was the love between a couple or lovers she couldn't understand. She'd seen couples, heard about troubles of love/crushes from others, and she even learned the art of seduction to lure targets. But she couldn't really get it, or why others acted such in a way towards another.

Ari at the time thought maybe it was like the feeling of when she was affected by the drug, if it was, she could understand but also didn't really enjoy the notion. Ari viewed everyone objectively and determined one's worth after at least several interactions. To her, she could agree when she came across someone with good looks, but that was all she would neither start an interaction or conversation with a person because of their looks or due to desire.

The relationship between a couple, she enjoyed reading romance story and found joy and amusement in the stories. She wasn't averse to the close interactions that couples had either. But Ari could never see herself acting in such a way towards another, and at the time she even found it hard to see herself in a romantic relationship the biggest reason the danger and work she needed to accomplish so she never explored it either.

But Roy almost essentially forced her hand in this matter. When he had kissed her Ari wasn't stupid, she knew the kind of relationship he wished and desired from her. That is why she felt guilty because she knew she would never be able to give him the relationship he wanted and that she also thought he deserved.

"Damn it, Roy… that really was a selfish act." Ari muttered as she ran her hand through her hair. Ari thought Roy probably also concluded what her choice might be, which made her feel worse.

Arianna let out a long-exasperated sigh escape from her lips, she was just very tired of it all. *Once this is all over… can I finally rest?* She wondered as she leaned forward as another sigh escaped and grabbed her helmet that rested on the ground. She reached inside and pulled out a single earpiece and turned it on completely allowing long distance communication.

Then the half screen that covered her one eye was flooded by messages. *It seems she got them back safe… hopefully she didn't strain herself… it's hard for mythics to remain here without a master from this world to supply mana to act as a stabilizer. Though broke some of those issues, but still.* Ari thought was she glanced as the numerous messages but didn't open a single one or reply despite the clear panic the later messages held.

Ari's eyes just glanced over the small notification of the message that held text. *If I'm going to do this and rescue him… I defiantly need inside help. They wouldn't let a Yano agent or really anyone slip through their hand easily, especially after the loss of Caden and Sean. Too bad for them I got an inside informant.* Ari hummed as she opened a new message. It was quick and simple. [Do they still have what was lost? Is it possible for pick up?]

Arianna closed her eyes as she took some calm breaths and felt energy around her brush against her skin, along with a slightly familiar energy that was almost encouraging her. She let a slight chuckle escape from her lips. She reached over and grabbed the other earpiece from her helmet and was surprised to find a speedy reply. [Still have it, they are near obsessed with it. Though the worry for such a lost thing is reasonable. Don't advise pick up, likely will thorns, little option.]

[Matter's not. Pick up is a must. Can't let them hold to something so valuable. Not to mention too big of a risk.]

[Pick up is likely impossible. Suggest back up.]

[Is breaking occurring?]

[Yes.]

Arianna looked down and over at her pistol. She knew the back-up but for some reason in her body she felt and odd tingling like a jolt of electricity as if in argument. Ari couldn't help but think back of what she saw earlier. Occurrences like that had become oddly common in the last few months but more so recently and when that happens its often like a warning. She felt like something inside her told her she couldn't trust it.

Ari knew she'd be unable to summon her partner Kailivrania for a while, just based on her own condition alone. Then a card slipped from her jacket pocket, she reached out and grabbed the card to look at it before she froze. Her eyes shock for a moment before they cold and became emotionless. *So that's what you're saying. You truly frightening in your foresight.*

The card a special item, at the time the single item it was more called a creature card, or a card from the deck of beings/mythics, and artifact created by the god Faradityx for the blood that could part the vail and command others. It was an artifact in the clan that had become legends as it was no longer used.

It was said to have been lost to time as well though that wasn't the case. They just had other means to summon creatures and it was a dangerous item that few could even use so new methods were made to do so. As such Arianna knew about them but it was the first time holding such a card.

The card in Ari's hand, the one Lumina had given her was something that sent a shiver through her. Ezec, master of the mind and rulers of the mental realm, the truest of tricksters, a creature from Canlonen legends and tales, one that was often used to scare young children.

[Is the lost item still where it was last left?] It took a moment for a reply to return.

[Currently… yes. But not for long. After the break in prior, moving is under way. They might ship out by tomorrow morning.]

Arianna paused as her eyes shook. *That means I have less than five hours to deal with this. I don't have time to formulate a plan, negotiate, or resupply. I don't even have time to go back. After five hours they will secure him in a high-grade cell that my current strength would have no chance breaking.* Arianna looked up and questioned if it was a test of her resolve or the *other's* meddling that brought this about, she concluded it was likely both.

I don't have a lot for me to use and I'm in really bad shape. But… I can't let this go. I can't let them have Roy. Not just because he's my friend, but because he had vital information that could killed thousands if it got into their hands. Ari growled as she punched the root of the tree with the side of her fist. She had limited ammo and was weak as she cursed under her breath in the realization.

If she hadn't passed out and went back to base to restock and get some healing items from the Yano to temporarily restore her body to peak strength she might not be in this situation. If she had only told the others her actual condition rather than hide it out of a mixture of fear, pride, and self-contempt this wouldn't have happened in the first place as she would have gotten one of those potions earlier.

Things were just spiralling out of control for her, and things had begun to slip from her fingers. Plan B of the Yano for captured allies, the release and silence of death, given to them from an ally. After all you could never tell how long till one would break, as in the end the silence would eventually break whether wished or not, especially against the Marione, as they have many ways to get the information they want.

[Do you happen to know where?]

[Three doors down from the kid with a broken door.]

So, three doors down from where Sean was being held... so 8D since it goes up till 20 till the next letter. Arianna thought. *I just hope that I don't need to use that card especially before its chained and tamed.*

Arianna wished to reduce the chance of being caught as she looked over at her helmet before she let out a sigh and hand lifted to her ears. Her hand moved over to her second set of ear-piercing something that was done months ago. The first were just a pair of studs with unique stones, the new piercing had a pair of small sliver hooped earrings with light blue stone in them.

The earrings were a prototype for a large project. She was requested to test it out as the earrings which had a pocket storage space. The item had little issue aside that the larger project was on the grand scale so earrings where not the best choice. But not only that there was very limited space due to the size and capacity and it easily 'overheated' so the cool down was long and the large the item or more transferred the longer it took before it could be used again.

Then it could also only store things under a certain weight. The range was also very short it could only store things she was holding. But Ari couldn't deny the usefulness of this new tech prototype, so she still used it despite the draw backs. She held her helmet and it was changed to a mask.

In the future she knew that greater tech would begin to appear and the same could be said for artifacts. As it was only the beginning as such being familiar with such for the future was the idea. The disguise and storage tech would only be the beginning. Her appearance then changed as she put on the mask before she climbed out from under the tree.

Arianna walked out of the forest to the point she could see the Marione base once more. She looked down at it with her fist clenched, she knew at the time what a head of her wasn't going to be nice, and that she was likely going to fail in some way but that didn't matter. Ari knew she had to try otherwise she would likely regret it or end up with many deaths on her hands due to her actions that caused this.

Under the mask the VHDS adjusted to the new 'medium' it now worked with. Arianna could feel her heart pound in anticipation as the night became deeper. Ari knew this would be her only chance for a long while as mercenary organizations rarely had above ground bases like this since they were so vulnerable to attacks.

Without a thought or recognition of where it was sent Ari sent a single message, with the idea of making it known to her co-conspirator of her intention. [Infiltration commence]. Her communication reduced and she then jumped from the ledge which she stood, towards the Marione base once more.

Chapter 41

Arianna couldn't really recall how she got there but she stood in front of cell 8D. She didn't delay or even acted cautiously as she pried open the panel and slashed all the wires ignoring the shock she felt for a moment. The door opened ad with no real hesitation she walked inside as the lights flickered on.

It hadn't even been a full 24 hours since Night had been captured but the room that was to be his was empty splattered with blood and chains that hung from the wall. Not even given the time to fully take in what was before her an alarm begun to blare out. At which she realised the alarm hadn't been disabled and she just alerted everyone that someone had returned to collect Night.

Ari went back into the hall and ducked into a different hallway. She weaved through the halls past the scrambling agents as she made sure to avoid as much suspicion as possible. Ari matched her movement pace to that which the agents were moving. As she made her way down slowly, due to the flow of people she needed to step off at each floor and move to a different set of stairs.

As she reached the third floor Ari's thoughts started to wander a little. It had become too dangerous for her to continue, before she even had a chance to even look, she had screwed up. Ari had let her nerves and emotions get the better of her and she acted impatiently making things worse. If she acted calmy she would have realized the alarm wasn't disarmed due to the lack of response from her help. If she did, she could have had the chance to look around for Night/Roy.

I'm a real mess, this isn't like me. And now I've blown my chance. I'm so sorry Roy, this is my fault. Darn it... I need to get out of here, now. Arianna thought as she shook her head lightly with her eyes closed. She had no choice but to leave him behind so she wouldn't get caught and make sure that his actions did not go down in vain.

Arianna's moment of distraction had become a pitfall, as if the jaws of something was desperately attempting to close itself around her and not let her escape. That distraction caused her to collide with a mid-level agent. The agent caught her out of reflex. "Watch were you're going idiot." They growled as they looked down at her. But then they started to look down at her and scrutinize her more.

"What?! I got more important things on my mind right now considering the alarm. So, what's your problem." Arianna growled as they started to grip her shoulder even tighter. She glared at him but quickly came to the realization that he wasn't about to let her go. She grabbed one of the needles from her forearm and stabbed it into his arm which forced him to release her.

"Get them!" they ordered as Arianna started to run with a click of her tongue. As she ran from the group of people that had begun to chase her. She paid no mind to where she was going or what direction she went she just ran. But eventually she ended up at dead end hall and the final door that appeared to be a set of stairs were locked. Ari started to curse profusely under her breath.

Ari's pursuers were getting close, and she would be caught if she did nothing. She was hesitant still to use her flames, but she'd rather not get caught. As she prepared and gathered magic energy to her hands she was suddenly grabbed and pulled away.

Arianna was suddenly pulled into a room from behind but knew she couldn't scream, so she struggled as much as she could against them. Then with all her strength she threw her arm back and sent her elbow into their guts causing them to let her go.

As she spun around her on her foot and swung her arm as a blade popped out from under her wrist. She slashed towards the one that grabbed her thinking them to be and enemy. The hidden blade grazed across their chest as they jumped back in surprise. "Calm down its just me."

"L … no Aether?!"

"It is you. But why are you surprised; you broke in here."

Arianna realised he never received her message. Though she didn't have the time to think about where that message actually went as there were more important things. "I came to rescue Night but set off the alarm by accident."

"Are you thick? What made you think this was a good idea. I would have watch out for that agent as a favour or is it that you don't trust me?"

"Well, no, I don't trust anyone truthfully but that's beside the point."

"Oh, and you probably trust him more since your lovers?"

"Wait what?! That's not… hold on what the Gods name made you think that?! Did you see him kiss me before he got captured? Jeez if you did, you clearly didn't hear anything we said though." Arianna muttered as she shook her hand and traced the nose line of the mask. "I'll assume that's what you're talking about. You don't need to really know this, but I'll let you know that's not what happened or the reason. We've known each other for a very long time that's all I'll say." She groaned.

"Take off the mask."

"What why?"

"Just do it."

"I seriously do not get what's going on in your head. Fine whatever." Arianna muttered as she just shifted the mask to the side to let him see her face. She crossed her arm and wore a very annoyed look. She knew this was fine since her disguise tech was working and they already acquainted. She had half a mind to do the same but held her tongue to get to the point.

"Your probably aware Night is a high-level Yano agent. The problem is that he doesn't work on infiltration and espionage style jobs or missions, as such he doesn't have the normal precautions. He has information that could kill around a thousand people at least, for both of our goals we need the Yano around. Then there is the personal relationship between us... I'd rather him not go through such a thing like Lumina, or others for that matter. Nor for him to feel guilt or worry about putting myself and everyone else he knows in danger."

"So, its sympathy."

"You can think that I don't care."

"Well, it's a little late the moment you set off the alarm they've likely secured him. So, he's likely out of your reach." Aether paused. "Why do you care so much? You're a codeless and nameless. Meaning you have little to lose even if he says anything. The Yano isn't your home or organization. I don't get your reasoning for putting yourself in danger like this."

"Maybe it's 'cause I have a death wish... haha." Ari replied sarcastically as she smirked. "No, it more because he's someone like family to me. And for someone that doesn't really have any family left at my side I'd rather not lose those I've come to consider as such. But for their own good and peace I will do what is necessary to give them sanctity." She glanced over at him.

"You probably still don't really understand. It's not something based on logic or reason but emotions and feelings. Because of our relationship, our past, what's he's done for me, all of that. I do not want him to regret his decision of choosing to be on my side, and for saving me. That is the reason I came back. And for those that are truly loyal to me I'll do anything for them, even if it means I might die." Ari smiled. "After all, I wouldn't still be a part of this line of work, if wasn't willing to take risks. Besides currently I have no plans to die... nor the ability to." She muttered under her breath.

Ari turned her head towards the door as she focused her attention out to the hallway. The sounds of footsteps and people yelling had died down at this point. "Well either way thank you for helping me out but it's time for me to go." Ari sighed as she grabbed the mask and about to slid it back over her face, but Aether grabbed her wrist, and action which caused Ari to shoot them a death glare.

"What are you going to do? I already told you that they've likely already secured Night." Aether asked as his grip was tight around her wrist. "It's pointless to try and save him now."

Ari pulled her wrist from their grasp and massaged it a little. "I'm already well aware of that. I'm not a complete and utter idiot. I know there is nothing I can do now." She replied, her eyes held sadness and guilt. "I need to get out of here."

Aether looked down at her, then took out a card. "The head of this base has closed off all other exits and the windows have been sealed after you last escape. The only why out now is through the hanger which is being used to transport things out the base. But being the only way out now I think you can understand how dangerous it could be. Use this key it will open the locked stairs. Destroy it once you're done it will not be usable after that anyways so no point holding onto it."

Arianna took the card from his hand and went to put the mask on. "Also, there's no point in using that mask. Those from that group aren't here. Its better if you just use your normal helmet."

Arianna paused and just removed the mask to switch to her helmet. She placed it on her head and closed the face plate. "How many of your people are here at the base?"

"I'm the only one that is still here."

"... Good, because I think I much just wreck house before I leave. Its best you get away soon too." Arianna muttered as she turned towards the door.

After a brief moment of pause Ari walked to the door, but then she stopped as she was in front of the door and turned back. "My reasons for this... whether its atonement... pity, guilt... it's hard to say in the very end its complicated. But... if you can... please just watch out for him." With that Arianna left the room and opened the door to the stairs.

The doors closed behind her, she walked over to the banister and looked down. *I could jump down from here... my body is in a good enough state now to handle this much. I should get to the hanger as soon as possible.* Arianna thought as she placed one of her feet against the lower bar of the railing. She let out a slight sigh as she placed her hands on the railing, she let out a slight huff as she jumped over the railing.

Her long coat fluttered in the wind as she fell from the third floor. She looked at her feet at the closing bottom floor, at the second to last railing she grabbed a hold and stopped her fall before she let go and landed softly to the ground. Ari looked up then moved over to the door before she begun to run down the hall towards the hanger.

Ari didn't notice the decrease in the people in the hallway as she ran as all that mattered was her escape. As she reached the door that led to the hanger, she slammed into it busting it open. There was oddly no one here even though it was the only main exit at the time but that wasn't something she could let herself be concerned with then and she just raced towards the large open door.

Arianna waved through the boxes and vehicles before she reached a large open space. But that's when the bay doors begun to close before her. She clicked her tongue and sprinted towards the door to try and slip out. Right as it looked like she was going to make it something hard slammed into her side. Hit aside like a fly she rolled along the ground till eventually she came to the stop. She looked up and saw as the bay doors slammed close.

When the doors closed that was when it was possible to see the people that were hiding in the shadows in wait. The lights of the hanger fully turned on and illuminated the hanger for all to be seen. And not far away from her in the large, opened area, stood a very tattered Imitator. From about she could hear clapping, she turned her head up to the upper deck where it came from. On the upper deck stood a man that looked down at her.

Chapter 42

Arianna looked up at the man, as she pushed herself to her feet. "So, you are the one. You came back here after you lost your ally didn't you. How loyal for one such as you. A codeless with no real code, do whatever they generally wish and want, like us. You'd think the bigger thorn in the side would be the Yano. But it seems to be you, whose worked for many at this point. The one that's stopped us at every turn to get a hint at elixir."

"I'm just doing my job. I'm a codeless after all. So why don't you let me go."

"Oh, I don't think I will for such a thorn. You've been such an annoying problem, its best to just get rid of you. After all you are the only one that's been truly capable standing against us. Its best for me to do what's best, for the organization."

"What give you right to determine the best course."

They snapped their fingers and Imitator swung down at Ari which caused her to jump back and avoid the attack that caused cracks in the ground. "Why I'm the leader of course. And I don't want some codeless scum to get in the way as we finally get so close after so many years."

Arianna could tell there was no reasoning with this man or even tricking him to be able to get out of there. She didn't like his eyes as they sent chilled down her back, they didn't feel right to her for some reason. But not only that she could feel the power the man had, and it was immense she barely stood close to him in strength. "So, your Anthelm Ivroeve the leader of the Marione, I've heard so much about. You're as imposing as they told me." Arianna spoked as she slid her hand into her pocket.

"Oh ho?! You've already heard of my name. Very few know of it now a days."

"But of course, I'm not the most famous codeless for nothing."

"No that's quite right, not to mention you are close with the Yano to even get a helmet."

"I've not sided with the Yano. I am codeless. I got this as payment for an incident years ago that they got me involved in. I was understandably left behind over one of their agents. A decision that went against the plan. A deviation that caused great problems and later caused me to sustain a great injury." Arianna spoke in a clam voice. "After all I'm sure many are aware of when I disappeared for a fair number of years. They owned me substantially after that, the helmet was just one such compensation."

"Oh, if that's the case why still work for them?"

"They pay quite well you know. A well money makes the world go round after all."

Arianna realized what he planned to do as he looked down at her with a frighting grin. As such Ari pulled out the teleportation amulet. But the Imitator swung as he and hit the amulet which caused it to shatter. Anthelm looked down at her and smirked. "Well, if that's the case why come for this." They spoke as Night was dragged out and showed off to her just to taunt her.

"Can't I have friends? Is it such an unreasonable explanation?" Ari replied as she shook her hand clear of the shattered items. "I'm not completely heartless that friends are an utter impossibility unlike some individuals." She replied snidely and Anthelm begun to laugh like a mad man.

"I like you. So fiery yet also as cold as ice. Your such an interesting contradiction... you remind me of someone from long ago.

Ah if only he didn't kill them all, I could have had a pet." Anthelm chuckled. "Let's make a bet, no deal."

"Deal… what is it?"

"I would like for you and Heron the Imitator to fight. The fight determines your fate." Anthelm said with a chilling smile. Ari clenched her fist.

"If that's the case… I'd rather have an Oath with you."

"An Oath… such gal."

"Yes, an Oath… after all I can't trust you in the slightest."

"You really are as sly and cunning as they've said." Anthelm chuckled. "Alright what are your conditions?"

"If I beat the Imitator neither you nor anyone in your organization or affiliated can kill the being that is known as Night in the Yano, as long as they are in your hands." Arianna stated with a clear voice. She didn't think Anthelm would agree to just hand him over so to her, her top concern was his safety till she could rescue him.

"Just beat… no. That's too much for something so small. You need to kill the Imitator for such a reward." Anthelm replied as he glared down at her. It was to be an impossible task as Anthelm had already revived the Imitator, but Arianna readily agreed. "Alright… then if Heron wins… you dear codeless will be ours to use. We are already aware of your… special capabilities."

Arianna glared at him, but she knew that she no longer had and easy chance to escape since Anthelm was here. "Fine I can agree to that."

"With thy blood thy makith an Oath with thee. An Oath with thy life blood it holds and sealed, and neither party can break lest death awaits for our soul and existence, in the void were nothing exists. We hold it to our ancestors and those higher that watch over. In the name of Faradityx and Vysdite we make this Oath." They both stated as blood pooled from there hand.

"At the loss of this battle I will give myself to the winners master."

"At the loss and death of my warrior in this battle, neither me or those that follow me as leader, those of my origination and those affiliated to me cannot kill or be the cause of death for the being known by the organization Yano as Night."

The pooled blood then begun to glow with magic and turned into a magic circle that wrapped around their necks. This was a true death Oath, an Oath that one could not break without death to follow. Something that even Anthelm would turn against. Anthelm then smiled down at her. "You truly messed up codeless you have no chance at winning. The Imitator has long lost to me and recently become a fine puppet in my hands." He laughed and the resounding laughter of those agents around on the side that watched laughed along.

"The fight hasn't even begun don't count me out so quickly old man." Arianna replied as she rolled her shoulders. She was calm as she looked at the Imitator who stood in front of her. Ari could tell that he was stronger than her if she was at full strength the gap between them would be less, but the gap in strength would still be present when fighting against the Imitator 'puppet'.

She reached behind her and pulled out her twin blades. The lights of the hanger shined against them as she twirled the blades and lunged forward.

Heron raised the large great axe they were using as Ari's blades clanged off it which caused sparks to fly. Heron then swung in a counterattack and Ari moved to have the axe blade just barely graze her side. It hurt like hell, but the rush of the fight made it possible to ignore the pain at the time.

Ari pivoted on her feet and spun around as she sent her foot into the side of his leg to cause it to buckle. But it didn't really work, and Heron grabbed her leg. She clicked her tongue as she stabbed her sword into his arm but also into her own leg at the same time. He released her leg and she slid it out for the blade as she pushed forward to slash her blade out of his arm and blood splattered the ground.

Heron's hand from that move was barely hanging on to his arm and just hung there to the side. He slammed the axe into the ground to cause a great tremor which caused Ari to jump back.

But that gave him time and she watched in shock as the severed part of his hand grew back together like strings, but flesh and blood. Heron's deathly pale skin and healing ability really matched the known features of greater ghouls.

Ghouls unlike zombies where in the most literal sense the living undead. Which made it possible for them to grow and heal, and very different from a zombie in different ways as well, one being the core that ghouls held being their life source.

But the ghouls Anthelm made were different from other ghouls as they were insanely strong for one, and their core was different. A core that could not easily be destroyed or found, to most they are beings that will never die.

Ari looked at Heron and could see the core in his body it was very similar to the one inside Lumina. She felt a chill at which she rolled to the side as a beam fell to the ground where she stood as Heron appeared forward and brought his axe down towards her. She had probably recovered yet from her last sudden dodge that she wasn't prepared for another.

Ari turned her blades and crossed them above her head. The axe collided with her swords and the metal screeched as they slid against each other. The force of the attack caused her legs to start to fall from under her as she felt a tingling sensation run through her arms. Heron then twisted his axe to free it from Ari's blades and slammed the blunt side of it into her ribs. The strength of the hit sent her back and slammed into a vehicle.

Heron begun to act like he won but Ari wasn't out and moved from the car and pushed off towards him. She slashed her blades down across his back causing deep bloody cuts from his shoulder to waist but this time the injury didn't quickly heal. Ari jumped back and a hidden smirk formed as the cut had been cauterized, almost immediately after her blade cut his back.

They jumped towards one another again and clashed blades with one another quickly. Sparks flew and metal clashed as on the two of them small knicks begun to appear on them both. Then Ari slide back and a trail of blood fallowed her it was clear she was more injured.

Even if she was more injured it didn't matter to her as such Arianna then jumped forward at Heron again. He swung at her with their weapons clashed in the air. But the resulting force sent her flying backwards and one blade left her hand. She pulled out her pistol and fired a full clip at Heron with most of them landing on him. Her blade stabbed into the ground as she fell and rolled back a little.

Ari felt sudden danger and rolled to the side as Heron's foot landed where her head was. She grabbed three needles that she coated with poison and stabbed into his leg before she scrambled to her feet and grabbed her blades. She was avoiding using her abilities as much as possible to have energy to spare, but things had begun to get problematic with Heron's ability to heal open and bleeding wounds so quickly.

Heron knock Ari's blades to the side out of her hands in a clang. She grabbed a dagger as slashed his mask causing it to break while also severing the part that was holding it in place. She then leaned back to avoid another slash before she went further and landed a kick into his jaw. The kick stunned him, so she ran and grabbed her blades, as she picked them up, she spun around and slashed him across the chest.

Heron had become faster; Ari felt a slight tremble though her body. But then she felt a sudden boost and could feel as she got stronger in tandem. She swung her swords at Heron and made deep slash in his leg. But he attacked as well, and his axe landed in her shoulder.

The blood trail down her skin, but she turned her blades and stabbed them into his stomach. She created a blast of fire from the blade that had the force akin to that of an explosion that it sent him backwards and tore the axe from her shoulder.

Ari panted as her wound stung and burned, she could feel the blood that was seeping from the wound as it traveled down her skin. It had managed to break some bones and it was possible to see stands and blood in the opened wound. She had nearly lost her arm from that attack, but it wasn't something she had the luxury to even think about.

Without much of a moment of rest or time to worry over her injury Heron had recovered and raced towards her. Primed and moved close to attack but Ari wasn't frozen in place from the wound. As Heron swung his axe she dodged, and it grazed past her. As the axe grazed past, she countered and strongly brought her blade down onto his wrist.

Her blades paused for a moment as they got caught in his wrist. She let go of her blade and ducked as the axe flew over her head at which she grabbed the blades at the went over her head the second time, she pulled against his momentum and the blade started to move from his arm. She was so close as she could hear the bone snap and flesh tare as blood fell on top of her, until she completely severed his hand.

The hand fell to the ground and tuned to ash. From the point that the arm was severed blood fell and pulsing flesh and bone could be seen from the point of separation. This action however caused Ari to lose grip on her blades and embed them into the ground before her and Heron's axe priced the ground into the wall behind her.

Heron pulled his axe from the wall as Ari rolled away and eventually turned back to face him. There was no weapon in her hand as she faced him so as he attacked once more, she had no way to defend herself. As he swung at her, he managed to hit her in one of the more major wounds that had yet to healed. The shock and pain caused her to freeze and tumble back along the ground.

Ari struggled to get up from the ground due to pain from her side. Heron quickly closed in, to where she had landed and was on top of her. He looked down at her for a moment before he kicked her in her stomach which caused her to roll back and slam into the wall.

As Heron went towards were Ari lied, he grabbed one of her blades that was embedded in the ground. As she fell from the wall to the ground, she was a little stunned her more injured arm held her stomach as she coughed, she didn't even notice Heron's approach.

As Heron stood before her once more, she noticed the shadow and looked up as he stabbed one of Ari's blades into her outstretched arm pinning it down and twisted it in. He planned to sever her hand like she had done to him, and she knew it too which caused her to tremble and think of the lab experiments she had gone through not even a week ago.

In this moment Ari felt utterly helpless, she was fighting a steep uphill battle. Her throat felt horse from her scream but felt and ember flicker to life inside her in defiance. It was as if it was to tell her that she cannot let it end so fight back. She pulled her injured arm out from under her slowly, so he didn't notice.

Ari turned her hand to have her palm face towards him then in a moment her hand shot up and moved closed to Heron's chest. Flames licked her hand and converged into itself and flared to create an explosion from the small fire in her hand. The explosion though small was strong and it sent him flying backwards with a large mark burned into his chest.

With this chance Ari grabbed the blade in her arm as Heron was stunned. Her hand wrapped around and gripped onto the blade, she held tightly causing the sharp edge to cut into her skin as she did so. It took some time but eventually she managed to pull the blade from her arm. The blade slipped from her hand as it was freed and landed on the ground before her, she forced herself up onto her feet and looked at Heron who stood in front of her.

With his single hand that remained her grabbed Ari's neck and slammed her back into the wall. He was stabbed and caused her blood to smear against it. The force against the wall she could hear the snap and crack of bone against the wall. It wasn't long before his grip begun to tighten around her neck.

Chapter 43

Heron's grip got tighter around Ari's neck his grip was so strong that it managed to slowly bend the metal alloy type protection that was around her neck. With the metal bent he did manage to choak Ari but only slightly which made it a little difficult for her to breath. She grabbed his wrist and begun to tighten her grip around it as she growled, "let go."

Flames begun to form around her hands before they eventually flared and badly burned his wrist. The flames had caused him to let go of her neck either from fear or out of pain. Flames held to his wrist even after he let go, and she fell to the ground with a light cough. This time she didn't paused and quickly pushed herself up and moved just in time to dodge his fist.

The two begun to fight hand to hand against each other. Kicking each other's chests and sweeping legs. Arianna slammed Heron into the ground. But at the time she noticed a familiar figure on the side lines watching, she knew the figure wasn't Night which caused her to pause in surprise. But it wasn't a good time as Heron hit her in the side and dug into her wound.

Heron managed to gain the upper hand and overpower her forcing her back. The two completely changed their positions as he placed his severed arm on her throat causing his blood to trail down the side of her covered neck. He was observant and located a weapon on Ari, he moved quickly and grabbed a dagger from Ari's boot.

With a dagger in hand, he stabbed it into her shoulder wound and dragged it down towards her breast as slow and painful as possible. The act caused her so much pain it was hard to think straight. She managed to gather herself enough kicked his stomach in an attempt get him off her, but it did nothing as she couldn't muster enough strength.

Tears laced her eyes as the pain she felt was immense. Her body was getting weaker with each moment and in her already poor state it wasn't good for the fight. It was a fight for her life. She could tell as her body became weaker that she would die here if she couldn't fight back against him. But her body from the injuries, loss of blood, and everything else she had to deal with in the last few months had begun to fail her.

The realization this might be it as she was going to lose let alone die. The thought of death didn't bother her rather the loss and being forced to follow Anthelm did. She didn't want that to happened, but she had not left to use, she was drained.

As if response to her desperation Ari could feel as energy begun to swirl and gather inside her to fill and give her the strength she had run out of. Though still not 100% she had strength and energy in her body to fight back. Though she had no idea how this came to pass, it didn't matter.

With this renewed strength she lifted her arms up to grab the dagger on in her shoulder. The other hand moved up towards the location that Ari could see the core. The hidden blade on her wrist slid out and pierced into Heron's chest.

Ari dragged the blade up and made and in scission in his chest. She then forced her hand with the blade still out into his chest and into the space. Large crackles of lighting and gusts of wind begun to occur around them the lightning licked the side of her helmet and the gusts cut her sides, but it didn't stop her. It became its own battle at the end, would Ari get choked out and pass out by Heron first or would Ari destroy Heron's core.

Her hand moved closer and close to the start like core inside Heron then the tip of the hidden blade grazed across it which caused Heron's body to shiver. The hidden blade couldn't pierce the core however no matter the force it didn't move. Eventually the blade slid back to the mechanism around her wrist Ari's hand moved closers as she ignored the shocking and stabbing pain that battered her hand.

Then Ari hand went around the star core she strengthened her grip around the core as large bolts of lightning shot off hitting anything it its path. It was stinging against the hand, as the core fought back against the touch. But eventually creaks begun to form and then like shattering glass it broke. Ari's hand went through to the other side of Heron's chest with the core in hand as it shattered in hand. The energy from the core disappeared and Heron's body turned to ashes on top of her as the pressure against her neck disappeared.

Arianna stood up and let the ashes fall to the ground as she pulled out the dagger in her large shoulder wound. She turned her head to Anthelm, he could feel her sharp and powerful gaze, in that moment he felt a chill run down his back like a powerful young beast was looking at him.

Ari grabbed her swords and whatever weapons she could along the way as she pointed up at Anthelm with the great axe resting on her uninjured shoulder. "Now! I've killed Imitator. Hand Night over."

"That wasn't part of the deal." Anthelm paused and concluded that Ari was too dangerous to leave alive. "I also never said you could leave alive either! Get that codeless and kill them! They are too dangerous to leave alive."

"You bastard!" Ari growled as the energy inside her begun to flare out. Marione agents from the side begun to just down and towards Ari. After the fight Ari initially felt tired but now, she was fine and with ease swung the great axe. She cut down several agents in a single swing and their blood flew. Some lost limbs will others were completely cut in half or decapitated. The area around Ari quickly begun to turn into a blood bath that she also was being covered in.

Arianna brought up her other hand and flames appeared flew at enemies, as a frosty mist formed off the axe blade. "CODELESS!" Night yelled out Ari looked up towards the upper deck at him to see as he begun to get dragged away fighting back all the while. Anthelm was leaving or really fleeing with Roy and others.

The area around Ari burst with a force that sent those close flying back. Vines then shot up from the ground and begun to piece and squish any agent they could get a hold of. She swung the axe down on the ground and a sheet of ice formed then with a flick of her wrist spikes shot up. The icy floor quickly got coated by blood. "M-m-monster!" Some Marione agents begun to scream as they raced off.

Arianna then begun to race forward and threw her injured arm forward and created a large, inclined icicle that she then jumped off. She jumped with as much strength as she could as she pushed off as she went towards the upper deck. She managed to grab a hold on the railing as she dangled over to floor of the hanger as she held onto the axe with her uninjured arm.

Ari then began to swing herself to then bring herself over the railing and onto the upper deck floor. She turned her head towards where Anthelm was escaping while dragging Night/Roy. "Stop them! Don't let them stop our escape!"

She looked at them as she grabbed her pistol and loaded a new clip. Ari raced forward towards the doors they were leaving from. She cut down and shot several agents that were in her way but there were to many, and she knew there was no way she was going to make it.

Ari did a large swing of the axe around her and cut down a number in front of her as she raised her pistol and aimed it at Roy. She looked down the sights at him and her arm started to tremble. *I can't let them take Roy.* She muttered she knew she needed to do this since it was her only chance since rescue was no longer an option.

As Ari tried to pull the trigger she couldn't. She had her finger against the trigger and her finger was trembling, but she couldn't. For some reason she physically couldn't pull the trigger and it was so frustrating to her, tears begun to fall. "Please..." she whimpered as she watched they take Roy further away.

The door had begun to close, and her arm fell to her side. "Why... what's stopping me..." she muttered as she looked at the gun. She pointed her gun at and enemy and could pulled the trigger, but it was just a click. *I'm out of bullets.*

Not only was there something physically that stopped Ari from shooting Roy, but she had also run out of bullets to even preform the act in the first place. She only had one option left she looked up and directly at Roy. *I'm sorry.* She thought as she dropped a flash bang and made a flash fire around her as the doors begun to close before her.

A card appeared in her hand the card in her hand begun to glow. "*Part the vail and come to me. I summon thee. Ezec.*" Arianna muttered as she released the card as it was consumed with icy blue flames, and it turned into a ball of light before eventually taking form before her.

In front of her eyes was a small creature that was like a cross of a fairy/pixie and imp, small and messy with multiple torn insect/fairy like wings, sharp teeth, point ears, horns, a tail, and long nails. The Ezec in front of her had short black hair. "Please... I know I haven't performed the proper steps... but I really need your help."

The Ezec's eyes opened, and its red eyes looked up at her. It was as if it looked into her mind even with her face covered. She felt chills run through her. *[Tamer... you do know for this a price must be paid.]*

"*I know... but I have no choice.*" She replied and the Ezec spoke again what they said caused her eyes to shake but she looked away for a moment. "*I understand. If that is the price... I have no choice either way, so I'll take it.*"

[You are quite interesting. I am Ragna... I look forward to when we seal our contract but for now... what is it that you wish me to do?]

"Ragna... no way?! N-no now's not the time for this." Ari told herself with a slight shake of her head. "*I need to you seal my friend Night... no Roy's memories and powers. It's the only way to keep him and everyone safe for long enough. Make it so only you can break the seal.*"

[... that man. I see. I can do that... but in moments of extreme the body might react and allow the use of his sealed powers.]

"That's fine as long as its only then that will be fine." Arianna muttered as she nodded her head. Ragna looked at her, he did look into her mind, so he knows the truth, but there are things to uphold, no matter what. After a few moments he flew off towards Roy to do as Ari requested.

When flash died down and others could see Ari swung the axe and cut the agents that had gotten close to her as she looked over at Roy. She could see Ragna next to him as it removed its hand from Roy's head and a whiteish-blue flame like orb was removed.

A momentary space was created by Ragna a mental realm. Ari could see Roy's face as both of their helmets were gone. She looked at him with teary eyes as she watched Roy's eyes blurred and dulled as recognition faded. "I'm sorry Roy... I'm so sorry. Even if I had no other choice... this is all my fault. I promise, I'll save you from them." Ari sobbed as she saw as his eyes back blank.

Ari closed her eyes, and everything returned to normal around her. *Thank you... thank you so much Ragna.* She thought as she watched Ragna disappear, and Roy slump down having fallen unconscious from what Ragna did. The door was sealed in front of Ari as Anthelm with high-ranking people escaped with Roy as their captive.

Ari lowered her head as she found it started to become difficult to breathe. Around her there was a large burst of energy. "It will fall." She muttered as fires begun to engulf things in the hanger and vehicles. Ice swirled out from around her and freeze those around her, and vines begun to shoot out from the ground.

There was no mercy as anything was killed or destroyed, vehicles exploded, things were impaled. Walls destroyed and those unlucky to be in the wrong place died in one way or another. Ari lifted her head up and tilted it as she watched those below. But it wasn't long before some agents rushed towards her. "Kill the monster!" they yelled.

It wasn't a small number that had made their way to her either. She raised the great axe up and pointed it towards the one that yelled out. "You all shall fall." Ari drawled out before she lunged forward then swung the axe killing many and caused their blood to fly.

Arianna moved different from how she usually did as if mechanical in a way. Despite her major injuries and what should be her weakened state not a single agents could get close to her. After some time, Ari begun to laugh out in an odd way that was chilling to those that heard it. Blood dripped from her axe but also from her arm that the large open wound was. Honestly were there wasn't blood on her at this point would be an easier question.

If one could see her eyes at this point you would see a slight daze with flicker of the surging energy inside her. Eventually there was no more screams from those that didn't escape from Ari's mad rampage. All around were dead, and she stood in the middle of a pool of blood as the building begun to collapse around her from the flames. A sigh escaped Arianna's lips as she regained her senses to a degree, she looked about her as she could hear the ceiling above her creak.

In remission she watched at the ceiling above her collapsed and begun to fall towards her. But something grabbed her shoulder without a single word. In the next moment she was enveloped in a white light and the ceil fell where she stood.

Chapter 44

Darkness was what greeted Arianna in the next moment. It was a brief moment of silence as her sense returned before her helmet was forcibly pulled off her head and thrown aside. She was then yanked up, held by her collar to the point her feet didn't touch the ground.

"WHAT THE HELL WERE YOU THINKING!" Alex growled she was pissed off at Arianna. "You should have waited for back up! Your fucking insane! Did you think you couldn't trust us! You sent us off then disappeared."

"Alex give her a chance to say something." Stan replied sharply though he didn't put Ari back on the ground either.

"She'll just lie or not tell us like usual since she knows what's the 'best' for everyone. You just can't handle giving another person control or trusting them. She's never told us the truth of herself but knows 'everything' about us!" Alex yelled as she glared at Ari. Ari glanced at Alex but didn't say anything. She knew anything she said would just be berated or attacked. Alex had completely turned against Ari and was treating her as an enemy.

"Arianna tell me where is my brother? Where is Roy." Stan asked as he looked at her, Ari knew he wasn't going to take no answer from her, and she knew at this moment even if she wanted to, she couldn't lie to Stan. But even so she didn't want to tell him.

"He isn't here." Ari muttered is reply as she looked away. It was the wrong answer as Stan threw her to the ground hard. Her badly injured shoulder hit but she didn't let a groan escape her lips.

"We're done with this Arianna. We are not in the mood for your games either. Now tell us." Stan growled she looked into his eyes before a laugh escaped her lips. It was very clear to her now. The emotions they kept buried, they had both turned on her. It felt like a knife was stabbed into her chest. She felt used and that it was unfair, but she also knew their anger was justified.

"I think you already know what happened. You just want to hear it from me... and give yourself validation to blame and hate me... like everyone else." Ari scoffed as she pushed herself up from the ground. But it wasn't even a second late that she was punched in the face the force which caused her head to turn to the opposite side. She turned her eyes that were ice cold at Alex who had just punched her.

"You're a real bitch! You don't even care about us. You don't even love Roy like I do or like Stan does. We've given up so much to reach this point, and have always helped you, you can't even give us this much."

"... You think I've given up nothing... tsk. As you said before you know NOTHING about me NOTHING! And your right I don't love Roy like you do, nor am I blood related to him like Stan is! But you truly think that. Heh. It's quite clear what you think of me."

Alex screamed as she tried to lunge at Ari and claw her face only to have Stan hold her back. "Just tell us what happened."

Arianna looked up her eyes were dark and the energy that came from her was chilling. "You want to know so much at this exact moment... fine!" she growled. "Roy sacrificed himself to save me since I was very weak. Kind of funny how he's the only one that noticed anything wrong really. I went back to save him and failed; I couldn't kill him either. So, I took his memories and power."

The moment she finished she got punched again this time by Stan which caused her to fall to the ground. Alex jumped on top of Ari and attacks her with no mercy. She got beat by both Alex and Stan to the point she spits blood. That was the only point

Stan stopped and pulled Alex back. But the look they both had towards her was dark and one of disgust. "Did you ever even think of us as your friends? How! How could you do that to him again. You forced him to lose everything again and sent him straight to hell! You're a monster."

Alex laughs out. "You though Arianna ever felt anything for us. She's a cold-hearted bitch with no blood. She's only ever put on an act. She never considered them anything close to finds just like how I have felt towards her." She laughed holding her stomach as she laughed out. She glanced at Ari with her purple eyes that were cold. "To her everything and everyone is just a tool. No emotions, a monster. It makes sense considering what she can do her powers. You can never trust a monster, or you'll end up just like Roy."

Arianna spit out blood and started to laugh she felt like she had been stabbed multiple times. She had no idea how Alex lead to such a conclusion... but that was how she truly felt towards her. She glanced over to Stan, and he looked away they had come to both think the same thing about her. That she was an emotionless monster that never told them anything true.

"Bahahaha! I see... I really was stupid. If only he could see this. Maybe he'd make a different choice. No... after all I'm just an emotionless unfeeling monster. I never had anything to lose in the first place now did it." Ari laughed before she clicked her tongue at them. "I get it loud and clear. Your no one to me any more... nothing more than strangers." Ari growled as she turned around.

Stan and Alex turn and start to leave but Stan stops for a moment. "The word monster really first you so well since not even poison could kill you." Stan scoffed before he left with Alex. She heard the door behind them close and there's footsteps fade away.

They would never have listened to anything I said in the first place. Even after how many times I almost died for them. Nothing... nothing I ever said to them did they actually believe. Hahahha! I couldn't believe I even considered to tell those traitor's my past after this was done. Arianna muttered as tears started to run down her face. "Haha... In the end... always alone." She let out a sad laugh.

Tear begun to fall from her eyes as she looked down blankly. "Haha... I think something just broke." She muttered as she placed her hand on her chest. Her eyes dulled a little, she collapsed to the ground as tears streamed down her face and her communicator went off.

White halls there were people in chairs crying, people in white coats and nurses rushing around and the smell of disinfectant filled the air. In Arianna's hand was some violet's as she walked through the halls of the hospital to a certain room.

Arianna let out a sigh as she walked into the room and placed the small had full of violets into a small cup of water. She looked over to the person in the bed. It was Sean he was still unconscious after what happened. It had only been a day or two by now and Ari could tell that he wasn't close to death rather the opposite as if waiting for something.

The bandage around Sean head was fresh she brough her hand up to move his bangs from his eyes and about to say something when another women burst into the room and grabbed Arianna by the collar. This motion irritated Arianna's injured shoulder more. "What the hell do you think you're doing here?!" Yavari yelled.

"You shouldn't yell in a hospital."

"A person like you, can't tell me what I can and can't do."

"It's called common curtesy, not, me telling you what to do."

"Well, you aren't family and you sure aren't friends miss Arianna Artusro. So, you should leave."

"I have no idea who you're talking about. They died." Arianna whispered with a smile. She then heard a groan and turned her head. "Ah." She gasped as she realized.

Sean groaned as he held his head and tried to sit up. Ari raced over and placed her hand on her shoulder. "Don't sit up to fast. You've been out for a few days after some head trauma. You might feel sick, wait till a doctor comes to check you." She told him as she pushed him back down into bed.

Sean looked at her in surprise, then Ari groaned for a moment as she closed her eyes. When she opened them, she noticed some colour attached to Sean that had come to turn completely white. She wasn't sure why, but she knew what it meant, and the colour disappeared without a word. She pressed her lips in thought for a moment.

"… You don't recognize anything do you?" Ari sighed as she ran her hand through her hair. Sean didn't answer but looked away, so she knew she was right. Ari sighed and shook her head. "Someone should call a doctor." She muttered.

Yavari stormed over to Ari and slapped her across the face. "This is all your fault you bloodless bitch." Yavari yelled. Ari's head was turned to the side as she turned her eyes and glared at Yavari. "Not saying anything. Good cause it is your fault that all this has happened to him, and that Caden died. Everything that's happened is you fault as you failed your job!" Yavari growled as she managed to poke into Ari's wound.

"You are a failure. An utter failure and monster. That's why your family left you an orphanage. They'd rather leave a worthless bitch like you to be another person's problem. Spineless wimps for a parent's that forced others to deal with children others have no blood ties." Yavari growled.

Ari's eyes glowed as she spun around and grabbed Yavari by the throat and lifted her up. "I don't care what dragger like words you say and throw at me. But DO NOT talk that way about my parents who are 1000 times better than a two-faced bitch like you. I knew the moment I arrived that you hated me! Everything I did, you hated and look down on just because I'm not your real child." Ari hissed as she dropped Yavari and turned toward the door.

Yavari then attacked Ari threw her into the wall. Ari slammed into the wall and let out a groan as her wound opened more and blood from the now reopen wound smeared the wall. Ari's head tilted down for a moment, she let out a sigh and slightly raised her head.

The disguise tech flickered for a moment due to a short letting Yavari and Sean see her real appearance only for a moment. Yavari stepped back in surprise as she saw real Ari's appearance. "N-no way! How is this even possible!"

Arianna glared at Yavari as her disguise tech activated again. She pushed herself up from the wall and held her right shoulder as she applied pressure to the wound. "Caden with mine and the Yano's help had finished the legal proceedings before he passed. All in part to all the evidence I managed to collect.

"Thanks to it… you Yavari have lost all legal rights to your blood retaliated children, Sean and Dave. They will be sent to Caden's parents to be raised. Now no longer will one need to worry about such treatment or your twisted ideals."

"You bitch! How could you even do such a thing! I'm their mother."

"You have no right to be a mother, you may have never treated your children like you did me but what you did do to them... You did this to yourself. All I did was collect the evidence to get legal recourse... also your marriage with Caden had also been broken. So don't expect anything."

Arianna walked over to the door. "Good to see you again after so long Yavari. It was nice to see you are as much as a bitch as I remembered." Ari paused and tilted her head back and smiled. "After everything you did to my mother. I've let you off easy just destroying that false life you made yourself."

Ari held the door. "Oh... and I know what you did to us. You're lucky I haven't killed you right here and now for it. It's your fault... so get your just deserts. As you will never rest easy again for it." She growled as she sent a murderous gaze at Yavari. "You should have listened to Caden back then because all of this both you and *her* fault."

Ari looked at Yavari with sharp eyes there was no kindness in them. Rather it was more an unending darkness. "With that my job is done. May we never meet again." She added as she left the room and let the officers enter the room to properly deal with Yavari. You could hear her screams of protest against the officers. It was a tickling feeling the very sound and sight.

Ari walked down the hall and told a nurse about Sean walking up and the officers also in the room for the adult women. With that finished she continued to walk down the hall towards the exit.

As she continued walking down the hall, she passed Sean's friend and brushed against Dave. They all stopped and turned.

"Arianna?!" Dave gasped as he turned. But no matter where anyone looked Arianna had disappeared as if she was never there.

"It was just and illusion Dave... s-she died in the fire at the school."

A woman with a large hat stood in a hallway not too far away but just out of there sight. They watched as they group turned around in sadness and disappointment. Not that long ago there was a funeral for those that died during the fire that occurred at the school.

Arianna Artusro was among the few missing and presumed dead from that day. The only reason she was added was the multiple statements from those in the school that placed her there, despite that she had been missing for months prior.

Since the body of Arianna was never found a few small group of people hoped that she had survived the fire. Though it was a vain hope, Arianna died that day or rather she never existed in the first place.

The women crossed her arms despite the pain and watch as Dave and the small group walked towards Sean's room. They didn't know about the fact that the room had become filled with commotion.

As the door opened, she watched as Yavari was dragged out in cuffs and a complete mess. She screamed bloody murder as she was dragged away. The women smirked before she turned around. She didn't see the expression of the group, nor did she really care.

"Violet! VIOLET! I'LL KILL YOU! I'LL YOU VIOLET ROTUSOLE!"

The mad screams echoed out but though some looked around in confusion the words fell on deaf ears. The women glanced towards the elevator before she looked back to see Dave and the others race into Sean's room once they realized that he woke up. *"May you live in peace after all the trouble caused from your parents. May Faradityx bless you two with a peaceful life from here on or as you so wish your life to be from here on."* The women muttered as she placed her hand on her chest.

As the door to the room closed and the mad screams were replaced with that of joy in Sean's room the women continued forward and walk out of the hospital without a look back.

Chapter 45

Dark sits in a waiting room with Icarus as they waited. Then finally for the first time in 24 hours the door to the interrogation room opened and Stan walked out. Stan's uncanny skill at being a walking person lie detector that never wrong was a heavy used skill by the organization back then. A skill that had just been in use, which was what the two waited for. "What's the verdict?" Dark asked.

The one inside the interrogation room was the man that Arianna brought with her from the Marione at Lumina's request. "They're clean. They aren't a spy for the Marione, they came here seeking refuge essentially. But they want to get back at the Marione."

"I see you can leave." Dark dismissed Stan, he them looked over to his brother. "He's not a spy but wishes to go against the Marione. Even though we know he isn't something to worry about… no one will take him just because of his prior relation with the Marione."

"You're right the number of Yano who've died at the hands of the Marione aren't small. And no one else knowns about this skill of Stanly's." Icarus agreed as he leaned back. "I can't take him with me since my unit rarely fights them in the first place.

"I can't take him. I'm the leader. I don't have a direct unit either so if I take him in the group will probably think he's the next head." Dark sighed as he covered his face. "But we can't just leave him."

The door to the interrogation waiting room opened. "If your so worried about that. I'll take him."

Months had passed as spring has turned to summer. In the usually busy Brightton City International Airport things moved around like normal. On one of the TV screens a news report played. "Chief of police Icarus Altshaler and detective Stanly Klipp both highly regarded officers apart of the Brightton City police have been missing for a full month now.

"Some have begun to wonder if the rumour of them retiring is true. Though it would be quiet disappointing with a such a young and accomplished officer like detective Klipp to retire so soon."

A young women turned her head from the news screen, there was a bandage around her neck and wrist as they looked over at their gate. Their mid-length black hair and dull red eyes were fairly eye catching as it was a combination that wasn't common to Canlonen.

They reached up to their right shoulder as they massaged it before she grabbed her bags and made her way to her gate. She arrived right in time for the international flight to London.

Without issue she boarded the flight and sat down in first class. They looked out the window with a straight face, but their eyes held a sad look to them. She reached back and pushed her hair behind her left ear to reveal the dangle white crystal earing pair with small silver hoops in her ear. Around the women's neck was unique sword looking necklace that was barely visible hidden under her shirt.

After some time and everything was loaded the plane begun to move back and eventually down the runway. As the plane left the ground she reached over and closed the window. It wasn't long before she pulled out and begun to read the old book in hand as the plane flew off into the sky further and further away from Brightton City and Canlonen itself. They didn't hesitate and never looked back.

An ending had arrived, an ending of many things. Yet… the end of one brought forth a new strong beginning. One which would be more dangerous than the last.

A decision made, and a new beginning starts. It is one beginning that rises from the ashes of another.

Words From the Author

There are several things I want to say in general, but also not sure what I should say here. So here it goes. To start I'd like to thank you for buying this book, though there are points and plans for more following.

This was something I wrote out of passion and entertainment, that I used to pass time and relieve stress, so I hope you enjoyed the story. Then there are people I want to thank my family, friends, and even online groups that I'm a part of that have given me encouragement and kind words over time it means a lot to me.

I as a person have had many ups and downs in my life already along with a fair number of setbacks, that without them I would have never made it to this point. Its thanks to them I brought myself here and to publish this so no matter what happens in the end of the day I am forever grateful for what they've done for me. They gave me the courage to fulfil a dream of mine, and though some many never know that I'm thanking them or will ever see this I needed to say it.

You might now that this book is self-published. I've wanted to try and publish a book for a while now to just really try it. An older version of this book when it was still called The Assassin was published for 2 or 3 contests back on the site called Ankit and had caught the attention of a staff for the sight and promoted the book on the blog and possible a few more times.

The book never won any contests of course, and despite knowing about other possible writing contests I didn't submit it to them. There wasn't really a good reason for it I didn't avoid applying for the contest or anything. It was probably more the fact of my lack of self-esteem.

I've wanted to publish this book and have edited it many times, even drew art for it, but I've always been on the fence needing that final push do such a thing. Some people online have encouraged me, some of my co-workers and friends as well when I've talked this story. By 2022 hopefully this story is published in some way for others to enjoy.

Now this isn't a biography so let's talk about the book itself as this book has been a long project of mine that has taken many years to complete to get to this point. The book itself has had several edits and re-writes at this point about 5 maybe 6, I believe, and it has changed a lot in many ways from the original idea. This book called Codeless was originally called The Assassin and the very first draft of the story began back in my 2nd half of my 11th grade year in 2015 with the first draft to be completed in summer of 2016, if I remember correctly.

The original concept idea of the story didn't have any fantasy elements to it when I began to write the first part of the original draft. It was to be an action mystery novel with a strong female protagonist. However, nearing the end of the writing first part of the book the genre changes to its main fantasy genre that it has now. I've always loved fantasy novels and I've written and made concepts for several stories that were heavily influence by that love of fiction fantasy that I've read since I was a kid.

Now the thing that turned this story to fantasy however might come from an unexpected place, back in 2015 I just happened to buy a pack of MTG cards at random as they had mention of dragons on the card booster pack. I just so happened to get a very rare card but also my favourite mythical creature as well from it, and to the point I couldn't help but bleed that love and excitement into the book to make it into what it is today.

As I've already mentioned this story is a self-published novel, so I am the author, editor, and artist for the book and trust me I wish I had an actual editor. In terms of English spelling and grammar are defiantly my worst areas despite it being my primary language and have many problems with it, things like tensing and such issue with, which some of you might have caught a few unintended errors over time. Not to even mentioned the initial issues of my Canadian English that till recent years was hated by spellcheck since it only had US or UK options, and Canadian is the mix of both styles. Though now a days spellcheck added my language of spelling, so this version re-write had less difficulty.

But that in the end it mattered little as I loved to write and have a very active imagination. Even with the numerous setbacks that I face, I still decided to do this and, in this version, turn such problems into more of an advantage for the books and to try to make the story a little more interesting. To that which I wonder if you've caught on.

Now there have been several changes made over time of the multiple draft edits and iterations I've made of this story to its current version. From the removal of chapters originally written, POV changes, changes of character stories, and how the character fit in the story/what role they are to play. Many things have changed over the about 6 years' worth of work on this story's universe. Till eventually it led to this point, this version of the story that has been completely essentially rewritten from the ground up from the last edit version.

When I say that, it's not a joke it took me 6 months to rewrite all the chapters and add about an additional month for all the notes, and plot ideas that I wrote out before I begun this rewrite. From its prior version its nearly a completely different story, key nearly as numerous things remain the same across the board.

In this draft to list a few major changes between the version you can look at the title itself. Originally the story was called The Assassin and it was going to remain as such till I got further along to change it to its current title of Codeless. The series name and the placement book itself has remain the same. Then there is also the POV changes that have occurred in the book from the original version, as originally the POV and tensing was completely different from what they are currently. Not just that but even several important characters have had name changes and/or their importance to the overall plot changed and the like. The most significate with a name changes from the original story are the main female lead protagonist Arianna, the 'problem' child Sean, and the secret rebel Lennox.

For many years and iterations of the story Arianna was named Roxanne along with a few other changes to the character today has (family, appearance etc.). But with this name change I was slightly forced to also change Sean's original name as he was originally call Ari. Even Dave had changes to his position and point in the plot from side supporting to a more leading role in the 2nd part. However, unlike these 3 that have generally remained in the same position for the plot of the story and what side they are one, one character has had the most change.

That character is Lennox the male character introduced in part 3. Originally, he was just call Loki a character who had a hostile relationship with the protagonist (Roxanne). He was more like an antagonist toward her even killing some other character's that had a close relationship with the protagonist. Eventually that changed however, one draft there was many shifts in the stories plot, but I liked the general concept of this character, as they themselves had a very interesting background concept that I really like and was important over all in the new and developing plot and universe of the story.

At this point he was given a new name of Kaiya and had the code name of Loki. His position in the plot had also shifted from antagonist to more neutral overall towards the protagonist (still named Roxanne). From this shift some other ideas for the character also came forward at this point. But his personality was almost completely different from what it currently is now. Eventually we get to this edit were his name changes to Lennox with a new code name as well, personality change, and some background character setting that of course I'll keep hidden for now.

At this point in writing the universe for this world is completed and I have a general idea for the entire series and some off shoot stories in the mix, so there shouldn't be any major changes going forward. Though I have generally made the time frame of the world, universe itself and the race a little unclear though slightly stated in the book. The are other things that should be in question over all as it will make certain occurrences clear and give insight to things going on and a few other things.

The art that is in the book was all done by me, from the maps, cover, and part images. My art style did slightly change over the course of the book which some might notice. I'll let you know now the images that I've drawn (though whether or not that are the best fit for the story as a whole), are more additional things for you guys to enjoy. I love art and often sketch/draw scenes I like or just to give me a clear and physical picture of characters. The only image that is a little outside of this, is the image for part 4 as there wasn't a particular scene, I wanted to draw but rather items to give a clear picture what I was thinking.

As I said the art of the book is in my style, I don't expect everyone to like how it looks. I can only do so much as I don't draw full realistic, rather a mix of that and an anime like style. To be honest for the story I wish my current style had or could do more of a realistic style to it. But in the end I wanted to add the part images anyways even if people didn't like it. I also needed to make a good cover for the book, and I just wanted to give some maps so you can picture the land that Codeless is taking place in either way. So, I just did it myself, since I can draw rather then get it commissioned, which is honestly something I normally do anyways with other things I work on.

Anyways make sure you keep an eye (and an ear) out for the future as this book series has only just begun. An if you liked my story and style its possible, I might do other things in the future as well, but it all depends.

Now be sure to keep an eye out and pay attention as there are many secrets to the universe that the Rise from Ashes collection of this series takes place. Even the books themselves. There is many things going on in this book and future installments that might hint to a bigger picture. But, be warry, they wish for this to be written but also for some to remain hidden. As there is always the possibility of deception and misdirection in their words that you read.

If you did enjoy this book if you couldn't tell this book isn't the end just the beginning of the tale. The next book shouldn't take me like 7 years to write and complete as the whole concept for the books fleshed out now. Though the process might not be as fast as some other, I got ideas for the next two books for this series even.

At the end of the day, I enjoy writing, and well just stories in general. Whether I become a professional or not, only time will tell. But in the end, I'll might pass the time writing something.

Now for a little bonus to you all, I have added part of the current first chapter of the next book in the series. I hope you enjoy this small sneak peek, what is planned to come in the future.

Dusk of Night

The World is not one of two colours. Light and dark; black and white; good and evil. Dividing it into such things will bring one to miss many other things that are occurring. There is no real clear-cut line in the sand.

In a corridor of white the sound of footsteps echoed as the entire building itself was in pure chaos. Racing down the hallway was a figure clad in all black, and in their arms was a girl with long green hair. Despite the chaos of the building and people yelled out to stop them, the figure remained moving forward and knocked whatever got in their way.

Back further down the hall from the direction the figure was running from a door burst open. "There they are! I have on sight confirmation that the subject is in sector 7D with the intruder. Active the sector defensives." A man exclaimed over his communicator. "What are you idiots doing! Stop them! They are attempting to escape with our newest subject! Subject LN!" He yelled pointing at the people acting like they're chickens with their heads cut off. The girl in the intruder's arms shuddered hearing their words.

"Worry not they will not get you back." They replied in a distorted voice as they held the girl tight to them. Bullets began to fly past them, extremely close as few grazed the intruder.

"Don't worry about the gunfire. They might hit but it will be nothing fatal. They want the girl alive and will try for you as well." An adult man's voice buzzed in the figures ear."

"Aye! I'm aware, such a thing like this doesn't bother me in the slightest."

The figure continued running ignoring the enemy fire that flew by them focusing more on the task in front of them. "Go down the next right. It will lead to the closest exit to the outdoors." Another younger male voice exclaimed in their ear. As they came up towards the right, they were informed of, they begun to slide slowing themselves down till they pivoted and immediately sprinted down the hall.

As they went down the hall they notices beams of light. "Lasers!" the girl exclaimed, but the figure continued forward and jumped right between the two laser beams. They landed on the ground uninjured. They looked over at the girl noting they were also uninjured and begun to run once again down the hall.

"Sorry. I got limited access right now. The map we have didn't show the lasers."

"It's fine we can work with what we have. Besides I'm fairly sure it's part of the defense system it wouldn't show up on the normal map. Just focus on what a head, and make sure they don't hack us back and gain access. If they do, we're done for."

"No pressure."

The intruder huffed in reply as they listened into the sound of approaching footsteps and focused their senses. They clicked their tongue realising that those chasing them were getting closer than they would prefer. "Hold on tight to me so you don't fall girly." They spoke low. The girl understanding wrapped her arms around their neck granting the intruder a single free hand.

With said free hand they got closer to the nearest wall and begun to run their fingers along it. At first it appeared as if nothing happened, but as people begun to near the start of were their fingers ran along people were slipping and falling to the ground.

The intruder then begun to skate along the ground as thin ice formed in front of them. Gaining enough forwards momentum, they spun around and raised their hand up. First as their hands raised up from the ground plums of water shot up. The intruder then closed their hand and the water turned into ice becoming and icy spike barricade. When that was finished, they turned back around before jumping up in the air. The moment their feet landed their boots had traction once more and began to run.

Fallowing the directions that the younger man told them for some time they were proceeding down a long hallway. From the side connecting hallways a group of people with guns filed out a distance away from them. The intruder recognized the problem and reached back behind them pulling out a blade. After a moment moving the blade in their hand along its edge it formed a slight white coloured glow.

Bullets flew by them, but they remained unfazed however the girl was less so burying her face into their firm chest. The intruder was facing down a firing line of gun man running towards them. By the gunman expressions they found it unnerving, even more so that they've yet to hit a shot. They were closing the distance quickly and when there were only a few meters left the intruder jumped up.

They held the girl close to them before rolling in the air as they went over their heads and slashed with the blade in hand. Parts of their guns fell off and to the floor while more of the unlucky ones sustained injury, losing an arm, or a finger or two, with only one person getting killed outright. However, despite getting cut with the sword their wounds had already been cauterized.

As they landed behind them the intruder attacked slashing another down that attempted to fire, while hitting a few of the others close by, which allowed another clear break. With that dealt with the intruder sheathed the sword to allow their hand to be free.

Manufactured by Amazon.ca
Bolton, ON

24889915R00199